ACCLAIM FOR BETH WISEMAN

HOME ALL ALONG

"Beth Wiseman's novel will find a permanent home in every reader's heart as she spins comfort and prose into a stellar read of grace."
—KELLY LONG, AUTHOR OF THE
PATCH OF HEAVEN SERIES

LOVE BEARS ALL THINGS

"Suggest to those seeking a more truthful, less saccharine portrayal of the trials of human life and the transformative growth and redemption that may occur as a result."
—LIBRARY JOURNAL

HER BROTHER'S KEEPER

"Wiseman has created a series in which the readers have a chance to peel back all the layers of the Amish secrets."
—RT BOOK REVIEWS, 4 1/2 STARS
AND JULY 2015 TOP PICK!

"Wiseman's new launch is edgier, taking on the tough issues of mental illness and suicide. Amish fiction fans seeking something a bit more thought-provoking and challenging than the usual fare will find this series debut a solid choice."
—LIBRARY JOURNAL

The Land of Canaan Novels

"Wiseman's voice is consistently compassionate and her words flow smoothly."

—*Publishers Weekly* review of
Seek Me with All Your Heart

"Wiseman's third Land of Canaan novel overflows with romance, broken promises, a modern knight in shining armor, and hope at the end of the rainbow."

—*RT Book Reviews*

"In *Seek Me with All Your Heart*, Beth Wiseman offers readers a heartwarming story filled with complex characters and deep emotion. I instantly loved Emily, and eagerly turned each page, anxious to learn more about her past—and what future the Lord had in store for her."

—*Shelley Shepard Gray*, bestselling author
of the *Seasons of Sugarcreek* series

"Wiseman has done it again! Beautifully compelling, *Seek Me with All Your Heart* is a heartwarming story of faith, family, and renewal. Her characters and descriptions are captivating, bringing the story to life with the turn of every page."

—*Amy Clipston*, bestselling
author of *A Gift of Grace*

The Daughters of the Promise Novels

"Well-defined characters and story make for an enjoyable read."

—*RT Book Reviews* on *Plain Pursuit*

"A touching, heartwarming story. Wiseman does a particularly great job of dealing with shunning, a controversial Amish practice that seems cruel and unnecessary to outsiders . . . If you're a fan of Amish fiction, don't miss *Plain Pursuit!*"

—KATHLEEN FULLER, AUTHOR OF
THE MIDDLEFIELD FAMILY NOVELS

AMISH
CELEBRATIONS

Other Books by Beth Wiseman

The Amish Secrets Novels

Her Brother's Keeper

Love Bears All Things

Home All Along

The Daughters of the Promise Novels

Plain Perfect

Plain Pursuit

Plain Promise

Plain Paradise

Plain Proposal

Plain Peace

The Land of Canaan Novels

Seek Me with All Your Heart

The Wonder of Your Love

His Love Endures Forever

Other Novels

Need You Now

The House that Love Built

The Promise

Novellas

A Choice to Forgive included in An Amish Christmas

A Change of Heart included in An Amish Gathering

Healing Hearts included in An Amish Love

A Perfect Plan included in An Amish Wedding

A Recipe for Hope included in An Amish Kitchen

Always Beautiful included in An Amish Miracle

Rooted in Love included in An Amish Garden

When Christmas Comes included in An Amish Second Christmas

In His Father's Arms included in An Amish Cradle

A Love for Irma Rose included in An Amish Year

Patchwork Perfect included in An Amish Year

A Cup Half Full included in An Amish Home

The Cedar Chest included in An Amish Heirloom

AMISH CELEBRATIONS

BETH WISEMAN

ZONDERVAN®

ZONDERVAN

Amish Celebrations

Copyright © 2018 by Elizabeth Wiseman Mackey

This title is also available as a Zondervan e-book.

Requests for information should be addressed to:

Zondervan, *3900 Sparks Dr. SE, Grand Rapids, Michigan 49546*
Library of Congress Cataloging-in-Publication
Names: Wiseman, Beth, 1962- author.
Title: Amish celebrations / Beth Wiseman.
Description: Grand Rapids, Michigan : Zondervan, [2018]
Identifiers: LCCN 2018002973 | ISBN 9780529118738 (paperback)
Subjects: LCSH: Amish--Fiction. | GSAFD: Christian fiction.
Classification: LCC PS3623.I83 A6 2018 | DDC 813/.6--dc23 LC record
available at https://lccn.loc.gov/2018002973

Scripture quotations are taken from the King James Version of the Bible.

Printed in the United States of America

18 19 20 21 22 / LSC / 20 19 18 17 16 15 14 13 12 11 10 9 8 7 6 5 4 3 2 1

To my readers

CONTENTS

The Gift of Sisters..1

A New Beginning...99

A Perfect Plan 217

A Christmas Miracle 327

GLOSSARY

ab im kopp: sick in the head

ach: oh

boppli: baby

bruder: brother

daadi haus: grandparents' house

daed: dad

danki: thank you

Englisch: those who are not Amish; the English language

Englischer: non-Amish person

grandmammi: grandmother

gut: good

haus: house

kapp: prayer covering worn by Amish women

kinner: children

maedel: girl

maeds: girls

mamm: mom

mei: my

mudder: mother

nee: no

Ordnung: the written and unwritten rules of the Amish; the understood behavior by which the Amish are expected to live, passed down from generation to generation. Most Amish know the rules by heart.

Pennsylvania Deutsch: the language most commonly used by the Amish

rumschpringe: "running around"; the period of time when Amish youth experience life in the Englisch world before making the decision to be baptized and commit to Amish life

schweschder: sister

sohn: son

wie bischt: hello; how are you?

wunderbaar: wonderful

ya: yes

THE GIFT OF SISTERS

CHAPTER 1

Rachel stared out her bedroom window into the darkness, a gentle breeze wafting through the screen. She bit her bottom lip and folded an arm across her stomach, determined to fend off the cocoon of anguish tightening around her.

Outside, her sister, Hannah, and Abraham Stoltzfus held hands in a swing Rachel's father had recently hung from a tree branch. There was only enough room for two people, as if their father expected suitors to line up seeking the girls' affections.

Rachel and Hannah would be sixteen and entering their *rumschpringe* soon. It was a time to experience things outside their district, and they would also be allowed to date. Their father had bent the rules a couple months ago and agreed to let the girls start dating early. The fellows in town had wasted no time asking Hannah out, even though she didn't accept any of them. But when Abraham Stoltzfus moved to town a month ago with his family, Hannah latched onto him right away.

No matter that Rachel had already fallen for him as soon as she'd seen him.

Jealousy was a sin, but as the emotion spread over Rachel like an infectious disease, she felt six years old again, fighting for attention on the playground, seeking acknowledgment from a boy.

Rachel's sister got everything she wanted. How could she not? Even in a world where vanity was discouraged, it was impossible not to notice Hannah's beauty, her high cheekbones, big blue eyes, wispy dark lashes, and wavy blond hair. Rachel had dark hair with split ends, teeth not nearly as straight as Hannah's, and a mole on her left cheek. Hannah always said the mole wasn't noticeable, but that was easy for her to say since Hannah's complexion was flawless. Rachel's sister had been spared from blemishes on her face when Rachel was constantly applying tea tree oil or honey to control her acne.

None of that should matter, but it seemed more important than ever as Hannah and Rachel's sixteenth birthdays approached. For two people who'd been born within minutes of each other to the same parents, they didn't look like they shared the same gene pool.

Until now Rachel had been content to walk in her sister's shadow. But as Abraham Stoltzfus stared into Hannah's eyes, his lips barely parted, his hand holding hers, something snapped inside Rachel. Despite her proper upbringing, an ugliness was boiling her insides raw.

Rachel loved her sister. But she also loved Abraham. There had to be a way to sway his growing feelings for Hannah.

She tapped a finger against her chin for a few moments, then looked up at the ceiling as the lantern cast bursts of dancing lights overhead. She closed her eyes and attempted to pray that she could accept God's will, even if it meant Hannah belonged with Abraham. But the resentment crept to the surface, and in the end Rachel prayed that Abraham would eventually choose her over her sister.

Hannah gazed into Abraham's brown eyes, flecked with gold from the pale light of the moon. Fireflies blinked on and off as a gentle breeze swirled around them. They'd been spending time together for the past month, and Hannah hadn't allowed more than a gentle peck on the lips. Mostly they'd gone to social events where displays of affection would have been looked down on.

But as Abraham's mouth neared Hannah's, she was sure this was the real thing. She tried to focus on what was about to be her first grown-up kiss. It should have been a euphoric moment filled with butterflies and anticipation. Instead, Hannah tried to harness irritation as her sister watched from the bedroom window. She cut her eyes up and to the right, willing Rachel to turn away.

"Don't let her bother you." Abraham nodded toward the window, then kissed Hannah gently on the nose before his mouth grazed her earlobe.

Hannah wasn't sure how she'd snagged the most handsome man in their district, but as Abraham covered her mouth with his, she allowed herself to fall into the moment. She closed her eyes and savored her first step into womanhood. As she did, she noticed Abraham's breathing become heavier than normal, the feel of his chest rising and falling as he pulled her closer. There would be a price to pay if either of her parents saw them from the upstairs window. But so far only Rachel eyed them, ogling with jealousy most likely.

After a few long moments, Abraham eased away as a bead of sweat trickled down the side of his face. His cropped bangs were damp as well, but his breathing began to slow down.

"I'm sorry she's spying on us." Hannah spat the words, then sighed as guilt tightened around her like a wet blanket of shame. Rachel had seen Abraham first and expressed an interest in him, but Hannah had gone in for the kill at the Sunday singing the first night they'd met Abraham. Rachel was withdrawn and shy most of the time when it came to guys, and Hannah had taken advantage of that by pursuing Abraham like a pioneer woman staking claim of her territory.

"She's just jealous." Abraham ran a hand through his crop of yellow hair, locks nearly the same shade of blond as Hannah's. She started to envision the flock of blond-headed children they'd have one day, but Abraham's comment invaded her thoughts.

"Maybe," Hannah whispered. It was true. Rachel had treated Hannah harshly ever since the singing when Hannah and Abraham had stayed to themselves in the corner of the barn. Rachel's fiery red face and stern stares in their direction had made that clear. And her attitude had only worsened over the past month. Now they were barely speaking.

Abraham lifted a hand to Hannah's cheek and brushed away a loose strand of hair that had fallen from beneath her prayer covering. "You're prettier than she is." He smiled, flashing a set of beautiful white teeth.

Hannah had been told she was pretty for as long as she could remember. More from the *Englisch* than those in her community, but plenty of young Amish men had commented on her looks at one time or another. Still, none of them had gone so far as to make a comparison between her and Rachel.

Abraham's comment made Hannah hurt for her sister. If those same men could see Rachel's heart, they'd choose her over Hannah for sure. Hannah's sister was a gentle soul who was always out to help others. Rachel was a better cook than Hannah, nimble with a needle and thread, and the vegetables she grew in their garden were always the largest and tastiest. Hannah's sister would make a far better wife than Hannah would.

But evil had been unleashed the day of the singing. Hannah had snatched Abraham from her sister before he had a chance to find out how great Rachel was.

Rachel pretended she was asleep when she heard Hannah coming up the stairs. She'd already extinguished the lantern. The hum of the battery-operated fan should have lulled her to sleep, but her distressed heart hammered against her chest with a vengeance Rachel couldn't corral.

As she squeezed her eyes closed, she tried again to pray, but her deepest desire was for Abraham to lose interest in Hannah so Rachel could try to win him over. And even through her pain, Rachel knew she should not pray for such things. At least, not again.

"I know you're not asleep." Hannah's clipped tone fueled Rachel's bitterness. "And I can't believe you were watching me and my future husband kissing outside."

Rachel's eyes popped open as she turned to face her sister. "'Future husband'? You've only been seeing him for a month."

"*Ya*, and I guess that's long enough since he told me he loves me and wants to be with me for the rest of his life."

Rachel was glad it was dark so Hannah couldn't see the tears pooling in her eyes. Nor could her sister feel the knife slicing into Rachel's heart. She wanted to tell Hannah that you can't fall in love in one month, but that wasn't true. Rachel had fallen in love with Abraham the moment she laid eyes on him.

Now she wished there was a way to divert Abraham's attention away from Hannah and in Rachel's direction. A tall order, since Rachel couldn't compete with her prettier sister. But she wasn't going to lose hope. Abandoning her earlier resolve, she closed her eyes and selfishly asked God to sway Abraham's thinking.

CHAPTER 2

Rachel finished cleaning the lunch dishes with her mother and Hannah, then asked her mother if she could use the spring buggy for a while. It was a sunny day without a cloud in the sky, and she was hoping the pleasant weather might help clear the fog from her mind and the bitterness from her heart.

"*Ya*, you can use the buggy. It's unseasonably cool for June." Her mother tossed the kitchen towel over her shoulder. "Might as well enjoy the weather before the heat of the summer settles on us."

Hannah put a stack of clean dishes in the cabinet. She had been unusually quiet, not saying much at breakfast or lunch. Normally Rachel could sense what was bothering Hannah, and vice versa. Their mother had more than once said she'd heard that twins sometimes felt things more deeply about each other than regular siblings. But today Rachel couldn't feel anything but anger toward Hannah, which probably blocked out any extrasensory skills she had when it came to her sister.

And it made sense to Rachel that her bitterness was also blocking the voice of God. She'd been praying more, but her prayers didn't feel genuine, even to herself. Even though she'd asked God for the strength to accept His will, the continued undertone of her prayers was for Abraham to want her instead of Hannah. God would surely tell Rachel not to interfere in Hannah's love life. And that wasn't what Rachel wanted to hear.

Sighing, she left the room. She'd already heard Hannah talking on her cell phone this morning, whispering so their father wouldn't hear. Mobile phones had become an accepted form of communication in their community, especially for those who ran a business—or were in their *rumschpringe*. But Rachel's parents weren't keen on the idea, and neither were most of the elders. Rachel and Hannah tried not to use their cell phones in front of them.

Hannah had been making plans with Abraham. He was supposed to be picking her up after supper and taking her to a movie. At least that's what Hannah had told their parents. But Rachel had overheard her sister say otherwise, something about being alone with Abraham. Rachel thought about exposing Hannah's plans to her parents, but that could come around and bite her back if she wanted to explore options during her running-around period.

Hannah considered spritzing perfume before Abraham picked her up but thought better of it. Her father might smell it on her way out the door and put a halt to her date. He'd already caught her wearing lip gloss once before, and he'd made her wipe it off before she went shopping with an *Englisch* friend. She reminded herself that her father was already being lenient by letting her date, even though her and Rachel's birthday wasn't for a couple more weeks.

Her parents hadn't asked where she and Abraham were going, and that was good. Hannah suspected they weren't going to be too strict about Abraham since his family was related to the bishop, one of the reasons for their move here. She'd already made sure Rachel overheard her talking to Abraham about going to the movies. Hannah didn't want her sister to know where she was really going. She was already feeling shameful about it.

Everyone knew that kids their age went to the beekeeper's cemetery to make out. The place was named for *Englischer* Bud Hawkins, who was buried there. He'd died from a thousand bee stings long before Hannah was born, and there were only a few other unmarked graves in the tiny cemetery, so there wasn't much reason for anyone to officially visit. Amish and *Englisch* kids went there because it was tucked away in a forest of oak trees that were centuries old. The enormous limbs had sloped and bent over the years, forming natural benches. It was rumored that during a full moon Bud Hawkins could be seen running through the cemetery with a swarm of bees chasing him. Hannah didn't believe that. But she suspected plenty of boys had lured girls into their arms by telling that story.

Hannah had never been there, and she was curious how Abraham had found out about the place so soon after he'd moved here.

She hurried downstairs when she saw Abraham pulling in the driveway. She was glad Rachel wasn't home yet. As usual when she met up with Abraham, Hannah wasn't feeling very good about herself, for the way she'd forcefully pursued him in spite of Rachel's feelings. She loved her sister, and no matter how happy she would be to marry Abraham someday, she still didn't like to see her hurting.

On the other hand, she was glad Rachel wasn't lurking around again spying on them.

She waited for Abraham to come to the door, but he stood beside his buggy like he was just waiting for her. Hannah wasn't sure exactly what proper dating protocol was, but she supposed there wasn't a reason for him to come to the door. Her parents already knew Abraham.

But still. She'd thought that's how it was done.

"What time will you be home?" Her father peered over his reading glasses from his recliner, a newspaper in his hand.

"I-I'm not sure." She also wasn't feeling good about herself for not being truthful with her parents about her plans.

Her father glanced out the window and scowled, perhaps wondering as she did why Abraham didn't come to the door. "You will be home at eight," he stated. That settled, he refocused on the newspaper, turning the page.

Hannah glanced at the clock on the mantel. It was five thirty. Tempted to argue for more time, she decided against it and gave a quick wave before she headed out the door.

"*Wie bischt,*" Abraham said as he opened the buggy door for her. Hannah slipped into the seat and felt like a proper lady. She was on her first real date. Even though she'd been spending time with Abraham, he'd never formally come and picked her up. They'd been meeting at coffee shops, had lunched several times near the lumberyard where he worked, and had visited here on the farm in the evening. But in her parents' eyes, this was the first date. Her father had scoffed at the first mention of it, but Hannah had her mother to thank for smoothing the way, reminding Hannah's father that he'd already agreed to let Hannah see Abraham, and that this was the next natural step.

Hannah had always thought her first real date would be supper and a movie. But she'd already eaten, and the plan was to go to the beekeeper's cemetery. And no matter where they went, the main point was that Abraham loved her and she loved him.

I think. She recalled what Rachel had said. Her sister was right. It had only been a month.

"You look pretty." Abraham smiled at her as he guided the buggy down the driveway.

"*Danki.*"

Hannah wasn't usually nervous around guys, but this evening her insides swirled with anticipation. She had lain awake reliving her kiss with Abraham over and over again, and envisioned the look on his face when he'd told her he loved her. She was already designing the blueprint for her life. Baptism, then a fall wedding.

"You had supper, right?" Abraham clicked his tongue and gave the horse a gentle tap of the reins to speed up as he guided the buggy across Lincoln Highway. "I'm happy to take you to eat if you haven't."

"*Ya,* I had supper. But *danki.*" Hannah pointed to a parking lot on her left. "If we decide to go to a movie or somewhere that's too far to go by buggy, we usually leave our buggies there and take the bus. The owner of that store has hitching posts, and he keeps an eye on the buggies and horses, even at night. He's a young guy who used to be Amish but chose not to get baptized into the faith. He has an apartment above his shop."

Nothing wrong with putting a bug in his ear for their next date.

Abraham turned toward her. "Why doesn't a driver just pick you up at home?"

Hannah felt her cheeks warming. "Drivers will pick us up at home, but some kids . . ." She shrugged, keeping her eyes down. "Some kids don't want their parents to know where they're going. And the drivers we use know our parents and would tell them if we went somewhere inappropriate. Our shop owner friend wouldn't do that. He's in his twenties, but he said he remembers how hard it was to get around during his *rumschpringe*."

Abraham clasped the reins in one hand as his other hand found hers. "Hannah, I'm happy to take you to a movie, if you'd rather do that." He smiled, squeezing her hand. "I just love you so much I don't want to share our time with anyone else."

Hannah smiled back at him as her heart rate soared. "I don't want to share our time with anyone else either." She couldn't wait to kiss him again.

Ten minutes later they pulled onto the road that led to the beekeeper's cemetery. It was just like she imagined it to be, mostly hidden with lots of trees that formed a canopy over the graves, and there were lots of places to sit on the enormous branches.

Abraham guided the buggy to the best spot—the best place to watch the sunset, he said, almost as if he'd been there before.

"I have to be home at eight." She cringed. "Since this is my first official date. So we're going to miss the sunset, I'm afraid." She glanced around but didn't see any other couples. They'd probably come later, closer to dark, she presumed.

"It's already six o'clock." Abraham frowned a little, but as he leaned over to kiss her, Hannah scooted closer. This kiss was longer, she noted, and even when she tried to ease away, Abraham cupped his hand behind her head and kept his mouth pressed to hers. She'd never kissed anyone before, just Abraham a few nights ago, so she could only trust that this was how it was done. But she jumped when he moved his hand down to the small of her back and pulled her even closer, pausing to take a breath. "I love you so much," he whispered as his breathing grew heavy again.

"I love you too," she said when she was able to ease away from him for a couple seconds. But as good as it felt kissing Abraham, she was aware of his hands, which were pushing boundaries Hannah had previously set for herself.

"Don't, Abraham." She didn't look him in the eye as she put her hand on top of his, sliding it to a more appropriate place.

"I just want to show you how much I love you." He kissed her again, longer, harder, almost forcefully.

"Stop." She put her hands on his chest and pushed him away.

"What? What's wrong? You kept me waiting a month just to kiss you." Abraham scowled as he leaned back. "I thought you loved me."

"I do." Hannah finally locked eyes with him. "But some things should be reserved for marriage."

He grinned. "That's sweet, Hannah, but we're grown-ups. And when you love someone, it's only natural to want to show that person. I've waited a long time."

A month is a long time? "I'm not comfortable with anything but kissing right now." Hannah swallowed hard as a lump formed in her throat.

Abraham scooted away from her and sighed, then mumbled something Hannah didn't fully understand. It sounded like he said maybe he'd chosen the wrong sister.

She blinked her eyes a few times. Surely she'd heard him wrong. "Um, what did you say? I didn't quite hear you."

"Nothing." Abraham sighed again.

Hannah took a deep breath, resolved that she'd misheard him. She didn't want to hurt his feelings. "Abraham, I'm sorry if I upset you or made you mad. I'm . . . I'm just nervous, I guess." She looked up at him.

Abraham moved toward her again, then gently cupped her cheek. "Don't be nervous. There's nothing to be afraid of." He kissed her softly on the lips. "I'll go slow."

Right away, though, Abraham's hands began to travel, and it took everything Hannah had to maintain her boundaries. Finally, she pushed him away again. "Stop, Abraham!"

He flung his hands up and shook his head. "*Ya*, I chose the wrong *schweschder*, that's for sure."

Hannah's jaw dropped.

"What? Why do you look so surprised? Your *schweschder* isn't as pretty as you, but I bet she'd be happy to go out with me."

Hannah's lip trembled for a couple of seconds before her shock and hurt turned into something else. She couldn't stand the thought of Abraham pursuing Rachel in such a way. It wasn't jealousy, though. It was a protective instinct. Hannah wasn't sure if Rachel would be able to resist Abraham's charms. She herself was having a hard time doing so. "I can't believe you just said that."

Abraham shrugged. "You knew we were coming here. What did you think we were going to do?"

"I thought we would get to know each other better. Talk. Kiss."

Abraham grinned. "*Ach*, well, I was *trying* to get to know you better."

Hannah gazed at the handsomest guy she'd ever seen,

knowing pride and vanity were not to be tolerated according to the *Ordnung*. Hannah had let him draw her in based on his charm and good looks, but now she questioned her judgment.

"Maybe you should just take me home." She pressed her lips firmly together to keep them from trembling.

Abraham raised one shoulder and dropped it slowly. "*Ya*, fine. But I thought you loved me."

"And I thought you loved me. But if you did, you wouldn't be acting this way."

He rolled his eyes. "Grow up, Hannah. When people love each other, they want to express that love."

"And they do. After they're married." She folded her arms across her chest as anger mingled with hurt, her eyes filling with tears. This wasn't how she'd expected her first real date to go. Her lip trembled, and she couldn't stop it this time as tears gathered in the corners of her eyes. "I want to go home."

"Fine. I guess we're breaking up."

Hannah sniffled. "I guess so."

Abraham shrugged. "Since we're broken up, then I guess I'm free to ask Rachel out."

Hannah snapped her head toward him, eyes blazing as she swiped at her eyes. "No, you aren't asking *mei schweschder* out."

"Like I said, she's not as pretty as you, but she's cute." He scratched his chin. "I bet she'd show a guy a little love."

Hannah forced a thin-lipped smile even though her heart was pounding in her chest. "She won't go out with you."

Yet even as she spoke, she knew that wasn't true. Rachel remained livid that Hannah had snagged the man Rachel picked out for herself. Would her sister go along with Abraham's advances, only to be devastated later on when she realized what you see isn't always what you get?

She waited for Abraham to say something, but to her surprise, he suddenly hung his head. They sat in silence.

Finally, he spoke. "I'm such an idiot." His voice was filled with remorse.

He lifted his head, and Hannah locked eyes with him. She didn't know what to say. *Idiot* wasn't a word they commonly used, but she knew what it meant, and he had certainly acted like one.

"Can we start over?" Abraham reached for her hand, and she let him take it in his. "I have had a horrible day, one of those days where everything goes wrong, and I don't mean to take it out on you." His words cracked a little as he squeezed her hand and hung his head again.

Hesitantly, Hannah squeezed his hand back. "I'm sorry you had a bad day." *Everyone has bad days.*

"And I am so sorry I brought up your *schweschder.* That was a terrible thing to do. It's you I love." Once again looking at her, he cupped her cheek. "I'm just frustrated because I want to *show* you how much I love you, and I guess I lost my head. Please forgive me."

Hannah wanted to believe him. But even more, she wanted to protect her sister. Maybe this was her punishment for stealing Abraham from Rachel in the first place. What if things hadn't happened exactly this way? It could be Rachel sitting in Abraham's buggy fending off roaming hands. Or would she have given in to him? Hannah wanted to believe that Rachel wouldn't have, but she didn't know for sure.

God always had a plan. Maybe Hannah was exactly where she was meant to be and this was the Lord's will for her.

She was lost in thought as Abraham again said he was sorry. "I only want to be with you." He leaned in to kiss her again, and Hannah didn't pull away.

But how far am I willing to go to protect Rachel?

CHAPTER 3

Rachel carried her small shopping basket to the front of the market and got in line behind an *Englisch* woman about her mother's age. The woman was tall and wide, and it wasn't until she bent over to unload her groceries that Rachel saw the cashier. *Gideon Lapp.*

The Lapp family had been a part of her life since she was born. In fact, Gideon, Rachel, and Hannah had grown up together and knew each other so well that their mothers had tried to play matchmaker over the past year. They'd set their *kapps* on a relationship between Rachel and Gideon. The two teenagers both loved to read, had a fondness for animals—even the not-so-friendly ones, like raccoons—and could play board games all afternoon. Hannah wasn't crazy about animals, and Rachel couldn't remember the last time she'd seen her sister read a book. So it made sense the moms would choose her for the match. But their tactics had often been embarrassing.

Rachel recalled a Sunday singing at Gideon's house. The social event for teens was scheduled to begin at four o'clock in the afternoon. Rachel's mother had told her three o'clock and dropped her off an hour early, forcing her to spend an hour alone with Gideon. In any other situation that would have been fine since they were really good friends. But the giddiness of their mothers had made the encounter awkward.

Another time, after church service, Gideon and Rachel had been talking about a book they'd both just read and had overheard their mothers talking about what beautiful children they'd make. Rachel had been terribly embarrassed. Judging from the redness in Gideon's face, so had he.

The attempts to pair them up in this year leading up to their *rumschpringe* had ended up backfiring. Rachel wasn't having any part of the matter, if for no other reason than the determination their mothers had displayed at the prospect of their children marrying. And the potential to share grandchildren.

"*Wie bischt,*" Gideon said after the *Englisch* lady left. He picked up a bag of sugar and scanned it.

"I'm *gut*. And you?" Rachel opened her small black purse and pulled out the cash her mother had given her for the items they needed.

Gideon shrugged. "Okay, I guess."

Rachel eyed him. Gideon's hair was the color of field oats and flattened from his hat, and his bangs were too long. He was tall and lanky, almost like he was still growing into his body. Today his blue shirt was untucked on one side even though he was wearing suspenders to hold up his pants. But despite his disheveled appearance, Gideon had an infectious smile and eyes that were either amber or green, depending on the light. Had it not been for the pushiness of their mothers, maybe they might actually have taken a liking to each other as more than just friends. "You don't sound okay."

"*Mei mamm* is sick." He didn't look up as he scanned a chocolate candy bar that hadn't been on the list.

"What's wrong? Does my *mamm* know about this?" Rachel put a hand to her chest. Marian Lapp wasn't just her mother's best friend. She was like an aunt to Rachel and Hannah.

Gideon shook his head. "*Nee*, she hasn't said anything to anyone about her illness. But can you please tell your *mamm*? I think she needs some support."

Rachel's heart hammered against her chest. "What's *wrong* with her?"

"She just found out she's diabetic." Gideon sighed as he shook his head, then held out his hand for the cash Rachel was holding.

Relief washed over her. "At least that's treatable, *ya*? I was afraid you were going to say cancer or something just as bad."

Gideon counted Rachel's change, handed it to her, then raised a bushy eyebrow. "The doctor said her blood sugar is dangerously high, and do you know anyone among us who enjoys baking and eating sweets more than *mei mamm*?"

"Hmm . . . you're right." Marian was always baking, like most of them were, but she'd always had a sweet tooth that seemed to bypass the norm. She was overweight, but Rachel wouldn't have expected it to affect her health. "But there are others in our district who have to watch their sugar. Like Big Jake Miller. He's been diabetic for years. *Mamm* said he mostly controls it with turmeric and cinnamon."

"I know. But she's real depressed about it. And the doctor has her pricking her finger all hours of the day to test her blood sugar. She's not happy."

A man behind Rachel cleared his throat.

"I've got a break in five minutes. Can you wait for me outside?"

Rachel nodded, then left the store.

Gideon scanned the older man's groceries as fast as he could, not wanting to keep Rachel waiting too long. His replacement cashier showed up five minutes late, so Gideon sprinted toward the exit as soon as he could, glad to see Rachel hadn't given up on him.

"Sorry," he said as he sat down beside her on a bench, catching his breath.

"It's okay."

Rachel's hands were folded in her lap, and she was deep in thought. He'd seen this look before, the serious way she pressed her lips together, the way her eyebrows drew inward. He'd always been attracted to Rachel. Hannah might be seen as the prettier sister by some people, but Gideon had been looking into Rachel's soul for a long time, and he liked what he saw.

Beauty was packaged from the inside out. If you were pretty on the inside, those qualities shone on the outside. He'd always wanted to ask Rachel out, and since her sixteenth birthday was right around the corner, now would be the time, before other suitors lined up. If she rejected him, he feared how it might affect the relationship with their families. But he'd come up with a safe way to test the water.

"I was wondering"—Gideon scratched his chin—"about a way to cheer up *mei mudder.*"

Rachel sat taller, twisting to face him. "How?"

He grinned, hoping his face wasn't turning red. "You know

how our mothers have been trying to fix us up for the past year?"

She lowered her gaze for a few seconds, nodded, then looked back at him.

"I thought of a way to lift *Mamm's* spirits." He raised an eyebrow and grinned. "If you and I started dating."

Rachel frowned, which was like a kick to Gideon's gut. Before she could object, he said, "I mean, we wouldn't really date. We could just pretend we are going out, to cheer up *Mamm*."

Scowling now, Rachel shook her head. "That sounds very deceitful. And then what would happen when we eventually broke up? Both of our families would be upset."

Gideon just needed a chance to spend time with Rachel to see where things might go, so he pressed on. "Our families wouldn't be upset if we dated, then realized we weren't meant for each other. We'd break up amicably, they'd quit trying to push us together, and hopefully by then *mei mudder* would be settled into her new diet and not be so depressed."

"It would be like lying."

Gideon's heart took another blow at the confirmation that she wasn't really interested in testing the water. "If two people enjoy each other's company and choose to go to the movies or out to eat, or shopping or something, then that's dating, and it's not a lie." He held his breath.

She pressed her lips together again and moved her mouth back and forth. He could practically see the wheels spinning in her head. "How long would we do this?"

How about forever? He swallowed hard and shrugged. "A month or so?"

Rachel chuckled and rolled her eyes. "I can already see my

mother. She's going to be so excited." She stilled her laughter, frowning again. "But it will probably break her heart when we break up."

Gideon held up one finger. "Not if we break up thoughtfully, and it will have served as a distraction for my mother, something to bring her out of the depression she's fallen into."

He sucked in another breath and waited.

Rachel's first thought was of Abraham. Although Hannah was doing her best to make sure Rachel would never know the feel of Abraham's arms around her. But dating Gideon could serve several purposes: it would cheer up Mrs. Lapp and maybe make more guys interested in dating Rachel after she'd dated Gideon. And best of all . . . maybe Abraham would be jealous. Plus, it would be good practice to pretend to date Gideon, since Rachel was often nervous around guys her age. Gideon was a good friend. Rachel was sure she was his second choice. His and Rachel's parents might think Gideon and Rachel were a good match, but given the opportunity, Gideon might have chosen Hannah. But he couldn't ask Hannah to be his pretend girlfriend now that she was seeing Abraham.

"Okay, but . . ." She paused as her pulse picked up. "No, uh . . . dating type stuff."

Gideon grinned. "You mean no kissing?"

Rachel nodded, even though she couldn't stop looking at his mouth now. "Public displays of affection aren't our way"—she made herself turn away—"so there shouldn't be a need for any physical contact." She raised her chin a little as her eyes drifted back to his mouth. Rachel had never kissed anyone, although her sister had probably done so enough for both of them recently.

She picked up the two small bags of groceries and stood. "So when will you be asking me out?"

"How about now?" Gideon's eyebrows went up as he stood and grinned again. He bowed at the waist as he tipped his straw hat. "Rachel, would you do me the honor of your presence this Saturday night? Would you allow me to take you to supper and a movie?"

Rachel chuckled as she curtsied. "Why, *ya*, dear sir. I would be equally as honored." She straightened, stood perfectly still, and tipped her head to one side. "Are we really going to go to supper and a movie? I've never been to a movie."

Gideon stepped closer. "We might be bordering on the edge of deception, but I'll never put you in a position where you have to lie. *Ya*, we are going to supper and a movie. And you can pick where you want to eat and the movie you want to see. I'll line up a driver."

Rachel giggled. "Okay, but we will go Dutch and each pay for our own."

Gideon shook his head. "*Nee*, that's not how it works. I'll be paying." He tipped his hat again, winked at her, and said. "See you Saturday."

This is going to be more fun than I thought.

Rachel started walking to her buggy. For the first time in a long while, she had something to look forward to. She wondered how Hannah and Abraham's date had gone, or if they'd skipped the movie and moved on to the other plans she'd overheard them making on the phone. Rachel had been too bitter to ask her sister much of anything lately. But maybe they'd seen a movie they could recommend.

And maybe Rachel could shed the anger she'd been feeling toward Hannah.

Closing her eyes, she prayed for just that purpose, thankful she could honestly ask for something different than the selfish requests she'd been sending up the past few days.

CHAPTER 4

Hannah set the table while her mother pulled the roast out of the oven. After Rachel filled four tea glasses, she called out to their father in the living room. "Supper is ready, *Daed*."

When they were all seated, Hannah bowed her head along with her family, and they prayed silently. Hannah thanked the Lord for the plentiful bounty spread before them and for her many blessings. *And God, please help me to avoid temptation where Abraham is concerned.* It was the same prayer she'd been silently reciting several times a day since their first date.

Hannah filled her plate with a little of everything—roast, potatoes, chowchow, and a slice of buttered bread—although she didn't have much of an appetite.

"Have you *maeds* thought about what you would like to do for your birthday? It's only a couple weeks away." *Mamm* looked back and forth between Rachel and Hannah. "I know we don't usually make a fuss over birthdays, but your sixteenth is special. We can have a small party, if you'd like."

"I don't want a party." Hannah spat the words before she considered that Rachel might feel differently. She glanced at her sister, but Rachel was taking a sip of tea, so Hannah refocused on her food, mostly moving it around on her plate.

"Rachel, how do you feel?" *Mamm* fixed her gaze on Hannah's sister, who shrugged.

"I guess it's whatever Hannah wants."

Hannah narrowed her eyes at Rachel. "Don't say it like that, like I always get what I want."

"That's not how I meant it." Rachel glared at Hannah from across the table.

"Well, that's how it sounded." Hannah lowered her voice when their father cleared his throat. "If you want a party, we'll have a party."

"I'm fine without a party." Rachel forked a bite of meat and stuffed it in her mouth.

"You're smacking your food." Hannah glared at Rachel across the table. "It's not very ladylike."

"I'm not smacking!"

"Enough!" Their father slammed his fork on his plate and stood up, pointing his finger back and forth between Hannah and Rachel. "I don't know what is going on with you two, although I suspect it has something to do with a fellow, but this is going to stop."

"She's mad because I'm dating Abraham." Hannah looked up at her father, who was scowling.

Daed narrowed his eyebrows at Hannah. "If that's true, then what are you being so unruly about?"

Hannah opened her mouth to say something, but she couldn't tell her parents the truth. No words came out as she swallowed the lump in her throat.

"Well, there's nothing wrong with me," Rachel said. "I'm not mad or upset about Hannah dating Abraham. As a matter of fact, I have some news to tell you all."

Their father slowly settled back into his chair and hesitantly picked up his fork as he kept his eyes on Rachel.

"I have a date Saturday night." Rachel looked at their mother. "I have a date with Gideon."

Mamm pressed her palms together, sat taller, and smiled. "Wonderful, just wonderful."

In spite of her irritation at her sister, Hannah's insides warmed. It had been obvious for a long time that Gideon was sweet on Rachel. He was a wonderful person, and for a time, Hannah had a crush on him. But it was clear that Gideon only had eyes for Rachel.

Still, Hannah was surprised that Rachel was finally giving Gideon a chance. She'd complained for the past year about how their mother and Gideon's mother kept trying to push them into a relationship, and how she wasn't having any part of it.

"I think that's great that you and Gideon are going out." Hannah forced a smile, even though Rachel had been dreadfully ugly to her lately. She was truly happy for her sister.

And maybe this meant she could break up with Abraham before things got out of control. So far she'd kept his roaming hands away, but she wasn't sure how much longer she'd be able to. Now it wouldn't matter. Abraham wouldn't ask Rachel out if she were dating Gideon. Hannah breathed a huge sigh of relief.

Rachel fought the snarly comments bubbling to the surface. *You're not the only one who can get a boyfriend.* But she smiled and tried to distance herself from the visions of Abraham and Hannah kissing.

"We're going to supper and a movie Saturday night," she said, keeping her gaze on her mother.

"How wonderful," *Mamm* said again, smiling. "Marian and I prayed for this."

Rachel took in a deep breath, feeling the weight of the deception pressing down on her. "We're not getting married, *Mamm*. It's just a date."

Her mother grinned, winking at Rachel. "*Ach*, well, you never know."

Rachel swallowed hard. Would her mother and Gideon's mother really be okay when they broke up? Or would the pretend relationship's demise cause more trouble than the temporary happiness?

"*Mamm*, I need to tell you something about Gideon's *mudder*." Rachel filled her lungs with air and blew it out slowly as all eyes landed on her.

"What? Is something wrong with Marian? She's been a bit of a stranger lately." *Mamm* dabbed at her mouth with her napkin but kept her eyes on Rachel.

"Gideon said she was diagnosed with diabetes."

Mamm sighed and hung her head. "Oh, dear. I bet Marian is devastated."

"*Ya*, Gideon said she's very upset and won't talk to anyone about it. He said her blood sugar levels are dangerously high." Rachel waited until her mother looked up at her. "Gideon thought I should tell you. He thinks she needs support from her friends. You know how much she likes to bake and eat."

Mamm shook her head. "Don't we all. I'll pay her a visit tomorrow. Does she know Gideon asked you out?"

"I don't know." Rachel placed her fork across her plate as she shrugged.

Mamm smiled. "Well, that news should cheer her up."

Rachel tried to smile but only half managed.

"That's terrible about Gideon's mother." Hannah shook her head before she took a tiny bite of buttered bread. "What movie are you going to see?"

"I don't know yet." Rachel raised one shoulder and dropped it slowly as she took a bite of roast. She waited for Hannah to tell them what movie she and Abraham had gone to, if they had, but her sister moved her food around on her plate and stayed quiet. But *Mamm* must have been wondering the same thing.

"Hannah, what movie did you and Abraham see the other night?" *Mamm* shook her head a tiny bit as she asked the question. Since movies were forbidden, Rachel glanced back and forth between her parents, catching a slight look of disdain from her father. But Rachel figured her mother couldn't help but be curious if Hannah and her date had at least chosen something without violence and bad language. Rachel was surprised her mother hadn't questioned Hannah before now. And despite her mother's eagerness for Rachel and Gideon to date, Rachel was also surprised that her mother hadn't balked—even a little bit—at Rachel's mention of a movie with Gideon.

Hannah's chair screeched across the wooden floor as she hurriedly backed up. "I don't feel well. May I be excused?" She stood up and put a hand across her stomach.

"*Ya*, of course." *Mamm* slid her chair back. "What's wrong?"

"*Nee*, don't get up." Hannah put a hand over her mouth, then hurried away, mumbling over her shoulder. "I just have an upset stomach."

Their mother stood up and peered into the living room as Hannah reached the stairs. Rachel also stood as she wiped her mouth with her napkin. "*Mamm*, I'm done eating. I'll go check on her so you can finish your supper."

Her mother nodded, and Rachel made her way across the living room, then took the stairs two at a time. She'd seen Hannah pull this trick before, faking sickness to avoid something. And Rachel was going to get to the bottom of whatever it was her sister was hiding.

Hannah closed the bathroom door behind her, but she could hear heavy footsteps on the stairs and knew it had to be Rachel. Her sister walked like an elephant. Or was it simply that everything Rachel did irritated Hannah these days?

"I'm fine," Hannah said when Rachel banged on the bathroom door.

"I'm sure you are."

Hannah stood up from where she'd been sitting on the edge of the bathtub, her temperature rising. "What does *that* mean?"

"It means that I've been your *schweschder* for almost sixteen years. You've been using the 'I'm sick' excuse to get out of everything from doing dishes to telling the truth."

Thankfully Rachel had lowered her voice. Hannah slung the door wide and swooshed past her sister, bumping her in the hip as she did. "You don't know what you're talking about."

Rachel followed Hannah into their bedroom. "You didn't even go to the movies with Abraham, did you?"

Hannah sat down on her bed, plumped up her pillows, then

swung her feet onto the bed and lay back. "It's none of your business what I did on my date." She smiled the fake sort of smile you thrust at someone you despise. "None of your business at all what *we* did, Abraham and I."

Despite her defiance, on the inside Hannah shuddered. What was she doing? Her stomach churned as she recalled the date. If Rachel only knew how uncomfortable the whole experience had been. And how scared Hannah was of what the future held. Again she wondered if she could and should break up with Abraham now that Rachel was dating Gideon. Then maybe things would get back to normal between the sisters.

"You went to the beekeeper's cemetery, didn't you?" Rachel's jaw hung low as she waited for Hannah to respond.

Hannah took a deep breath and avoided Rachel's accusing stare. They had pinky sworn a long time ago that they'd never let a boy take them there. Even though pinky swearing was something they'd learned from an *Englisch* friend when they were younger and wasn't something their parents would likely approve of, they'd kept their promise to each other. Until now.

"And what if I did?"

Rachel sat down on the edge of Hannah's bed. "Is Abraham so good-looking that you've forgotten the way we were raised? Have you forgotten what happened to Sarah?"

Hannah squeezed her eyes closed as she pictured Sarah being sent to live with her *Englisch* grandparents in Iowa because she'd gotten pregnant. "I'm not going to let anything like that happen."

"I hope not." Rachel spoke quietly now.

"Can you get on your own bed, please?" Hannah glared at Rachel, suddenly resentful of all she was doing for her sister.

She'd been planning to keep dating a guy who was a jerk just to make sure he didn't hurt Rachel. She wondered if Rachel would protect her in such a way. Or would Hannah's sister be so desperate to have someone like Abraham pursue her that she'd think only of herself? Hannah didn't want to believe that, but love was turning out to be a confusing thing when it came to guys.

It will all be over soon. After I break up with Abraham.

Hannah waited until Rachel was sitting on her own bed, then rolled onto her side and faced the window. Orange hues became one with the clouds as the sun began to set, and Hannah still needed to take a bath. For now she just wanted to lie quietly.

She hoped she could break up with Abraham before their next date, scheduled for Saturday. Now that she'd seen how he reacted when things didn't go his way, she feared what might happen when she told him.

It didn't matter anymore. She just wanted out of the relationship and away from Abraham Stoltzfus. And she wanted to talk to her best friend, her sister. But as a tear rolled down her cheek, she stayed quiet.

CHAPTER 5

Rachel finished ironing her favorite maroon dress. Her date with Gideon would begin in about an hour. "Aren't you going to get ready for your date with Abraham?"

Hannah didn't move from her spot on the bed where she'd been lying for the past hour, staring off into space while she pretended to read a book she was holding. "I *am* ready."

Rachel ran the iron over her dress once more, then set it aside. She really hadn't heated the iron long enough to do a good job, but she didn't think guys noticed a few wrinkles. She eyed her sister's tangled hair fanned across her pillow like plucked angel wings, wondering if Hannah would brush the knotty mess before she pinned it beneath her *kapp*. And had Hannah ever taken a bath last night? Rachel didn't think so.

"You don't look ready," Rachel said in a whisper as she removed the blue dress she was wearing. She tossed it in a pile of clothes near the corner of the room, then pulled the freshly ironed dress over her head. When she finally looked at Hannah again, her sister hadn't moved. Normally such a comment would have sparked a feud, or at least a retort.

Rachel sighed softly. She'd watched her sister all week, and something had obviously been bothering her. Rachel wanted to ask her what was wrong. Prior to Abraham Stoltzfus, she would have. They'd never kept things from each other. But things had been differently lately.

Rachel stuffed the urge to ask Hannah what was going on. She had more important things to think about, like her first date. Even if it was just a pretend date. That was probably why she wasn't nervous, the way she'd expected she would be the first time she went out with someone.

But this was her friend Gideon. They'd had the chicken pox at the same time, back when the community was still debating about vaccinations. They'd spent six days together at Gideon's house when they were five, since they couldn't be around other children, some of whom hadn't received the vaccination either. Rachel recalled her mother waiting and waiting for Hannah to break out with the itchy red spots, but she never did. *Mamm* finally took Hannah to get the vaccination. Rachel still had tiny scars from the pox.

Of course Hannah was spared.

Rachel and Gideon continued to hang out together after those six days together. They learned to read sitting side by side in the one-room schoolhouse. They always picked each other for softball or volleyball teams. When Gideon broke his arm, she'd been the first person he'd wanted to sign his cast. And Rachel knew that Gideon would eat most anything, except for pickled beets. They were friends—really good friends. There'd been an interlude when her body was changing and she hadn't wanted to be around boys. But once into her teen years, she and Gideon had begun to hang out again.

Finally, Rachel couldn't take it anymore. "Hannah, what's

wrong? You look like something the cat dragged in, and you don't seem to have any interest in your date tonight. Are you sick?"

Hannah rolled her eyes, blew out a big puff of air, and sat up on the bed. "I'm not sick. I'm fine."

Rachel started to tell Hannah she didn't look fine, but thought better of it. She'd probably said enough. "Okay, well . . ." She shrugged. "I guess I'll go downstairs and wait for Gideon." She was almost out the door when she turned back around and peeked inside the bedroom. "I hope you have fun tonight." She said it with as much sincerity as she could muster. She waited for Hannah to respond, but her sister just shrugged and lay back down.

No matter how angry she'd been at Hannah, Rachel walked down the stairs on shaky legs. She and Hannah might have been distant lately, but Rachel could feel something wrong with her sister, and without knowing what it was, it scared her. She stopped at the bottom of the stairs, thinking it over, then gasped, quickly slamming a hand against her mouth. Maybe Hannah really was sick because . . .

Because . . . she's pregnant.

Who knew what Hannah and Abraham had been doing all those times they'd been hanging out before Rachel saw them kissing out the bedroom window. And maybe Hannah *hadn't* been lying when she said she wasn't feeling well the other night. Maybe she was lying now. Was it possible?

Rachel shook her head so hard, she almost lost her prayer covering, but she still couldn't shake loose of the thought swirling like a tornado in her mind. She took a deep breath and made her way across the living room when she saw her date pulling into the driveway.

Gideon parked his spring buggy in front of Rachel's house. In spite of himself, he was nervous. Even though he'd turned sixteen two months ago, this was his first date.

He tethered the horse, thinking about how long he'd wanted to go out with Rachel. He smiled. *Probably since I was five.* If it was possible for two five-year-olds to bond, he and Rachel had done so when they'd had the chicken pox. He remembered how every morning Rachel's *mudder* had dropped her off, since Gideon didn't have any siblings and they were trying to keep the illness from spreading. The details of that time were sketchy now, but he remembered telling his *mudder* he was going to marry Rachel someday. *Mamm* had glowed with happiness, and Gideon wondered if he'd set the stage for her matchmaking a long time ago.

"You look beautiful," Gideon said when Rachel opened the front door. He'd told her before that maroon was her best color. He wondered if she'd worn the dress for him, then reminded himself that this wasn't a real date.

"*Danki.* And you look pretty spiffy yourself."

Gideon chuckled. "Spiffy?" He shrugged. "Okay. *Danki.*"

"*Mamm* and *Daed* said to apologize that they couldn't be here when you arrived." Rachel lowered her gaze, her face turning pink. "You know, since it's my first date, they wanted to be here, but they had supper plans with the Bylers."

Gideon waited until she looked back at him. "That's okay. There's no one I'd rather be going on a first date with." He waved his arm for her to go ahead of him. They'd just started to cross the yard when Abraham turned in the drive. "I guess Hannah has a date tonight too."

Rachel didn't say anything for a few seconds as she stopped and watched Abraham pulling his buggy down the driveway. "*Ya*, she does."

Gideon took a deep breath. Rachel's tone hadn't gone unnoticed. She'd surely rather be with Abraham. But Gideon wasn't going to hold back in his effort to show Rachel that they could be a real couple.

He walked with her to Abraham's buggy.

"*Wie bischt*," Abraham said as he stepped out.

Gideon nodded, forcing a smile. He'd seen Abraham at church service every two weeks over the last couple months, but that was it, since his family had only recently moved here. Gideon was over six feet tall, but Abraham was even taller. And the guy practically oozed charm. Gideon thought he could be pretty charming himself sometimes, but Abraham's perfect smile, combined with the confident way he held himself, left Gideon standing way outside of this guy's circle of winning attributes. No wonder all the girls were going crazy over him.

Rachel included. He'd seen the way she watched him at worship services.

They all turned to the porch when the screen door slammed closed. Hannah hurried down the steps toward them, but Rachel grabbed Gideon's hand and said they needed to go. He gave a quick wave to Hannah, then told Abraham bye as Rachel dragged him to his buggy.

After they were on the road, he said, "What was that all about? Are you and Hannah fighting or something?" *Probably over Abraham.*

Rachel shrugged, her gaze straight ahead. "*Nee*, not really."

Something was wrong, but Gideon wasn't sure if he should

push her on it. He wanted this to be a good first date for both of them. He cleared his throat. "So, where would you like to go?"

Her head snapped around toward him, her eyes wide. "You said we were going to eat. Aren't we going to supper? Because that's what you said. You weren't expecting to go anywhere else, were you?"

Gideon realized his mouth was open, so he closed it. "Uh, I thought we were going to eat."

She brought a hand to her chest and let out a breath she seemed to be holding. "*Ya,* right. That's what I thought."

"I just meant what restaurant?" He paused, flicked the reins, and got them across the highway and onto a side street with less traffic. "But we can do something else if you want to."

"*Nee!* Supper is *gut.* I want supper."

They were quiet for a few minutes, and Gideon was surprised that Rachel seemed so nervous, steadily twirling the string of her *kapp.* Maybe that was a good thing. He wasn't sure. But he'd known Rachel all his life. Something was bothering her.

"Do you want to tell me what's wrong now, or wait until we get to the restaurant?" He glanced at her, then back at the road, not wanting to miss her reaction, but also not wanting to get them killed. A car had just whizzed by and spooked the horse. It took Gideon a minute to get him calmed down.

"I'll tell you what's bothering me when we get to the restaurant. That way you can focus on getting us there in one piece."

Gideon nodded, but his stomach churned. They hadn't been gone five minutes, and already there was a problem. Rachel's scowl had deepened, her lip folded under into a pout that would leave any guy worried.

Maybe the date hadn't been such a good idea after all.

CHAPTER 6

Rachel couldn't shrug the thought that Hannah might be pregnant. It went against their upbringing and their beliefs. Surely Hannah wouldn't have crossed that line. But the more Rachel thought about it, the more worried she became. They were always within a week of each other for their monthlies, but this past time Rachel couldn't recall Hannah mentioning anything. Usually they both had horrible cramps.

Still, if she was wrong, what a dishonor it would be to Hannah to even mention anything to Gideon.

After they ordered iced tea, Gideon looked at her and grinned. "This is a nice place. I've never been here."

"Me either." Rachel had chosen a restaurant that she had heard good things about but that wasn't expensive. "Another first for both of us." She smiled, then refocused on her menu, which consisted of a little bit of everything—chicken, fish, steaks, burgers, and appetizers.

They each ordered a burger, then talked about the weather, gardening techniques, books, the movie they were planning to see, and other topics that couples might talk about on their first date to get to know each other.

Finally, Gideon leaned back against the seat of the booth. "So . . . what has you troubled?"

Rachel was still leery about saying too much. Maybe she was way off about Hannah and Abraham. "I'm worried about Hannah. She just hasn't been herself lately."

Gideon drew his eyebrows together. "Is she sick?"

Rachel tried to read Gideon's level of concern. They might have been the best of friends, but now that they were old enough to date, maybe Gideon was hoping it wouldn't work out with Hannah and Abraham. That had certainly been Rachel's hope—that it wouldn't last. But Hannah's troubled mood had cast those thoughts aside for now. In spite of everything, Rachel just wanted her sister to be happy again.

Rachel shrugged. "I'm not really sure if she's sick. She's been snappy, but it's not even really that. She seems . . . depressed."

"That doesn't sound like Hannah. She's always upbeat."

They paused as the waitress arrived and set their plates in front of them.

"Most of the time, she is." Rachel picked up a french fry and blew on it before putting it in her mouth. After she finished it, she snuck a look at Gideon as he took a big bite of his burger. He'd gotten a haircut, and she'd thought she smelled a hint of spice, like cologne, earlier when they were in the buggy. Rachel had been guilty of spritzing herself with a lavender body spray earlier. Colognes and perfumes weren't normally allowed, but she supposed it was another one of the things that would be overlooked as she breezed into her *rumschpringe*.

She tried not to read anything into either of their grooming preparations. They both knew this wasn't a real date.

"I'll pray for her, that whatever is wrong, she'll be feeling better soon."

"*Danki*. This just isn't like her. She always tells me everything, and I always tell her everything." She smiled a little. "Hannah is like a diary of my life. She knows everything about me. And I know everything about her. Or, I thought I did."

She took a sip of tea, then sighed. She really needed to stop focusing on her worries and instead put her mind toward having fun this evening. She took a breath and lightened her tone. "I'm sorry. I should have asked how your *mamm* is doing. *Mei mudder* went to see her the other day, but your *mamm* wasn't home, so I don't think they've actually spoken or *mei mudder* would have mentioned it. Is she feeling better about her diagnosis?"

"I don't know." Gideon chuckled. "But her spirits lifted considerably when I told her we were going out tonight." He nodded his head. "This was a good plan. Even if it's just temporary, I think it will give her something to be happy about while she adjusts to a new way of eating."

"I just hope this doesn't backfire on us and we don't do more damage, like really upset her even more when we break up." Rachel laughed. "My *mudder* was pretty excited, too, when I told her we were going out."

"So, now we have to decide what movie to see. I have a driver meeting us back at my house. I didn't want him to have to wait while we ate, so I only hired him to take us to the movies. It's Arlen Walsh, an *Englischer mei daed* knows. He lives close to the movie theater, so he'll just go home while the movie plays, then come back and get us." Gideon lifted a shoulder and lowered it. "That way, you can say hi to my parents before we go to the show. My *mamm* will like that." He reached into the pocket of his black slacks and unfolded a newspaper clipping. "Here's what is playing." He handed it to Rachel. "You pick."

She set it on the table in front of her and clapped her hands lightly together. "Yay! I get to pick. But I want it to be something you'll like too."

Gideon took another bite of his burger, then wiped his mouth "You know, you've done that since you were little, clapping your hands together when you're happy."

Rachel smiled. "I guess you're kind of like a diary of my life too." Even though there were plenty of things she hadn't shared with Gideon, he knew a lot about her. He knew which books were her favorites and that she snorted when she laughed too hard—an embarrassing thing not many people had witnessed. And he knew that for a while she'd wanted to leave their district to be a veterinarian. That childhood ambition had been quashed the first time she saw blood, and besides, she wanted to be close to God in the community she'd grown up in.

It was also Gideon's shoulder she'd cried on when her grandmother died. Her mother had been overwhelmed with grief, and Hannah and her father did their best to comfort her at the time. But Rachel had been particularly close to her *grandmammi*, and she'd spent a lot of time in Gideon's arms after she died. It hadn't seemed odd at the time, but when she thought about it, she wondered how it would feel now.

Rachel was still having trouble keeping her eyes off Gideon's lips. She had always assumed there would be a kiss after a first date. But this was different, and she suspected they'd hug on the front porch when the date was over. Especially since Rachel had already told him no dating-type stuff.

Unlike Hannah and Abraham.

No, she wouldn't think of them. Instead, she studied the movies that were playing in Lancaster. But every time she started to read a description, her traitorous mind drifted to Hannah. The more she thought about her sister, the more her heart started to race. In the past, that had always been an indication that something was wrong. As the hammering in her chest worsened, she found it difficult to focus on anything else.

Hannah pushed Abraham away, burst into tears, and covered her face with her hands. "I want to go home," she said with muffled cries. "Just take me home."

"What's wrong?"

Hannah lowered her hands and gazed into his dark eyes, unable to tell if he was sympathetic to her tears or angry. She suspected the latter. "You know what's wrong."

They were sitting next to each other on a yellow-and-blue pastel quilt Abraham had brought. He'd spread it out on the ground. Hannah was never going to own a quilt with those colors.

"I don't think this is working out, Abraham." She sniffled, then swiped at her eyes. "I think things are different here than where you came from."

Abraham's bottom lip twitched. "Things are the same everywhere, Hannah. You've just led a sheltered life." He threw the words at her like a reprimand, but he flashed a slight grin. "Are you trying to break up with me?"

"*Nee*, Abraham. I'm not *trying* to break up with you. I *am* breaking up with you." She pulled a tissue from the pocket of her white apron and dabbed at her eyes. "I'm sorry," she repeated.

He touched her arm, and she flinched. "Hannah, I understand that you're scared about what's happening between us. I
am too. I've never loved anyone the way I love you."

Hannah closed her eyes for a few moments, drawn in by the
tenderness in his voice, and then she met his gaze, his eyes like
magnets, pulling her to a place she shouldn't go. It was early, and
the sun had barely begun its descent. Hannah could see her reflec-
tion in Abraham's eyes, but she wasn't sure she liked what she saw.

"Please don't cry." He spoke in a whisper as he gently kissed
her on the cheek. "I'm sorry if I get carried away sometimes. It's
just . . ." He lowered his gaze, then looked back at her, tears pooling in the corners of his eyes. "You're just so beautiful, and I love
you so much."

Hannah took a deep breath. "If you loved me so much, you
wouldn't keep pushing me to do things I'm not comfortable
with. Things *you* shouldn't be comfortable with either."

He raised both palms and smiled. His tears vanished as
quickly as they'd appeared. "I surrender. I promise. I'll be good.
Let's don't break up."

This was the Abraham she'd fallen for. Confident, charming, and more good-looking than anyone she'd ever seen. But
the more she saw what was inside him, the less and less attractive
he'd become.

She took another deep breath. "I'm sorry, Abraham, I really
am. But I am breaking up with you. I don't want to date you anymore. And I want to go home."

Abraham was eerily quiet, his eyes fused with hers, his
expression difficult to read, like the calm before a big storm.

Hannah had been really afraid twice in her life. Once when
she cut her leg climbing over a barbwire fence. The gash had

been deep, and she'd never seen so much blood. The other time was when Rachel was sick and ran such a high fever that she hallucinated and talked to people who weren't in the room.

Next to those two events, the look on Abraham's face molded into an expression that now held the number three spot on her list, and she trembled.

Abraham's nostrils flared as his lips thinned with anger. His brown eyes turned black with fury as he clenched his fists at his sides. "No one has ever broken up with me, Hannah King."

Now it was Abraham trembling, but Hannah didn't think it was because he was afraid. She closed her eyes and prayed.

Gideon finished the last of his burger and fries, but Rachel had barely touched any of her food.

"Do you want me to take you home?" Gideon swallowed hard when Rachel looked across the table at him with tears in her eyes. She was upset about Hannah, but he wondered if there was more to her mood. "Maybe this wasn't a *gut* idea. I don't want things to be weird between us, and—"

She shook her head. "It's not you or the date. It's . . ." She blinked her eyes a few times. "Do you think it would be okay if we don't go to a movie?"

Gideon drew in a deep breath and blew it out slowly as he struggled to hide his disappointment. This was going worse than he could have imagined. "*Ya*, sure, that's fine. I'll take you home in the buggy. I can get word to the driver."

She stared at him for a long while. "Do you think we could go to the beekeeper's cemetery?"

Gideon's eyebrows lifted so high in surprise he thought his temples might explode from the pressure. He'd dreamed about kissing Rachel for years, but everyone knew what went on at the beekeeper's cemetery, and Gideon wasn't able to hide his shock, even though a tiny part of him wanted to bolt out the door with her right now.

Rachel covered her face with her hands for a couple of seconds, and when she slowly moved them, her face was as red as a freshly painted barn. "*Nee*, it's not what you think. I'm worried about Hannah, and I think that might be where she and Abraham are." She put a hand across her churning stomach. "I can feel it when something is wrong with Hannah. I'm so worried, Gideon. And I'm so sorry. I was looking forward to seeing a movie."

"*Nee, nee*. Don't be sorry." He reached across the table and found Hannah's hand and squeezed, something that came as natural as breathing, when he wasn't analyzing how things should be on a date. He motioned for the waitress. "We'll leave as soon as I pay the bill."

Gideon worried all the way to the buggy, hoping he would be able to reach their driver before the guy showed up. He had to leave a message, but a few minutes later, they were on the road in his buggy. He could feel the anxiety radiating from Rachel like steam off a hot bath.

"I'm sure she's fine," he said, holding her hand. He was surprised Hannah would go to the beekeeper's cemetery, since the place had such a bad reputation that seemed to follow anyone who went there, but he knew she was a good girl. As was Rachel.

Gideon let go of Rachel's hand when she started to cry, and he coaxed the horse into a fast trot, hoping there wouldn't be much traffic when they neared Lincoln Highway. Sometimes the wait could be awhile, and even worse, impatient *Englischers* often spooked the horses by honking.

"Don't worry. I'll get you there safely and as fast as I can."

"I haven't been very nice to Hannah lately." Rachel found his hand again and held it tightly as Gideon wondered why the sisters had been at odds and if it had anything to do with Abraham. "I don't know what I'd do if anything happened to her."

"I'm sure she's fine," he repeated and squeezed her fingers.

Still, Gideon had seen this play out before. Rachel and Hannah seemed to know when the other was hurt or sick, or if something was wrong. Most recently it happened when Rachel missed a church service a few months ago, which wasn't like her. Gideon had seen Hannah fidgeting throughout the service. About thirty minutes into the worship service, she'd bolted out the door with no explanation. Gideon later learned that she found Rachel at home hallucinating with a high fever.

He could recall multiple incidents like that one, though not all that severe. Mostly it was Hannah running somewhere out of fear for Rachel. Everyone joked that it was because she was the older sister by eight minutes. But right now there was no mistaking the panic in Rachel's eyes or the way her lip trembled. She was scared for Hannah.

Gideon wasn't sure why. Abraham was admired by everyone in the community, even though he'd been here only a month or so. All the girls were smitten with him. But maybe Rachel knew something Gideon didn't. He picked up speed, and Rachel's grip on his hand tightened.

CHAPTER 7

Dusk was settling in by the time Gideon turned on the asphalt road that ran south of the cemetery.

"Stop the buggy!" Rachel screamed. Gideon pulled back on the reins, and the horse lifted its two front legs, neighing and kicking as if fending off an intruder. But it was Hannah who appeared before them, limping, her dark-green dress ripped at the seam. She was missing one of her black loafers.

Rachel jumped from her seat in the topless buggy and ran to Hannah with shaky legs and outstretched arms. "Hannah!" Her heart slammed against her chest as she stopped in front of her sister and latched on to Hannah's forearms. "Are you okay?" She inspected Hannah from head to toe, her eyes homing in on Hannah's scraped knee and the blood trickling down her leg. Tears streaked her sister's face, and a force rose inside Rachel that she didn't know existed. "Who did this to you? Did Abraham hurt you?"

Hannah shook her head. "*Nee, nee.* I fell down." She looked at her one bare foot. "And I twisted my ankle."

"Move." Gideon slid between them, scooped Hannah into his arms, and started walking toward the buggy so fast that Rachel could barely keep up. He gently eased Hannah into the back seat and told Rachel to get in the front. "The horse is spooked. It's almost dark. And I can see headlights in the distance. We need to get going."

After they started down the road, Gideon and Rachel looked over their shoulder at the same time, and both asked Hannah again if she was okay.

Sniffling, she sat up. "I was running from the cemetery, and when I got to the road, I tripped and fell on the asphalt."

Rachel reached behind her and handed Hannah her handkerchief to put on her knee. "Where is Abraham? What happened?" Rachel brought a hand to her chest, hoping to calm her racing heart. "Why were you running?"

Hannah cried harder. "I broke up with Abraham, and he got really mad. He was shaking and yelling at me, and—and I got scared." She sucked in a gasp of air. "So I ran away." She sobbed for a few moments. "He didn't even come after me or look for me, that I know of. And I'm glad." She scrunched up her face, wincing as she dabbed at her knee. "I never want to see him again."

Violence wasn't their way, but Rachel envisioned a baseball bat in her hand as she took a big swing at Abraham.

After the horse was moving in a steady trot on the main road toward home, Gideon reached his arm into the back seat and touched Hannah's arm. "Thank goodness Rachel got that feeling she gets and insisted we head this way. Do you want to stop for a few minutes to gather yourself before we get to your house?"

Hannah shook her head. "*Nee*, I just want to get home."

Rachel took a deep breath, faced forward, and tried to lose the image of herself with the baseball bat. Hannah was okay, and that was all that mattered.

She closed her eyes and slid her hand across the seat in search of Gideon's. When she touched his leg instead, she pulled back and glanced over her shoulder. Gideon's hand had found its way into Hannah's grasp.

Rachel fought the familiar jealousy bubbling to the surface, fearing she was going straight to hell if she couldn't corral her emotions when it came to Hannah and guys. But even though she knew it was probably only Gideon's way of comforting his friend, she couldn't help but wonder, was it more?

Then again, why shouldn't Gideon go after Hannah now that Abraham wasn't in the picture? Hannah was a catch. And Rachel remembered the crush Hannah had on Gideon in the eighth grade. Both sets of parents would be thrilled if Gideon dated Rachel or Hannah. Either sister would surely do. Gideon and Rachel were only friends anyway.

They were quiet as Gideon turned on the road to Rachel and Hannah's house. As discreetly as she could, barely moving her head, Rachel cut her eyes to Gideon's arm, trailing it all the way to his hand, which was still holding on to Hannah's. She took a deep breath, faced forward, and thanked God again that Hannah was okay.

In the yard, Gideon was quick to get out of the buggy. He helped Hannah to her feet, keeping an arm around her shoulder. Rachel walked behind them as Hannah's arm circled Gideon's waist, her head resting on his chest.

"What should we tell *Mamm* and *Daed*?" Rachel was still struggling to control her pulse as she trailed behind them.

Hannah pointed to the living room, then the downstairs bedroom. "The lights are all off. They're already in bed."

Rachel doubted they were asleep, knowing her mother

wouldn't close her eyes until she knew both of her daughters were home safely.

"We'll be really quiet and hurry up the stairs," Hannah said. "We can figure out what to tell them later."

"The truth sounds *gut*," Rachel said, probably much too sarcastically.

Gideon helped Hannah up the porch steps and eased open the screen door, then the wooden door. He waited until Hannah lit a lantern and headed upstairs before he turned and headed back outside.

Rachel followed him. A faint light from the solar lantern in the yard provided enough light for her to see his eyes changing from amber to green. And now that she knew Hannah was okay, once again she couldn't stop looking at Gideon's lips. "That was some kind of first date, *ya*?"

A muscle in Gideon's jaw flicked. "I can't believe Abraham treated Hannah this way."

Rachel shifted her weight, putting herself an inch or two closer to Gideon. She twirled the string from her *kapp* around her finger. "Well, you know Hannah. She'll soon be on to the next fellow in line." She cringed at her own words. Hannah was probably upstairs bawling her eyes out. "I'm sure she'll be okay."

It was surprising how quickly she'd gone from a doting and terrified sister to a jealous shrew. She had proclaimed for a year how she wasn't interested in Gideon, but she couldn't stand the thought of Hannah trying to snatch him away too. Maybe she could salvage the night. She inched closer to Gideon, but he seemed to be looking somewhere over Rachel's shoulder, his wandering gaze traveling up. To the light of the lantern in the girls' room.

Rachel recalled how she had sat in that same spot watching Hannah kissing Abraham. Now the situation had reversed, and she hoped Gideon would kiss her good night.

"I guess I'd better go," he finally said, snapping his attention back to Rachel. "I'm sorry this happened to Hannah. You better go on in and tend to her." He glanced up again at the lit window. "I hope Abraham feels bad for the way he acted."

Then he turned and walked toward his buggy.

Strangely disappointed, Rachel went back to the porch. She was almost up the stairs when Gideon called her name.

"Do you want to try this again next Saturday?" he asked in a loud whisper.

Rachel glanced up at Hannah, who was staring out the window, then back at Gideon. "Sure."

He tipped his straw hat and waved.

Easing open the screen door, Rachel trudged inside, the weight of her guilt pushing her lower and lower. Hannah had endured a horrible night. She might be pregnant. And all Rachel could think about was how she'd feel if Hannah and Gideon got together.

It wasn't even a real date.

Her thoughts tumbled as she recalled how jealous she'd been of Hannah and Abraham. And now, it didn't sound like Abraham was the *gut* person she'd thought him to be. Had his looks overshadowed his personality, tricking them both?

And what about Hannah? If she was finished with Abraham, was she making a move on Gideon?

But Gideon had asked Rachel out again, so maybe she'd been wrong to think there was anything more to his actions with her sister than being a nice guy.

Unsure of her reasoning, Rachel made a decision. She wasn't going to tell Hannah about her and Gideon's arrangement.

Hannah gazed out the window and smiled. Gideon was a good guy, and she hoped it would work out for him and Rachel.

Sniffling, she sat down on her bed and waited for Rachel to get upstairs. Her sister was going to have a lot of questions. She bit her bottom lip and stifled the tears threatening to spill again. She wasn't sure she ever wanted to get involved with another guy. Could any of them really be trusted? *And can I trust myself to choose without losing my head over a man's looks?*

Abraham had seemed so nice in the beginning, so charming, so giving. But as she recalled the warning signs, which were clearer now, she admitted to herself that she'd overlooked some of his less attractive qualities. For example, Abraham had commented that Hannah was prettier than Rachel. It was one thing to say Hannah was pretty, but to compare the sisters was horrible. She'd thought so at the time, but she'd let it go. What did that say about her?

"*Wie bischt.*" Rachel walked in carrying a lantern and closed the door behind her. "Is your knee all right?" She sat on her bed and placed the light on the bedside table between their beds, next to Hannah's lantern.

"*Ya*, it's okay. I just scraped it pretty bad. I put some of *Mamm's* salve on it." Hannah tried to smile. "I'm sorry I messed up your date with Gideon, but I'm so grateful you showed up. I was mostly just upset, and I would have found a way home. But . . . I'm glad it was you and Gideon who found me since I was in such a bad way."

"I just had that feeling." Rachel sighed, and Hannah knew what she meant.

Hannah took off her prayer covering and removed her hairpins, then set the items on the bed, letting her blond hair fall well below her shoulders. Running her fingers through it, she tried to block out the events of the evening, but Rachel's questions would be forthcoming any minute, so she braced herself.

"I can't believe Abraham got so mad about you breaking up with him, mad enough that he scared you." Rachel shook her head. "I never would have thought he would be like that." She raised her eyes to Hannah's and squinted. "Why did you break up with him? Had he gotten angry with you like that before?"

Hannah couldn't tell Rachel how ungentlemanly he'd acted last week. Or that she'd decided to continue dating him to protect Rachel. "He just wasn't the right person for me."

Hannah had fallen asleep as soon as her head hit the pillow, but Rachel was wide awake. If Hannah was pregnant, she might not have broken up with the baby's father, even though he was a jerk. So maybe she wasn't pregnant after all.

Or maybe she was. Maybe she didn't realize she'd missed her monthly and didn't know she was with child.

It was all too much to dive into tonight after what Hannah had been through.

Rachel snuffed out Hannah's lantern but kept hers lit on the table. Reading made her tired, so she opened a magazine to an article about summer gardening tips. After ten or fifteen minutes, she was dozing off sitting up. But she jumped when something hit the window. Straightening, she closed the magazine and sat perfectly still. It happened again—a pebble hitting the glass. The battery was dead on the clock they kept on the nightstand, but Rachel figured it to be around ten.

Hannah snored lightly as Rachel tiptoed to the window and peered into the darkness. She didn't see anyone at first, but then someone shined a flashlight at her, blinding her for a moment. Once the light was out of her face, she saw someone standing in the yard, near enough to the propane lamp that she was finally able to make out who it was.

She looked over her shoulder at Hannah, still sleeping soundly, then, quiet as a church mouse, she slid her dress over her nightgown, grabbed the lantern, and left the room to go outside.

CHAPTER 8

R achel tiptoed through the living room in the darkness, deciding not to use the lantern for fear of waking up her parents. She shined a small flashlight at her feet to guide her steps and held her breath until she'd quietly closed the front door behind her.

Trekking across the yard, visions of a baseball bat again came to mind.

"What are you doing here?" she asked Abraham in an angry whisper. Then she pointed toward her right, away from the propane light in the yard, but also away from her parents' open window. She motioned for him to follow her.

"I wanted to make sure Hannah is okay," Abraham said once they'd put some distance between them and the house.

Rachel could barely see his face in the darkness. "*Nee*, she's not okay. She has a twisted ankle and a scraped-up knee from running away from *you*." She pointed the light at his face. He threw up a hand to block the glare, so she lowered it.

"I don't know why she ran away. I looked everywhere for her. She just got really upset when I told her I didn't want to date her anymore." He took off his straw hat, hung his head, then ran a hand through his hair, sighing. "I didn't know she would take it so hard."

Rachel was quiet for a few seconds as she tapped a finger to her chin. "She said *she* broke up with *you*." She raised her eyes to his, momentarily taken aback by how good he looked, even sweaty and breathless, like he'd run all the way here. "Hannah said you got really mad and scared her."

"What?" Abraham's jaw dropped. "Scared her? If anyone was scared, it was *me*." He blew out a long burst of air, shaking his head. "Hannah is a great girl, and I've enjoyed spending time with her. But we just don't have a lot in common, and I think she was already planning our wedding."

Rachel recalled Hannah's comment about Abraham being her future husband, but she stayed quiet. Then he put a gentle hand on Rachel's arm, which sent a jolt of adrenaline soaring through her. But she took a step backward and focused on Hannah and the look on her face when Rachel and Gideon had found her.

"She was *ab im kopp*, Rachel." He'd taken a step toward her again. "She went crazy when I tried to explain why I didn't think it was going to work out between us. She started punching me and screaming at me." He pointed to his right forearm, so Rachel shined the flashlight there, illuminating a purple bruise the size of an orange. "She can throw a pretty good punch too." He shook his head. "Maybe things are different here, but where I come from in Ohio, people don't do things like that. The *Ordnung* teaches us to be passive."

Rachel leaned closer to his arm, keeping the flashlight in place. She had seen Hannah lose her temper, but she couldn't imagine her sister hitting another person. For any reason.

Except . . . *She did hit a wall once.* But a friend had just been killed in a buggy accident.

"You should probably go home, Abraham." Rachel took a deep breath, even though her eyes found their way to Abraham's lips. Just as her traitorous eyes had found their way to Gideon's lips. It was as if they had a mind of their own. Desperation for a first kiss was mounting.

Abraham hung his head, sighing. "I can't believe this happened. Maybe I should have broken the news to her more gently about breaking up. I just had no idea . . ." He lifted his eyes to Rachel's. "Can you please just tell her that I am really sorry? I guess there isn't a *gut* way to break up with anyone. When she ran off, I tried to find her, but it took me a while to ready the horse."

"She shouldn't have been at the cemetery. That place has a bad reputation." Rachel's thoughts went full circle as she wondered again if Hannah was pregnant. It was seeming less and less likely.

Abraham shifted his weight and shook his head again. "I just thought it was a quiet place to talk . . ." He grinned a little. "And maybe to kiss."

Rachel adjusted the flashlight so her face wasn't in the light. She could feel the warmth of a blush creeping up her neck to her cheeks.

"But I didn't know it had a bad reputation. An *Englisch* guy told me about it, someone I work with at the lumberyard." He blew out an air of frustration. "It's true. We are unequally yoked with them—the *Englisch*—and we shouldn't be so trusting."

Rachel nodded. Her family had many *Englisch* friends who were very good people. But a few had crossed them over the years, usually for financial gain.

"Anyway." Abraham tipped his hat to her. "I'm sorry I got you out of bed so late. Please tell Hannah that I wish her nothing but the best. I don't want things to be awkward between us." He put a hand over the bruise on his arm. "And I'd never do anything to embarrass her. I won't tell anyone how she reacted to the breakup."

You just did.

"I'm only telling you so you can be there for her. I thought you should know how upset she is."

"What if she'd been the one to come outside?"

Abraham sighed again. "I would have told her again how very sorry I am and encouraged her to find someone else more suited to her." He tipped his hat again before he turned to go.

Rachel waited until he'd walked down the driveway and was out of sight before she went back inside. When she eased open the bedroom door, Hannah was standing at the window.

Hannah trembled as she turned to face her sister. She'd fought the urge to hurry downstairs because it sounded like one of her parents had gotten out of bed. The pipes rattled the way they did when someone flushed the commode. She was already afraid one of them would find Rachel out in the yard with Abraham. So she'd stayed where she was.

"What was he doing here?" she asked through gritted teeth.

Rachel pulled her dress over her head, then sat down in her nightgown on the bed. "He came to say he was sorry for breaking up with you."

"*What?* He didn't break up with me. I broke up with him."

She scurried to Rachel's bed and sat down beside her sister, twisting to face her. "He's lying, Rachel. And he can't be trusted."

Hannah's sister didn't say anything.

"He's just trying to make himself look good by saying he broke up with me." She paused, sniffling. "I wouldn't lie about this."

Rachel was still quiet, avoiding Hannah's eyes.

"You cannot, under any circumstance, go out with him. No matter how hard he might try to pressure you. I know you're dating Gideon, and I think he is perfect for you, but I also know how charming and convincing Abraham can be." She pointed a finger at Rachel. "Don't let him sway you to his evil way of thinking." Shaking her head, she repeated herself. "Evil, evil, evil."

Rachel stared at her for a few moments. "Um, I'm pretty sure I can go out with whomever I want."

Hannah's jaw dropped as tears filled her eyes. "After what he did to me, you'd go out with him?"

"Even though we've never been allowed to date until now, you've never had any guy reject you. They followed you on the playground when we were young. They offered you desserts from their lunch pails. And the older we got, they practically salivated while they followed you around." Rachel paused, bit her lip, then went on. "I'm just saying breakups must be hard, no matter who is doing the breaking up."

Hannah stood up and looked down at her sister as she felt her heart breaking. "Really, Rachel, are you saying you don't believe my version of the story?" She shook her head when her sister raised an eyebrow. "That's not what I meant to say. It's not a version of the story. It is the truth."

Rachel rubbed her nose, a habit she had when she couldn't make up her mind about something.

"I can't believe you let Abraham sway your thinking. I'm your *schweschder*. What reason would I have to lie about whether I broke up or he did?" Hannah swiped at her eyes.

"You knew I wanted to go out with Abraham, but you swooped in and snagged him like a witch on a broom." Rachel stood up and faced off with Hannah.

"Like a witch on a broom?" Hannah's jaw dropped. They didn't celebrate Halloween, but they had plenty of *Englisch* friends who dressed up for the holiday. "That's just mean, Rachel."

"Well, it's hard always being in your shadow, Hannah. You're the prettier one, the one all the boys have always gone after." Rachel's eyes pooled with tears.

Hannah tried to touch Rachel on the arm, but her sister jerked away. "That's not true." She began to list all the reasons Rachel would be a better wife than she would, and as Rachel's tears dried, Hannah said, "Gideon has always liked you, even when we were young. He's such a *wunderbaar* person. He's sweet, polite, he works hard, and—"

"I guess now that I have Gideon, you want him too!"

Hannah's mouth fell open again. "*Nee!* I don't. I'm just explaining how right you two are for each other and that Gideon has always had eyes—"

They both jumped as the door burst open so hard it slammed against the wall. Their father, wearing wrinkled black pants that he'd likely pulled from the laundry hamper, stepped over the threshold. His face was red as he ran a hand through his salt-and-pepper hair.

"Your *mamm* and I can hear you *maeds* arguing from

our bedroom downstairs." He looked back and forth between Hannah and Rachel. "This bickering between the two of you has been going on for months." He stomped one of his bare feet. "It ends now."

Hannah and Rachel sat down on their respective beds and nodded.

"And another thing . . ." *Daed* pointed his finger at Rachel, then at Hannah. "The next time I see a boy over here late at night, especially one throwing rocks at the window, I'm going to bolt out of this *haus* in my underwear and embarrass the both of you." He scratched his head, then ran his hand the length of his beard. "Whose boyfriend is he, anyway?" He looked at Hannah as his bushy eyebrows leaned into a frown.

"I broke up with him. He's not my boyfriend." Hannah shrugged.

Their father glowered at Rachel. "Is he your boyfriend now?"

Rachel stared significantly at Hannah, and Hannah sighed. "*Daed*, he's neither one of our boyfriends. You don't have to worry about him. Neither one of us plans on dating him."

Their father grumbled. "Well, *gut*. Maybe you two can get straight with each other now. Being *schweschders* is a gift from God, and when you treat each other the way you two have, it disappoints the Lord, and it hurts your *mudder* and me."

Hannah and Rachel both said they were sorry, and their father left. Hannah was ready to sleep, but as she got comfortable on her bed atop the covers, Rachel didn't move. Hannah could feel her glare. "What now?" she asked.

"You can't control who I date. Why did you tell *Daed* that neither of us plans on dating Abraham?"

Hannah squeezed her eyes closed, tempted to start yelling at

Rachel, but that would only get them in more trouble. "It doesn't matter anyway. You're dating Gideon."

There was a long silence, and Hannah was grateful for it. Yawning, she settled into her pillow, hoping Rachel would extinguish the lantern and get to sleep as well.

"I'm not really dating Gideon."

Hannah rolled onto her side and faced Rachel. "You were just out with him when you found me. And you said he asked you out for next Saturday. That sounds like dating to me." She yawned again.

Rachel smirked as she folded her arms across her chest. "We are just pretending to date."

Hannah blew out a big breath of air, rolled her eyes, and sat up. "What does that even mean?"

"It means that Gideon and I are pretending to be dating to cheer up his mother. It was his idea. He said she is really depressed, and he thought that maybe us spending time together might lighten her spirit and motivate her to accept the changes she needs to make in her life because of her diabetes."

Hannah put her hands over her face, fighting the urge to scream.

"So, if Abraham were to ask me out, I'd be free to go. Gideon and I would just pretend to break up sooner than we'd planned."

"That's the stupidest thing I've ever heard. Did it occur to you that Gideon might just be saying that, about cheering up his mother, because he really does want to date you but didn't know how to ask you?"

Rachel shook her head. "*Nee*. It's not like that with Gideon and me. We're like best friends. He wouldn't need to make up something like that."

"I disagree. But you would be silly to stop seeing someone like Gideon and start dating Abraham." Hannah lowered her head, her mind reeling in defeat. No way was she going to start seeing Abraham again. Especially after Rachel seemed to believe his lies.

"I'll date whomever I want."

Rachel snuffed out the lantern, and Hannah settled back into her pillow. "*Gut.* So will I." She thought about all she'd put up with, the effort she'd put forth to keep Abraham's roaming hands off her and the mean things he'd said to her. All sacrifices to protect Rachel. But rage and self-pity were percolating now. "Maybe I'll even date Gideon now that I know he's available."

Rachel called Hannah a name she'd only heard used by the *Englisch*. And Hannah threw it right back at her.

Their father was wrong. Being Rachel's sister wasn't a gift. It was a curse.

CHAPTER 9

By the time Saturday came around, Rachel didn't feel as though she had a sister. She and Hannah weren't fighting, but they weren't speaking either, and they both made every attempt to avoid each other, although they were careful to be civil in front of their father. But as Hannah used the treadle sewing machine in the corner of the bedroom, Rachel had no choice but to share space with her sister. Rachel needed to get ready for her date with Gideon.

Earlier in the week, Hannah had taken the bottle of essential oil out of the bedside table drawer. Their mother had been making a concoction of rose, lavender, and cloves since they'd started having monthlies, so Rachel could now rule out any possibility that Hannah was pregnant. Apparently Abraham had been telling the truth, saying all he and Hannah had done was talk and kiss. And if he'd been telling the truth about that, then maybe everything else he'd said was accurate and Hannah was bitter because a guy had broken up with her. In a community where pride was frowned upon, Hannah had an overabundance of it.

Rachel pulled a dark-green dress from the rack on the wall and started ironing. It wasn't even a minute later when Hannah pushed back her chair, bit the thread from whatever she was working on, and then huffed her way out of the room.

Good riddance. Even as Rachel had the thought, it seemed to swirl around her heart and squeeze. She wasn't sure how much longer this could go on. She missed Hannah. She missed her sister.

Show me how to fix it, she prayed. Although, to be truthful, she already knew the answer.

Hannah sat on the porch step in her bare feet and wiggled her toes, leaning back on her palms as the sunrays beat down on her. This part of the day was always the hottest, and the first week of July was giving them no mercy. But she was prepared to sit in the heat for however long it took. She wanted to be the first one to welcome Gideon. She wanted to ask him if it was true that he and Rachel were only pretending to date to cheer up his mother.

But if Rachel had lied, then it would only hurt Gideon's feelings to mention anything. She'd have to figure out another way to find out.

When she saw Gideon's buggy coming up the driveway, she stood and put a hand to her forehead, shading her eyes. A part of her wanted to throw herself at Gideon because she was so angry with Rachel. But her protective side—the side that had been winning out lately, despite everything—wanted to test Gideon's intentions. Was Rachel truly his first choice? Or given the opportunity to choose, would Rachel drop into second place?

As she plotted, she had to question why she was really doing this. Were her own intentions aimed strictly at protecting Rachel, making sure her sister was number one to Gideon? Or did she hate to see a great guy like Gideon slip out of reach for herself?

Did she hate to see *any* guy slip out of reach? A battle raged inside her as she considered Abraham. How much of her time with him had been solely to keep him away from Rachel? And how much was because Hannah had enjoyed their time together, at least at the beginning? She questioned whether or not she'd been truthful with herself.

Shaking her head, Hannah walked toward Gideon's buggy, wondering when all the lying and secret keeping had inched into all their lives. But it didn't stop her from swaying her hips a bit more than necessary as she made her way across the yard.

"*Wie bischt,*" she said when Gideon stepped out of his buggy. He would go to the door most likely, the way he did last time he picked up Rachel.

Unlike Abraham.

Hannah took a deep breath. She'd have to see Abraham tomorrow at worship service unless she feigned being sick, and she wasn't sure she could heap another deception onto the pile. She forced the thoughts aside, blinked her eyes at Gideon, and smiled.

"Hi, Hannah. Are you feeling better than the last time I saw you?" Gideon grinned as he loosely tethered his horse, then leaned his elbows on the top rung of the fence.

"*Ya,* I am. And *danki* for taking such *gut* care of me." She lowered her eyes. "It's embarrassing that I let myself get into a situation like that."

"I'd like to have a word or two with Abraham about it." Gideon straightened, puffing out his chest.

Hannah shook her head. "*Nee,* please. Let's just leave it alone.

I don't want to draw attention to it. I'm already afraid Abraham is going to make things up about me because he was so mad that I broke up with him."

Gideon nodded. As much as he disliked Abraham for what he'd done to Hannah, it was probably best to let the situation die down. "I won't let him talk badly about you. If I hear him doing that, I'll speak up. But otherwise I won't approach him. Does that sound fair?" Gideon came around the fence and into the front yard.

Hannah nodded before she edged closer to him and put her arms around his waist. She laid her head against his chest. "*Danki* for being so *gut* to me."

Gideon had hugged Hannah and Rachel before over the years. Funerals, baptisms, or maybe a quick congratulatory hug for a winning shot over the volleyball net. But this hug felt different, especially the way Hannah nuzzled her cheek against his shirt. He put his arms around her so as not to be rude, then gave her a cautious pat on the back. "I'm just glad you're okay."

Over his shoulder, Rachel opened the front door and stepped onto the porch. Gideon dropped his arms to his sides, but Hannah only held on tighter. He gently latched onto Hannah's arms and finally eased her away, although she frowned once she was facing him.

But Gideon's attention quickly shifted to Rachel. His date stomped across the yard swinging her arms back and forth, taking long strides toward them. Rachel squinted her eyes, but Gideon didn't think it was from the sun. Her lips were pressed together, and it looked like she might be gritting her teeth.

"Let's go," she said as she walked around Hannah and grabbed Gideon's hand, pulling him to go with her, so hard he almost lost his footing.

"Bye, Hannah." Gideon forced a smile, but Rachel yanked him along even harder.

"Hey." He jerked his hand out of hers when they reached the buggy. He looked behind them, but Hannah had already turned to go back in the house. "What was that all about?"

"Nothing." Rachel walked to the passenger side of the buggy and got inside. Gideon untethered the horse.

"It didn't look like *nothing*," he said as he backed up the buggy, then flicked the reins once he was ready to head down the driveway.

"Well, it's nothing to worry about." Rachel folded her hands in her lap atop her small black purse and looked straight ahead.

"Why are you and Hannah fighting?"

Rachel turned her head and glowered at Gideon. "Now that Hannah isn't dating Abraham, maybe you'd prefer to date her instead?"

Gideon narrowed his eyes. She hadn't called it pretend dating, so that was a good thing. But although the apparent jealousy was flattering, it was unbecoming just the same. "I don't have any interest in dating Hannah."

She lifted one shoulder, then lowered it slowly. "It didn't look that way."

"Hannah hugged me as a thank-you for getting her safely home after what happened with Abraham." He glanced at Rachel, but she was staring straight ahead again. And if Gideon was being truthful with himself, Hannah's hug had felt more intimate than any other time they'd hugged.

"It would be just like Hannah to go after someone I'm dating, or someone I like, the way she did with . . ." She bit her lip but cut her eyes slightly in Gideon's direction.

Gideon coaxed his horse to pick up speed as they crossed the highway, and then settled him into a steady trot, trying to calm the irritation funneling around him. "First of all, we aren't really dating, so if you want to go out with a jerk like Abraham, we can end this charade and break up. My *mudder* was happy to hear we were going out, but I don't think she's going to fall apart if we stop seeing each other. Her friends—your *mamm* included—forced their way back into her life, and she's leaning on them a lot. She's even baking again and learning how to cook a different way, without sugar."

Rachel raised her chin and didn't look at Gideon. "Abraham came to our house last Saturday night to explain what happened between him and Hannah, and his version of the story is very different from my *schweschder's.*"

Gideon had expected Rachel to comment on his mother's improvement, but she'd stuck with the part of the conversation about Abraham. "I hope you didn't believe Abraham over your *schweschder.*"

"I don't know what to believe." She turned to Gideon. "Hannah has always gotten what she wanted, and if Abraham broke up with her, she might try to twist things around."

Gideon wanted to tell her that was unlikely, but the more he thought about the way Hannah had hugged him, the more confused he was. "That doesn't sound like Hannah."

"You don't know her the way I do."

Gideon glanced at Rachel, unable to keep from scowling. "I think I know her pretty well since we all grew up together."

"So, you don't think Hannah would lie to save herself from the embarrassment of a breakup?"

"*Nee*, I don't. You saw how upset she was when we found her that night."

Rachel huffed. "Abraham said she was upset because he broke up with her and that she ran off before he could get the horse tethered. He looked for her, but when he couldn't find her, he showed up at our house to make sure she was okay."

Gideon shook his head. "I don't believe that." He glowered at Rachel. "And you shouldn't either. Hannah is your *schweschder*, and—"

"Don't tell me sisterhood is a gift. Because it's not. Hannah takes what she wants."

Gideon was quiet. This wasn't a pretty side of Rachel. But he was trying to figure out what she was most upset about—if it was about Abraham or the way Hannah had hugged Gideon.

"You and Hannah have always been close. It's a shame that Abraham is getting between you."

"That's Hannah's fault. She knew I liked him, but she sank her hooks into him. Of course I didn't stand a chance after that." She grabbed both strings of her *kapp* and held them in one hand. A topless spring buggy was a better choice than a closed buggy since the heat was brutal, but in such cases ladies often had a time keeping their hair beneath their prayer coverings.

"Why would you say that you didn't have a chance?" Gideon's heart was taking a beating. He wondered if he should just tell Rachel that he'd always wanted to date her. But if it was Abraham she wanted, even after hearing what he'd done, maybe Gideon didn't know Rachel as well as he thought he did.

Rachel snapped her head in his direction. "Everyone, including me, knows that Hannah is the prettier *schweschder.*"

Gideon sighed. "I'm sorry you see it that way. It isn't true, but it shouldn't matter. You know we don't pride ourselves on looks. I know that attraction either comes naturally or not, but it doesn't define a person's feelings, and sometimes a person becomes even more attractive based on what's inside."

He turned to her in time to see her roll her eyes.

"You would think that's how it should be, but even in our community Hannah has always outshined the other girls, and it's impossible not to notice."

Gideon pondered the thought. It was true that Hannah's looks didn't go unnoticed, but for her own sister to be degrading her in such a way felt wrong. Rachel's ugly comments were fueled by hurt, so he tried to think of something to soften her tone. "Did you notice that I chose you to have these pretend dates with, and not Hannah?"

She chuckled as she rolled her eyes again. "Our mothers paired us up a long time ago, and it didn't have anything to do with whether or not we were attracted to each other. They think we have a lot in common."

Gideon wanted to tell her that wasn't true, that Rachel had always been his first choice. But he stayed quiet, thinking this date was turning out worse than the first one. He looked for a way to change their present course. "We *do* have a lot in common, in case you haven't noticed that over the years." He smiled, still hoping to cheer her up and move the conversation away from anything to do with Hannah and Abraham.

She turned toward him and smiled back. It didn't look friendly. "*Ya,* I know. And I know you're a *gut* man. Hannah reminded me of that last night when she was telling me she forbids me to date Abraham."

Gideon's temperature rose. Rachel's hostility stemmed from the fact that she wanted to go out with Abraham. Through gritted teeth, he asked for confirmation of this. "Do you want to date Abraham?"

She shrugged. "I don't know. Maybe. If he asked."

"Well, he's not going to ask you out if he thinks you and I are dating, so let's break up." He pulled back on the reins, slowed the horse's gait, and guided the buggy onto a side road that would lead them back to her house.

Her eyes locked with his. "What about supper and a movie?"

"I don't think this is a *gut* idea. It was a dumb idea to cheer up *mei mudder*, but I think she just needed time to get used to her health issues. I'll tell her it isn't working out with us." He paused. "You know, like we planned, *ya*? You can tell your *mudder* the same thing. They'll get over it." His jaw clenched as he took in a deep breath. "Then you can go after Abraham the way you want to."

Rachel stared at him. "I never said I would definitely date him. But Hannah can't make those decisions for me. I should be able to choose. You and I don't have to stop dating though."

Gideon wanted to find hope in her comment, but his own hurt bubbled to the surface. "We aren't really dating, remember?"

"Then we aren't really breaking up either."

He swallowed hard. "*Ya*, I think we are." He glanced at Rachel, surprised to see her blinking back tears.

"Are we still going to be friends? You're acting like we aren't." Her voice cracked, which caused Gideon's chest to tighten.

He turned on the street to Rachel's house. "I'm tired of being your friend, Rachel. Don't you see that? I like you. I've always liked you. You've always been number one to me. I thought that maybe by pretending to date, you'd see my feelings for you. But . . ." Sighing, he pulled the horse to a stop. "I think your feelings are for someone else."

Rachel stared at Gideon for several long moments. "I saw the way you looked at Hannah today. I can't be number two to you or anyone else." She climbed down from the buggy, then paused and looked up at him. "Maybe I need to move far away so that people see me for the person I am, not the *other schweschder* who isn't as pretty."

"*You* are the only person who doesn't see you as you are." Gideon lowered his eyes. "Bye, Rachel."

CHAPTER 10

Rachel and Hannah sat side by side at worship service, along with their mother. Their father was on the other side of the room with the men. Gideon and Abraham were also with the men but sitting on opposite sides of the room from each other.

Church service was being held in the Millers' barn, and despite the misting water fans, Rachel's clothes stuck to her, and sweat pooled at her temples. She could barely hear the bishop over the hum of the generators fueling the fans. She couldn't focus anyway. Gideon's good-bye the night before was like a bee in her bonnet, words trapped inside her head, stinging over and over again.

"You are the only person who doesn't see you as you are." Was it really true? Had she truly spent all her time worrying about an issue she'd created in her own mind? Was she destroying her relationships and possibilities over nothing?

The thought exhausted her.

She glanced at Hannah, but her sister was fidgeting with the hem of her white apron. Hannah had bitten her fingernails to the quick, something she'd always done when she was upset. They still hadn't spoken to each other in days, and Rachel wondered if any guy was worth this. She'd been jealous of Hannah all her life, but she loved her sibling with all her heart. That had to be more important, right?

She closed her eyes and once again asked that God would show her a way not to be envious of Hannah. She felt like she'd prayed it a thousand times. Jealousy was a sin, and Rachel was drowning in it, like quicksand slowly taking her under.

When she looked up, her eyes darted back and forth between Gideon and Abraham, landing on Abraham. He smiled and winked at her.

It was an inappropriate gesture for worship service, but Rachel returned the smile as she again considered whether he'd told the truth about him and Hannah.

By the time worship was over, everyone in the barn was dripping wet, and as Rachel exited the barn with everyone else, she was glad it was cloudy and breezy. The women headed straight for the Millers' kitchen to start carrying trays of food out to the tables that were already set up beneath the trees in the yard.

After all the children and men were served, the women began to seat themselves. Abraham motioned at the empty chair to his left, grinning. Rachel considered sitting by him, but she didn't want to stir things up with Hannah, so she headed off in another direction—until she saw Hannah sitting down next to Gideon. Rachel did an about-face and hurried to the empty chair by Abraham.

"What about your boyfriend?" Abraham whispered in her ear.

Rachel swallowed hard, but she was unable to take her eyes off Gideon and Hannah. "We broke up," she finally said, still staring at her sister and her friend. Abraham was talking, but she wasn't really paying attention. Gideon leaned closer to Hannah, said something to her, and she laughed.

Despite everything, seeing Hannah smile warmed Rachel's heart. Hannah hadn't shown much joy lately. Still, Rachel's chest ached when she thought about Hannah and Gideon dating. She turned it all over in her mind as she reached for a piece of buttered bread. This was different from her hostility about Hannah dating Abraham. This hurt far worse. But as Rachel watched them talking and laughing, she decided right then and there that no matter her feelings for Gideon, no matter her own pain, she was not going to interfere with what might be brewing. She was going to fight the bitterness she'd let dictate her decisions.

I will at least try.

"Hello? Did you hear me?"

Rachel turned to Abraham. "Uh, sorry. Um. What did you say?"

He flashed his smile at her. "I was asking you out, for next Saturday."

Rachel had waited a long time for Abraham to show an interest in her, and it should have lit up her life. But her eyes kept drifting to Hannah and Gideon.

"I guess we are trading." Abraham nodded toward Rachel's sister and Gideon.

Rachel stared at them. "I guess so," she said softly.

"So, that means you'll go out with me?" Still grinning, Abraham passed her the bowl of chowchow when she reached for it.

"Sure," she whispered as she waited for feelings of euphoria to wash over her. But instead she found herself wondering if this was a bad trade.

Or was Rachel just programmed to want anything Hannah

had? She'd accused her sister of exactly that, but now Rachel wondered if she was guilty instead. "I'm not going to the beekeeper's cemetery," she added, still whispering.

"Of course not. I'd never take you there."

But you took my schweschder. Because she's prettier?

Rachel could feel God's disappointment in her. Again. She glanced at Hannah and Gideon, still smiling and enjoying each other's company. She wasn't hungry anymore.

Hannah gave Gideon the last of her turkey. It wasn't something they'd normally have at a meal following church service, but John Zook had found one of his turkeys badly injured in a barbwire fence, and he'd had to put the bird out of its misery the night before. Hannah loved turkey, but she'd served herself way too much.

"*Danki* for sitting with me and staying close to me today, Gideon." Hannah glanced at Rachel sitting next to Abraham. The thought of him being around her sister made Hannah's stomach queasy. "I just don't want Abraham to confront me." She sighed. "Although I'm sure Rachel is fit to be tied that I'm sitting here with you."

Gideon shook his head. "I doubt it. I told Rachel how I feel about her, but it was clear to me that she prefers Abraham."

"She doesn't know him." Hannah picked up her napkin and dabbed the sweat on her forehead. "It upsets my stomach to think about Rachel getting involved with Abraham."

"Maybe she'll have to find out for herself."

Gideon forked the last bite of turkey Hannah had given him

while she thought about all she'd done to keep Abraham and Rachel apart. Hannah was tired of all the competition over boys. She just wanted her sister back.

"Um . . ." Gideon wiped his mouth with his napkin. "I probably won't be at your birthday party next week. *Mei mamm* said your parents are having a small gathering to celebrate." He shook his head. "But things are already awkward with Rachel and me."

Hannah wondered what kind of celebration it would be since the two birthday girls weren't even speaking to each other. "I understand."

"But I do want to get Rachel a gift." He grinned. "You, too, of course. But do you have any ideas for Rachel? Is there something she might want?" He looked over at Abraham and Rachel. "I'm choosing to believe in Rachel, that she'll see through Abraham's charms and see the real guy. So even if I'm not at the party, I want to give her something."

Hannah smiled weakly. Rachel had told Hannah repeatedly what she wanted for her birthday. So Hannah told him.

Rachel brushed by Hannah with an empty pitcher and two glasses. They barely made eye contact, much less said anything to each other. As the women cleaned the tables, older children gathered up the younger ones. Everyone would be heading home soon, and Rachel tried again to capture any sense of joy that she should be feeling about Abraham. But there was an emptiness inside her that she couldn't get rid of, as if a part of her were missing.

By the time they'd cleaned things up, Rachel had made up her mind that she wasn't going to go out with Abraham. It was her and Hannah's birthday on Saturday, and even if the date was in the evening after the party, Rachel didn't want to go. That would make it a horrible birthday, worse than she already anticipated it would be. She still wasn't convinced about who broke up with whom, but if she had to choose between them, Rachel was going to choose her sister.

She scanned the area and looked for Gideon and Hannah but didn't see them. Maybe they were off holding hands or sneaking a kiss behind the house. Rachel took a deep and determined breath and again promised herself and God that she was not going to interfere with Gideon and Hannah if things were moving in a romantic direction. Rachel didn't like the person she'd become, and this time she was going to pray for Hannah's happiness before her own.

Only a few folks were left when Rachel finally spotted Abraham. He was talking with the Lapp brothers, Isaac and Paul, and they walked along the side of the house before disappearing into the backyard. Rachel feared this might be the only chance she'd have to tell Abraham she couldn't go out with him Saturday.

She was grateful her parents hadn't invited him to the birthday party. They were aware that Hannah and Rachel had been fighting about him. But now she'd have to find a tactful way to tell him that she couldn't go out with him and also be careful not to extend an accidental invitation. And she hoped Abraham didn't invite himself, because Rachel wouldn't know what to say. Gideon would be there, so that would further complicate an already complicated birthday party.

Rachel had already told her parents she would walk the short distance to their house. She would be drenched in sweat by the time she got home, but the time to herself would give her a chance to think. She'd had a knot in her throat all the way to the service that morning, and she wasn't sure she could sit next to Hannah again without bursting into tears.

She heard Abraham's voice, even though she couldn't see him, so she walked toward the sound. But before the boys came into view, Abraham mentioned Hannah, so Rachel slowed her steps and listened.

"*Ya*, she's pretty, but a bit *ab im kopp*." Abraham chuckled. "I sent her on her way. I'm going out with her *schweschder* Saturday."

Rachel clenched her fists at her sides. She didn't feel good about herself when she talked badly about Hannah, but hearing someone else do it was almost unbearable.

"Hannah is a nice girl. We've known her our whole life," Isaac said.

Paul and Isaac were both a year older than Rachel and Hannah. Rachel relaxed a little when Isaac defended her sister.

"*Ya* . . ." Paul cleared his throat. "Ain't nothing crazy about Hannah or Rachel. Any fella would be blessed to date either one of them."

Abraham laughed again. "*Ach*, well . . . I guess I'm doubly blessed that I dated Hannah, and now I'll get to go out with her sister. Maybe Rachel will be a little friendlier than her *schweschder*."

Rachel put a hand to her chest. *Hannah is always friendly to everyone.*

"What do you mean, *friendlier*?" Isaac asked.

"*Ach*, you know . . . maybe be interested in more than just kissing."

Silence. Rachel was holding her breath and wishing she could see Isaac and Paul.

"I know you're new here," Isaac said. "But the *Ordnung* is universal and clearly says such things should be reserved for marriage."

Good for you, Isaac.

Abraham mumbled, but Rachel couldn't make out what he said.

"Where'd you get that bruise on your arm?" Paul asked.

"Lifting a fence post. I was throwing it over my shoulder and it slipped and caught my arm."

That's not what you told me. Abraham said Hannah hit him. It seemed far-fetched at the time, but his sad eyes had told a different story.

If he'd lied about that, had he lied about everything else?

Their voices were muffled again. Then all three of the guys stepped around the corner, and Rachel wished the earth would swallow her up as her eyes widened.

Abraham frowned. "Rachel." He looped his thumbs beneath his suspenders. "How long have you been standing here?"

Her heart hammered in her chest as she willed it to settle down. She said hello to Paul and Isaac before they shuffled past her. Abraham took a couple steps toward her, then kept coming until he was right in front of her.

"*Ach*, finally . . . some time alone with you." He winked at her the way he'd done during worship service, and it didn't seem any more appropriate now than it had then. As a devilish grin filled his face, Rachel bit her lip until it throbbed like her pulse. He was close enough to kiss her, and she shuddered at the thought. Abraham's true colors were shooting from his pores and creating a rainbow full of lies.

But before she could unscramble her thoughts or emotions, Abraham leaned down and cupped his hand behind her neck, pulling her to him.

CHAPTER 11

Hannah lay on her bed and stared out the window. Sunday afternoons were a restful time, and usually Hannah napped while Rachel read a book. But Hannah had no interest in sleep today. *Where is Rachel?*

Her parents said Rachel would be along later, but they didn't realize how dangerous Abraham Stoltzfus was. Hannah and her family loved the bishop, so it was hard for her to believe Abraham was related to him.

She jumped when the bedroom door opened, and relief washed over her when Rachel came into the room. Then her sister burst into tears.

Hannah was off the bed and pulling Rachel into a hug in two seconds. "What did he do to you?" She let Rachel cry on her shoulder for a minute before she eased her away. "Are you okay?"

Rachel nodded, sniffling. "Hannah, I miss you! I'm so sorry about everything."

"I've missed you too." She wrapped her arms around her sister, and they both cried for a long while before they sat on their beds facing each other.

"I'm never going to allow a man to get between us again, ever. You were right about Abraham." Rachel shook her head, starting to cry again. "He's not a *gut* person. I don't know what kind of Amish community he came from, but . . ." She shook her head. "I'm so thankful I got away from him when he tried to kiss me. I couldn't bear it if he was my first kiss."

Hannah lowered her head, embarrassed, wishing Abraham hadn't been her first kiss. But when a glazed look of despair spread over Rachel's face, Hannah realized Rachel hadn't said it to hurt her. She leaned toward her sister, putting a hand on her leg. "I think there are *gut* and bad people everywhere. Maybe Abraham isn't bad. Maybe he's just lost."

"I overheard him talking to Paul and Isaac Byler, and he wasn't saying nice things. Then he tried to kiss me, and when I wouldn't let him, he got mad." She found Hannah's hand and squeezed. "Hearing some of the things Abraham said made me sick to my stomach. And I kept picturing you with blood running down your leg and seeing how hard you were crying. Hannah, I'm so sorry." Rachel covered her face with her hands.

"I'm sorry too. Let's never argue or fight or compete for boys again. I shouldn't have gone after Abraham when it was plain to see that you liked him."

Rachel smiled a little. "That was bad judgment on my part."

"And mine." Hannah shook her head.

"But, Hannah, I need to tell you something." Rachel sighed. "Gideon and I are friends. *Ya,* I think something more was happening between us, but I saw the hug you gave him, and I saw the two of you together today. I feel like it's hard with Gideon, to know if it's friendship or . . ." She shrugged. "Or another kind of love. So, if Gideon has asked you out, or if you are interested in

him, I'm not going to cause any problems, and I would only wish
you the best."

Rachel choked back another sob in her throat. She wanted to
make up for the way she'd treated Hannah, but giving up Gideon
so easily was harder than she'd thought it would be. She waited
for Hannah to tell her she had no interest in Gideon, but her sister only nodded, which sent Rachel directly to prayer.

*God, I don't ever want to be jealous about anyone or anything.
I pray for Hannah's happiness, even if it's with Gideon. Please,
God, help me to stay true to Hannah—and myself.*

"I just want us to put all of this behind us." Hannah paused
as her eyes clouded with tears again. "Abraham was saying bad
things about *me* to Paul and Isaac, wasn't he?"

Rachel nodded but then smiled. "It would have warmed your
heart, though, to hear Isaac and Paul saying nice things about
you, and about me. I suspect anytime Abraham tries to spread
lies, the community members we know and love will brush his
comments under a dirty rug."

They were quiet for a while, then Hannah said, "Only six
more days until we're sixteen. Our official *rumschpringe* will
begin. What's the first thing you want to do?"

"Go to a movie." Rachel smiled. "Twice, I've tried, but neither time worked out. What about you?"

"The same. I want to go see a movie." Hannah held up her
pinky. "Let's promise not to ever be ugly to each other again over
a guy." Rachel curled her finger around Hannah's. "And let's
promise that the first movie we see will be together."

"It's a promise."

"Should we go talk to *Mamm* about our birthday party on Saturday? Maybe she'll make us red velvet cake." Hannah pressed her palms together and smiled.

Rachel nodded, then reached under the bed and pulled out a small red suitcase filled with things from their past and hopes for their future. She shuffled through drawings they'd done in school, pushed a faceless doll they'd named Mary out of the way, then dug a little deeper until she found a list titled "16th Birthday Party." Red velvet cake was at the top.

Rachel could already feel things returning to normal. She silently thanked God for gifting her with a sister like Hannah, and she asked His forgiveness for ever thinking the blessing was a curse.

Gideon clocked out at noon, the way he did every Saturday. Usually he'd go straight to the deli a few doors down from the construction company where he worked and get a sandwich, too hungry to wait until he got home. But today he didn't have much of an appetite. Rachel and Hannah had been on his mind all day. It was their birthday, and the party was starting in an hour. Gideon wanted nothing more than to give Rachel the birthday gift she wanted, but since that wasn't possible, he'd bought both her and Hannah trinket boxes, a suggestion from his mother, who promised to deliver the gifts. His mother had been disappointed that Gideon wasn't going but said she understood. Instead of telling her he and Rachel had broken up, he'd told her the truth: how they had pretended to date in an effort to cheer her up. His mother was more disappointed that Gideon had lied than she was about him not dating Rachel.

He untethered his horse, readied his buggy, then set off for home, wondering if his father had gone to the party. Gideon hoped so. He wanted to go upstairs and be alone.

Hannah kept looking out the window, hoping Gideon would change his mind and show up, but they were almost an hour into the party, and she was losing hope. Gideon's mother and father had come. Not long after Hannah and Rachel had opened their gifts, their father had taken Gideon's father out to the barn to show him a table he was building. Now it was just girls— Hannah, Rachel, their mother, Gideon's mother, four girls they'd grown up with, and three cousins.

As everyone moved into the kitchen for cake and ice cream, Hannah walked to where Rachel was standing at the window. "I'm sorry you didn't get the present you wanted for your birthday."

Hannah had sewn Rachel a jacket to use when things cooled down. It had been an effort since Hannah wasn't a very good seamstress, and sewing a jacket when it was so hot had taken discipline. Rachel said it was the best gift ever, but Hannah knew there was something she'd wanted more.

"Having you back as my *schweschder* is gift enough for me." Rachel smiled, but her eyes drifted back out the window.

"Should we join the others for cake? I'm sure they are waiting on us." Hannah put an arm around Rachel, and when they walked into the kitchen, their mother lit the sixteen candles on the cake while everyone sang "Happy Birthday."

After Hannah and Rachel blew out the candles, everyone clapped. When the noise settled, Gideon was standing in the doorway.

"Sorry I'm late," he said as his face reddened. Hannah supposed he expected at least one other man to be here.

"Your father and mine are out in the barn," Hannah said. She then thanked him for the trinket box.

Gideon nodded, but his eyes were on Rachel, and when Hannah caught the look that passed between her sister and Gideon, she smiled.

Gideon gobbled his cake and ice cream as fast as he could so he could excuse himself and get to the barn where he belonged. The kitchen was like a henhouse. Even though he couldn't keep his eyes off Rachel, there was a pain in his heart knowing that they'd ended their conversation badly the last time they'd spoken. If Gideon couldn't have Rachel as his girlfriend, he still wanted to be friends.

Rachel had thanked him for the trinket box, but she wouldn't keep her eyes locked with his. Before all the pretend dating and breaking up had started, Rachel used to stare into his eyes, and Gideon was pretty sure she could see all the way to his soul. Maybe he'd been too harsh to push her away. Surely she would see Abraham for the man he really was—or wasn't. Either way, he'd decided to attend the party so he could get things right with Rachel, whether as friends or otherwise.

"*Danki*, all, so much for everything." Rachel glanced at Gideon, and he wasn't sure, but he thought there were tears in the corners of her eyes. *Happy tears?*

Hannah was smiling, too, so the girls must have made up.

"I'm going out to the barn to see if the other men are ready for cake and ice cream." Rachel scooted past him, and out of the corner of his eye, Gideon saw her bolt down the porch steps, then to her left. Not anywhere near the barn.

The hens began to cluck—as his father would say—about sewing, the next Sister's Day, an upcoming quilting party, and other girl stuff. Gideon slipped out of the kitchen without notice, then stopped at the window. Rachel was standing in the yard, facing away from him, not moving.

He jumped when Hannah eased up to him. Hannah had been overly friendly lately. There was the hug and also the time they'd spent together after worship service. He wasn't sure what her intentions were, and he didn't want to do anything to hurt her feelings.

"Go to her," Hannah said softly. "Give her a chance to make things right."

Gideon shook his head. "*Nee*, she has a date with Abraham tonight." A thought that caused his stomach to churn.

"*Nee*, she doesn't."

Gideon turned to face Hannah. "What happened?"

Hannah smiled. "Let's just say she saw Abraham's true colors."

"Did he hurt her?" Gideon clenched his fists at his sides, but Hannah shook her head.

"She was wise enough not to give him a chance. I don't think Abraham will be giving either of us any trouble. I don't think our community will allow it."

Gideon took off his straw hat and ran a hand through his damp hair, then put the hat back on. He scratched his chin. "I'm not sure my heart can take it if Rachel doesn't want to try to be more than friends." He sighed. "But I also don't want her not in my life, so I guess I need to accept it if that's all she wants. We'll be friends."

"Only one way to find out." Hannah nudged him with her shoulder, grinning.

"And, uh . . ." He needed to know that Hannah was okay if there was something between him and Rachel, but he didn't know how to ask her. Maybe Gideon had misinterpreted Hannah's hug and the attention she'd given him after church service. But he wasn't going to do anything that was going to drive a wedge between the sisters, even if that meant walking away from Rachel for good. "Are you sure you're okay if . . . uh . . ."

Hannah blinked her eyes a few times. "Rachel has always been the one for you, Gideon. We all see that. It's just taken my *schweschder* longer to realize it." She dabbed at one eye with her finger to snub a tear, and Gideon thought he might cry himself. He loved Hannah. Just not the same way he loved Rachel.

Hannah sniffled but smiled. "However, rest assured, if Rachel didn't come to her senses, I wasn't going to let a *gut* guy like you get away." She bit her lip for a moment and gazed at Gideon. "What are you waiting for?" She shoved his arm gently. "Go."

Gideon held Hannah's gaze for a long while, then he kissed her on the forehead, followed by a quick hug. "*Danki*, Hannah." Then he rushed for the door.

Rachel wiped her eyes on the sleeves of her dress when she heard footsteps, then turned around. Gideon was walking toward her.

"Why are you crying?" he asked when he reached her.

Rachel put her hands on her hips and stared at the ground, shaking her head. "Because I have messed everything up." She looked up at him, and it took everything she had not to fall into his arms. "With you and me."

"I didn't exactly handle things very *gut* either."

"*Nee*, it was me. I was consumed with jealousy, and I wanted everything Hannah had, mostly because Hannah had it." A tear rolled down her cheek. "I almost lost my *schweschder*, and as much as I love you, if you and Hannah choose each other, I will not interfere with that in any way. I want Hannah to be happy. I want you to be happy. I had my chance, and I behaved badly."

Gideon rubbed his chin. "You mean, like, um . . . you love me like a friend?"

"*Ya*, I love you like a friend"—Gideon's eyes left hers—"*if* you love Hannah as more than a friend. I will always love you as a friend if that's the case. And I mean that."

"Hannah knows who I love. And I told you that I want to be more than your friend, Rachel." He took his thumb and wiped away a tear that slid down her face.

"I want to be more than friends, too, Gideon. I've been confused about friendship love and romantic love, and I wasn't sure how to tell the difference."

He cupped her cheek. "I think a relationship should have a foundation of friendship before the rest can come." He smiled a little. "And in case there is any confusion about friendship love and romantic love, I say we put it to the test right now."

When Gideon's lips met with Rachel's, she thought she heard music, and the earth seemed to shift beneath her feet as her knees began to shake.

"Friends?" Gideon smiled as he brushed back a strand of hair that had fallen from beneath her *kapp*. "Or more?"

"Definitely more," she said, breathless.

"Happy birthday, Rachel. Did you get what you wanted?"

Rachel smiled. "It's what I've been telling Hannah I wanted—my first kiss. So, *ya*, I got what I wanted, and more. Best birthday ever."

She looked toward the house and caught Hannah watching from the window. Hannah smiled and gave a quick wave before turning away. Rachel silently prayed that Hannah would find her perfect person soon too.

Gideon kissed her again, and there was no mistaking that friendship love was well on the way to romantic love.

EPILOGUE

R achel hurried down the stairs when her mother called out that Gideon was pulling in. "Coming!"

She ran through the living room and past her father, who was reading the newspaper. He didn't ask anymore when Rachel would be home. Saturday nights were date nights, and Gideon always had Rachel home at what her father called a reasonable hour. They'd been dating for two months now, and although Rachel didn't want to count her eggs before they hatched, she was pretty sure a proposal was on her horizon.

Abraham and his family had moved away last month. No one was quite sure why, but there was a rumor that Abraham got into some trouble with some *Englisch* boys in Bird-in-Hand. Rachel didn't wish bad will on Abraham, but she and Hannah were both glad he was gone.

Rachel ran across the yard and jumped into Gideon's arms. "I'm so excited! I can't believe it's taken two months for us to see a movie."

Gideon kissed her before she eased out of his arms. "*Ya*, my work schedule was such a mess while we were taking inventory. *Danki* for waiting on me. Finally, we are going to the movies." He grinned. "It's okay with your parents, right? Did you tell them it's a Christian film?"

Rachel nodded. "*Ya*, I told them. They knew this was coming, so they were happy we chose a faith-based movie."

They turned when another buggy pulled in the driveway, and seconds later Isaac Lapp stepped out. Hannah strode more patiently toward her date, but at the last minute she picked up her pace and gave him a quick kiss. They'd been dating almost as long as Rachel and Gideon, and Rachel had never seen Hannah so happy.

"*Wie bischt.*" Isaac shook Gideon's hand, then the men tethered the horses and checked that the water trough was full. A few minutes later, a blue van arrived.

Hannah cupped her hands around her mouth. "Gideon, Isaac! The driver is here!"

They waited for the boys, then they all walked to the van.

Hannah held up her pinky, and Rachel latched on with hers. "Pinky swears forever. Our first movie and we are going to it together, like we promised."

Rachel nodded, smiling. "And *schweschders* forever."

A New Beginning

CHAPTER 1

Noah's heart palpitated. He was excited and nervous about attending this party with his *Englisch* friend. He'd lived in Lancaster County his entire life, but as Gavin wound his car around the semicircle driveway, Noah was sure this was the biggest house he'd ever seen. A huge two-story structure encased in white stone with ornate columns and decorative pillars that ran the length of the front porch.

"What did I tell you?" Gavin put the car in park near the entrance and looked at Noah. "It's a massive place with a pool in the backyard, and there's going to be tons of food and girls."

Gavin left the car running and stepped out. Noah followed his friend's lead, looking down at his blue jeans and flip-flops before he smoothed the wrinkles on the front of his yellow T-shirt. All loaner clothes from Gavin. The jeans were a little big, but when Noah suggested he might wear suspenders, Gavin frowned and told him that wouldn't be cool.

A man hopped into the driver's seat and drove the car around the driveway, passing a fountain shaped like a giant pear. Colorful summer flowers filled the area around the water, which flowed into a small pond outlined in lights.

Noah followed Gavin across the threshold and into a spacious living room filled with fancy furniture in shades of white and gold. A large crystal chandelier hung in the entryway, and he saw another one in the distance. Loud music and a haze of smoke assaulted his senses as they made their way through the crowd of teenagers, Gavin edging some of the kids out of the way with his elbow.

"The beer is out by the pool," he yelled above the music.

Gavin was what the *Englisch* girls called a ladies' man. He was tall and muscular with sandy blond hair that was just wavy enough to look good without being too girly. Gavin strutted as he walked, kind of a swagger, his shoulders squared, and with an air of confidence Noah wished he had. Gavin's teeth were perfectly straight and white, from braces he wore when he was younger. When Gavin smiled, girls seemed to melt like butter in his presence.

Noah had always liked Gavin. He was a nice guy and always the first person to offer to cover Noah's shift if he needed to be off work. And Noah needed to be off a lot during the fall harvesting season that was coming up.

Noah hurried to keep up with his friend, as his temples pounded and his heart hammered against his chest. His parents would be disappointed that he'd agreed to come. Rebecca would be even more upset, but Noah had worked at the hardware store with Gavin for almost a year, and Gavin told him this was the party of the year and he'd be crazy not to go. He'd turned down his friend at least a dozen times before, but since Noah hadn't really taken advantage of his *rumschpringe* over the last couple years, he decided to tag along to see what one of these parties was like while he still could. Soon these kinds of things would be forbidden, and this might be his last chance to experience the *Englisch* world before he was baptized and married Rebecca.

He tried to hold his breath as clouds of cigarette smoke wafted in every direction. People were talking loudly and yelling over the music, and about a dozen or so kids around his age were wiggling their hips and swaying to the beat, most with a cup in hand.

Noah followed Gavin out the patio door straight to a big keg of beer. But his eyes kept drifting to the pool. The girls there barely had on any clothes—skimpy swimsuits that didn't leave much to Noah's imagination. He'd never seen that much of Rebecca, much less strangers, and he was going to marry Rebecca. Girls in their community wore bathing suits, but not the kind these girls were wearing.

"Watch out." Gavin nudged Noah and grinned as he handed him a plastic cup filled to the rim with beer. "You'll turn to stone if you stare too long."

Noah glanced down, swallowed hard, and wondered if his cheeks were turning red.

"Relax, man. I know you're getting married in a couple months. But I guess it doesn't hurt to look, as long as you're respectful, so you might as well get an eyeful now." Gavin nodded toward the far end of the pool. "That's who I've got my eye on. Penny Schroeder."

"*Ya*, she's pretty." Noah wasn't surprised Gavin was going after the prettiest girl he'd seen at the party so far. Penny had long blond hair pulled into a high ponytail, and from what Noah could see of her waist-up in the water, she had a great figure. He lowered his gaze as guilt rushed over him. He was going to be a married man soon.

Gavin pointed to a guy who had just jumped into the water,

grabbing his knees in midair, which caused a tidal wave across the pool.

"I'd run if I was that guy." Several girls pushed back groomed hairstyles that were now soaked, and two of them had lost their sunglasses and now yelled at whoever had just splashed them.

Noah took a sip of his beer. He'd only had the beverage one other time, when he and Jacob Lapp each drank a bottle behind Jacob's barn early into their *rumschpringe*. Jacob had gotten an older kid to buy it for them. Noah liked the taste then, and he liked it now. And he wouldn't have to have just one this time. There were two other kegs at the other end of the pool. He drank what was in his glass and went to fill it up again.

"Easy there, dude." Gavin grinned. "We've got all night, so you'd better pace yourself." He motioned for Noah to follow him. "Let's go see Penny and her friends."

Noah was a bit shaky, so he chugged more of the beer and stifled a burp, hoping it didn't slip out the second he opened his mouth. He watched as Penny got out of the pool, and he could see that everything below her waist was well proportioned too. Although her bikini bottom looked too small—

Noah forced himself to look away, worried about turning shades of red again. But almost against his will, his eyes ventured back, and she smiled.

"Hi. Are you Noah? Gavin said he might be bringing a friend." Penny held out her hand. "Welcome to my house. Please make yourself at home." She pointed to a large covered area to her left with a bunch of tables and chairs set up, although not many people were over there. "The guy we hired to cook will be firing up the barbecue pit soon, but there's tons of appetizers if you're hungry now."

Noah had been so mesmerized by Penny that he hadn't noticed another girl join them. She could have been Penny's sister. The same blond hair, gorgeous smile, and nice body.

"This is McKenna." Penny nodded at her look-alike friend. "And that's Noah, a friend of Gavin's."

McKenna edged closer to Noah, her eyes lifting slightly above his. Noah hadn't been able to do much about his cropped bangs, which surely gave him away as Amish, since he didn't know any *Englisch* guys with his haircut. He'd tried to comb them to the side, but they just kept falling forward, so he finally gave up.

Noah took a nervous drink from his cup, and a tiny bit of liquid dribbled down his chin, which he quickly wiped away. But McKenna just smiled.

"Uh, hey . . ." Penny blinked her eyes at Gavin. "Why don't the four of us go up to the video room. It's off-limits for parties, but I live here, so"—she shrugged, grinning—"I say we can go." She nudged Gavin. "It's also where my dad's liquor cabinet is. But since his heart attack, he doesn't drink anymore, so he won't notice if a little tiny bit is missing."

"Sounds good." Gavin sounded smooth as he winked at Penny, but Noah thought he caught a twinge of something less sure in his friend's expression as Gavin turned away.

Noah drank more beer and realized he wasn't nearly as nervous as he'd been earlier. He followed Gavin and the girls toward the house and stayed close as they elbowed their way to a spiral staircase. Once on the landing upstairs, they started down a long hallway, and Penny opened double doors on the right that led into a room that reminded Noah of a mini movie theater. He'd been to the movies before—one of the things he'd taken advantage of during his *rumschpringe*. Once he'd gone by himself, and twice he'd taken Rebecca.

They hadn't been in the room two minutes when Penny asked Gavin to follow her to another room. Right before Gavin stepped into the hallway, he turned to Noah and McKenna and pointed a finger at McKenna.

"Hey, no taking advantage of this guy. He's engaged to be married soon."

Penny slapped Gavin playfully on the arm. "Leave them alone. They'll be fine. And the booze is over there." She pointed to a cabinet to the right of the theater seats. "Have fun." She gave a quick wave, and they were gone.

Noah felt light on his feet and a little foggy, and it didn't take a genius to figure out he was in dangerous territory. He swallowed hard as McKenna walked toward him, her eyes locked on his. She stopped a few inches away from him and bit her bottom lip, her eyes slightly glassy. Noah's gut told him to take a step backward, but his feet were rooted to the floor. He'd never been this close to a girl who had such little clothing on, and his heart started pounding again.

"I know you're engaged," she said as she put a hand on his arm. "So, if us being alone together makes you uncomfortable, we can rejoin the party."

Noah wondered if she could hear his heart. He opened his mouth to tell her he wanted to go back to the party, but his mind couldn't seem to organize his thoughts into a sentence.

McKenna just smiled.

CHAPTER 2

Rebecca ran her finger down her to-do list of the things she needed to take care of before the wedding and was pleased at how much she'd accomplished. Then she looked at her brother's list and huffed.

"*Mamm*, Paul hasn't done any of the things on his list."

Rebecca's mother wiped her hands on a dish towel as she leaned against the kitchen counter. "There are still two months until the wedding, *mei maedel*. I'm sure your *bruder* will take care of his responsibilities."

"*Ya*, I hope so. But Paul waits until the last minute to do everything, and *Daed* insisted he get the fence painted, and that's not even on this list."

Her mother smiled. "Are you going to be like this for the next couple months? I promise you, everything will be fine."

Linda Fisher was the calmest woman Rebecca knew, and the perfect person to help plan a wedding. Rebecca wished she was more like her mother, but she had a tendency to worry about everything, even though she knew it was a sin. Little things got her all worked up, especially things out of her control.

She took a deep cleansing breath and blew it out slowly.

Noah had fallen in love with her just the way she was, but she wanted to be the best wife possible. She'd been practicing being calm. But when it came to her brother, procrastination was his middle name.

"I know. Everything will be fine." Even as she said the words, she had a niggling feeling deep inside that something was going to happen to mess up her wedding.

"*Ya*, it will be." Her mother draped the dish towel over her shoulder and blew a strand of hair from her face, then took the corner of the towel and dabbed at sweat on her forehead. "At least by October the temperatures will have cooled down." She tucked a few loose hairs back into place beneath her *kapp*.

"Besides, I think your *bruder* is seeing someone, although I haven't a clue who it might be. He's so tired after he works in the fields with your *daed*, but he still always wants to run any last-minute errands for me, especially if it involves going to the market." She paused, smiling. "Maybe it's one of the girls who works there. Maybe Mary Lapp? And he goes to the library a lot too." She tapped a finger to her chin. "But I'm not sure any of our people work at the library."

"Who knows. Paul is so secretive when it comes to girls." Rebecca's brother was three years older than her, and he'd had a long string of infatuations well before their parents would have allowed it. Rebecca recalled his first real love interest when Paul was fifteen. He wasn't old enough to date, but he'd thought he was madly in love with Elizabeth Troyer, a girl two years older than him. But it didn't take long before Paul moved on to someone else. "You can always tell when he is smitten about someone. He walks around with that goofy smile on his face. But he never dates anyone for long."

Her mother chuckled. "*Ya*, and he has that look on his face now. But we'll know if it's serious if and when your *bruder* publishes any intentions."

Rebecca appreciated her mother's optimism, but she wasn't sure her brother was ever going to get married. "Word slips out long before publishing a wedding announcement takes place." Rebecca grinned. "*We* always know. It's you parents who remain in the dark."

"*Ach*, I wouldn't say that's true in every case. We were sure you and Noah were going to get married, way before you announced it."

"That's because Noah always picked me up here for our dates by himself. Lots of kids go out in a group to cover up who might be seeing whom."

Mamm narrowed her eyebrows into a frown. "Where is Noah anyway? He hasn't been by for a few days."

Rebecca shrugged as she read through her brother's list again, strumming her fingers on the kitchen table. "I don't know." She lifted her head and frowned. "It has been a few days, hasn't it?" Usually he came by on Tuesdays and Thursdays because he got off work early on those days. Today was Friday. She leaned back in the chair and folded her arms across her chest. "I'd know exactly where he is and what he's doing if you and *Daed* would let me have a cell phone."

Mamm shook her head. "You know how your *daed* feels about mobile phones."

Rebecca sat taller. "*You* could talk *Daed* into allowing them. It would be so much easier to take care of things for the wedding."

Her mother chuckled. "This isn't the first wedding in our community, and somehow we've managed just fine all these years without mobile phones." She walked to the stove and turned down the burner under the pinto beans she was cooking for supper. "I'm sure once you're married, that will be the first thing you buy."

"Noah has one already."

"*Ya*, I know. And Noah also has a job." *Mamm* scowled. "Not only are those things a disruption to our way of life, but they are expensive."

Rebecca sat taller. "So, are you saying that if I had a job and saved my money, I could get one?"

"It's a moot point, Rebecca. You couldn't save that much money before you're married anyway, and your father doesn't like the phones."

"We are living in the past." She frowned and shook her head. "The bishop allows cell phones, and *everyone* has one."

Her mother sighed. "*Ya*, the bishop allows them, but they are supposed to be used for business and emergencies. Your *daed* and I are trying to hold on to values that were instilled in us when we were *kinner*, like staying detached from the outside world and not allowing too many people into our circle who are unequally yoked. But things are changing." She pointed out the window. "There's your fellow coming up the road now. I always recognize that beautiful black horse way before I can see Noah's face."

Rebecca whipped her head around and smiled as her heart fluttered, the way it always did when she saw Noah. She was sure it would be that way for the rest of her life. She scooted her chair back and hurried through the living room toward the front door.

"Tell Noah we send blessings to his family. I haven't talked to his mother in a month since I was sick and missed the last worship service."

"*Ya, ya,* okay." Rebecca pushed the screen door open and

skipped down the porch steps. She was waiting in the yard when Noah pulled his buggy to a stop. She looked over her shoulder to be sure neither of her parents were watching out the window. She wanted to welcome Noah with a big hug and kiss.

"Thank goodness," Rebecca said as she walked toward him. "I thought you'd been kidnapped by aliens." After another quick look back at the house, she threw her arms around his neck, pushed up on her toes, and kissed him on the lips. "I've missed you." She stared into Noah's dark eyes before she tucked his brown hair behind his ears and laughed. "You need a haircut."

Noah untucked his hair until the long strands were free again. "*Ya*, I know. I'll get *Mamm* to do it."

Rebecca kept her arms around his neck. "I told you I would cut it."

Noah rolled his eyes and grinned. "Uh, I was there that day you trimmed Paul's hair. You snipped his ear and it bled forever."

Rebecca dropped her arms to her side and sighed. "He moved his head. That's the only reason that happened."

Noah put his hands on Rebecca's arms and pulled her into a hug, and she immediately felt that he was trembling. She eased him away. "What's wrong?"

Her fiancé lowered his gaze and kicked at the grass before he looked back at her. "You look pretty."

Rebecca's stomach churned. Something about the sober expression on Noah's face made her insides roil. "Noah, is something wrong? And where have you been all week? I didn't see you Tuesday or Thursday. Have you been sick? Working overtime at the hardware store?"

She took a deep breath and reminded herself not to get worked up, no matter the reason. She'd been guilty of flying off the handle over little things—like Noah being late to places, not calling when he said he would, or forgetting appointments. These were things Noah needed to work on, true. But Rebecca needed to work on her reactions to his shortcomings. She certainly had her own.

He shook his head. "*Nee, nee.*" He paused, scratching his chin. "I've just been thinking about things."

Alarms rang in Rebecca's head as worry wrapped around her. But this was the man she planned to marry, and she refused to let unjustified anxiety rise to the surface. "Thinking about what?"

Noah's bottom lip trembled. Rebecca had never seen that before. She was starting to think this wasn't idle worry. Something was up. "You're scaring me. What's wrong?"

"I-I'm not sure I want to be baptized." Noah was staring at the ground again.

Rebecca swallowed hard and took a deep breath. Then she playfully poked him in the chest. "Well, that's silly. If you don't get baptized, we can't get married."

Noah was quiet. Rebecca's insides were now a swirling tornado as she waited for the man she loved to look at her. "Noah?" Her voice cracked as she said his name barely above a whisper. "Noah?" she asked again when he didn't respond. "What are you saying?"

He finally looked up at her, and the tears in his eyes caused Rebecca's knees to go weak. "I'm sorry, Rebecca. I'm so sorry."

Rebecca brought a hand to her chest, hoping to slow the beat of her heart. Tears filled her own eyes. "Just say it, Noah. Whatever it is, I know we can work through it."

He stood taller and lifted his chin. "I told you. I don't know if I want to be baptized."

His voice was more forceful, and Rebecca couldn't stop the tears from trailing down her cheeks. "Just say it."

Noah blinked his own watery eyes. "I don't want to get married."

Rebecca had been dating Noah for over a year. They'd known each other their entire lives. She thought she knew him. "I-I don't understand. Don't you love me?"

Noah blinked his eyes a few more times, obviously trying to control the tears pooling. "*Ya*, I do. But I'm just not ready to get baptized and married."

Rebecca took a step backward, glaring at him as she cried.

"I'm sorry," he repeated, although the words barely came out.

Rebecca spun around and ran to the house, waiting for Noah to call after her.

But he didn't.

CHAPTER 3

McKenna had just finished painting her toenails when Penny walked into her bedroom and folded her arms across her chest, frowning. "Your mom told me to come on in. Do you have something you want to tell me?"

McKenna looked back at her toenails and began fanning them with a file folder. She shrugged, trying to decide if she liked the dark shade of blue. "No. Why?"

Penny flopped into McKenna's pink beanbag chair and slung her purse on the floor next to her. "It's exhausting being your friend." She crossed her legs and kicked her foot into action.

McKenna loved Penny. They'd been friends for years. But Penny's overly dramatic displays could be annoying. "Then don't stay friends with me."

Penny rolled her eyes. "We'll always be friends. I'm sure of that. But the Amish are different from us. Yeah, they get to run around and pretend they're normal for a while, until they get baptized and choose someone to marry." She paused, sighing. "We've lived in Paradise, Pennsylvania, all our lives. And the Amish guys almost always choose a good Amish girl to marry. You know that. You were just supposed to entertain Noah so

Gavin and I could be alone for a while. Now Gavin told me Noah called off his wedding. I'm sure he's just a play toy for you, but you messed up his life."

McKenna tossed the file folder on the bed as she scowled at her friend. "*Play toy*? That's just mean, Penny. I'm not sure exactly what you're accusing me of, but I assure you, nothing happened."

"Nothing?" Penny glared at her. "Then why did Noah call off his wedding less than a week after the party?" She pointed a finger at McKenna. "*Something* must have happened."

McKenna's chest tightened as she considered the accusation. She didn't want to be responsible for anyone's breakup. As she recalled her conversation with Noah, she was sure she hadn't led him on. "Nothing happened. I promise. If Noah decided to break up with his girlfriend, it had nothing to do with me."

Penny lifted an eyebrow, her leg kicking the air harder as she twisted her mouth from side to side.

"We talked for the two hours you were off doing whatever with Gavin," McKenna continued.

"Talked about what?"

McKenna glowered at her friend, at the accusing tone digging further underneath her skin. "Lots of things. He said I was easy to talk to, although he did most of the talking. He's a super nice guy. But we didn't do anything—not even get into your dad's liquor cabinet. We'd both had a couple beers and decided that was enough."

Thinking about that, McKenna frowned, wishing she had avoided alcohol completely that night. It wasn't her thing. Again, she tried to remember if she might have been flirty with Noah. *No, I wasn't.*

"You should be thanking me for keeping him company instead of accusing me of seducing him or something. I didn't even want to go to the party." She cringed when Penny's expression fell. "I'm sorry. I just wasn't in the mood, but since it was at your house, and you wanted me to go, and . . ."

Penny uncrossed her legs, stood up, and folded her arms across her chest. "My second cousin is Amish, so I've probably been to more Amish events than you have. They are simple people and quite sheltered. Did you kiss him?"

McKenna stood up and faced off with her friend. "No!"

"That's not what I heard."

"I hugged him good-bye, kissed him on the cheek, and told him it had been great talking with him." She threw her hands in the air. "I made a new friend, that's all. You know I hug everyone, and sometimes I kiss people on the cheek." She shrugged. "It's like a handshake to me when I like a person." McKenna hadn't received many hugs growing up. Showing warmth was important to her.

"Well, apparently for an Amish guy that little show of affection was enough for him to call off his wedding. You need to get ahold of him and tell him the hug and kiss didn't mean anything so he'll come to his senses and go back to his fiancée."

McKenna was quiet, but she finally looked at Penny. "Quit being so mean. I'll talk to him." She tucked her hair behind her ears. "But if one simple peck on the cheek and a hug were enough to make Noah ditch his girlfriend, maybe he was just looking for a way out."

Still, McKenna was going to be more careful about whom she hugged from now on.

Penny shook her head. "I don't know, but Gavin made it

sound like the breakup was your fault, and apparently Gavin works with Noah and they're pretty good friends. And I don't want Gavin holding me even partly responsible for your boo-boo, because you know I really like him." She chuckled, then sighed. "I doubted you were pursuing an Amish guy. They have those funky haircuts. They're super religious, and . . ." She frowned, shaking her head. "Can you imagine life without a car, air-conditioning, makeup, and blow dryers? Not to mention the sack dresses they wear."

McKenna wasn't about to tell her friend that she could imagine all those things and even longed for them some days. "It was just a little peck, Penny. I'll talk to Noah to make sure he didn't misunderstand anything. So, how'd it go with you and Gavin?"

Penny smiled, practically glowed. "It was awesome. He's not just handsome. He's truly such a nice guy." She held up her first finger. "And he's a gentleman."

They were both quiet for a few seconds. McKenna watched as Penny burrowed herself into the beanbag chair and closed her eyes. She always wanted to come to McKenna's house, which was probably a fifth the size of the mansion Penny's family lived in. Penny said her house was good for parties and that was about it. Her parents fought a lot, and McKenna had seen some of the arguments, so she sort of understood. Her own house was quiet, just her and her mom. And they barely spoke to each other.

McKenna sighed, frowning. "I'm glad things went well with Gavin, but now I'm feeling kind of bad. I still can't believe that simple gesture was enough for Noah to call off his wedding." McKenna only had eyes for one guy, and she hadn't even told

Penny about him. She thought a moment. "Noah's Amish, but does he have a cell phone? Or how do I talk to him?"

Penny smiled, reached into her purse, and pulled out a folded piece of paper. "Gavin gave me his number. He has a cell, like half the Amish do." She frowned. "So many gray areas with those people. Sometimes I think they make up the rules as they go along." She unfolded the paper and handed it to McKenna. Then, her mission accomplished, she stood and slung her purse over her shoulder. "Obviously, your interest in Noah—or the interest he *thinks* you have in him—was enough to make him question his relationship with his fiancée. But I'm glad to hear that you'll talk to him."

McKenna suspected that Penny's intentions were more about not upsetting Gavin than about repairing Noah's love life.

Penny grabbed her purse from the floor and bit her bottom lip. Then she pointed to McKenna's nightstand. "Do you actually read that?"

McKenna zoned in on what Penny was looking at. "The Bible? Yes, I do sometimes, especially when . . ." She shrugged. "It just helps me."

Penny tapped a finger to her chin. "Helps you how?"

McKenna couldn't recall ever having a conversation like this with Penny. "It helps me feel closer to God."

Penny stared at the book for a while.

"Do you want to borrow it?" McKenna had notes written inside, but if it would offer some comfort to her friend, she'd part with it temporarily.

"I don't know." Penny finally looked at McKenna, more sullen than she'd ever seen her.

"You can take it, Penny. If you want," McKenna added

carefully. She knew better than to push anything on Penny. Her friend was a bit of a rebel sometimes.

Penny offered a weak smile. "I'll think about it."

McKenna waited until after Penny was gone before she changed from her worn T-shirt and shorts into jeans and a light-blue sweater. She wasn't sure how to interpret her quick exchange with Penny about the Bible, but the fact that she'd shown even a slight interest was promising. McKenna had asked Penny to go to church with her in the past, and she had declined every time. Of course, McKenna didn't get to go every Sunday herself. It depended on the situation with her mother that day.

She ran a brush through her hair and put on some lip gloss, then found her car keys and purse. After she'd slipped into her sandals, she went down the hallway and stopped at her mother's bedroom. "Mom, I'm going out." She spoke loud enough for her mother to hear her through the closed door.

"Okay."

McKenna stood at the door a few seconds, her hand on the knob. She already felt bad about any misconceptions Noah had perceived at the party. If she walked into her mother's bedroom right now, she was pretty sure what she saw would make her feel even worse. So she took off down the hallway.

She suspected Noah worked at the hardware store on Saturdays, like Penny said Gavin did, and she decided she'd forgo the phone call and talk to him in person. She might not be able to do anything to help her mother, but if she'd played any role, even if unintentionally, in Noah breaking up with his fiancée, McKenna wanted to fix it now.

Rebecca's emotions had gone full circle in less than twenty-four hours. For the rest of the day Friday, she'd cried and begged her parents and Paul to just leave her alone for a while. Saturday morning she'd woken up crying, but by midafternoon, anger found its way into her heart, and she wanted to unleash it on someone. Her parents had left after lunch to go to an auction in Bird-in-Hand. She shuffled down the stairs and straight to a plate of cinnamon rolls in the middle of the kitchen counter. She'd barely sat down when she heard footsteps.

"*Wie bischt*, Becky." Paul reached for a pastry. "I'm sorry about you and Noah."

Rebecca could feel the venom at the tip of her tongue, ready to spew. "I *hate* being called Becky. Why do you keep calling me that when you know I don't like it? Everyone else calls me Rebecca." She glared at him. "Why can't you call me Rebecca? Do you do it just to make me mad?"

Paul stared at her, finished chewing, then said, "I'm going to let that go because I know you're hurt, *Rebecca*."

She covered her face with her hands. She'd already had her own private temper tantrum upstairs—the kind she'd sworn off in her attempt to be calmer and more levelheaded—but she was pretty sure this situation had warranted her fit.

Her brother sighed, then pulled out the chair next to her at the kitchen table and placed a hand on her shoulder. "Maybe Noah just has cold feet. Remember Katie and Jake? Jake broke up with her because he thought he wanted to live like the *Englisch*, but a week later he'd changed his mind and they were back together."

Rebecca uncovered her face and sniffled. "I remember that. But I thought I knew Noah so well. I just don't understand. We've been planning a life together, and . . ." She covered her face again, glad Paul was the only person seeing her like this.

"Becky . . ." Paul touched her shoulder again. "Sorry. Rebecca. If Noah doesn't change his mind, then it's just not God's plan for you. It just means there is someone better out there for you."

Rebecca lowered her hands again and reached into her apron pocket for a tissue, then blew her nose. "*Nee*, there isn't anyone else for me. I can't imagine being with anyone but Noah."

"You can't imagine it *now*, but that doesn't mean there isn't someone else." Paul stood up, went to the refrigerator, and poured himself a glass of milk. "But I am a little mad at him for hurting you like this."

Rebecca stared at her brother as he downed the milk. She thought about all the hearts he had broken since his *rum-schpringe* started six years ago. Most folks in their community were baptized and married within a couple of years of their running around period. At twenty-two, Paul seemed to fall in and out of love faster than anyone she'd ever known and had yet to settle down. He was the last person who should be giving her advice about anything related to love and loss. And the last person who should be mad at Noah. But she didn't say anything.

"Maybe he slept on it and realized he made a terrible mistake." Paul reached for another cinnamon roll. "I have to go to town. *Daed* asked if I could go look at Abram Troyer's two mules he wants to sell. Why don't you ride along? It's Saturday, so Noah is working. I can drop you at the hardware store to talk to him."

Rebecca shook her head. "I don't know. I can't make him love me." She started to cry again.

"People don't just fall in and out of love overnight. There has to be something else going on." Paul grabbed another roll and took his hat from where he'd hung it on the back of the kitchen chair.

Rebecca dropped her jaw, unable to keep quiet any longer. "You fall in and out of love more than anyone I've ever known."

Paul scowled. "I've dated a lot of women, and I loved some of them. But there were things missing in the relationships that led me to know it wasn't right for either of us."

Rebecca raised her chin as she sniffled. "Hearts were broken just the same."

Paul shrugged. "And those girls went on to find someone else. Everyone I ever dated is married now."

Rebecca thought about the girls Paul had gone out with, or at least the ones she knew about. "I guess they are all married now."

Her brother smiled. "*Ya*, see . . . all part of God's perfect plan." He reached for the doorknob that opened to the front porch. "You can either sit here and cry all day, or you can talk to Noah and try to find out why he changed his mind."

Rebecca dabbed at her eyes and stood up. "I guess you're right. What do I have to lose? I just need to get cleaned up."

Paul nodded as he took his hand from the doorknob. "Be quick."

She took a deep breath and trudged to the stairs, then picked up the pace when Paul cleared his throat. She hoped this wasn't a mistake.

CHAPTER 4

Paul pulled his buggy into the parking lot of the hardware store, happy to see a hitching post available. Merchants had learned a long time ago that if they didn't have a place for buggies to park, most folks would find somewhere that did. Paul hoped this didn't take too long so he could go see about the mules, then get to the library.

"You haven't said a word the entire ride." He stepped out of the buggy to secure the horse.

"I was thinking about what to say to Noah," Rebecca said as she caught up to him.

"Well, did you come up with anything?" Paul gave Daisy Mae a scratch behind her ears. It was a girlie name for a horse, but he'd gotten her for a good price, and she never let him down, even when he got caught in a snowstorm two years ago. She plowed through it and got them both home safely. He probably needed to retire the old girl, but he wasn't ready, and he didn't think she was either. He nuzzled her nose with his. "Be back soon."

He turned just in time to see Rebecca roll her eyes. "I think you love that horse more than you've loved any of your girlfriends."

Paul chuckled as he walked toward the building. "That's because Daisy Mae doesn't get jealous, doesn't argue, and doesn't demand an unreasonable amount of attention."

Rebecca pulled on Paul's shirt and forced him to slow his stride. In a few more feet, they'd pass by the glass window of the hardware store. "I don't know what I'm going to say," she said, tugging on his shirt until they were stopped inches away from the window.

Paul had never been on the receiving end of a breakup, but he tried to recall some of the questions he'd been asked when he ended a relationship. "Just ask him what happened to cause him to change his mind."

"I already did."

"Ask him again." Paul looked her in the eyes. "But be prepared for an answer that might hurt more than not knowing."

He hoped that wouldn't be the case for his sister, but he could still remember Annie Byler pushing him for a reason after he'd broken up with her. She wouldn't let it go, so Paul finally told her he loved her, but not enough to spend the rest of his life with her. It was only a partial version of the truth, but Annie was a great girl, and the expression on her face at that moment had haunted him for years. Now Annie was happily married. And Rebecca would find someone else, too, if Noah really had changed his mind.

"Maybe it's not me." Rebecca still wasn't moving forward. "Maybe he just doesn't want to be baptized into the faith. Maybe he loves me but doesn't want to remain Amish."

Paul tipped back his straw hat and scratched his forehead. "Did he ask you not to be baptized and to run away with him somewhere?"

"*Nee.*"

Paul raised an eyebrow and let that sink in for Becky, mentally reminding himself to stop calling her that.

Rebecca squeezed her eyes closed. "I think I've changed *mei* mind. I should give him some time. I'll look desperate if I bother him at work."

You are desperate. And Paul couldn't really blame her. Noah had been his sister's only true love. Part of him wanted to go in the store and give Noah a piece of his mind, but that wouldn't help Rebecca's cause. "Well, I need two hinges to fix the gate, so I'll run in and get them if you want to wait here. It's on that list of yours. Maybe Noah will open up to me."

Rebecca's bottom lip trembled, and Paul could have kicked himself. "I'm sure all those repairs need to be made," she said in a shaky voice. "But there doesn't seem to be an urgency anymore."

Paul sighed. "Go wait in the buggy. I'll run in and get the hinges. I'll let you know if Noah says anything."

Rebecca tucked her chin, nodded, and shuffled back to the buggy.

Sighing again, he walked toward the front door but slowed his step as he passed the window and looked in.

What in the world?

Shocked, his heart pounding in his chest, he scrambled backward until he wasn't visible. He waited a couple seconds, then inched his head forward until he could see Noah and the woman again. His sister hadn't even considered that maybe Noah had fallen for someone else. But when he saw Noah wrap his arms around the woman and pull her close to him, Paul's eyes widened. Then Noah kissed her. The way they were standing, Paul couldn't tell if the kiss was directly on the mouth or nearby on her cheek. Either way, he'd kissed her. Had Noah been cheating on Rebecca? Or did he break up the day before so he could be with someone else now? Did it even matter?

And by the looks of her jeans and long blond hair, she was *Englisch.*

Paul tried to pull his eyes away, but his pulse picked up when he recognized the familiar stance of the woman and the way her hair fell to her waist, just curling at the ends. The hug seemed to go on forever, but when Paul finally saw the woman's face, he grew weak in the knees and rushed back to the buggy.

"Oh no. Oh no." Rebecca brought her hands to her chest. "That was fast. What happened? What did he say? Did you even get the hinges? What happened?"

Paul didn't want to lie to his sister, but he needed time to process what he'd just seen. "Noah was busy with someone, and I feel sick to my stomach all of a sudden. I think I need to head back to the house."

"*Ya*, okay. Do you want me to drive the buggy?"

He shook his head. "*Nee.* Sorry about this."

"You probably ate too many of *Mamm's* cinnamon rolls. They're so good, but they are very rich. I got a stomachache from eating too many one time."

Paul nodded and tried to lose the image of McKenna and Noah. *His* McKenna. The woman he hadn't told anyone about. The woman he really and truly had fallen in love with the moment he laid eyes on her at the library a few months ago.

CHAPTER 5

McKenna wiggled out of Noah's embrace, tried to smile, and attempted to swallow back her shock. It hadn't been a "Hi, how are you?" hug. It was more like an "I've missed you so much" hug, one that would have gone on forever if she hadn't ended it. And she wasn't sure if the kiss on the cheek had been intended for her mouth. She turned her head when she sensed it coming.

Noah picked up his straw hat from the tile floor. He moved toward her, and McKenna tensed but resisted the urge to take a step backward.

"It's so *gut* to see you. I realized after the party that I didn't get your phone number, so I asked Gavin to make sure Penny got it to you."

McKenna took a deep breath. "Um, yeah. She did. But I decided to just stop by."

Penny was right. Noah had taken a hug and simple peck on the cheek way out of context. Now McKenna wished she'd just called him. The Amish weren't fond of public affection. She especially knew that from the time she'd spent with Paul. McKenna and Paul had spent hours together talking, and only recently had he hugged her good-bye when they were out of sight from people in the library. A few times they met at the market in Bird-in-Hand, but there were too many people around, and it wasn't really a good place to talk. Outside wasn't a good option either because the temperatures hadn't cooled down enough to get rid of the mosquitos. But even when they'd been alone, Paul hadn't so much as held her hand. Noah seemed to be acting very out of character for an Amish man.

"I haven't been able to stop thinking about you since the party." Noah smiled as he waved a hand around the store. "It's Gavin's day to get off early, and the cashier wasn't feeling *gut*, so I've been running the place by myself. I guess I just took advantage of the opportunity to give you a hug."

McKenna took a deep breath. Noah had been such a sweetheart at the party, and he was a really nice guy. She searched for words that wouldn't hurt him but would make it clear she didn't have any romantic interest in him.

"Listen, Noah . . ."

She paused when a muscle twitched along his jaw, and his expression grew sober. "I'm sorry. The hug was too forward. I was just surprised to see you, and happy."

His soul-searching dark eyes seemed to beg for forgiveness. McKenna recognized that expression. She'd seen it plenty of times on her mother's face. "It's okay. But . . ." She still couldn't think of a way to tame any feelings he might think he had for her.

He grinned a little. "*Ya*, I moved way too fast. We haven't even had a first date."

McKenna's jaw dropped. She decided a partial version of the truth was going to be the easiest for Noah to handle. "I'm seeing someone. I can't go out with you." She wasn't sure if meeting

Paul at the library and market constituted dating, but it seemed less cruel than saying she wasn't interested in Noah romantically. She raised her chin and pressed her lips together, even though she was trembling on the inside.

"Oh." Noah rubbed his chin as his face turned red. "I-I didn't know that. You didn't mention it at the party."

McKenna set her purse on the counter nearby and sighed. "I know we didn't talk about your fiancée much, mostly about your way of life, my way of life, and how different our lives are. But . . ." She raised a hand to her chest. "Penny told me you broke up with your girlfriend. Is that true?"

His eyebrows drew in as creases deepened across his forehead. Noah was still sporting a tan in September. She knew the Amish worked hard in the fields, but for a nineteen-year-old, the effects of too much time in the sun were already showing. Even his eyes had tiny lines beginning to feather from the corners.

Paul worked outdoors a lot, too, but McKenna couldn't recall if there was even the tiniest wrinkle on his face. Probably because it didn't matter. For once in her life, she'd fallen for what was inside a guy, not just his outer good looks, which Paul just happened to have as well.

"*Ya,* I broke off our engagement." Noah gazed over McKenna's shoulder, seemingly lost in memories or regrets as his face grew somber. "There wasn't an easy way to do it, and I'm sure she's heartbroken."

"Why did you do it?" McKenna held her breath. "Please say it didn't have anything to do with me."

He locked eyes with hers. "It had everything to do with you."

McKenna blinked in disbelief, afraid she might cry.

"That didn't come out the way I meant it to. What I meant

to say is that if I'm attracted to someone else, how can I marry Rebecca?" He shook his head. "It wouldn't be right."

McKenna felt a bit of relief and took a deep breath. "Have you ever had a girlfriend before Rebecca?"

"*Ach, ya,* a couple." Noah looked away as he scratched his chin. The Amish weren't supposed to lie, but McKenna wasn't sure she believed him. "No one as special as Rebecca." His face lit up a little, and McKenna was hopeful.

"Noah." She spoke gently. "We are all attracted to people physically from time to time, but it's what is on the inside that truly sparks a flame. And you don't know me at all." *Or the baggage I come with.* She hadn't even told Paul about her mother, and she'd told him things she'd never told anyone.

Noah took off his hat and set it on the counter by McKenna's purse, then ran a hand through his dark hair, sighing, before he looked at her. "McKenna, I think you are beautiful, and from what I saw at the party, you're beautiful on the inside too."

McKenna opened her mouth to reiterate that he didn't know her, but Noah held up a hand, signaling he had more to say. "But my breaking up with Rebecca wasn't only because of you, so please don't feel guilty. I shouldn't have said that the breakup had everything to do with you. There was more to it than that."

"Like what?" More relief washed over her, but somewhere there was a girl she didn't know who was heartbroken.

He folded his arms across his chest and leaned against the counter. "I am supposed to be baptized in a few weeks, and that is a lifelong commitment that we take very seriously."

"I know." She shifted her weight and mirrored his stance, crossing her arms over her chest. "And I know you have to get baptized before you can get married, right?"

Noah nodded. "I love Rebecca, but sometimes I feel like I'd be more suited to the *Englisch* life, and I'm not going to ask her to leave a life she loves."

Without thinking, McKenna gave Noah a few gentle pokes on the chest. "More suited to the *Englisch* life? Are you *kidding* me? You went to one party, had some beer at a swanky house, and now, all of a sudden you're ready to live like that?"

Noah grinned. "I've been in my *rumschpringe* for three years. That wasn't my first party. I hadn't been to anything that fancy, but I've hung out with *Englischers* off and on since I was sixteen. But it's more than that." He shook his head. "It has to do with my faith, and you wouldn't understand."

McKenna frowned. "I grew up in a home without faith, and I've worked very hard the past few years to have a good relationship with God." Although she was disappointed in herself for drinking at Penny's party and wondered if she'd let God down. "I don't think you should say I wouldn't understand."

He cringed. "I'm sorry. You're right. That was one subject we didn't talk about at the party." The hint of a smile lit his face, quickly replaced with another sour expression. "Maybe I was kind of using you as an excuse to get out of baptism and marriage."

McKenna raised an eyebrow as she tapped a foot up and down. "Gee, just what every girl wants to hear."

Noah chuckled, which was nice amid the tension. McKenna dropped her arms to her sides and relaxed a little.

"I was super glad to see you when you walked in. I guess I just really enjoyed our talk, and there's no denying you're very pretty. But I wish you well with your boyfriend."

McKenna picked up her purse and slung it over her shoulder.

"Aw, thanks. And this guy isn't exactly my boyfriend, but I'm hoping he will be one day. Right now we spend a lot of time together." She didn't see how she and Paul could ever be a couple, but the vision still strolled into her mind often. For now the possibility of it was what Noah needed to hear to help him make long-lasting decisions without an infatuation dictating his actions.

He smiled broadly. "Your face lights up when you talk about him. Anyone I know?"

"I doubt it." McKenna and Paul hadn't exchanged last names, which seemed a bit odd now that she thought about it. But it was almost like an unspoken rule to keep a little distance between them. It would be embarrassing to admit to Noah that she didn't know Paul's last name—a guy she just said she hoped to have as a boyfriend. And that wasn't a lie. If only things were different.

Paul was a common Amish name in Lancaster County. There were probably dozens in Paradise and Bird-in-Hand alone. But she didn't want to chance anyone finding out about their secret meetings, mostly at the library. She wanted to get off the subject and get home. She'd been nearly sick all the way to the hardware store. She felt a little better now but needed to say one last thing to Noah.

"Think long and hard before you choose to give up Rebecca. And think even harder about giving up your faith. It's all that's kept me going at times." McKenna thought about the inner peace she struggled to maintain each day she lived with her mother. From the moment she opened her heart to the Lord, things had begun to change. She felt a peacefulness she hadn't known and had a best friend to whom she could tell anything without being judged. Even though she didn't understand why God hadn't helped her mother.

"I'll never give up my faith. It's how I choose to practice it that has me confused."

McKenna stared at Noah for a moment, trying to read his expression, which looked as muddled as his comments about his faith. She wondered if maybe he was more grounded in his religious beliefs than he wanted to admit right now. Maybe he was saving face in front of her, downplaying a temporary infatuation by questioning his faith. Or had this fairly insignificant event caused him such disappointment in himself that he wondered if his Amish life was right for him? If God would forgive him?

She smiled. "I'm going to pray for you, Noah, but just remember that God forgives every mistake we make, even when we question our motives. Don't let a little slipup derail you from your plans."

Noah lowered his eyes for a few moments, and McKenna felt like maybe she'd hit the nail on the head about him wanting to save face a little. When he looked back at her, his shy smile said she might be right. "*Danki* for saying that. I hope things work out with your friend too. Is there anything I can pray for you specifically?"

McKenna's prayer list was especially long these days, but she wasn't going to burden him with anything but the need at the top of her list. "Yes, there is. Can you pray for my mom?"

"*Ya*, sure. Is she sick?"

McKenna swallowed hard. "Yeah, I guess you could say that." Even Penny didn't know about McKenna's mother, just that she slept a lot. Too much to hold down a job. But McKenna tried to count her blessings. Without her grandmother's inheritance, she and her mother would have starved a long time ago. The money paid the mortgage, they always had food, and McKenna earned enough at her part-time job to pay for a few college classes over the summer. Her mother controlled the household expenses, and a large chunk of the budget went toward her pills. McKenna was looking for a full-time job now, hoping she could take some classes in the evenings.

"I'll pray for your mother." Noah smiled. "And for you."

"Thanks. And I'll pray that you feel peace about the decisions you're making and that you'll make the right ones."

Noah stuck out his hand. "Friends?"

McKenna shook his hand and gave him a taut nod, grinning. "Friends." This time she withstood the temptation to give him a hug or kiss.

She doubted she'd ever see Noah again. Unless they both ended up at another party together, which seemed unlikely. McKenna was done with parties. They were always the same, everyone drinking, smoking, and making idiots of themselves half the time. She'd been guilty of all that in her early teens, but watching her mother sinking further and further into an abyss over the past couple of years had caused her to rethink her life. And her time with Paul had also influenced her goals. She wasn't ever going to be Amish, but she craved the peacefulness that went along with the Amish lifestyle.

As McKenna left the hardware store and walked to her car, she prayed for Noah and Rebecca. She prayed for her mother to get well. And she asked God to stay by her side. She hadn't found the Lord until recently, and McKenna had a long way to go before she felt worthy of all God had to offer. But she planned to keep trying to better herself.

She started her car, glanced at the time on her dashboard, and headed toward the library. Seeing Paul was always the highlight of her day. She'd never felt like this about anyone before. And that was a problem because he was Amish.

CHAPTER 6

Noah rang up Doc Tyler's order—two boxes of nails, some screws, and a few paintbrushes. The *Englisch* man was a regular and was always working on a new home improvement project. He was a retired psychiatrist, soft-spoken, and friendly. Doc Tyler had a long gray beard, and on the days he wore suspenders, he could almost be mistaken for an Amish man, except he parted what was left of his gray hair to the side.

Doc Tyler's appearance and mannerisms reminded Noah of Bishop Lapp. But Noah didn't think the retired psychiatrist or the bishop could get his mind right, even if they were all locked in a room together for hours. Noah's faith and his mental state felt in jeopardy.

After the doctor left, Gavin rounded the corner carrying a box. He set it on the counter, then ran the sleeve of his shirt across his forehead. "That's the last of the tiles. I just have to go stack them with the rest of the order."

Noah nodded. "*Ya*, okay." He slammed the cash register drawer, noticing it didn't close the first time. It took two more tries before it finally clicked into place.

"I'm not sure what the cash register did to deserve that, but maybe your anger is directed somewhere else. Like at yourself?" Gavin raised an eyebrow as he folded his arms across his chest. "I know this breakup with Rebecca is eating you up. Why don't you just go talk to her?"

Noah didn't say anything.

"Penny told me you and McKenna talked. Dude, there isn't a guy out there who hasn't been influenced by a woman or made a knee-jerk decision that turned out to be a mistake. McKenna's beautiful, so you were momentarily swept off your feet. But I know you're still in love with Rebecca, so I don't understand why you haven't told her you made a huge mistake."

"I do love her. I'll always love her." Noah kept his eyes cast down. "It's just not that simple. I hurt her really bad." He finally looked up at Gavin. "Maybe I don't even deserve to be baptized." Noah sighed. "I can't imagine walking away from my community."

Gavin shook his head. "None of us are deserving of God's blessings, so don't beat yourself up. But you'd get ousted, or shunned if you left, right?"

Noah shook his head as he sat down on the stool behind the counter, wishing the cashier would get back from lunch so he could avoid having to talk to anyone. "*Nee*, I wouldn't get shunned because I haven't been baptized yet. I could still see my family. But . . ." He took off his straw hat and scratched his head. "It's a lifelong commitment to the church and to Rebecca." He locked eyes with Gavin. "What if I change my mind in five years? What if I realize I made a mistake?"

"We all feel that way sometimes. I'm sure whenever I ask someone to marry me, I'll be terrified of the same thing."

"But you could get a divorce."

Gavin scowled. "Believe it or not, my religion frowns on divorce too. And I would still feel like a failure in God's eyes."

Noah had never had a conversation with Gavin about anything to do with God or religion. "Do you go to church?"

"Yeah. A couple times a month." Gavin grinned. "Just like you do."

Noah smiled. *Englisch* people who grew up in Lancaster County, like Gavin, knew the Amish had worship service every other Sunday. "*Ya*, well, ours is three hours long."

Chuckling, Gavin picked up the box of tiles. "I know. That's reason enough not to be Amish." He shook his head. "Seriously, though, you've been miserable since the party. Nothing happened, Noah. Maybe you thought you'd messed up and would just try to roll with it, but put it behind you. Get on with what your heart says. I think you should talk to Rebecca. If you live your life based on 'what-ifs'—'What if I get divorced? What if I fall out of love?'—and so on, you're never going to be happy."

Noah nodded. Gavin was right.

Rebecca eyed all the things she'd laid out on her bed to be boxed up. Her wedding dress, her silly lists of things to do before the wedding, her new prayer covering, and her new shoes. Tears trickled down her cheeks, and by the time she'd packed the last of her wedding items, she was sobbing.

"Becky, he isn't worth your tears."

Rebecca spun around, glowered at Paul, then swiped at her tears. "How would you know? Every time you get close to someone, you break off the relationship."

Paul stepped across the threshold as his eyes hardened and his nostrils flared. "That doesn't mean I'm not hurt when a relationship comes to an end."

Rebecca turned back and eyed her box of wedding things, lowering her chin. "I'm sorry." True or not, it was a hurtful thing to say.

Paul sat on the edge of her bed. "I think Noah is seeing someone else."

Blood pounded in Rebecca's temples as she considered the possibility. She shook her head. "*Nee*, not Noah. He would never cheat on me." She took a deep breath to calm her racing heart.

"I'm not saying he was cheating on you. I'm saying maybe he broke up with you so he *could* see someone else."

Rebecca brought a hand to her chest as she locked eyes with her brother. "Who?"

"You don't know her." Paul avoided her eyes. "She's *Englisch*."

As anger comingled with hurt, nasty bile grew in Rebecca's throat until she thought she might choke. If ever she needed to force herself to stay calm, it was now. "I know lots of *Englisch* girls."

"Not this one." Paul stood and walked across the room toward the door.

"Wait a minute." Rebecca took a few steps toward him. "Why do you think he's seeing an *Englisch* girl?"

Paul looked down at his worn work boots, then back up at her, a sorrowful expression on his face. "At the hardware store, the reason I didn't go in was because I saw Noah hugging an *Englisch* girl with long blond hair."

Relief began to flood over Rebecca like water putting out a fire. "There's nothing wrong with having an *Englisch* friend.

Noah sees a lot of people at the hardware store." She clenched her hands at her sides. "I can't believe you let me get this upset over a hug." She rolled her eyes and drew in a deep breath.

"It didn't look like that kind of hug to me. He had his hand cupped behind her head, and he was holding her close."

Rebecca focused on something in the distance as her bottom lip began to tremble, her hands still fisted at her sides as she took in the comment like a punch to her gut. "That's the way he hugs me, with a hand on the back of my head." She locked eyes with Paul as a tear slipped down her cheek.

"I'm sorry." Paul looked away, blinking as if trying to hold back his own tears, and despite her despair, it touched her that her brother felt her hurt so deeply.

"I'll be okay." It was a lie, but she wanted to ease Paul's suffering, and maybe if she repeated the words over and over again, they'd become true.

Paul hurried out of Rebecca's room before his emotions bubbled to the surface in front of his sister. As he'd been doing since he first saw them, he wondered why McKenna had been embracing Noah. He thought he and McKenna had been making a real connection over their past months together. But there she'd been . . . *connecting* with Noah. Why?

He rubbed his face. Maybe McKenna was one of those women who wanted to marry an Amish guy. He'd seen it happen plenty of times, and it rarely worked out. Outsiders glamorized the Plain lifestyle, and then when they realized how much work was involved—the early hours, the harvest, giving up modern luxuries, and a host of other challenges—they chose to go back to the way of life they knew and understood. Perhaps McKenna thought she could beat the odds. And maybe Noah was her backup plan if things didn't work out with Paul.

Still . . .

He pulled off his work boots, dropped his suspenders, and untucked his shirt. As he lay back on the bed staring at the ceiling, he wondered if he'd misread the situation with McKenna and Noah. If so, he'd upset Rebecca even more than she already was.

He scratched his chin, yawning even though it was early afternoon. How well did he really know McKenna? He mulled over all the things he'd learned about her during their conversations. She loved books. Obviously, since they met at the library. She adored animals but didn't have any pets because her mother wouldn't allow it. She was beautiful inside and out. She hadn't talked about her mother much, just that her father died when she was young, and it had been her and her mom since then, living in the same small house just outside Bird-in-Hand where she was raised.

Most important, McKenna's face always lit up when she saw Paul, and a strange feeling swept over him every time he was with her.

The more he thought about it, the more recollections came to mind. McKenna talked a lot about how much she admired the Amish way of life. She knew almost as much as Paul. Most *Englischers* here did. But she knew more than most.

She is *looking for an Amish husband.* Maybe as a way out of whatever secret she was keeping. Paul was sure there was something she wasn't telling him about her life. Was it about Noah?

His head spun, and his heart hurt. He glanced at the small

clock on his nightstand. The battery was going dead, so it stayed about ten minutes behind. McKenna would be at the library any minute.

He closed his eyes and thought about what could have been. If anyone knew the real reason he'd broken so many hearts in his community, they'd understand his dilemma. In any case, even if he'd been wrong about the hug, it was probably best that he stopped meeting McKenna.

McKenna waited at the library for over an hour, her head buried in a book even though she couldn't focus on what she was reading. A pang in the pit of her stomach told her something was wrong. She'd been meeting Paul on the self-help aisle—which they laughed about—for weeks now. They'd both been looking for the Christian fiction section and bumped into each other, literally.

She looked at the time on her phone again. Paul didn't have a cell phone, but he had her number. He could have found a phone and called to let her know he wouldn't be here.

How could it be that I never asked his last name? She bounced every Amish surname she could think of around in her mind— Beiler, Lapp, Stoltzfus, Troyer, Hostetler, King, and others—trying to remember if he might have mentioned it.

After another hour she was sure he wasn't coming, and her foot had fallen asleep as she sat on the floor against a shelf. She forced herself up, put the book in its place, and headed home.

It was Saturday, and Saturdays were always the worst for her mother. And for McKenna. That was the day Evan always showed up.

CHAPTER 7

McKenna pushed on her earbuds until she was sure they wouldn't go any farther, then she turned up the music until she couldn't hear her mother and Evan in the next room. McKenna hated Evan, and she'd told him so more than once.

She closed her eyes, tuned out the music for a few moments, and asked God for forgiveness. She was hurting herself more than Evan by hating him. But it was hard not to since he was killing her mother. They would be up all night, high on whatever stimulant Evan brought. Then they'd eventually wind down with pills. And then, before he disappeared, Evan would leave McKenna's mom enough pills to get her through the week.

McKenna tried not to think about what went on in the next room. She tried to find things to do on Saturday nights, but the only thing going on tonight was another one of Penny's parties, and McKenna wasn't up for that.

She scrolled through new posts on Facebook. Some of the Amish kids who were in their *rumschpringe* had pages, so she looked for pictures of Paul that anyone might have shared, but after an hour, it seemed pointless. He'd obviously changed his mind about wanting to be her friend.

And yet . . . Her heart flipped in her chest as she worried something might have happened to him. She resumed her Facebook search after remembering Paul had often mentioned a sister named Becky. Maybe she had a page.

Rebecca had a sore throat Sunday morning. It wasn't bad enough to miss worship service, but she made out like it was, exaggerating a cough that came up overnight. As curious as she was about the blond girl and Noah, she wasn't ready to face her former fiancé. She'd likely burst out in tears at the sight of him. And he'd already told her he didn't want to get married. She poured herself onto the couch and squeezed her eyes closed.

He doesn't want to marry me. He doesn't want to marry me.

No matter how many times she forced the truth into her mind, it just didn't ring true. Something big had happened. And the only thing big enough to change his mind had to be that he wanted to be with someone else.

She kicked her bare feet up on the coffee table, something her mother didn't allow. She thought she would enjoy having the house to herself, but it was giving her too much time in her head.

Will Noah talk to Paul at worship service? Will they avoid each other? Will Paul have information to share with me when he gets home?

Rebecca looked over her shoulder in surprise when she heard a car turning in the driveway. They weren't expecting any *Englisch* visitors—most folks would presume everyone was at worship service. The car continued toward the house, though, and she hurried to find a scarf and did her best to tie her hair in a knot before she draped the beige cloth over her head.

When a blond *Englisch* girl came up the sidewalk, Rebecca put a hand to her chest, hoping to stop the pounding that was getting worse with each step the woman took. There were hundreds or thousands of pretty *Englisch* girls with long blond hair in Lancaster County. The odds were stacked in Rebecca's favor that this wasn't Noah's girl, but her pulse raced just the same as she waited for the woman to knock.

She did, and Rebecca eased the door open.

"Are you Becky Fisher?"

Rebecca nodded, even though Paul was the only person who still called her Becky. The woman introduced herself as McKenna Young. She had stunning blue eyes, a flawless complexion, and just enough makeup on that it almost looked like she wasn't wearing any. "Can I help you?"

"Do you have a brother named Paul?"

Rebecca gasped. "Did something happen to him?"

"No, no. I'm so sorry. I didn't mean to scare you. I'm a friend of his, and I got worried when he didn't, um . . . show up at the library where we usually meet on Saturdays."

Oh dear. So that's where he goes on Saturdays. Now her brother had taken to breaking the hearts of *Englisch* women. He'd probably run out of Amish girls to date.

Rebecca motioned for the woman to step back so she could open the screen door. "Please, come in." She closed the door behind her visitor. "That's such a pretty name, McKenna."

"Thank you. I'm sorry for this intrusion. I was just worried. Is Paul here?" McKenna bit her bottom lip, her eyes wide and inquiring.

"*Nee*, I'm sorry. He and *mei* parents are at worship service this morning."

McKenna grunted, then frowned. "I always get the Sundays confused."

Rebecca suspected the reason for McKenna's visit, but this was a distraction from her own worries. "Do you want a cup of coffee?"

McKenna tucked her hair behind her ear on one side, revealing a gold looped earing. "I'd love some, if it's not too much trouble."

"*Nee*, not at all. I have some freshly made."

As McKenna sat in a chair by the table, Rebecca poured them each a cup then sat across from her guest, prepared for the barrage of questions she knew was coming. How many Amish girls had sat at this table fishing for information about Paul? She was tired of covering for him and making excuses for his behavior when he abruptly stopped seeing someone.

"So, you said you're a friend of Paul's?" Rebecca grinned. "Or more than a friend?" Surely Paul wouldn't venture into such dangerous territory—to date an *Englischer*. Even though Noah apparently had.

McKenna smiled, her eyes cast down as she circled the rim of her cup with her finger. "We're good friends." She looked up at Rebecca. "I felt like it was turning into more, but when he didn't show up yesterday . . ." She lifted one shoulder, then lowered it slowly. "I don't know what to think. He has my phone number." Pausing, she shifted uncomfortably in her chair. "I mean, I know he doesn't have a cell phone, but I thought he might borrow one or something."

Rebecca was already feeling sorry for this stranger. Maybe

it was because Rebecca was still grieving the loss of her own relationship. "I'm afraid this is what Paul does sometimes."

McKenna's bottom lip twitched. "What do you mean?"

"I'm afraid my brother is what you *Englisch* might call a 'love 'em and leave 'em' kind of man." Rebecca took a sip of coffee. There was no way to ease this woman's suffering, so getting to the point seemed best. If she had known Paul's latest fling was coming over, she'd have put a box of tissues on the kitchen table, like she'd done in the past.

McKenna's lip went from a twitch to a tremble. "He doesn't seem like the type," she said barely above a whisper as she stopped running her finger around the cup's rim, her eyes locked with Rebecca's as if she might not believe her. Or was she challenging her for more information?

"Paul is a wonderful man, and I love my brother very much, but he has a history of this. He just can't seem to commit to anyone long term."

McKenna blinked her eyes a few times. *Please don't cry.* Rebecca would end up crying with her, and she'd done enough of that recently.

"I'm sorry." McKenna dabbed at the corner of one eye. "I feel silly, and I shouldn't have come."

Rebecca got up, walked to the living room, and returned with a box of tissues.

"I just wanted to make sure he was okay, for starters. But I also wondered why he just didn't show up. Am I overreacting?" McKenna leaned forward a little, once again searching Rebecca's face for answers.

Rebecca had sugarcoated details to Paul's girlfriends in the past, but she was finished doing that. "I don't think you are overreacting. We have a phone in the barn Paul could have used to call you." She cringed. "Sorry to be the one to tell you that."

McKenna took a tissue and dabbed at her eyes. "I feel so dumb." She lowered her eyes and shook her head. "I'm not sure I realized how much I care for Paul until this moment."

You and so many others.

"We met at the library," McKenna said with the hint of a smile on her face.

Rebecca forced her own smile. She had to hear the "before" stories a lot of times too.

"We've been meeting there every Saturday for the past couple of months. We haven't even gone out on a date or anything." McKenna sniffled. "It's probably just as well, for obvious reasons." She coughed, sniffled, and raised her chin. "But maybe there was a reason he just didn't show up, or—"

"Don't do this to yourself," Rebecca said. "We have a phone. He could have called. And he didn't." She shook her head, sighing. "Paul gets close to someone, and then . . . I don't know exactly what happens, but he ends the relationship early on." Rebecca knew this next part would sting, but maybe it would help McKenna get over Paul. "Lots of girls have sat where you are right now." She pointed across the table before she went on. "I'm sure you are as lovely on the inside as you are on the outside. Otherwise Paul wouldn't have allowed you to get close to him. I'm truly sorry he hurt you." Rebecca scrunched up her nose, then gritted her teeth a little. "But, like you said, it's probably for the best." She paused. "Unless you would have been willing to convert to our faith."

"You're right." McKenna finally took a sip of her coffee. "I really felt like I was falling in love with Paul." She pointed to her watery eyes. "As you can tell. But deep in my heart, I knew there was eventually going to be a parting of ways." She chewed on a fingernail for a couple of seconds. "I guess I just wanted it to go on as long as it could before I had to give him up."

Rebecca nodded. This woman was much more logical than the others had been, so Rebecca threw her a bone. "Most of Paul's girlfriends didn't last more than a few weeks. Since you and he had been seeing each other for months, maybe Paul was falling for you, too, and this was the easiest way for him to sever the relationship." *Although I doubt it.*

A tear rolled down McKenna's cheek. She didn't even try to stop it. Instead, she locked eyes with Rebecca. "You know, I didn't even know Paul's last name. I spent hours on Facebook last night. I know sometimes you guys have Facebook pages—I mean, if you haven't been baptized yet, right?" Rebecca nodded, even though she'd never had such a page. "So I took a chance and searched for Pauls in Lancaster County." She smiled a little and finally dabbed at her eyes again. "There are eight hundred and twenty-two Pauls in our county, so I abandoned that course of action and decided to talk to an Amish friend I've known for years—Mary Zook. Do you know her?"

"I'm not sure." There were thousands of folks in Lancaster County, but the *Englisch* presumed they all knew each other personally. "I know several Mary Zooks. It's a very common name."

"I guess it doesn't matter, but I described Paul to her and that he'd mentioned a sister named Becky. This friend was rushing to get her daughter to a doctor's appointment and said she couldn't think of anyone. But just as she was loading her daughter in the buggy and I was getting in my car, she said the man I described might be Paul Fisher on Black Horse Road. She was in such a rush, I didn't push her further, but I drove down your road until I saw Fisher on the mailbox."

Rebecca scrunched up her face again. This woman had gone to a lot of trouble to find a man she'd only been meeting at the library a few months.

"I hear how desperate that sounds." McKenna shook her head. "But there was something about him. He's compassionate, kind, smart . . ." She paused, smiled a little. "And handsome."

"And very dangerous for you to fall for unless you are willing to live a life like we do," Rebecca said again.

McKenna shook her head again. "I admire all of you, and I think a lot of people seek the peacefulness you seem to have. If I had been raised that way, it would be different. But to make all the changes required to marry an Amish man . . ." She covered her mouth with one hand. "I barely know Paul. I can't believe I just said that."

Neither can I. Rebecca swallowed hard. This one had it bad for her brother.

McKenna abruptly stood up. "You have been so nice to me. Thank you for the coffee and conversation."

Rebecca rose too. She liked this woman more than half the women in her district who had fallen for Paul. At least McKenna was levelheaded about it. Rebecca reminded herself to be more like McKenna regarding her own situation. "You're welcome. I'm sorry I didn't have better news for you. I just didn't think beating around the bush would help you get over him."

"You're right." The other girl hesitated, then threw her arms around Rebecca. The move caught her completely off guard, so it took a few seconds for her to hug back—which instantly brought her thoughts full circle, back to Noah in the arms of another woman.

McKenna eased away and sighed. "I don't want to ask you to lie, but could you maybe not mention I was here? I already feel silly." She smiled. "And who knows, maybe he will be at the library next Saturday."

Rebecca admired McKenna's optimism, so she forced a smile, knowing it wouldn't be the case.

After McKenna left, Rebecca sank onto the couch again and propped up her feet. She wasn't going to tell Paul about McKenna's visit. They'd just get into an argument about the way he handled his love life. Or the way Rebecca had just handled it for him.

When she heard the buggy turning into the driveway a half hour later, she moved her feet off the table, straightened the few gardening magazines back into a pile, and waited patiently as Paul and her parents came up the porch steps.

When her parents were out of earshot, she asked Paul in a whisper, "Did you see Noah?"

He nodded before he took off his hat and hung it on the rack by the door.

"Well? I'm going crazy. Did you talk to him?" Rebecca's heart pumped harder.

"*Ya*, I did."

Rebecca stomped her foot. "Can you quit dragging this out and just tell me what he said?"

"I will. But you're not going to like it."

CHAPTER 8

Paul had listened to Noah pour out his heart to him after worship service. Even though it was an honest confession, Paul still felt the urge to punch him through most of the guy's ramblings. The vision of Noah and McKenna was etched into Paul's mind, no matter how hard he tried to erase it.

"Noah went to an *Englisch* party, and he met a girl there." Paul sat down at the kitchen table, glad to see more cinnamon rolls on the table, even though he'd stuffed himself during the meal after church. "Apparently they talked for hours, and he admitted to me that he felt an attraction toward her."

If Noah and McKenna had talked for hours, Paul wasn't surprised Noah felt drawn to her. Paul had noticed McKenna's outer beauty right away, but once they spent time talking, he saw her inner glow. He imagined McKenna had that effect on most people.

Rebecca stood in the kitchen, not moving, her hands clenched at her sides. Paul wasn't sure she was even breathing.

"He said it was just an infatuation. But it concerned him that he'd let those feelings in, and that he was so quick to break up with you. And now he's questioning everything."

Rebecca still didn't move.

"He still loves you, Becky. He's just confused." Paul sighed, wishing he'd met McKenna at the library. Noah had insisted nothing happened between them. Paul told him he saw the embrace, but he never let on that he knew McKenna. Noah explained about McKenna going to the hardware store to make sure Noah hadn't broken off the engagement because of her. "I misunderstood the hug, though. It was just a friendly hug. He's not involved with the woman." He reached for a cinnamon roll. "You just need to talk to him."

Rebecca's hands were still fisted at her sides, but at least she wasn't crying.

"Say something," he finally said with a mouthful of roll.

"I despise a woman I don't even know." Rebecca relaxed her stance but quickly folded her arms across her chest. "And maybe Noah shouldn't have been so forthcoming about his feelings for her, even if he was being honest."

Paul understood his sister's dilemma, but he felt a huge relief knowing there wasn't anything going on between Noah and McKenna. And now he wasn't sure whether or not to call McKenna and apologize for not being at the library. Noah said she talked a lot about the Amish way of life that night at the party, and warning bells were still going off in Paul's mind, that McKenna might just be in search of an Amish husband. She was keeping a secret. Paul didn't know what it was, but he feared she was running away from something.

"Noah isn't perfect." Paul pulled his suspenders off his shoulders and let them drop to his sides, then untucked his shirt. Sunday was a day of rest, and he was heading upstairs to take a nap. "And neither are you. None of us are. Maybe you need to hear him out."

Rebecca sat down at the kitchen table after Paul went upstairs. Her parents were in the living room talking about something that happened at church, an incident with Bishop Lapp and his wife in which they'd overheard them arguing.

As Rebecca bit into a cinnamon roll, she went over everything in her mind. It sounded like Noah had fallen for an *Englisch* girl, then that girl had put him in his place, and now he wanted to get back with Rebecca, who had somehow slipped into second place. What if the *Englisch* girl had wanted to be with him? Rebecca felt the sting of tears building as she swallowed the bite of cinnamon roll, but she blinked her eyes and fought off the urge to cry. She'd shed enough tears over Noah.

Then she thought about McKenna, who was beautiful, kind, and seemingly in love with Paul. It angered Rebecca that her brother hadn't had the courtesy to call her. It was a disastrous situation with a no-win outcome, but Rebecca liked McKenna, and her heart hurt for her. She considered telling Paul that McKenna came to the house, but there didn't seem to be much point. Rebecca's brother would likely offer up an excuse that would make her feel even worse. He was honest to a fault sometimes. Best to just let it go.

Rebecca was holding on to a despicable loathing of whatever woman Noah had so quickly fallen for. But could she place all the blame on the woman? Even if she had seduced Noah— and it didn't sound as though she had—he should have fought off any temptations if he really loved Rebecca the way he had proclaimed.

Even if Rebecca's feelings were misdirected, they didn't

diminish what she felt—jealousy, betrayal, and anger all rolled into a ball of repugnance. She made up her mind that she was going to be baptized as planned since that was the one thing she was sure of: her commitment to God and the church. But she was rethinking her choice to marry Noah, even if he came crawling back to her.

Noah slunk around the house most of Sunday afternoon. He left two messages on the answering machine Rebecca's family had in the barn, asking Rebecca to call him. Maybe no one had gone to the barn since returning from church. Or was she choosing not to call him? If Paul filled her in on what Noah told him, the latter was entirely possible. Noah wondered how much his friend told Rebecca. Probably everything. They didn't always see eye to eye on things, but they were close. Noah shouldn't have been so forthcoming with Paul. He should have just told his future brother-in-law that he'd had a moment of confusion and was past it now.

Noah could only hope Rebecca would take him back.

He cringed when he remembered the look on Paul's face when Noah told him he'd temporarily fallen for McKenna. He was lying on his bed chastising himself for the whole ordeal when a knock sounded at his bedroom door.

"Come in."

His mother walked over and sat on the bed next to Noah. "You need to go talk to Rebecca, *sohn*. I spoke with her *mudder* at church and asked if Rebecca was okay. Linda said she woke up sick this morning, but I think we all suspect she just didn't want to face you. You are as miserable as she is, so rather than continue this, maybe go talk to her."

"I talked to Paul, and I'm sure he relayed my feelings to Rebecca." He looked out the window to avoid his mother's expression, which looked like sympathy trying to mask irritation. Noah had been such a cad. "And I've left two messages on the recorder in their barn."

Noah hadn't shared details with his mother about the breakup, just that he was confused. Both of his parents loved Rebecca, so the split was hard on them too.

Mamm patted him on the knee, sighed, then stood to leave. "I hope things work out for you and Rebecca."

Me too.

Rebecca's mother came in the back door and told her there were two messages on the answering machine, both from Noah. "He wants you to call him." *Mamm* hung her cape on the rack, then shivered. "I was ready for some cooler temperatures, but this little cold front was unexpected." She put her hands on her hips and gazed out the living room window, then shook her head. "Your *daed* and *bruder* are outside repairing the fence, even though Sundays are supposed to be a day of rest. Paul took a short nap, but your *daed* has been working on one project or another all day long."

"The fence was number six on my list of repairs to be made before the wedding. The wedding that's no longer happening. So I don't know why *Daed* is killing himself on home repairs." Rebecca wasn't ready to call Noah. She chose to change the subject. "An *Englisch* woman came by this morning while you were at worship service. She's probably about nineteen, around my age. She was looking for Paul. Apparently they had been seeing each other, mostly meeting at the library on Saturdays."

Her mother sat in the wooden rocking chair, crossed her legs, and pushed the chair into action. "I knew that boy was up to something. Was she just a friend? I hope so since she's *Englisch*."

"I think her feelings ran deeper than friendship. Paul didn't show up yesterday, so she decided to come talk to him. But then I told her Paul had a history of breaking up with people when they got too close to him, and she actually cried."

"Rebecca!" Her mother stopped rocking and glared at her. "Why did you do that?"

"You know it's true, *Mamm*. And it seemed less cruel to tell her that was just the way Paul is and that it wasn't anything she'd done. I liked her a lot. She seemed very sweet." Rebecca recalled how transparent McKenna had been and the way she'd hugged her. It felt genuine. "And she was wearing a cross necklace, so she's probably Christian."

Her mother nervously kicked her foot out, starting the rocker up again. "But it's probably for the best since she isn't Amish. I hope Paul will find someone special and finally commit."

"*Ach*, well, I think he's gone through just about everyone around here."

Mamm stood. "I'm going to say one thing about you and Noah, and then I'm going to stay out of it."

Rebecca doubted that. She lay her head back against the couch, sighing as she waited.

"In life and in marriage, there will always be situations where forgiveness is not only an option but required if you plan to continue working toward the peace we all strive to have. Your *bruder* told me what Noah said, and Noah's *mudder* said he is as miserable as you are, although I don't think she knows exactly what happened, so I didn't say anything."

"I'm sure Noah is too embarrassed to tell his parents he broke off our engagement because of an *Englisch* girl he met at a party." Rebecca scowled. Her logic for despising that woman was unfounded, but the emotion was still there anyway. "What if that girl had returned his affections? He told me he wasn't even sure he wanted to be baptized, much less marry me." She kicked her feet up on the coffee table but removed them right away when he mother cleared her throat. "So, now that we know the *Englisch* girl wasn't interested in him the way he'd hoped, he's going to crawl back to me, his second choice? That's not right, *Mamm*."

"*Nee*, it's not." Her mother rubbed her chin for a few seconds. "Maybe there is more to it."

"I don't see how there is more to it."

Her mother frowned. "Well, you'll never know unless you call him." *Mamm* stood up and brushed the wrinkles from her black apron. "Whatever you decide to do, can you please go tell your *daed* and Paul that supper will be ready in about fifteen minutes?"

Rebecca nodded, then forced herself off the couch.

After she relayed her mother's message, she walked to the barn, then stared at the phone and answering machine. She finally listened to Noah's two messages asking her to call him. Just hearing his voice caused her to burst into tears.

CHAPTER 9

Noah sat next to Rebecca on the porch swing in front of her house. Gavin had helped him plan what he was going to say, but now that he was here, he wasn't sure his explanation was going to be enough to get him back into Rebecca's good graces. He took a deep breath.

"I'm sorry for breaking up with you. I'm sorry I said I didn't want to be baptized. It's just . . ." He paused, trying to recall all the times he'd practiced for this conversation. "I got cold feet." Squeezing his eyes closed, he cringed. Nowhere in the planning had the term *cold feet* been considered. "Well, not really cold feet, more like *cool* feet." He shook his head. "*Nee*, that's not what I mean either."

Rebecca twisted to face him, her hands folded in her lap, careful not to so much as brush his knees with hers as she repositioned herself. "Let me help you." Glowering, she raised her chin. "I think what you're trying to say is that you found an *Englisch* woman more attractive than me, and you were completely taken in by her, enough so that it caused you to question whether or not you wanted to be baptized and marry me."

She'd practically quoted what he'd told Paul, but it was

inaccurate. He just wasn't sure how to explain to Rebecca in a way that she'd understand and still want to be with him. "*Ya*, I was attracted to her, but not just the way you think." He cast his eyes down. "I was able to tell her things I can't tell you."

"Like what?" Rebecca's tone was clipped, and Noah knew he had a long way to go to win back her affections.

"I've always wanted you to love everything about me. I didn't think you needed to know my every thought, my every fear, or all the things I question about our life." She raised an eyebrow but also tipped her head to the side a little, seemingly prepared for him to go on. "To be able to talk to someone so openly about my fears and the things that worried me felt freeing."

"*Freeing*?" Rebecca gritted her teeth. "It felt freeing to be able to talk to a stranger about your innermost feelings?"

"*Ya*, it did." He held up a palm when she opened her mouth to say something. "Just let me finish. When—"

"Did you drink alcohol at that party?" Rebecca clenched her lips together, which Noah had always thought was cute. Right now it was plain scary. Lying wasn't going to win him any points. Rebecca would see right through him, and God would frown on it.

"*Ya*, I did, but not much. And if it makes you feel any better, I was sick as a hound dog the next morning."

She smiled a little, which was the only encouragement he'd received since he arrived, even if it was a little coldhearted.

"My point is we ended up stuck in a room together because neither one of us wanted to drink anything else, and Gavin and this girl named Penny wanted to be alone, so we just talked. She didn't know me, and I didn't know her. But we fell into an easy conversation, and before I knew it, I was telling her things I'd always been afraid to tell you."

"Like what?"

Noah tipped the rim of his straw hat back and scratched his head, not because he needed a recollection of the conversation. He remembered it clearly, and he remembered the way McKenna had listened and not judged him. "You've told me over and over that you can't sleep unless everything is completely black, total darkness." He paused, feeling his face warming. "I can't sleep without some kind of light on. I usually leave a flashlight on shining across the room, and I have a drawer full of batteries so I can do that every night."

Rebecca's eyes widened just as she broke out in laughter.

Noah folded his arms across his chest and refused to look at her. "See, that's why I never told you." He twisted to face her just as she put a hand over her mouth. "There's more, so I might as well get it out in the open." He took a deep breath. "I don't want six to eight *kinner* the way you do. I'd be happy with one or two. I feel like I'm going to faint when I see blood. Not very manly." He shook his head. "There's just a bunch of stuff I didn't want to tell you because I wanted to be everything you ever wanted me to be."

Rebecca stared at him for a long while. "What made you tell a perfect stranger these things? What exactly is so intimidating about me that you felt you couldn't talk to your future wife?"

Noah felt a little relief that she'd referred to herself as his future wife. "Because I didn't know her. I didn't really care what she thought. It just felt good to tell someone things no one knew." He shrugged. "Well, *mei mamm* knows about the flashlight, but I don't think she'd ever say anything." Sighing, he went on. "But the surprising thing is that when that woman said she totally understood, didn't judge me, and was so nice, I guess I didn't realize how much I'd been craving that kind of emotional intimacy. For months, all you and I have talked about is wedding plans. I've got things I'm worried about. What if I don't have enough money saved to take care of you the way you deserve? I've had all these worries bottled up inside, and I guess I wanted someone to listen and care.

"And not only did I open up to her, but she opened up to me. She's got a really bad situation at home with her mother, who is hooked on drugs. Her *mamm's* been in and out of rehabilitation facilities, and she's involved with some bad people. She opened up to me the same way I did to her, since she said she hadn't been able to do that with anyone. And she has a boyfriend. I didn't know that at the time, but she did tell me she was telling me things she'd never told anyone."

Rebecca had inched slightly closer to Noah, but she wasn't giving him as much understanding as he'd hoped for, mostly just staring at him and listening.

"Rebecca, she's a pretty woman, but she's not as pretty as you. I was drawn to the person inside because I felt like I could be honest, and it felt good." He hung his head. "I guess I was a little infatuated at first." Looking up at her, he said a quick prayer that he wouldn't cry. "But you're the only woman I've ever loved, the only woman I'll ever love. I just want to be able to tell you anything."

Unexpectedly, a tear dribbled down Rebecca's cheek. "Have I always been so unapproachable that you felt you couldn't talk to me? And don't you think I have fears, things that embarrass me, and worries about making a lifelong commitment? But I just figured we would work through things after we were married, that we would grow in our faith and in our marriage."

"That's what I want too." He looked away as shame wrapped around him.

Rebecca couldn't shake the image of Noah in the arms of another woman, although it sounded innocent enough. But worse than the vision was that Noah had talked so intimately with another person, and the thought fueled the jealousy bubbling up inside her like oil and water that were never going to mix. But she loved Noah, and she didn't want to spend her life without him.

"Noah, I love you." Rebecca swallowed the sob in her throat when Noah covered his eyes with one hand, his shoulders shaking.

He leaned over and pulled her into a hug. "I'm sorry. I love you, too, and want to marry you more than anything. I don't know what happened. I-I don't know."

His hat slid off, and Rebecca kissed the top of his head, then lay hers against his damp hair. After a few seconds, Noah eased away, his eyes moist, lip trembling. "I almost lost you."

Rebecca brushed back his bangs. "*Ya*, you did. But I forgive you. So forgive yourself." Noah tended to hold on to things, and despite her hurt and anger, Rebecca was sure he would lug this guilt around like a bag of cement. But equally as cumbersome was the load Rebecca couldn't seem to shed. "But I reserve the right not to like that woman, at least for a while longer."

She took a deep breath, hoping she never met the woman who had threatened her future, even if unintentionally. She couldn't recall feeling jealousy before. Rebecca had always felt solid in her relationship with Noah, confident that they would be baptized, married, fight and argue like all couples, but always be together. That stability had shifted. Rebecca thought about the provocative way some of the *Englisch* women dressed. Was it Noah's fault he'd been lured under her spell? It would be easier for her to stomach if Noah had been a victim, had been slipped some kind of love potion or something. But everyone faced temptation, and Noah hadn't walked away from it.

She decided to give herself time to unload the bitterness she felt toward a woman she'd never met, whom she never wanted to meet.

McKenna packed the last of her belongings in a small red suitcase she kept under her bed. She gazed at a picture of her and her mother at the beach a few years ago, during one of her mother's many remissions following a rehab program. She placed the frame on top of a soft white sweater, then folded the sweater around it, hoping the glass wouldn't break. A tear trickled down her cheek, and she quickly wiped it away when she heard footsteps.

"I can't believe you're doing this to your mother." Evan's voice sent goose bumps all over McKenna's skin, and the hair on the back of her neck prickled as she started to tremble. He'd hit her before, and it might happen again before she was safely out of the house, but she'd made up her mind that if he laid a hand on her, this time she was going to fight back.

He poked her in the back. "Hey. Did you hear me?"

McKenna turned around on shaky knees. "I called the police. I told them there are enough drugs in this house to build a bonfire. You've got about ten minutes to get out of here and never come back."

It was the biggest lie McKenna had ever told, but when a siren sang in the distance, Evan's eyes went wild. McKenna silently asked God to forgive the lie and also thanked Him for His perfect timing.

Evan shot from the room, and not a minute later she heard the front door slam, followed by his squealing tires as he spun out of the driveway. He would assume that McKenna's mother would go to jail. McKenna knew Evan well enough to know he'd leave her mother to rot in a cell before he'd help her. He'd always been happy to leave her drugs in exchange for whatever her mother gave him on the weekends, but McKenna was pretty sure Evan was gone for good now.

She clicked the locks on the suitcase, glanced around the room, and thought about what her future held as she made her way down the hall. She'd have to quit college, save money, and get a place of her own. For now Penny said she could stay with her. It wouldn't have been McKenna's first choice. She hated to hear Penny's parents fighting all the time, and she didn't know how Penny lived with it. But Penny was obviously used to it. Maybe they had always fought and it was just a way of life for her.

She'd briefly confessed about her mother when she asked to stay with her. Penny had been unusually quiet on the phone. McKenna wondered if Penny, or her parents, didn't want McKenna staying there. But then Penny said, "It'll be fun. We can party every night."

McKenna worried she was jumping from one hotbed to another, but as she slowed her stride and stopped at her mother's bedroom door, she let the built-up tears fall. "Bye, Mom," she whispered.

Her mother was lying on her side facing the window. McKenna didn't know if she was awake, too high to hear her, or just didn't care that she was leaving. But she watched her shoulder rise and fall. She was breathing.

McKenna went to the living room and sat on the couch. Sniffling, she swiped at her eyes as a car pulled in the driveway.

When she opened the door, Loraine was standing there with open arms, and McKenna fell into them. "I didn't know who else to call."

"You did the right thing. Once a sponsor always a sponsor. One of these days I hope after your mom falls she'll stand up and stay that way. But you need to go on with your life."

McKenna wasn't sure how she was going to do that, but she trusted Loraine to do what was best for her mother.

She glanced at the time on her phone, then checked her text messages and missed calls. Nothing. This was the time she and Paul met at the library. She considered going, to see if maybe Paul was there. But she'd already done that the Saturday before and he'd never shown. And he hadn't called. She'd obviously misread any feelings she thought he might have had for her. And based on what his sister had said, it was probably for the best.

But her heart was heavy as she drove to Penny's house. She slowed as she passed by the library. There were two buggies tethered to the side of the building. All Amish buggies looked mostly the same, gray and uniform in design. But Paul's had a tiny yellow sticker on the back, the remnants of a price tag, he'd told her.

She slowed down more.

CHAPTER 10

Paul went to the self-help aisle and pretended to peruse the books. In his heart, he knew McKenna wouldn't be there, and that was probably for the best. But he hadn't been able to stop thinking about her. At the least he needed to explain to her why he hadn't shown up the past Saturday or called. He would have called if he hadn't left her number in the pocket of his slacks, which had gone through the wringer that morning. Maybe that was God's way of telling him to force her out of his heart, that she wasn't the one. But it sure had felt like she was.

He walked around the library, stopping here and there to look at books he wasn't interested in, and he wasn't really paying much attention when he found himself on the romance aisle. After a few strange looks from the women nearby, he decided to leave. But he continued to search his mind for anything else about McKenna, chastising himself again for never asking for her last name. He wanted to clear her from his thoughts, but instead of aiding him in that effort, God seemed to be working against him, almost prodding him not to give up on her.

By the time he pulled in the driveway at home, his despair had crept up on him, merged with bitterness, and he was ready to lash out at the first person he saw, which just happened to be Becky. He went out to the backyard where she was hanging clothes on the line and recognized his pants right away. He'd found them in a pile of wet clothes in the laundry room that morning and had pulled out McKenna's phone number, smudged and illegible.

"*Wie bischt,*" she said, smiling.

Paul had already heard the news that the wedding was back on, and he was happy for his sister, but his own heart felt permanently damaged.

"Why are you doing clothes on a Saturday?" Monday had been washday for as long as Paul could remember.

Becky finished clipping a blue dress to the line, then turned to face him, pulling her black sweater snug. "It rained Monday and on and off the rest of the week. Once it rained after I'd already hung everything out to dry. *Mamm* and I were busy finishing a quilt for Mary Mae anyway." She smiled. "And it's a *gut* thing we did because the baby arrived yesterday." His sister lifted a pair of their father's slacks, gave them a good shake, and proceeded to pin each leg to the line. "I had to run everything back through the wringer this morning since they weren't drying very well hanging in the house. They smelled funny too." She looked up at the partly cloudy sky. "It'd better not rain again."

"Are you the one who took the pants in my room?" He nodded at his black pants, the ones with a worn spot on the knee, the ones that had previously held McKenna's phone number.

"*Ya,* it was me." She didn't look at him, just lifted another dress from the basket.

"Don't you check the pockets?" Paul's nostrils flared as he clenched his fists at his sides.

Becky draped the dress over her arm and turned to him. "I

try to remember to check the pockets, but you and *Daed* need to do that before you toss your clothes in the hamper."

"My pants weren't in the hamper. If I want my clothes washed, I'll put them in the laundry room. Don't take clothes out of my room."

She raised her eyebrows and clamped her lips tight before she said, "Here's a better idea: why don't you just wash and dry your own clothes!"

Paul didn't know the first thing about doing laundry, so he decided to soften his voice. Besides, yelling at Becky wasn't really justified. He'd lost McKenna on his own by not calling her or showing up at the library the previous Saturday. "Sorry. I lost something important that was in my pocket." He turned to go to the house.

"Wait."

Paul turned around as Becky walked toward him. He folded his arms across his chest and scowled. "What?"

"What was in your pocket?" Becky narrowed her eyes. "Although whatever it was, I don't think you should be mad at me."

"A phone number." He looked down and kicked at the grass. When he looked up, Becky was grinning.

"A girl's phone number, no doubt."

"*Ya*, a girl's phone number, and it's not funny, so quit smiling."

Becky shrugged, then headed back to the clothes. "I'm sure there is another girl waiting in the wings," she said over her shoulder. "There always is."

Paul's blood boiled as he marched back over to his sister. "You think you know me so well, that I dump every woman who gets close to me, just so I can move on to the next one. But maybe you don't know me very well at all."

Becky faced off with him. Even with her chin lifted, she was a foot shorter. "Then why do you keep dating? You break those girls' hearts, and it doesn't seem to bother you."

"I told you before, it always hurts me too. But none of them want the same things I do, and that ultimately ends the relationship."

"*You* end it every time. It's a pattern. And I feel very sorry for all those women whose hearts you've broken. And I really liked the last one, even though she was *Englisch*. She cried when she left here, after I told her this is how you are. I'm not even supposed to tell you she came by. You get close and then break up. And—"

Paul grabbed her arm, then quickly let go when she flinched. "There was an *Englisch* girl here, looking for me?" His heart pounded against his chest. "What was her name?"

Becky squeezed her eyes closed like she was trying to remember. "McKenna. That was her name."

Paul drew in a deep calming breath, even though he was shaking with anger. "What did you tell her?"

"The truth," Becky said defensively as she lifted her chin again. "She said you were supposed to have met her at the library, and she was worried because you hadn't shown up. It was earlier in the week. She was so sweet. I liked her very much."

"Me too!" Paul closed his eyes for a few seconds and tried to relax. "What else was said?"

"Paul, do you know how many of your ex-girlfriends I've had to console? I just wasn't up for it again, and besides, she was *Englisch*, so the relationship had nowhere to go anyway. So I told her that was how you are—'love 'em and leave 'em,' like they say."

"She was crying?" Paul couldn't stand to think about that.

"*Ya*. But why would you want to drag it out with her? The

Englisch have feelings, too, and it was obvious that she cares a lot about you. It just seemed mean to mislead her unless she was planning to convert to our ways. She seemed to agree with that, that she couldn't join the Amish faith."

Paul's stomach roiled even more. "She said she doesn't want to be Amish?"

"*Ya*, she did. So I did you a favor." Becky glowered at him as if waiting for an apology.

"*Nee*, Becky, you didn't do me a favor. At first I thought she was one of those girls who just thought she wanted to be Amish. Now you're telling me she doesn't. You probably ran off my only hope at true love." He waited for a reaction from his sister, but she just dropped her jaw. Then her eyes widened as it all seemed to fall into place for her.

"That's why you ran those girls off." She gasped, still wide-eyed. "It's why you're twenty-two and still haven't been baptized. You plan to leave. You want to live in the *Englisch* world." His sister took a step back, her expression evolving into something bordering on hysteria, as if Paul had killed someone or something.

Paul took a few steps toward her and gently latched onto her arms. "Becky, if I had been baptized, I would have been shunned later because I don't belong here. But I haven't been baptized, so I will always be able to be a part of your life even if I do choose to be baptized into a different faith."

"Then why date all those girls in our community?"

Paul shook his head. "If I was hiding such a big secret, I wondered if any of them were too. I never would have encouraged any of them to leave, and once I realized each of them was firmly grounded in their faith, I let go of them. And it hurt me every single time." He sighed. "But I didn't feel about any of them the way I feel about McKenna. And now I have no way to find her. I don't even know her last name." He turned to leave. He'd already said too much, and Becky was sure to tell their parents.

"Young."

Paul didn't slow his step. He was done talking about it.

"Young!" she said louder. "That is McKenna's last name. Young."

He stopped and said a quick prayer of thanks.

CHAPTER 11

Paul had looked every place he could think of to find Noah, his only link to McKenna. Although Becky had no idea where Noah was, she'd offered up some places he might have gone. But after several hours of looking, Paul started a search of his own. He found seventeen families in the Paradise phone book with the last name Young. But among a population of eleven hundred people, it was like finding a needle in a haystack. Lots of *Englisch* folks no longer had a landline, only a cell phone. And if McKenna and her mother did have a home phone, it was likely listed in her mother's name.

But he'd called all seventeen numbers from the phone in the barn before he set out in his buggy. Twelve people who answered said they didn't know a McKenna Young. The other five numbers had been disconnected. He jotted down those five addresses and decided to drive by each house, hoping to recognize McKenna's blue car in one of the driveways.

He was nearing the second house on the list when his horse decided to relieve herself, which meant he had to reduce his speed considerably or prepare to be sprayed. Just as he was slowing down, a woman emerged from the house toting a suitcase, frowning when she saw Paul's horse relieving more than just her bladder. He thought people should be used to it, but Paul supposed he could understand her feelings. It was right in front of her house.

"Ma'am, I'm sorry about this," he said out the window of his buggy. Amish generally avoided traveling through neighborhoods if it could be avoided and opted for farm roads instead. Or at the least, they used a manure bag, which Paul had forgotten in his rush to find McKenna.

"Trade hazard," the woman said as she opened the car door and flung the suitcase inside.

Paul figured now was as good a time as any. "Does McKenna Young live there?" He held his breath, but when the woman nodded, he released the breath and quickly stepped out of the buggy. He held his horse by the bit. "Is she home right now?"

The woman shook her head. "No. I just came by to pick up a few things, and I'm leaving too."

Paul didn't have anywhere to tether his horse, or he would have walked closer. But even in the distance, he could see that McKenna's mother looked older than he'd imagined. Gray hair in his district was common for women even in their thirties. But the *Englisch* were known to dye their hair as soon as any gray began to show. This woman had gray hair that hung almost to her shoulders.

"Can you tell me where I might be able to find McKenna? I'm a friend of hers."

Scowling, the woman walked closer to Paul. "I honestly don't know where she's at."

He wanted to say it seemed odd she wouldn't know where her daughter was, but he thought better of it. "I lost her phone number. Could you possibly give it to me again?"

McKenna's mother folded her arms across her chest, the wrinkles on her forehead turning into deep lines of irritation. "McKenna is staying with friends for a while. I'm sure she'll call you when she can."

Paul recalled McKenna mentioning a friend of hers, but he couldn't remember the girl's name. And he wasn't ready to give up his only lead. "Mrs. Young, it's important I talk to her."

The woman chuckled. "Oh, I assure you, I am *not* Mrs. Young. I'm a friend of the family. Mrs. Young will also be away for a while." She held up a hand. "Look, I'm sure you're a nice enough fellow, but that's all I can say right now."

Paul opened his mouth again to ask the woman to give McKenna his phone number, but she held up a hand before she quickly walked back to her car and left. Paul crawled back into his buggy, tempted to follow her, but if she turned on the highway, he'd have no chance of keeping up with her in his buggy.

He sat there for a while and thought about any other way he might find McKenna, but when his horse neighed, he figured he better get out of the neighborhood before he left another reminder of the visit. He clicked his tongue and gave a gentle tap of the reins, sending the horse into a slow trot. He would recheck the places Becky had told him Noah might be. If he still couldn't locate him, he'd try to find a phone and call him again.

But maybe this was God's way of telling Paul that he and McKenna weren't meant to be after all.

Rebecca decided to surprise Noah at work the next day. She'd packed a lunch and hoped he could slip away for an hour. Maybe they could go eat at the park around the corner. His coworker Gavin was at the front desk when Rebecca walked in the hardware store carrying a picnic basket. Gavin reminded her of someone who could be on the cover of a fancy magazine. He was tall, muscular, and carried himself with confidence. His blond hair framed his handsome face. He'd always been very nice to her, but today she was fighting the urge to feel resentment toward him since he was the one who'd taken Noah to the *Englisch* party. In her heart she knew it wasn't Gavin's fault Noah chose to find comfort with a stranger.

"Hey, Rebecca. You missed Noah. He just left for lunch." Gavin smiled. Even his teeth were nice looking, white and straight.

"*Ach*, okay. It wasn't a planned lunch. I had to pick up some fabric nearby, so I just threw a little something together before I left home." She glanced at the basket. "Chicken salad sandwiches, chips, and some apple pie."

Gavin shook his head. "His loss. I've tasted your apple pie." He chuckled. "He gave me a bite once in the break room, but it was a very small bite. Stingy fellow." Gavin laughed again.

Rebecca had no reason to verify what Noah had told her, but an opportunity was presenting itself. "I have more errands to run in the area. Do you want to eat lunch with me?"

"Sure. Noah will probably kill me for eating his pie, but I'm going to. And I love chicken salad." He glanced at the front door. "It's usually slow right now. We can eat in the back, but I'll have to jump up and run to the showroom if someone comes in. There's a buzzer in the back, so I'll know."

"Great." Rebecca followed him through a door that led to a small room with a table and chairs, sink, small refrigerator, and microwave. She'd eaten lunch here with Noah several times before. As she lay out the food, Gavin found two paper plates, then grabbed them each a soda, which was a real treat since her mother didn't approve of the drinks.

Rebecca lowered her head, surprised when she looked up that Gavin had lowered his head in prayer also. It shouldn't have surprised her. There were plenty of *Englischers* who prayed before meals. A reminder that there were a lot of good people in the world who weren't Amish. Rebecca laughed when Gavin tore into the pie.

"I'm not taking any chances Noah will return and want his lunch. I'm going to finish off this pie first." He smiled with a mouthful, then swallowed and said, "And it's just as good as I remember."

Gavin was a charming and handsome man. Rebecca remembered Noah mentioning a girl named Penny who Gavin was interested in. "I think Noah mentioned you have a girlfriend. I think he said her name was Penny."

"I'm working on it." He shrugged. "She's not really my girlfriend." He shook his head. "She is absolutely gorgeous, but she's got some issues. A little too much partying for my taste." He raised an eyebrow as he peeled the plastic wrap from the sandwich. "Don't get me wrong, I enjoy a beer as much as the next guy, but she's all about having fun every night, and I gotta work. Penny's parents are wealthy, so all she has to do is manage to hit a couple college classes in the afternoon. But we'll see how it goes."

Rebecca fought the vision of Noah and another girl chatting it up while Gavin and Penny were in a different room, but she smiled, then took a bite of her sandwich. She'd already decided to leave her piece of pie for Noah.

"Yeah, Penny's got this girl living with her for a while." Gavin took a sip of Coke. "And she's not the big partier like Penny, so I'm hoping maybe McKenna will be a good influence on her."

Rebecca stopped chewing, sat taller, and after she swallowed, she said. "That's not a very common name, McKenna." She thought about Paul and how badly she'd messed things up for him. "My brother has a friend named McKenna. He seemed to really like her, and I accidentally lost the phone number he had for her. He's been running all over town for days trying to find her." She shook her head, glancing at Gavin, who was busy with his sandwich. "Those things usually don't work out, when one person is *Englisch* and the other is Amish." She recalled what Paul had confessed, and for her brother's sake, she pressed onward. "Does her last name happen to be Young, by any chance?"

Gavin nodded. "It sure is." He chuckled. "Small world. I have McKenna's phone number if you want to give it to him."

Rebecca let out a small gasp. "That would be wonderful." *A way to redeem myself after all the terrible things I said about Paul's womanizing.*

"Let me go get my phone. I left it on the counter, and I have her number stored in it since she's friends with Penny. I don't really know McKenna all that well, but she seems like a really sweet person."

Rebecca smiled. "She actually came by our house looking for Paul, but I had no idea Paul really cared for her, so I didn't encourage the relationship, which still worries me, for the reasons I mentioned. But I liked her very much."

Gavin wiped his mouth, then frowned a little. "I didn't realize you'd met McKenna. Noah told me what happened. He said you'd freaked out about him spending time with her at the party. I think you're an awesome person to put that behind you. Noah loves you, and he'd be a miserable soul without you. After you two broke up, he moped around here for days."

Rebecca forced her jaw closed, reeling on the inside that Paul's McKenna was also Noah's mystery girl. She could feel the color draining from her face as she swallowed hard. The sweet woman who had come to visit Rebecca was starting to grow horns in Rebecca's mind.

"I'll go get the number." Gavin stood, and as he was leaving the room, he said over his shoulder, "Anyway it was just a hug and a kiss, nothing more. Noah would never really cheat on you."

Rebecca's heart was pounding against her chest. *A kiss? I thought it was just a hug.* Horrified, she scurried to stuff containers back into the picnic basket, and by the time Gavin returned, she was packed up and ready to go.

"Here you go." He chuckled again. "Wow. Such a small world," he repeated. "And thanks for lunch. I plan to rub it in to Noah that I ate his pie."

Rebecca accepted the paper Gavin had written McKenna Young's phone number on. Then, pausing only a moment, she picked up her pie and stuffed it in the basket with the rest.

"*Danki,*" she whispered before she left.

Outside, she took a breath. No way was she going to give Paul that phone number and be subjected to seeing that woman on a regular basis on the off chance that they became more involved—which would be stupid for both of them. Things would be better this way.

After she left the building, she crumpled up the piece of paper and tossed it in the nearest trash can.

CHAPTER 12

McKenna lay on one of the queen-size beds in Penny's room. Her friend's bedroom was bigger than McKenna and her mother's living room. It had been two weeks since Loraine took her mother to a rehabilitation facility and helped McKenna get the rest of her things out of the house before it foreclosed. Loraine said there was no money left in her mother's account. Grandma's inheritance was gone. And McKenna knew where most of the money had gone.

Penny was sitting on her bed drinking a beer, citing that it was okay to drink in the early afternoon because it was Saturday. McKenna was searching for full-time jobs online. At least she still had her computer to peruse possibilities.

"I told you not to worry about finding a job." Penny sighed. "My parents said you can stay here as long as you like. You might as well take advantage of no rent or bills. My dad said he'd pay for your cell phone and car insurance, and I'm sure he'd take care of anything else too."

McKenna was grateful she had a place to stay and for Mr. Schroeder's offer to help her, but she didn't want to stay in this house one day longer than she had to. The fighting between Penny's parents was almost unbearable at times.

"Why didn't you tell me things were so bad with your mom?" Penny grimaced. "I mean, I kinda knew she was a druggie, but it seemed to make you uncomfortable when I asked about her."

"It's embarrassing, and it's heartbreaking too. She's still my mother, even if she's not a very good one." McKenna didn't look up when Penny popped the top off another bottle of beer. "Isn't that like your fifth one?"

"I don't need another parent. I already have two too many." Penny wound her long blond hair on top of her head and secured it with a clip. "Let's do something. I heard Frank Lymer is having a party tonight, but I'm bored now. We could go to the mall."

"Well, clearly I'd have to drive us." McKenna didn't have any money to shop, so that didn't sound appealing. But about every five minutes, she eyed the time on her computer. It was nearing two o'clock, and she wanted to go to the library. She doubted Paul would be there, but she'd yet to get him out of her mind.

Finally, she made a decision. "I'm going to the library."

"Oh, wow. Really? You're still hung up on that Amish guy? Even if he's there, the relationship has nowhere to go."

McKenna had told Penny a little bit about Paul, but when her friend made disapproving remarks, McKenna shut down the conversation and hadn't brought it up again. "I don't know how to explain it. There was just something about him."

"They live very differently than we do, but yeah, I've found most of them to be nice. Even that Noah guy Gavin brought to my party seemed okay."

McKenna recalled her time with Noah and the intimate hug

and kiss on the cheek. "I thought he was very sweet. Maybe a little confused about his life, but nice."

Penny swung her feet over the side of the bed and slipped her feet into a pair of flip-flops, even though it seemed too chilly outside for sandals. She picked up her purse from the nightstand and stood. "Well, I'm off to the mall. Maybe I can find something to wear to the party tonight." She put a hand on her hip and scowled. "You're going, right?"

McKenna sighed. "I don't know." Penny seemed to live for the next party, and she didn't have enough responsibilities to occupy her time. Maybe if her parents enforced a few rules, things would be different.

But then again, maybe McKenna should've done the same with her mom. She spent the majority of her life watching her mother go downhill, first with drinking, and then adding pills to the mix. She remembered the look on Evan's face when she sent him packing. She regretted not doing something about him sooner. McKenna wouldn't be able to see or talk to her mother for the first thirty days of the rehabilitation program. It was a voluntary facility, meaning her mother could walk out at any time, but so far she hadn't. McKenna called to check on her every day.

"I'm outta here." Penny dug her keys out of her Michael Kors purse. McKenna glanced at her own worn-out knockoff designer bag she'd bought at Penny's insistence.

"I don't think you need to drive anywhere. I can drop you off at the mall on my way to the library."

"I'll be fine."

Before McKenna could object, the bedroom door opened and Mrs. Schroeder walked to the middle of the room to face off with her daughter. The woman folded her arms across her chest, a sour expression on her face that McKenna had come to recognize. Penny's mom was getting ready to scold her for something, and she didn't have a problem doing it in front of McKenna.

"What?" Penny said as she rolled her eyes.

"I believe you have taken something of mine." Mrs. Schroeder's eyes blazed as she lowered her arms to her sides, clenching her fists. "You know exactly what I'm talking about."

"I haven't taken anything of yours." Penny spat the words at her mother—which resulted in a hard slap across the face.

McKenna's jaw dropped as she froze on the bed, unsure whether to excuse herself or run interference. Evan had hit her before, but her mother had never laid a hand on McKenna, except maybe a spanking as a child. She never even told her mother about Evan's actions for fear things would get worse for her, or for her mother.

Penny's eyes watered as she reached up and cupped her red cheek. "I promise, Mom. I haven't taken anything. What exactly do you think I've taken?" Her voice trembled as she spoke. McKenna had never seen her friend like this. Penny sported more of an attitude than anything else—an attitude that had now fled the scene and been replaced by fear.

Mrs. Schroeder relaxed her stance, took a deep breath, and looked at McKenna. "I'm sorry about this, McKenna, but Penny has stolen from her father and me before, and we simply won't tolerate it anymore."

McKenna couldn't imagine why Penny would want or need to steal anything. Her parents provided her with everything she wanted or needed. *Except maybe love and affection.*

Penny's mother refocused on her daughter, her mouth set in a straight line. She stared at her for a few seconds, then a tight-lipped smile filled her face. "Fine, you can tell that to your father later." Mrs. Schroeder made an about-face, left the room, and slammed the door behind her.

McKenna rushed to Penny and wrapped her in a hug. "Oh, Penny. I'm so sorry."

Penny eased away, pulled her purse up on her shoulder, and shrugged. "Not like it's the first time." She locked eyes with McKenna as a tear ran down her cheek, which she quickly swiped away. "I've never stolen anything from her, I promise. And I have no idea what she's talking about." Her lip trembled. "But maybe I should take something since I get accused all the time . . ." She touched her cheek again. "And slapped for things I didn't do."

McKenna reached for her own purse. "Come on. I'll go to the mall with you."

"No." Penny shook her head. "No. I just want to be alone." Without another word, she left, pulling the door shut behind her.

McKenna sighed as she watched her friend leave. She definitely wanted to talk to Penny more about all of this, but it was obvious Penny wasn't ready. McKenna worried, though—especially because Penny had been drinking. She'd begged her not to drive after partying plenty of times before, but she always did.

Keep her safe, God.

After Penny was gone, McKenna left the house too. Penny's parents were yelling in the living room, so she left via the back door in the kitchen. It was unlikely Paul would be at the library, but she had another motive for going. Some of those self-help books might be useful now. McKenna needed to start her life over. A new life, one that didn't depend on her mother or Evan.

Noah trudged up the porch steps to Rebecca's house. He thought they were behind this whole McKenna incident, but when Gavin told him about his conversation with Rebecca in the lunchroom, Noah was sure he was in hot water again.

Rebecca opened the door before he had a chance to knock. She stepped over the threshold and went to the rocking chair on the porch. Noah obediently followed, sat down in the other rocker, and waited for the lashing that was sure to come. He knew better than to start the conversation. He'd let Rebecca take the lead so he could get a feel for exactly how mad she was. Maybe he should have mentioned the kiss.

Noah cringed and continued to wait.

"We have a problem." Rebecca said softly, glancing his way, a sober expression on her face. "And I don't know what to do about it."

"It was one kiss on the cheek, Rebecca. I regret it. I'm sorry, but telling you when you were so upset just didn't make sense at the time." He took off his hat and set it in his lap. Even though the temperatures were cooler, Noah had sweated buckets all the way here as he wondered if Rebecca was going to call off the marriage again. "I didn't lie. I just didn't mention it."

She turned to face him, still not letting her expression give anything away. "When you first started working at the hardware store, I fantasized sometimes about kissing Gavin."

Noah's jaw dropped, but he quickly snapped his mouth closed when Rebecca frowned.

"But I was in love with you, so it was just a passing thing I never would have acted on." She locked eyes with him. "But I thought about it. And I'm not sure that if Gavin had tried to kiss me that I would have stopped him."

Noah's heart pounded against his chest. "So, uh . . ." He scratched his forehead, unsure where she was going with this. Hearing about her attraction to Gavin stung, probably the same way he'd hurt her with his infatuation with McKenna. "What are you saying, that you want to kiss Gavin so we'll be even?" Noah could hardly bear the thought, but he didn't want this hanging over them for their entire marriage, which he hoped was still going to happen.

Rebecca rolled her bottom lip under and frowned. "Of course not." She shook her head as she maintained her look of total disdain. "I'm only telling you this because I'm not perfect either."

They were both quiet for a few minutes.

"Are we still getting married?" Noah asked, and held his breath.

"We're not going to talk about that right now." Noah's heart sank as Rebecca's face relaxed, but it was clear to Noah that she had more on her mind. His heart began to hammer in his chest, wondering what else was coming. Maybe she had an entire list of men she'd thought about kissing.

"I've met McKenna."

Noah's chest tightened even more. This was not going to go well. "When?"

"A few weeks ago." Rebecca twisted her mouth back and forth as her eyebrows drew together. Noah recognized that look. She was deep in thought.

"Uh-oh." It was all he could think to say, but he was caught off guard a little when Rebecca smiled.

"Noah, I love you, and I know you love me. We are going to be baptized, and then probably get married. If we do, we're both going to make mistakes, and your little indiscretion with McKenna isn't going to stop that from happening." She paused, crossed one leg over the other, and started to rock, keeping her eyes in front of her. "But I feel like I'm going to be sick to my stomach every time I think about her in your arms."

Noah was still waiting to hear about Rebecca's meeting with McKenna and how that had come to be. But he'd given her the lead, and he was going to let her keep the reins.

"McKenna came here looking for Paul." She glanced at Noah. "She's very beautiful, and she was a very nice person." Then Rebecca scowled. "Of course I didn't know that Paul's McKenna was your hugging girl."

Her voice got louder, and Noah felt like he was in quicksand now, but he had to ask. "Why was she looking for Paul?"

"I think they're in love with each other. But when McKenna came here looking for him, I told her some pretty awful things about my brother. She said they'd been meeting at the library, having lunch, and that she really liked him." She turned to face Noah. "You know how Paul is, how he dates someone for a short time, then breaks up with her. I was sick and tired of hearing from all the brokenhearted women left in his path, and I thought I was doing McKenna a favor by telling her Paul was basically a womanizer and she should forget about him. McKenna left crying, and she asked me not to mention her visit to Paul. So I didn't . . . at first. I thought I was doing them both a favor. She said she didn't want to be Amish, so there was nowhere for their friendship to go."

Noah thanked God that this conversation had taken a turn,

but he felt like something bad was coming, so he took a deep breath and stayed quiet.

"It wasn't until later I found out how much Paul cared for McKenna, how for the first time he seemed really and truly in love. I'd accidentally washed his pants with her phone number in the pocket, so he didn't know how to get in touch with her. But I remembered her last name, so I encouraged him to go find her." She blinked back tears. "Especially since he confessed he does not want to be baptized into our faith."

Noah's eyes widened as his jaw dropped. He wouldn't have expected that from Paul, a man who had always seemed grounded in his faith. "Uh, I missed several calls from him, but he left messages and said he was using borrowed phones and would try again. But I didn't hear from him."

"I want *mei bruder* to be happy. I don't want him leaving us, but I could tell his mind was made up, with or without McKenna." She swiped at her eyes. Noah wanted to believe he was in the clear, but he couldn't shed the sense that there was more. "And it gets worse."

For who?

Noah was happy the focus was off him, but he didn't like seeing Rebecca so upset.

"Gavin gave me McKenna's phone number. Apparently she is staying with her friend Penny." She raised sad eyes to Noah's. "And I threw it away. I didn't tell Paul where to find her even though he's been moping around and so unhappy."

Noah looked down. This felt like a trap. Was Rebecca trying to find out if he had McKenna's phone number? And, if so, would it be for Paul, or to pull the noose tighter around Noah's neck?

"If you feel bad and want Paul to have her number, just ask Gavin again." Noah hoped he'd dodged the hanging.

"For all I know, you have it." Rebecca sniffled again. "But I don't even want to know."

Sure you do. Noah did have McKenna's number, and his silence surely solidified Rebecca's suspicions. He waited for her to pounce.

"So, here is the problem . . ." Rebecca took a deep breath.

Noah's stomach churned. It sounded like there was more than one problem, but he was overly anxious to hear what was on the top of Rebecca's list.

She stared at him long and hard. "I want *mei bruder* happy, but what if they are meant to be together and she sticks around for a while?" She threw her hands in the air. "What if they even get married?"

Noah reminded himself to breathe. He didn't want to say the wrong thing. "Uh . . ."

Rebecca sighed. "Then I would be forced to be around McKenna, possibly forever, and all I would ever see is her lips on yours, a constant reminder that you kissed her."

"It was just one kiss, kinda on the cheek." From her expression, Noah was sure that was not the thing to say. He had to do something, and he was down to his last option. On an exhale, he stood up, then reached for Rebecca's hand. "Come on."

She let him help her from the rocker, still sniffling, but she walked down the porch steps with him. "Where are we going?"

Noah sighed. "To fix things."

CHAPTER 13

McKenna walked to the self-help aisle at the library, and for the first time, she was interested in some of the titles. She was nineteen, on her own, living at a friend's house, which was far from ideal, even though McKenna was grateful. She needed a full-time job, and she didn't want to abandon all her hopes and dreams about college. But she wondered if she would end up like her mother. McKenna had loved her grandmother, but she'd probably been an alcoholic. McKenna just hadn't realized it when she was younger. The signs were there, and even as a preteen, she'd recognized alcohol abuse. And now her mother was battling substance abuse. McKenna didn't want to go down that road.

She chose a book about breaking the chains of a dysfunctional family, then leaned against the shelf and held the book to her chest. She closed her eyes and prayed that God would show her the way.

"McKenna."

That voice was so familiar.

Fearful she'd imagined it, she slowly opened her eyes. She fought the urge to jump into Paul's arms and instead smiled.

He stepped closer and stared at her with an intensity McKenna had been feeling since the day she met him. But had his sister been correct, that he dated women and discarded them after only a short time? Was she setting herself up for disappointment?

Neither of them said anything, and McKenna wondered if he could hear her heart pounding against her chest. He opened his mouth to say something, but then closed it, tipped back the rim of his hat, and gazed into her eyes. She tried to imagine what was on his mind. Was this a courtesy visit to tell her he cared about her, but things would never work out because they lived in two different worlds? Would he just apologize for not ending their friendship in a more civil manner, as opposed to just disappearing? She could stand there all day long analyzing, or she could just tell him the truth.

"I missed you," she whispered, glancing to her left where two older women were scanning the shelves. She momentarily wondered what kind of book they were searching for.

Paul inched closer to her until the familiar smell of the lavender soap his mother made wafted around her. "I'm sorry."

McKenna swallowed the lump in her throat. This was it, the courtesy breakup of a relationship that had never really gotten off the ground. They'd never even kissed. She waited for Paul to elaborate on the apology, to say he couldn't see her anymore because she wasn't Amish, or because he'd already found someone else, someone more suited to his way of life, one of his own people.

"I think I mistook a hug between you and Noah as something more, and I decided you were looking for an Amish husband."

McKenna sucked in a breath so hard she almost choked.

"Why in the world would you think I would intentionally pursue an Amish man?"

Paul shrugged. "*Ach*, well, you were seeing me, and I'm Amish. Then I saw you with Noah." He lowered his gaze and shook his head, starting to grin. "It sounds silly now." He looked back at her. "But, believe it or not, there are people out there who are running—from something or someone—and they think all of their problems will be solved if they convert to our way of life. So by the time I found out you didn't want to be Amish, your phone number had gone through the wash, and I didn't know how to reach you. My sister finally told me you came to our house looking for me. I've been trying to find you ever since."

"I guess I should have assumed you might know Noah, but he's just a sweet guy who was confused about his commitment to the church and upcoming marriage to a girl named Rebecca." McKenna tipped her head to one side. "You saw us at the hardware store? Why didn't you come in? I could have explained."

"I had Becky with me." McKenna wasn't following, and he must have tuned in to the confused expression on her face. "My sister is Rebecca. I think I'm the only one who calls her Becky."

McKenna put a hand over her mouth and stared at him a few seconds, her eyes wide. "Your Becky is Noah's Rebecca?"

"*Ya*. And when I saw you, uh . . . in Noah's arms, I didn't want her to see that, even though I told her about it."

"It was just a friendly hug and kiss on the cheek." McKenna lowered her gaze, but Paul gently cupped her chin and lifted her eyes to his.

"I don't care about that, and I think that Beck—Rebecca—and Noah are working things out. But I have to know . . ." His brown eyes twinkled amber in the bright lights of the library, and McKenna saw fear in them. "Did I imagine things between us?"

She shook her head. "No."

His expression became even more pained, the lines on his forehead deepening. "Sometimes the *Englisch* idolize our way of life, and it doesn't turn out to be what they expected. Becky told me you don't think you could ever convert to our faith. Is it true, that you don't want to be Amish?"

Tears filled McKenna's eyes. This would likely be the last time she'd see Paul Fisher. "I don't want to be Amish." Paul smiled a little. And now McKenna had questions as well. "Is it true that you've dated a lot of women and broken their hearts?"

He nodded. "Most women in our district are baptized by the time they are my age, twenty-two. Those women, *mei* parents, and even *mei* sister should have at least suspected I wasn't going to be baptized into the faith, ever. I love God. I like to think I'm a good Christian. But I feel God calling me in another direction. At first I thought you were wanting to get involved with someone mostly because they were Amish, and then when I saw you with Noah, I thought for sure you were. But once things were straightened out, I started looking for you. I had to know if our long talks, the things I felt—if they were real."

McKenna nodded. "They were for me."

"I found your house, and I went by, but you weren't there. A lady said you and your *mudder* were gone."

McKenna took the book from where she still had it pressed against her chest, and she turned it toward Paul. "My mother is in a rehab facility. It's the one thing I never told you. My time with you was an escape from that situation, and I didn't want it muddied up with my baggage."

Paul glanced at the books on the aisle, then grinned. "Do you want to go somewhere else? Maybe coffee and a whoopie pie?"

McKenna smiled. "I would love that." Her phone buzzed in her purse. "I need to see who this is. It might be about my mom." She found the phone, read the text message, and put a hand to her chest. "Oh no. I have to go."

Paul touched her arm. "Is everything okay?"

McKenna shook her head, grabbed his hand, and hurried him out of the library. "No, everything is *not* okay."

Rebecca wasn't sure why they were at the hardware store, but whatever Noah had on his mind about fixing things was quickly forgotten when they entered the store.

"We gotta go." Gavin's eyes were red, almost like he might have been crying.

"What's wrong?" Noah and Rebecca both asked at the same time.

"Can you get me to the clinic up the road in your buggy? My car won't start. I've tried three times. I think it's my battery." Gavin was turning off lights as he hurried around the store, then practically pushed Noah and Rebecca out onto the sidewalk while he flipped the sign on the door to Closed and locked up. "It's Penny. She overdosed, and her parents took her to the nearest place, which is Stoltzfus Clinic. The only reason I even know is because her mother found my number on Penny's phone and called to yell at me, accusing me of supplying her with pills." He grunted. "I'm guessing Penny's mother has enough pills in her medicine cabinet to overdose a horse, so maybe she should have checked her own prescriptions."

Rebecca gasped as she threw her hand over her mouth.

"Of course, we'll take you anywhere you need to go." Noah worked quickly to untether the horse, and Rebecca climbed in the back seat so Gavin could ride up front.

"Maybe I care more about that girl than I thought, because I feel like someone's punched me in the gut." Gavin spoke in a shaky voice as Noah clicked the reins and headed in the direction of the clinic. Rebecca knew the place well and had been there plenty of times herself for minor things. The owner used to be Amish and had opened the clinic to accommodate the Amish, but lots of *Englisch* folks went there too.

Fifteen minutes later, Noah pulled into the parking lot. He pulled up to an available hitching post, and Gavin hurried out of the buggy and ran toward the building.

"This is terrible," Rebecca said as Noah tethered the horse, then filled a pan with water he kept in the buggy. Noah had pushed the animal hard to make good time. "I hope Gavin's friend is okay."

"Me too." They walked hand in hand to the clinic. Whatever Noah's idea had been to fix things, it no longer seemed important. Rebecca thought about the pettiness of her choices recently, when inside the clinic a young woman was fighting for her life. She wondered if the overdose was accidental or intentional. She'd never met Penny, but she silently fell into prayer for the woman.

Her prayers were cut short when they entered the waiting room. It was empty except for two people sitting next to each other. Her brother and McKenna. Gavin must have gone to see Penny.

Rebecca waited for McKenna to sprout horns or show her fangs, but instead she just smiled, reminding Rebecca of how nice she'd been when she visited their house. Rebecca glanced at Noah. Her fiancé was as white as the walls.

Everyone exchanged pleasantries, although they seemed a bit strained, especially for Noah, who looked everywhere except at McKenna. Rebecca wasn't sure how everything panned out, but it eased her guilt that Paul and McKenna had somehow found each other. Still, she didn't know if she could get past the intimacy McKenna had shared with Noah. It was a selfish thought to have when a young woman was in such a desperate situation.

Rebecca's eyes drifted to McKenna, and she saw the sorrow on her face, similar to the expression she'd had the day she visited looking for Paul. Rebecca then noticed the way her brother was looking at McKenna, the way he pushed back her hair and whispered something in her ear.

Before she had time to ponder what Paul might have said, the door leading to the examining rooms opened, and Gavin burst out. It didn't look like he'd been crying. He *was* crying.

CHAPTER 14

Noah stood tall, but he was trembling on the inside. Rebecca was staring at McKenna a lot, and Noah wondered if his fiancée was going to blow up. It wasn't their way, but it had been known to happen.

Penny was released an hour after they all arrived.

"I can't believe you thought I overdosed." Penny rolled her eyes as she reached for Gavin's hand. "Apparently I'm allergic to Benadryl."

Even though Penny was trying to play off the incident, her bottom lip was trembling. She had smudged makeup under her eyes, and her long blond hair wasn't the smooth and shiny mane it usually was. Noah wondered if she was telling the truth about an allergic reaction.

Loud voices sounded from behind the closed door that led from the exam rooms to the waiting room, and a few moments later, a man and woman pushed through the doors.

"Let's go, Penny." The lady, presumably Penny's mother, grabbed her daughter by the arm, but Penny jerked away and kept her hand in Gavin's.

"No." Penny's eyes filled with tears. "I'm not going with you."

Penny's father, a well-dressed *Englisch* man with graying hair, walked past them without a word and left the building.

"Uh, yes, young lady, you are coming with us." Penny's mom waved toward the exit door. "Your father is livid and embarrassed. Why would you do something like this?"

Noah kept his eyes down, his heart hurting for Penny, a girl he barely knew. He couldn't imagine his parents speaking to him like that in front of his friends, or even privately for that matter.

Penny leaned closer to Gavin, and he wrapped his arm around her.

Penny's mother threw her arms in the air. "Unbelievable. What in the world would make you take a bunch of pills like that? I'm sure having your stomach pumped wasn't a pleasant experience, but at least you survived."

Noah glanced around the room. Penny's head was buried in the nook of Gavin's arm, and she started to cry. Rebecca's eyes filled with tears, and so did McKenna's. Paul had his arm around McKenna.

"I'm leaving, Penny. Are you coming or not?" Penny's mother waited, and Penny eventually shook her head. "Fine." The woman stormed out of the building, and within seconds the yelling started again, fading after a few moments.

Penny lifted her head from Gavin's chest but wouldn't make eye contact with any of them. "I'm sorry." Tears poured down her cheeks. "I wasn't trying to kill myself. I promise. I just wanted the pain to stop."

Rebecca dabbed at her eyes. McKenna eased away from Paul and walked over to Penny, gently coaxing her friend away from Gavin a little. She pushed hair away from Penny's face and kissed her on the cheek before she pulled her into a hug.

"I love you, and everything is going to be okay." McKenna's nurturing, sweet voice seemed to calm Penny, and she fell into her arms.

Gavin, Noah, and Paul stood quietly nearby, but none of them said anything. Rebecca wasn't sure what to say or do either. It felt intrusive to even be here. She didn't know Penny, and she'd held on to awful thoughts about McKenna for much too long. It was obvious, though, that McKenna was just an affectionate person. Rebecca recalled their conversation in the kitchen and how much even she liked McKenna. If Rebecca was honest with herself, she could see Noah's initial attraction to her. Kindness radiated from her.

Rebecca could feel the bitterness draining from her mind.

"I can't go back there, McKenna." Penny lowered her head to her friend's shoulder. "I can't be around all of the fighting. It's nonstop." She sobbed. "My parents are so messed up." She grunted, then looked into McKenna's eyes. "I assure you . . ." She glanced around at all of them. "Money does not buy happiness. I . . ." She took a deep breath. "I want peace. I want a different life. I don't want this one anymore. I'm tired of feeling this way. I want—No. I *need* God's love in my life."

Rebecca was sure she wasn't the only one with tears in her eyes at the admission.

Penny began to cry again, then whispered to McKenna, "We don't have anywhere to go. My parents are probably canceling my credit cards on their drive home."

"We will figure it out." McKenna tucked Penny's tangled masses of hair behind her ears. "I have enough money for a cheap hotel for tonight, and you need to rest."

As Penny and McKenna continued to talk quietly, Rebecca let go of Noah's hand and walked over to where Paul was standing, then leaned up and whispered in his ear. After he nodded, she went to McKenna and Penny.

"We have a place where you can both stay as long as you want to." Rebecca lifted her chin, fighting tears of her own.

Penny sniffled. "You don't even know us."

McKenna touched Rebecca's arm and smiled slightly. "I know her, Penny. She's Paul's sister, Becky, and she's gracious and kind." She turned around and her smile grew as she locked eyes with Paul. "And so is her brother."

Rebecca lowered her gaze as shame took hold of her. She fought to shrug it off, but it would take time for her to forgive herself for the horrible thoughts she'd had about McKenna.

When she looked up again, she saw the way Paul gazed at McKenna. Perhaps they were all smitten with her in their own ways, but Rebecca had never seen Paul look at a woman the way he was gazing into McKenna's eyes.

"The *daadi haus* on our property is empty. Paul and I are sure our parents won't mind if you both stay there awhile." Rebecca put a hand on Penny's arm. Her people weren't affectionate by nature, especially in front of others, but Rebecca felt the tension leaving Penny from that simple gesture. "So please be our guests for as long as you'd like."

Penny wrapped her arms around Rebecca's neck and cried. "Thank you," she whispered. "I'll find a way to pay you. I just can't go back to my house."

"There are no worries," Rebecca said. "You need rest."

McKenna looked at Paul. "I have my car, so I can take the three of us girls. Paul made arrangements to have an Amish friend at the library take his horse and buggy home." She looked at Noah. "Can you take Gavin and Paul in your buggy?"

Noah nodded, the color having returned to his face. Whatever his idea had been to fix things between them, God had had other plans. They were all exactly where they needed to be at this moment.

Rebecca reached for Penny's hand, then McKenna's. She squeezed both, then guided these two lost souls out of the building, feeling a purpose arising in her that snubbed out the bad feelings she'd had, along with the shame.

After they were in the car, McKenna assured Penny and Rebecca she could drive. On the way to Rebecca's house, McKenna talked about her mother and the situation she'd been living with for years. Penny shared about life at her house too. Rebecca shuddered at some of the stories, but she'd never felt more blessed in her life, and she prayed for these women to find the peace they both so desperately needed. Rebecca had heard Penny's plea loud and clear. *I need God's love in my life.*

Rebecca wanted that for both of them.

Noah's heart was heavy as he flicked the reins and pushed the horse to go a little faster. Dark clouds were forming, and he hoped to get Gavin back to the hardware store, and Paul and himself home before it started to rain. He was glad the girls were in McKenna's car.

Gavin planned to finish his shift at the store and had arranged for his father to pick him up later, but Noah's friend hadn't said much, so Noah spoke up.

"Did you know things were that bad at Penny's house?" He recalled the lavish party he'd attended and the temptations that abounded everywhere. The fancy house with technologies Noah hadn't seen before, the drinking, and the evidence of wealth.

Sitting next to him on the front seat of the buggy, Gavin shook his head. "I mean, I knew Penny had issues, but I'm as shocked as everyone else that she took it this far. I realized early on that she partied a lot—more than I'm comfortable with—but it was obviously an escape for her. Still, I like her a lot. The few times she's shown the real Penny, I've liked that person even better than the one who is always trying to be cool. But it tore me up to see her like that today, especially when she broke down the way she did." He looked over his shoulder at Paul. "Do you really think it's going to be okay with your parents that Penny and McKenna stay there?"

Noah had wondered the same thing.

"*Ya*, it will be okay when Becky and I explain the situation to them."

Thinking about the temporary living arrangements, Noah recalled his plan to fix things between himself and Rebecca. In light of the seriousness of the past few hours, it now sounded silly, but he'd thought if Rebecca hugged and kissed Gavin on the cheek, then they'd be even and she could put it behind her. But something had happened tonight, and he was still trying to wrap his mind around it. He knew Rebecca well, but he'd seen a side of her he hadn't seen before tonight, a compassion that touched his heart. In spite of her feelings about McKenna, Rebecca had been the one to reach out to her and Penny and offer a solution. The gesture made him love her all the more.

After a few more moments of silence, Noah glanced at Paul. "So you and McKenna looked pretty cozy."

Paul cleared his throat. "*Ya*, I like McKenna a lot."

"But she's *Englisch*," Noah said.

Quiet again.

Then Paul sighed. "*Ya*, she is."

I guess Rebecca was right about Paul not planning to join the church.

When Noah stopped in front of the hardware store, his friend thanked him for the ride and for being there.

"It was nothing," Noah assured him. He paused. "Rebecca and I are going to be baptized Sunday during worship service. I heard what Penny said about needing the love of God."

"Yeah, I was surprised about that," Gavin said, scratching his chin before he opened the door of the buggy. He turned to Noah and smiled. "Surprised in a good way."

Noah nodded. He'd always suspected Gavin was in a good place with the Lord. "Baptism is a blessed and holy event for us. I think it will be impossible not to feel the love of God during the ceremony. I don't think the bishop would mind if you and Penny attended. I can explain to him that I work with you, and you and Penny are friends."

Gavin stepped out of the buggy, closed the door, then leaned in the window. "I think that would be great. I'll talk to Penny."

Even after Noah dropped off Paul, he couldn't stop thinking about the events of the day. Rebecca had been so upset about McKenna, and then she'd transformed in front of his eyes. Penny wasn't the rich girl who had everything, the way Noah had assumed. McKenna and Paul were clearly smitten with each other, but that was a complicated situation. In the end, six friends and acquaintances—*Englisch* and Amish—had bonded together for the good of all.

Noah cringed as he thought about how close he'd come to being sucked into a world that he now knew he wasn't a part of. He prayed Rebecca would become his wife, but one thing he was sure of was that he was going to be baptized on Sunday.

He felt a new closeness with God. Something deeper. *For where two or three are gathered together in my name, there am I in the midst of them.* Paul, McKenna, Penny, Rebecca, Gavin, and Noah—each person in that waiting room had been there for a reason, and the grace of God shone down on all of them.

CHAPTER 15

Sunday morning arrived with crisp fall weather, and as the clouds parted, sunshine found its way between the cracks in the barn where the worship service was being held. Rebecca could feel God's presence, and it was everything she could do not to cry when the bishop's wife blessed her with a holy kiss on the cheek. She glanced at Noah just as the bishop blessed him with a holy kiss.

Rebecca and Noah hadn't talked about wedding plans, and she was happy about that. She wanted to know that she and Noah were both being baptized for the right reasons, and not just because they wanted to get married. Everything was in order for a wedding, but on hold. Penny's and McKenna's situations had taken priority. Both girls wore dark circles under their eyes today, and Rebecca suspected they stayed up late talking.

As was normal, the women were on one side of the room and the men on the other. The bishop and deacons were in the middle, along with Noah, Rebecca, and the bishop's wife.

Rebecca glanced at Penny and McKenna as the bishop said his final prayer. McKenna's expression was sober, as if she was in deep thought. Penny wept openly. Rebecca had been witness to a lot of baptisms over the years, and each time the Holy Spirit had been present. She could recall that even as a child she'd been overwhelmed with God's love during a baptism. The first attendance to such an event, as it was for Penny, was always special. Almost as special as this day was for Rebecca. She prayed again for peace for McKenna and Penny. Then, seeing Paul across the room, his gaze fixed on McKenna, Rebecca prayed for her brother and McKenna too.

Gavin was standing next to Paul and had the same serious expression McKenna did. His eyes never left Penny.

But despite Rebecca's baptism and the love she felt swelling in her heart, there was still something she had to take care of. She waited until after the meal was served before she found McKenna and asked to talk to her privately. McKenna followed her out of the barn until they were a few feet into the front yard of the Petersheims' house.

"Thank you and your family again for letting me and Penny stay in your extra house." She touched Rebecca's arm. "I will get a full-time job and pay back any rent, or whatever arrangement your parents are willing to work out until we get on our feet."

Rebecca tried to smile but failed and instead blinked back tears. "I've held ill will against you, and I want to say I'm sorry."

McKenna pulled her jacket snug, glanced at the ground, then back at Rebecca. "I know this is about the hug and kiss, but I promise you, nothing happened, and it never would have."

Rebecca nodded. "I know that now, but at the time, I let jealousy latch onto me, and I laid misplaced blame on you. I want you to know I'm sorry." She lowered her eyes. "And I'm ashamed."

McKenna touched Rebecca's arm and spoke softly. "Please

don't apologize. Any ill will you felt toward me was understandable. But don't let shame bring you down. It can be like a weight around your neck. I've always been ashamed of my mother's behavior, even though I love her very much. I struggle with shame, too, and it's a horrible emotion brought forth by the enemy."

"I guess . . . I guess I just need you to forgive me."

McKenna smiled. "There's nothing to forgive, Becky."

Rebecca huffed, grinning. "There is one other thing."

McKenna's eyebrows drew in as she brought a hand to her chest. "What is it?"

"Can you please call me Rebecca? I'm not sure if Paul calls me Becky just to irritate me because that's what big brothers do, or if he really can't shrug the habit because he's called me Becky since we were kids."

McKenna laughed. "I can do that, Rebecca." Then she pulled Rebecca into a hug, and without a moment's hesitation, Rebecca returned the embrace.

Paul was glad to see McKenna and Rebecca hugging. He needed the two women he loved to have a good relationship. Across the yard he saw that Noah had slipped out of the barn at some point, the way Paul had. Noah was also watching the women talk and embrace, so Paul walked toward him and put a hand on his back.

"Everyone is going to be okay," Paul said. "And congratulations on your baptism."

Noah nodded. "*Danki.*" Then he refocused on the women, who were still chatting, before he turned back to Paul. "I am sure about my decision to be baptized into our faith, but I'd be lying if I said I didn't want desperately to marry Rebecca." He hung his head, sighing. "If she'll still have me."

Paul chuckled, which caused Noah to raise his head and lift an eyebrow.

"You're still getting married next month, even if Rebecca hasn't formally said so." Still grinning he said, "She has this list of everything that needs to be done before the wedding. She's been driving everyone crazy. So I think it's safe to say that the wedding is back on."

Noah smiled. "I hope so. What about you and McKenna?"

"It's too soon to know for sure, but I feel good about the future." Paul had already spoken privately to his parents and confessed that he wasn't going to be baptized into the Amish faith. He'd waited for his mother to blow up and blame McKenna, but instead she offered him a weak smile and said they had suspected his hesitation for a long time. She admitted to hoping Paul would change his mind but assured him she didn't blame McKenna. And Paul was glad about that because he could see McKenna and him together in the future.

After the women cleared the dishes following the meal, Noah found Rebecca. Folks were already getting in their buggies to head home, especially the families with young children. It was always a long and wonderful day of worship, but the little ones were tired after a three-hour church service and the meal.

"It was a *gut* day." Noah gazed into Rebecca's eyes, hoping she could feel how much he loved her. He'd said he was sorry dozens of times, but today he wanted to focus on the celebration of baptism. He continued praying that Rebecca would still become his wife, though. He hoped Paul was right, that plans were moving in that direction.

"It was a *gut* day." She smiled in the same manner she had before Noah had almost ruined things. He tried to keep his mind on the blessing of baptism, but it was hard not to drop to his knees and beg Rebecca to commit to him for a lifetime.

The short conversation ended when Gavin and Penny walked up to them. Gavin shook Noah's hand. "Thank you for having us at your baptisms. It was a wonderful experience."

Penny was looking at the ground, sniffling. Noah had seen her crying throughout most of the ceremony and even occasionally during the meal. The majority of the service was in Pennsylvania *Deutsch*, but the few *Englisch* visitors who attended Amish services were always deeply affected. Noah thought maybe for some it was their first time to feel the Holy Spirit and the oneness with God.

"What did you think, Penny?" Noah tried to read her expression, but he could barely see her face until she lifted her head and looked into his eyes.

"Do you think it would be possible for us to come back?" Penny's voice seemed almost desperate, pleading.

Noah couldn't recall the bishop allowing *Englischers* to attend regularly, but these were odd circumstances with Penny and McKenna both trying to start out on their own, away from parents who had negatively influenced them. "I will talk to the bishop," he said.

Penny hugged him. "*Danki*," she whispered.

Most outsiders knew a little bit of Pennsylvania *Deutsch*, and he appreciated the fact that Penny spoke a word in their dialect. But he eased out of the hug fairly quickly as he recalled the trouble of his last hug in the arms of another woman. Thankfully, when he looked at Rebecca, she was smiling the same smile, and glowing.

"We're going to go, but God's blessings to both of you." Gavin hugged Rebecca before they left.

After they were out of earshot, Noah shook his head. "They are a hugging bunch of people."

Rebecca laughed, which was nice to hear. "*Ya*, they are." She paused. "And I think that's *gut*. Maybe our people should do more hugging."

"Do you think Penny will be okay?" Noah glanced around, and when he confirmed that no one was watching, he reached for Rebecca's hand.

"*Ya*, I do," she said. "And I think McKenna will be all right too. They are both strong women."

Rebecca's eyes drifted somewhere over Noah's shoulders, and when he turned around, he saw McKenna and Paul talking. "What about them? Do you think they will be all right too?"

Rebecca kept her gaze on her brother and McKenna. "*Ya*, I do. Maybe not in the way I always thought, but this is Paul's journey, and he has to follow his heart and God's guidance."

Noah was having a hard time keeping his emotions in check as he swallowed back a lump in his throat, still fighting the urge to ask Rebecca if they were going to be married for sure.

"I see lots of new beginnings in the works for all of us." She smiled as she squeezed his hand. "Now let's get down to business." She reached into the pocket of her black apron and pulled out a piece of paper. Grinning, she said, "There's this list I need to talk to you about. There are several items you need to take care of."

Noah smiled as he silently thanked God for the day's many blessings.

EPILOGUE

Rebecca and Noah bustled about the house, readying things for their first formal supper gathering with friends. They moved into the main house a month ago when Rebecca's parents insisted they were ready for a slower-paced life. "Semiretirement," her mother called it when they moved into the *daadi haus*, leaving Noah in charge of the farm. Like Paul and Rebecca, their parents had been tending the farm since they were children. Rebecca was sure they would still be actively involved but was happy to see them slowing down.

Paul moved out and bought a small house in Bird-in-Hand right after Christmas, and he had taken the blessings of his family with him. He and McKenna were still dating, and Rebecca was excited to be playing hostess to them in her own home. She and Noah had lived with her parents in the months after the wedding, so it still felt strange with just her and Noah.

She raced to the door when she heard the knock.

Paul laughed as she threw open the door. "It still feels weird to knock on the door of the house I grew up in."

"I told you, you don't have to knock." Rebecca waved an arm. "Come in." Then she hugged McKenna, and McKenna kissed her on the cheek the way she always did.

"It smells so good in here." McKenna brought a hand to her chest, and it was impossible not to notice the ring on her left hand. Rebecca couldn't contain her gasp, and McKenna grinned, then held out her hand for Rebecca to see."

Both women embraced. "I'm so happy for you." Then she hugged her brother. Rebecca had grown to love McKenna just like a sister, and now she would be. "Do you have a date?"

McKenna smiled. "Actually, we do, but not for a wedding. We were wondering if you and Noah would come to our baptism at the church we belong to."

Rebecca blinked back tears. "Of course we will." She knew her brother and McKenna attended a nondenominational church in Bird-in-Hand that they really liked.

"We were going to wait until Gavin and Penny got here to make the announcements, but I guess the ring gave it away." McKenna glowed, and Rebecca bubbled with happiness.

"They're always late to everything," Noah said when he walked into the room. He shook Paul's hand, then hugged McKenna, knowing the kiss on the cheek was coming, and also knowing no one thought a thing about it anymore. Occasionally, Rebecca recalled the way they'd all been brought together by just such an embrace. If things had happened any other way, they wouldn't be exactly where they were meant to be. "I hope Penny doesn't bring a dessert." Noah rolled his eyes.

Rebecca frowned at him. "You will eat it if she does."

Noah cringed. "She's an awful cook."

McKenna and Paul laughed. "We'll struggle through it somehow," Paul said.

Penny had reconciled with her parents but told them she was never going home. She had other plans for her life, and she'd made good on them. She'd married Gavin two months ago. They were all thrilled for the couple.

McKenna's mother had completed a recovery program, but she'd recently relapsed, and it weighed heavy on McKenna's heart. But Rebecca's future sister-in-law was also pursuing her own life. McKenna was back to attending college courses after she'd acquired a full-time job at the Pequea Valley Public Library, the place she and Paul had met.

Life had truly been good to all of them.

"Knock, knock, it's us." Penny burst through the door, Gavin trailing behind and carrying a cake. Unlike Rebecca's brother, Penny always announced herself and stepped over the threshold before anyone responded. Always a ball of energy, she blew a wisp of hair that had fallen from beneath her *kapp*. Rebecca was still getting used to seeing Penny wearing Amish clothes. If anyone had told her a year ago that Gavin and Penny would end up being baptized into the Amish community, Rebecca never would have believed it. But it fit for them. They'd attended worship service every other Sunday since the day of Noah and Rebecca's baptism. After they attended classes to prepare for their own baptisms and completed the ceremony, they were married.

Penny still carried some of her sassiness around, but everyone in the community loved her. She had worked hard to master their dialect, but her cooking and baking skills left much to be desired. None of them had the heart to tell her so, least of all Gavin, who adored her.

"What do we have here?" Penny marched to McKenna and grabbed her hand, then jumped up and down. "You and Paul are getting married!"

"We are." The women embraced.

Once everything settled down, they all moved to the kitchen of the home Rebecca and Paul had grown up in. They'd chosen different lives from each other, but all were in God's plan.

They bowed their heads before the meal, and Rebecca knew in spite of their various paths they were united in their prayer.

Thank You, Lord, for your abundant blessings. And for new beginnings.

A Perfect Plan

PROLOGUE

Priscilla glanced around the yard at all the guests. Warm August temperatures allowed for an outside celebration, and it never rained on her special day. *Mamm* went all out for birthdays, but this year was the biggest yet. In addition to a beautiful pineapple layered cake that her oldest sister, Naomi, made, there was a ham, barbecued string beans, scalloped potatoes, creamed celery, homemade breads, jams, jellies, chowchow, and a variety of pies and cookies. She smiled as she turned away from the main food table.

Ten oblong tables spanned the front yard, topped with simple white coverings. On each table, *Mamm*'s blue Tupperware party bowls were filled with peanuts and chips, with a platter of pickles and olives in the center. Everything was perfect, right down to the decorations. Her sister Hannah had been put in charge of filling the balloons with helium, and yellow and blue bundles were tied to the head chair at each table. Priscilla's place setting had double the balloons from every color in the rainbow.

"I think everything turned out lovely." Naomi waved her arm around the yard. "And look how many guests showed up. There must be a hundred people here."

Priscilla took another look around the crowd and was happy to see that some of the folks were starting a game of volleyball on the far side of the yard. Then her eyes landed on someone. "What is Chester Lapp doing here?"

Chester Lapp was handsome and well-respected in the community. He was a fine carpenter. Her father had purchased two rockers from Chester for the front porch. But he was nineteen. Why would he want to come to her sixteenth birthday party?

"Why shouldn't he be here?" Naomi folded her arms across her chest and grinned. "Our family has known his family forever. We even share a phone shanty."

"I know that." Priscilla rolled her eyes. "I'm just surprised he's here. I mean, I rarely see him socially. Just at worship, and he hardly ever goes to Sunday singings. I wonder who invited him."

Naomi scratched her cheek as she took a deep breath and looked away.

"You did, didn't you? *Why?*" Priscilla narrowed her eyebrows at her sister. Naomi was twenty-two and always playing matchmaker for someone. "I barely know him."

"Maybe you should get to know him better." Naomi breezed across the yard, turning back once to wink at her sister.

Priscilla sprinted a few steps to catch up with her. "Why do you say that? Has he said something? Tell me, Naomi."

Naomi stopped alongside Priscilla and whispered, "Let's just say he has asked about you more than once."

"When?" She tried not to get too excited as her eyes drifted in Chester's direction.

"Once when I saw him in town, a couple of months ago. Then I ran into him last week at the hardware store in Bird-in-Hand.

He asked about you then too." Naomi shrugged. "So I invited him to your birthday party."

Priscilla twisted her mouth from side to side as she studied the tall, handsome man. "I'm still surprised that he came."

"I'm not." Naomi grinned, then walked away.

Priscilla kept her eyes on Chester, but jumped when he turned around and caught her staring. She quickly looked away and began straightening one of the paper tablecloths that had blown up in the wind, but she could see him moving toward her out of the corner of her eye.

"Happy birthday."

She looked up and smiled. *"Danki."* Then she began to line up the bowls and pickle tray so that everything was evenly spaced on the table. She could feel Chester's piercing blue eyes on her, and slowly she lifted her eyes to his again. An easy smile played at the corner of his mouth as he looped his thumbs beneath his suspenders. If it weren't for his traditional clothing, Chester wouldn't look much like an Amish man. Most men kept their hair in a bobbed haircut, bangs in the front, straight on the sides. Chester's hair was dark and curly above his brows and ears; his wavy locks didn't resemble much of a bob. Priscilla wondered if his beard would be curly as well someday, after he was married.

"It's a great party."

Priscilla pulled her eyes from his and went back to the task at hand. *"Ya,* it is. *Danki* for coming." She pushed one of the blue bowls an inch or so to the right, making sure it was the same distance from the pickle tray as the other bowl.

"What are you doing?" Chester folded his arms across his chest, still grinning.

"What?"

"You've been moving those bowls not even a quarter-inch back and forth. I think they are perfectly spaced now."

Priscilla felt the heat rush from her neck to her cheeks. "I wasn't doing that."

"*Ya*, you were."

"No." She folded her arms across her chest, mirroring his stance. "I wasn't." She pulled her eyes from his and kicked at the grass with her bare foot.

He was right. She needed things to be in perfect order, but she wasn't going to apologize for it. She enjoyed organizing things. She'd recently alphabetized recipe cards for Naomi, and her mother was thrilled when Priscilla organized her sewing supplies, grouping her thread colors together and sorting material by color and fabric. Other people appreciated her need for things to be in order—but Chester was making fun of her for arranging a couple of bowls.

"Are you gonna be at the singing on Sunday?"

Priscilla found his eyes and wanted to look away, but couldn't. "Uh, *ya*. I usually go."

"How about going with me?"

She opened her mouth to speak, but nothing came out. Chester Lapp was older, handsome, and asking her to be his date for a Sunday singing. She'd be wound up like a top in preparation for it. Finally she took a breath and spoke. "I can't. But *danki* for asking me." She turned and darted off before he could say anything more.

Chester tipped back his hat and watched Priscilla hurry across the grass. Even in her haste, she was as graceful as a snowflake riding the breeze on a winter morning. He pulled off his hat, scratched his head, then replaced the hat, all the while keeping his eyes on her.

He didn't know that much about her. Beautiful, yes. She was petite with strawberry blond hair, and her blue eyes gleamed when she talked. It seemed like she'd blossomed into a young woman overnight, and she was old enough for him to ask out now. He'd accepted Naomi's invitation to the party hoping to get to know Priscilla a little better. Maybe asking her to a Sunday singing was too forward. But Chester knew that he had more in common with Priscilla than she realized.

While Chester was talking with Naomi, he'd casually mentioned that he planned to go skydiving before he was baptized into the faith. Naomi had burst into laughter. When she came up for air she said, "My sister has always wanted to do that. We think she's *ab im kopp*, but she says she will do it before she's baptized."

Chester didn't know any other young Amish woman who would consider such an endeavor, though it was perfectly allowable prior to baptism. This Priscilla King intrigued him.

Priscilla balanced her youngest sister, Sarah Mae, on her hip as she chatted with her guests. Her best friend, Rose, walked up and whispered in her ear, "I need to talk to you."

Priscilla excused herself, and she and Rose eased away from the crowd.

"I just overheard Chester Lapp telling Naomi that he asked

you to a Sunday singing." Rose thrust her hands onto her hips. "And you said no! Why?"

"I don't know him." She thought about the way Chester made her uncomfortable earlier, teasing her about the bowls.

Naomi walked up to them then, her lips pinched together in a frown. "Did you really decline an offer from Chester?"

"Why are you trying to fix me up with him? We barely know each other." Priscilla set Sarah Mae down in the grass beside her. "Good looks aren't everything." She raised her chin, not wanting to admit that Chester made her nervous.

"Too bad." Naomi tucked a strand of loose hair beneath her prayer covering. "Because the two of you have a common goal."

Priscilla rolled her eyes. "What might that be?"

"You both want to go skydiving. I don't know of any other two people in our district who share such a crazy goal." She shrugged. "I just thought it might be worth a mention." Naomi picked up Sarah Mae, grinned, and walked away.

Rose's eyes grew round. "You've wanted to go skydiving ever since Barbie and Elam's wedding."

"That doesn't mean that I should go on a date with Chester Lapp." Although she had to admit, he'd suddenly grown more interesting.

Priscilla had tried and tried to find someone who would jump out of a plane with her. Ever since she'd attended her *Englisch* friend's outdoor wedding, where a man jumped from a plane and right into the reception area, she'd dreamed of doing that herself. To freefall through the air, soar like a bird . . . such freedom. Priscilla had talked to the man with the parachute for nearly an hour—and she'd left with a business card and phone number to call if she ever wanted to jump.

"I gotta go." Rose gave her a quick hug, wished her happy birthday again, and headed to her buggy. Priscilla stayed where she was, watching Chester talk with her parents across the yard. When he walked away from them, Priscilla hurried toward him.

"Chester! Wait!"

CHAPTER 1

Hiccup . . .

Priscilla covered her mouth with her hand—not so much to stifle the intermittent spasms in her diaphragm, but to keep from exploding at her five-year-old sister. She took a deep breath as she studied the scene before her, then closed her eyes and blew the air from her lungs in an effort to calm herself. It didn't work.

"What have you *done*, Sarah Mae?" She stepped forward to where the little girl was sitting in the middle of the sewing room. *Hiccup . . .*

Sarah Mae's big brown eyes filled with tears. "What's wrong?" She blinked a few times, her bottom lip quivering. "Why are you using your mean voice?"

Priscilla took another deep breath, hiccuped again, then rubbed her tired eyes. "I'm not using a 'mean' voice, Sarah Mae."

"*Mamm* said I could have these scraps to make a dress for Lizzie Lou." Sarah Mae lifted up the finely sewn blue material for Priscilla to see.

226

It was the left arm of Priscilla's wedding dress, perfectly stitched and ready to attach to the body of the outfit she planned to be married in. In all her nineteen years, she'd never crafted a finer long sleeve.

"See, I made armholes for Lizzie Lou." Sarah Mae nodded toward her doll, which was propped up against a chair to the left. The rag doll with flowing brown hair went everywhere Sarah Mae went. And Lizzie Lou had many outfits—dresses for working in the fields and going to church service, along with brown, black, and white aprons. Lizzie Lou also had two *kapps* and a black jacket.

Priscilla cringed as Sarah Mae pushed her small fingers through slits on either side of the sleeve. "Sarah Mae . . ." *Hiccup* . . . She clutched her chest and tried to control her voice. Then she pointed with one hand toward a pile of scraps to her right. "Those are the scraps *Mamm* meant for you to use." She glanced about at the pieces of material scattered around Sarah Mae until she spotted her other sleeve. She squatted down next to her sister, picked it up, and poked her fingers through the holes on either side.

"That's Lizzie Lou's Sunday dress." Sarah Mae tucked her chin, then lifted her watery eyes to Priscilla's.

Priscilla handed what used to be the sleeves of her wedding dress back to her sister. She scanned the area around Sarah Mae, hoping and praying that the body of her dress was still intact.

"Sarah Mae," she said softly, following another hiccup, "there was another piece of sewn material, a much larger piece. Where is it?"

Sarah Mae stood up, tucked her chin again, then walked across the room. "Lizzie Lou wanted a hammock and a blanket."

"Sarah Mae! No!"

The dress was cut in half, one piece tied between two chairs, the other piece on the floor below the "hammock."

"How could you do this? That was my wedding dress, Sarah Mae! Not scraps!"

"I'm sorry, Sissy! I'm sorry!" Sarah Mae threw her little arms around Priscilla's legs and looked up, tears pouring down her face. "I'll make you a new dress for your wedding."

Priscilla patted Sarah Mae on the back as she thought about the time she'd spent on her wedding dress. "It's all right. I'll make an even better dress." She forced a smile for Sarah Mae. Four weeks until the wedding. It was doable. It might not be as finely stitched as the one that now served as two dresses, a hammock, and a blanket for Lizzie Lou, but it could be done. "Maybe Lizzie Lou needs to get married in her new dress," she mumbled under her breath.

"Sissy?" Sarah Mae pulled her arms from around Priscilla's legs and stared up at her sister. "I'm sorry."

"I know you are, Sarah Mae." She realized her hiccups were gone. She leaned down and kissed the little girl on the cheek. "You stay here and play. I'm going to go help *Mamm* with supper."

And after the meal and cleanup, Priscilla would go meet Chester at the phone shanty that bordered both their homesteads—as she always did on Tuesdays and Thursdays. She smiled. She was the luckiest girl in the world to be marrying Chester Lapp. If this was the worst thing that happened to disrupt the wedding she'd been planning for the past few months, she could live with it.

Chester arrived at the shanty about ten minutes early, anxious to hold Priscilla in his arms. In only a month she'd be his *frau*, and there'd be no more sneaking off to the shanty.

He leaned up against the structure, which resembled an old outhouse—a tall, wooden boxlike building that housed a telephone and a small stool. Most families had phones in the barns these days, but his father, along with Priscilla's father and the Dienners and the Petersheims, chose to keep with tradition, holding on to the shanty they had shared for years.

As he leaned against the weathered wood, he looped his thumbs beneath his suspenders and watched the sun setting in the west, leaving a warm glow atop the fields stretched before him as far as he could see. Tall green grass speckled with brown was evidence of the recent first frost and seemed a prelude for a hard winter.

Chester closed his eyes and imagined curling up on the couch beside Priscilla in front of a warm fire this winter. He was close to finishing the house he was building for them. The building inspector was coming tomorrow to check the electrical wiring. Installing electricity was required, even though they would never turn it on. And should they decide to sell, the resale value would be better if it was wired for electricity. But Chester was counting on spending the rest of his life in that house with Priscilla. He'd worked hard to make it everything they'd dreamed of. Four bedrooms would be enough room for the *kinner* they planned to have.

He heard movement and turned to his left to see Priscilla moving through the field like a beautiful butterfly, her arms swinging back and forth as she lifted her legs high through the pasture, a pallet of orange dusk behind her.

My sweet Priscilla.

Chester had loved Priscilla since she was sixteen. That was when he started courting her, carrying her home from Sunday singings and making plans for their future. But since he was three years older than she, he waited until she was nineteen to propose. As he watched her hurrying toward him in a dark green dress and black apron, his heart skipped a beat, the way it always did when he first saw her.

She came to a stop right in front of him, breathless and beautiful. "How long have you been waiting?"

"Not long." He cupped her cheeks in his hands and gently kissed her on the mouth, lingering for much longer than he should.

She pulled back and smiled at him. "We'll be married soon enough, and you can kiss me like that all the time."

Chester would be lying to himself if he denied the fact that her looks had drawn him to her initially. She stood out among their people with her strawberry blond hair and stunning blue eyes. A natural blush filled her cheeks atop her ivory complexion.

Despite her comment, Chester kissed her again. She giggled and pushed him away. "Chester Lapp, you better behave yourself."

She was small and flowerlike, but Chester knew better than to be misled by her dainty appearance. Priscilla was as strong a woman as he'd ever met—inside and out. He recalled the day not long after her sixteenth birthday when they held hands and jumped out of a perfectly good airplane together.

His future wife could also swing a baseball bat like no woman he'd seen and outrun most of her teammates. She spoke her mind when necessary, yet was the most compassionate person he knew. She was organized and punctual, and expected others to be. She could obsess on details sometimes, that was true, but in Chester's eyes . . . she was perfect.

"Have I told you lately how much I love you?"

She tapped her finger to her chin and twisted her mouth to one side. "Hmm . . . I can't recall."

He cupped her cheek in his hand. "I love you with all my heart. Forever."

Priscilla put her hand atop his, then pulled his hand to her mouth and kissed it tenderly. "I love you, too, and I can't wait to be your *frau*." Then she let go of his hand, stepped back a bit, and frowned.

"What is it?"

"Something happened today. With my wedding dress." She let out a heavy sigh. "Sarah Mae used it to make doll clothes, along with a hammock and blanket for her doll's enjoyment."

It wasn't funny, but Chester stifled a grin just the same. Priscilla came from a family of girls. Naomi—the oldest at twenty-five and still unmarried—lived in the *daadi haus* on the family's property where she ran a bakery business. Then there was Priscilla's married sister, Hannah, who was twenty-two. Then Priscilla, and then Sarah Mae—her parents' little surprise.

Priscilla folded her arms across her chest. "Chester, are you laughing?" She tried to make her voice sound stern.

"No. Not laughing at all." He held his palms toward her. "Besides, you'll be beautiful on our wedding day no matter what you're wearing." He reached for her hand, then squeezed.

"I can make a new dress." She scowled a bit, then her eyes brightened. "The inspectors come tomorrow to look at the house, no?"

"*Ya*. I think everything will be fine, then I can move forward with the finishing touches for my bride-to-be." He hoped that everything would in fact be fine. With his father's help, they had done most of the wiring themselves. It would be a huge setback if something was wrong. He wanted to whisk Priscilla into their new home as soon as possible.

"Do your parents know you meet me here on Tuesdays and Thursdays?" Priscilla bit her bottom lip, then grinned.

"I think so. Do yours?"

She giggled. "*Ya*. We don't speak of it, but they know I'm not just going for a walk." She hugged herself and shivered. "I forgot my sweater."

Chester wasted no time taking off his black jacket, regretful he hadn't done it as soon as she arrived. He draped it around her shoulders.

"*Danki*." Priscilla settled into the jacket, smiling. "I hope the weather is nice for our wedding day. It might be a little cold, but I'm hoping there won't be any rain. I want everyone to be able to gather in the barn or outdoors following the ceremony."

"It will be a perfect day." Chester latched on to the collar on both sides of his jacket and pulled it snug around her. "You warm enough?"

"*Ya*. I'm *gut*."

Then she hiccuped, and he laughed. It was the cutest little sound he'd ever heard, and her eyes widened as she cupped her hand over her mouth.

"This is the second time this has happened today." Her cheeks flushed a bright pink. "How embarrassing."

"It's cute," he said as another hiccup escaped. "*Daed* always tells us to eat a spoonful of sugar when we get the hiccups."

Chester's family was small by comparison to others in the district—only Chester and his brother, Abraham.

"Abe used to get the hiccups a lot."

"*Nee*, I don't know how cute it . . . *hiccup* . . . is."

They both laughed again, but jumped when the telephone in the shanty rang.

On the third ring, Chester stepped inside the booth and picked up the receiver. He said hello, then his smile faded and he tightened his grip on the receiver.

CHAPTER 2

It was almost dark by the time Priscilla eased up the porch steps. She hung her head as she opened the door and moved inside. Naomi was peeling potatoes at the kitchen table.

"Why so sour?" Naomi wasn't wearing her *kapp*, and strands of her dark brown hair had fallen forward from the bun atop her head.

Priscilla and her sister didn't look anything alike. Naomi had dark hair, dark eyes, and an olive complexion, just like Sarah Mae and Hannah—and like their mother. Hannah used to tease her when they were young, telling her she was adopted.

Priscilla pulled out a chair across from Naomi at the large kitchen table. She sat down, propped her elbows on the table, and rested her chin in her hands. "I was with Chester at the phone shanty."

"Really? I'm *so* surprised." Naomi smiled. "I think we know where you go on Tuesday and Thursday nights, Priscilla." She set a peeled potato in the pot beside her, then her expression grew solemn. "Did something happen? You look sad, *maedel*."

"I'm okay, I guess." She bit her bottom lip. "Chester is pretty upset, though. The building inspector is coming tomorrow to check the wiring, and we've been nervous about that, praying everything would be up to code. But tonight Zeke called and said there's a problem with the roof."

Chester's cousin Zeke was in town for the wedding, and he just happened to be a carpenter who specialized in roofing. Chester had asked him to check out the roof on the house.

"What's wrong with it?" Naomi sliced off a sliver of potato and handed it to Priscilla; she was the only one in the family who liked raw potato.

Priscilla waited to swallow before she answered. "The storm last week blew off some shingles. Zeke said he would help Chester repair it, but I know Chester wasn't expecting to have to fit that in. His job at the furniture store takes up most of his time, plus the chores around his house, and . . ." She sighed. "And now he has to fix the roof."

"God often challenges us, but I'm sure you and Chester will have a fine home." Naomi began cutting hard-boiled eggs on a chopping board.

"Potato salad?" Priscilla eyed the mayonnaise and jar of pickles on the table beside Naomi.

"*Ya. Daed* asked if I would make him some." Naomi carried the pot of potatoes to the sink, filled it with water, and put it on the stove.

Naomi took most of her meals with the family at the main house, even though she lived in the *daadi haus*. She also ran a baked goods business from her home, and she was a wonderful cook.

Priscilla let out a heavy sigh. "Did you hear what happened to my wedding dress?"

Naomi grinned as she sat down again and continued

chopping hard-boiled eggs. "I did . . . something about clothes for Lizzie Lou?"

"Don't forget the hammock and blanket." Priscilla shook her head. "I was so upset with her, but when she started to cry, I thought . . . well, I guess I'll just have to make another dress. A better dress."

Priscilla reached for half a boiled egg, only to have Naomi playfully slap her hand. "*Ach.* No, *ya* don't. I have just enough." She pulled the plate of eggs closer. "I pulled a honey bun cake from the oven. Go get yourself a piece."

"We just ate supper."

"Then why are you trying to eat my eggs?"

Priscilla shrugged. "I don't know."

They were quiet for a few moments.

"I have a lot on my mind about this wedding. First my dress today, and then problems with the roof."

"Everything will be fine, Priscilla. You worry too much."

They sat quietly as Naomi chopped the eggs for the potato salad. Priscilla knew her sister was right. But when things didn't go as planned, she wondered if she was on the right path, the one God had planned for her.

Priscilla tapped her finger to her chin. "Remember how everything went wrong with Hannah's wedding?"

Naomi chuckled. "*Ya.* The church wagon showed up late with the supplies, we ran out of propane for the extra ovens *Daed* rented . . ." She shook her head. "And the poor groom was battling the flu."

"It's not funny, Naomi. I don't want those troubles at my wedding."

Naomi stopped chopping the eggs and locked eyes with

Priscilla. "Hannah didn't let it bother her, Priscilla, because she loved Leroy and just wanted to be with him. You should be glad you found someone to spend your life with and stop fretting about everything. You know worry is a sin."

"I know." Priscilla sighed again. "Why do you think I'm like that? I mean, I always pray that everything will go smoothly, even though I know we're not here on this earth to have an easy life."

Naomi handed her a piece of egg and a sympathetic smile. "Priscilla, where were you while we were growing up? Did you not listen at all? We cannot understand God's plan for us. Everything is His will. It might seem like things are falling apart sometimes, but often God has something better in store for us down the line." She sat taller and smiled. "You will enjoy life much more if you will just relax."

Chester climbed up the ladder and joined Zeke on top of the roof. Zeke had come from Ohio to serve as one of Chester's attendants for the wedding, and Chester was sure thankful that his cousin was in the construction business.

"I'm surprised more of these shingles didn't blow off during the storm." Zeke pointed to the section of the roof over the kitchen. "Look. See how different some of them are? You need to talk to the person who sold these to you."

Chester rubbed his forehead, wondering how neither he, his father, nor his brother had noticed the difference in the shingles. "*Ya*. You're right."

"Don't worry, cousin. I can help you with this."

"*Danki*, Zeke. Since Abe broke his wrist, he hasn't been able to be of much help." Abe had fallen from the roof a few weeks earlier, and they were grateful that his injuries had been no worse.

They climbed down the ladder, and Zeke followed Chester to the front door. He turned the knob and motioned Zeke ahead of him and into the living room so Zeke could see the progress he'd made the past week.

Zeke scanned the room, then raised a brow toward Chester. "Mighty fine." He ran his hand along a built-in bookcase on the far wall. "And a bit fancy."

"Priscilla's idea." Chester stepped next to Zeke and eyed the floor-to-ceiling bookcase. "She likes to read, and she said she hopes that our *kinner* will too."

Zeke grinned. "Planning to start a family right away?"

"As soon as possible." Chester smiled back at his cousin, thoughts of Priscilla and their wedding night swirling in his head. He allowed himself the vision for a couple of seconds, then added, "We want lots of *kinner*. Priscilla will be a fine *mamm*."

Zeke put his hand on Chester's shoulder. "I'm happy for you."

Chester showed Zeke the rest of the house. The kitchen was large and spacious with plenty of room for the table and chairs Priscilla's parents gave them as a wedding present. As he waited for Zeke to have a good look, he pictured Priscilla cooking their meals and tending to their *kinner*. Their wedding couldn't come soon enough.

Following supper cleanup on Thursday, Priscilla brushed past her mother in the kitchen, anxious to meet Chester at the phone shanty. She pulled her black sweater from the rack by the door, and she'd almost made a clean getaway when her mother cleared her throat. After holding her breath for a moment, Priscilla eased around and faced her.

"Priscilla, before you go on your *walk* . . ."

Mamm folded her arms across her chest and held her chin high in such a way that Priscilla knew she was trying to be firm—but Priscilla saw the slight twinkle in her eyes.

"I'd like for you to stop by the Zooks' house. I have something for you to take to Rachel."

Priscilla glanced at the clock hanging on the wall in the kitchen. She loved Rachel Zook and enjoyed visiting with her, but Chester would be waiting.

"That boy will wait, Priscilla." *Mamm* grinned as she left the kitchen, leaving no doubt that she did indeed know about the meetings at the shanty. She returned a moment later with a small lap quilt.

Priscilla had seen *Mamm* working on a pink quilt—of course it was for Rachel. Everything in Rachel's life was bright pink, even her clothing, shoes, and socks. The walls of Rachel's room were also painted pink, and everyone in the community contributed to the pink décor.

Bishop Ebersol allowed Rachel to dress in the untraditional color, and he often referred to her as one of God's special blessings, which she truly was. Rachel was the same age as Priscilla, but in her mind she was only about five years old.

Priscilla took the quilt from her mother and studied it for a moment. She couldn't believe how many different shades of pink formed the stars and border. "It's beautiful, *Mamm*. I'm sure Rachel will love it."

Her mother smiled. "I loved making it for her."

Priscilla headed out the door, wondering how she could keep her visit brief. She wasn't sure she'd ever had a short visit with Rachel.

She'd barely cleared the porch steps when she took off in a run. The Zook place wasn't far down the road, but it was in the opposite direction from the phone shanty. She'd have to hurry.

Five minutes later she arrived on the Zook porch and tried to catch her breath. She folded the quilt over one arm and patted her cheeks for a moment, trying to ease the sting from the cool wind. She knocked on the door.

Mary and John Zook had fourteen children—more than anyone else in their district. Priscilla figured John Zook was happy that nine out of fourteen of those *kinner* were boys. Lots of help in the fields.

Priscilla wanted a large family, too, but she thought six or seven *kinner* would be enough. She wasn't sure how Mary kept up with fourteen, especially since they all still lived at home. Priscilla was pretty sure that Annie had just turned two, and the oldest boy, Ben, was twenty-one.

Priscilla tucked a strand of loose hair beneath her *kapp* as the wooden door opened. Mary Zook smiled through the screen, with Annie on one hip and two slightly older girls standing beside her. A smile lit the woman's tired face.

"Priscilla, come in." Mary eyed the quilt draped over Priscilla's arm as she shifted Annie on her hip. "What've you got there?"

"*Mamm* made it for Rachel," Priscilla said as she stepped into the large living room. She offered the quilt to Mary, hoping to make a quick exit. But Mary shook her head.

"Let me have one of the girls go get her. She'd be so disappointed if she knew you came calling and she didn't get to see you." Mary set Annie down as she spoke to one of the older girls—either Frieda or Elizabeth. Priscilla couldn't remember who was who. They weren't twins, but they looked a lot alike.

"I don't want to disrupt your household so soon after the supper hour." But Priscilla knew it was too late. Rachel would be downstairs soon. *Wait on me, Chester.*

Mary picked up Annie again, then eased her into a playpen filled with toys. "Are you excited about your wedding?"

"*Ya.* Very excited." Priscilla felt her cheeks warm a bit, the way they did every time someone asked about her upcoming nuptials. She couldn't wait to be Chester's *frau.*

"I remember our wedding day like it was yesterday." Mary's brown eyes took on a faraway look, then she met eyes with Priscilla and laughed. "But we've stayed busy since then."

Priscilla felt even more heat in her cheeks, unsure if Mary was referring to all the children they'd had or something else. Before she had time to decide for sure, she heard a familiar voice. And even though she knew she'd be late to meet Chester, the sound of Rachel's sweet voice warmed her heart.

"Pre-Ceelia!" Rachel ran to Priscilla the way she always did and threw her arms around her. Rachel was several inches taller than Priscilla, and overall a large girl. As always, she was dressed in a bright pink dress with matching pink shoes and socks. Her prayer covering was white, but there were two pink flowers sewn on either side. Priscilla couldn't breathe for a moment as Rachel engulfed her in a big hug.

She'd grown up with Rachel, but she couldn't recall when her friend became so obsessed with the color pink. It must have been when they were both very young, because for as long as Priscilla could remember, Rachel required pink—on her person, in her room, and basically everywhere she went. Priscilla had comforted Rachel many times when they were places that weren't pink. About five years ago, when Mary was sick, Priscilla and her mother took Rachel to the doctor for a cold. Rachel pulled a pink crayon from the pocket of her apron and colored on the *Englisch* doctor's pretty white wall. She carried a pink crayon everywhere she went.

Mary tapped Rachel on the shoulder and spoke to her tenderly. "Careful, Rachel. You don't want to hurt Priscilla."

"I love Pre-Ceelia!" Rachel finally released Priscilla from the embrace.

"I love you, too, Rachel." She held the quilt out to her. "*Mei mamm* made this for you."

Rachel brought both hands to her mouth and gasped, then she slowly took the quilt from Priscilla and brought it to her face. She inhaled as she pressed her face into it and mumbled something Priscilla didn't understand.

"Move the quilt, Rachel, so we can understand you." Mary tapped Rachel on the shoulder again, and Rachel brought the quilt away from her face.

"*Danki* to Pre-Ceelia's *mamm* for my present." Rachel buried her face in the quilt again.

Priscilla glanced at the clock on the fireplace mantel. "You're welcome, Rachel. I'll tell *Mamm* how much you like it." She smiled at Mary. "I guess I better go."

Mary nodded, but Rachel pulled the blanket from her face like it was on fire. Her eyes grew round as she spoke. "I have something for you too!" She bounced on her toes. "I have a present for Pre-Ceelia!" She turned to Mary. "It's in *mei* room, *Mamm*. I go get it!"

Rachel ran to the stairs and bolted up them two at a time. Priscilla bit her bottom lip and looked at the clock again.

"You've always been one of Rachel's favorite people," Mary said.

Priscilla smiled as guilt pinched at her heart. She shouldn't be in such a hurry to leave, but Chester . . . he was surely at the phone shanty wondering where she was. "Rachel is one of my favorite people too."

Rachel returned and handed Priscilla a letter-sized envelope. *To Priscilla* was written across it with pink crayon. "For your marriage day. Not to open until your marriage day!" She raised her shoulders, then dropped them slowly as she smiled. "It's from God."

"*Danki*, Rachel. This is very special." Priscilla pressed the envelope to her chest. "Are you sure you don't want me to open it now?"

Rachel shook her head so hard that Priscilla worried she would have a headache. When she finally stopped, she pressed her lips together and frowned. "No! God said only to open on your marriage day!"

Priscilla touched Rachel on the arm. "Okay. I promise to open it on my marriage—wedding day." She looked at the clock again.

Rachel let out a heavy breath and nodded, and Priscilla put the envelope into her pocket. "I'll see you soon." She turned to leave, but Mary snapped her fingers.

"*Ach!* I almost forgot. I have two of your *mamm*'s bowls from our last gathering. She sent home the leftovers with me. Let me just run and get them." Mary eased around the playpen and scooted past Priscilla, Rachel, and the other girls toward the kitchen.

Priscilla forced a smile before her eyes landed on the clock.

Wait for me, Chester . . .

CHAPTER 3

Priscilla ran as fast as she could, lifting her legs high as she made her way across the hayfield to the phone shanty. And for the third time this week, she had a case of the hiccups. Yards before she reached the meeting place, she could hear the phone ringing, but there was no sign of Chester. She picked up the pace as she wondered if maybe Chester stopped somewhere to try to call the shanty. Lots of folks in their community had cell phones, but neither Priscilla nor Chester did. Mostly it was out of respect for their parents, who were against any type of phone near the house. The families sharing the shanty also chose not to have an answering machine, even though Bishop Ebersol didn't have a problem with it.

She stepped into the shanty and reached for the phone hanging on the wall just as another hiccup echoed within the small space. *Please be Chester.*

"Hello."

"I'm looking for Chester Lapp."

She stifled a sigh. "He's not here right now. Can I take a message for him?" Priscilla picked up the pencil that was beside a small pad of paper they kept on a shelf underneath the phone.

"Yes, if you don't mind. This is Joel Cunningham. I'm the building inspector, and we met yesterday."

Priscilla took a deep breath, then blew it out slowly, afraid to ask . . . but needing to know. "Is everything okay? Did the house pass the inspection?" To her embarrassment, she hiccuped into the phone, then squeezed her eyes closed as she spoke. "I'm so sorry."

There was a slight chuckle on the other end of the line. "No problem. Eat a spoonful of sugar."

That was the second time she'd heard that. Before she could respond, the man continued.

"There are a few things I need to go over with Chester. Can you take my number and have him give me a call?"

Priscilla wrote down the phone number, promised to have Chester call him tomorrow, and hiccuped as she hung up. She tucked the number in the pocket of her apron with Rachel's envelope before she headed for home, sorry she had missed Chester and fighting worry about what problems the building inspector may have found. Instead, she thought about what Naomi had said.

Friday morning Chester finished sanding a bench he'd been working on all week. It was a special order, and Mr. Turner said it needed to be finished today so that the customer could pick it up Saturday morning. He knew it might mean staying late tonight, and he had hoped to get off early to go check on Priscilla. She'd never missed one of their Tuesday or Thursday meetings at the shanty. But Mr. Turner's snappy tone didn't leave much room for an argument. His boss hadn't seemed himself lately. The elderly man had even barked at a customer for slamming the door when he entered the store. Chester wasn't surprised that the patron left without buying anything.

He heard the bell chime on the front door, but he knew Mr. Turner was there, along with two other employees, so he didn't get up, but instead started staining the bench with a light walnut color. He heard a woman's voice talking to Mr. Turner . . . and then recognized it as Priscilla's. He wiped his hands on a towel and turned around to see her entering the work area in the back of the store.

"I'm so sorry I missed you at the shanty." She glanced over her shoulder and waited until the door shut behind her, then threw her arms around his neck. He squeezed her tightly before gently easing her away.

"Is everything okay?" He kissed her softly on the lips before she answered.

"*Ya*. I'm sorry. *Mamm* wanted me to take something to Rachel Zook, and it was hard to get away." She grinned as her cheeks flushed a light pink. "I missed you."

Chester kissed her again, keeping one eye on the door. "I missed you too."

She bit her bottom lip. "The phone at the shanty was ringing when I finally got there. It was the building inspector."

Chester tipped back the rim of his hat and rubbed his forehead. "*Ya*. He called me here at the shop this morning."

Priscilla stared at him. "How bad is it?"

"It could have been worse, but *Daed* and me are gonna have to do some rewiring upstairs." He shook his head. "Seems like a lot of work when we won't be using electricity."

"I know." She frowned. "I can't imagine us not living there forever."

After everything he'd put into building this house for them, he sure hoped that they would live there forever. But now he could add wiring repair to the roof repair. It was going to be a challenge to have everything done by mid-November.

It was tradition for the bride and groom to spend as long as three months living with the bride's parents. During that time, they would visit family and friends—sometimes stopping at several homes in one day. It was also when they would collect the bulk of their wedding presents. But both Chester and Priscilla were hoping to move into their new home two weeks after the wedding.

He cupped her cheek in his hand and gazed into her beautiful blue eyes. He didn't want to think of the problems he'd had with the house—beginning with the foundation, which didn't set right. Then the lumber for the frame was delayed, putting him behind schedule on the entire project. And now, these latest issues.

He pushed the thoughts from his mind, resolved to focus on the future and his new life with Priscilla. After a tender kiss, he said, "Do you know how much I love you?"

She smiled. "With all your heart."

He reached down and squeezed her hand. "I guess I better get back to work. But I'll see you at your *haus* on Sunday." He gave her a quick wink.

As was customary, the church deacon would announce to church members on Sunday that Priscilla and Chester were getting married. Then her father would stand up and announce the date and time. Communion was held in October, and wedding publications were always announced during worship service within a few weeks after that. Most of the community already knew about the upcoming wedding, but publication was a long-standing tradition, and those who didn't already know would clear their calendars for the first Tuesday in November. On the day of publication, Priscilla and Chester were allowed to skip church service and spend time alone at Priscilla's house, and Priscilla would cook them a fine meal. He was looking forward to spending some time alone with her.

Priscilla stayed in the sewing room for most of the afternoon and tried to work on a new wedding dress, but the treadle sewing machine kept locking up. After a while, she gave the foot pedal a swift kick and moseyed to her room. She plopped down on the bed, her head filled with wedding plans. She was thankful that she'd already made her bridal attendants' dresses. Naomi's and Rose's dresses were safely put away, with no chance of becoming doll clothes for Lizzie Lou. She was also thankful that Hannah had decided early on that she didn't want to be an attendant because her baby was due the same week as the wedding. That had made it much easier on Priscilla. Otherwise, she would have been forced to exclude either one of her sisters or her lifelong best friend, since only two attendants were allowed.

After leaving Chester earlier in the day, she'd spent the morning helping her mother and Naomi clean the basement. With the wedding now three and a half weeks away, *Mamm* wanted every nook and cranny in the house clean. But Priscilla knew she needed to finish her wedding dress too.

She ran her hand along the intricate stitching of her red-and-white Lone Star quilt, knowing that she wouldn't be sleeping alone beneath it for much longer. She couldn't wait to be in Chester's loving arms for the rest of her life.

Once they were in their own home, they would share Chester's king-size bed, one he'd made just for them. Her furniture would nicely fill one of the extra bedrooms in their new home. Leaning back on her hands, she studied her bedroom. Everything was in the proper place, and not much had changed over the course of her nineteen years. But as she took inventory of the life she'd lived in this room, somehow everything looked different to her today, each piece of furniture and keepsake reflective of her life up until now.

Daed had made her full-size bed when she seven years old, replacing Hannah's hand-me-down twin bed. She could still remember the first time she slept in the "big girl bed," tucked beneath a new set of sheets and quilt. She glanced at the matching oak dresser that came a few months after the bed; the top three drawers were stuffed with undergarments, extra *kapps*, socks, tights for the winter, and sweaters. The bottom drawer was filled with letters from relatives, Christmas cards she'd received, and books. The rocking chair in the corner of the room once belonged to her grandmother, and the clock hanging on her wall was a gift from her mother just last year. Her family and friends knew how much she loved clocks, especially handmade ones like the one from *Mamm*—enclosed in cedar with delicate gold hands, keeping the world on schedule. Priscilla loved to fall asleep at night to the gentle ticking.

It would all be going with her to her new home, and she was thankful for the familiarity her possessions would provide. She glanced to her left. Rachel's envelope was on her nightstand. She thought about opening it, but recalled the promise she had made. *Sweet Rachel.*

It would be time to go help with supper soon, but for just a moment, she decided to indulge herself. She lay back on her bed and closed her eyes, visions of her wedding day swirling in her mind. Naomi and Rose would be by her side. Zeke and Abe would serve as Chester's attendants. *Mamm* would cry, of course—just as she had when Hannah got married. Her friends and family would all bring lavishly decorated cakes and keepsake containers filled with candies, cookies, and all kinds of special goodies to be passed around the *eck*. There would be a meal of *roascht* and all the fixings bountiful enough to feed the family and friends in attendance. It was a perfect plan, and it was going to be a great day.

Hiccup. Not again! Her chest rose and fell with each spasm. She'd never had the hiccups so much in her life.

She heard the murmur of voices across the hall, but she didn't budge as she continued to envision her wedding day. Then the voices became clearer.

"I hope we're not going to have a repeat of Hannah's wedding."

Priscilla's eyes flew open at the sound of her mother's voice. She didn't move, just listened as Naomi answered.

"I'm sure everything will be fine, *Mamm.*"

"I hope so. Poor Chester is having all kinds of trouble with the *haus.*" Her mother paused, and Priscilla cupped her hand over her mouth and hiccuped again. "You know what happened with the wedding dress. And now this."

What? Priscilla bolted off the bed and held her breath as her heart raced. She could tell from the sounds coming from across the hall that *Mamm* and Naomi were straightening Sarah Mae's room.

"I don't know if we should even tell Priscilla just yet that her favorite *aenti* and *onkel* won't be able to come." *Mamm* sighed deeply. "You know how much your sister worries."

No! Not only were *Aenti* Rebecca and *Onkel* John her favorite kinfolks, but her aunt was supposed to be making Priscilla a special cake topped with candied yellow roses. Priscilla stood quietly, her hand firmly across her mouth, and listened. Her body jerked with another spasm.

"No problem, *Mamm*. I'll make Priscilla a special cake."

Priscilla pulled her hand away and smiled at Naomi's offer. *Hiccup!* Her eyes widened as she realized how loud it was this time. In seconds her mother and Naomi were standing in her doorway.

"I thought you were downstairs in the sewing room working on your dress." *Mamm* put her hands on her hips and frowned.

"I was . . ." She paused as her chest heaved in and out. "But the sewing machine kept locking up on me. Now, please tell me why *Aenti* Rebecca and *Onkel* John aren't going to be at my wedding." Priscilla put her palms on her chest and held her breath, but it didn't go any good. *Hiccup.*

Mamm walked to the bed and smoothed the quilt where Priscilla had been sitting, then she turned around and folded her hands in front of her. "Rebecca is going to have a baby, and the doctor in Middlefield told her she shouldn't travel."

Priscilla cringed. "What? *Aenti* Rebecca is pregnant? She's . . . she's nearly *your* age, *Mamm*. How can that be?"

Mamm slammed her hands back to her hips as she cleared her throat. "I assure you, Priscilla, women can get pregnant at the age of forty." She stared at Priscilla, raised her eyebrows, and stood taller.

Priscilla sat back down as she quickly calculated her mother's age. Forty-five. "*Ach, ya.* Sarah Mae." She grinned.

Naomi stepped forward and put a hand on Priscilla's arm. "No worries, Priscilla. I'll make sure there are candied yellow roses on one of your cakes."

"*Danki*, Naomi."

There was no doubt in Priscilla's mind that her sister would make a great cake. *Hiccup!*

"That's a terrible case of the hiccups," Naomi said as she sat down in Priscilla's rocking chair.

"Please don't tell me to eat a spoonful of sugar. I've already heard that twice." *Hiccup.*

Naomi kicked the floor with her bare feet until the oak rocker swung into motion. "I can't even remember the last time I had the hiccups."

Her mother sat down beside Priscilla on the bed and crossed one leg over the other.

Priscilla hiccuped again, and they all chuckled. "Until lately I can't remember the last time I've had them either. But I got them when I was at the phone shanty with . . ." She shifted her eyes toward her mother, who was grinning. ". . . with Chester. He got the call that there were problems with the roof. Oh . . . and before that I got them when I found Sarah Mae cutting up my wedding dress." She tapped her finger to her chin. "And I when I answered the phone at the shanty when the building inspector called with bad news." Her expression dropped. She glanced back and forth between her mother and sister. "And now I have them again when I hear this sad news about *Aenti* Rebecca and

Onkel John." She sat up taller and gasped. "Every time I get the hiccups, something bad happens with the wedding."

Mamm slapped her playfully on the leg. "*Ach*, Priscilla. You're being superstitious. That's nonsense."

Maybe.

But just the same . . . she was going downstairs to eat a spoonful of sugar. And she would pray for no more embarrassing eruptions.

CHAPTER 4

Saturday morning Priscilla pulled her black jacket snug around her as she walked down the road toward Rose's house. She needed to talk to her best friend—specifically, she needed Rose to convince her that she'd lost sleep last night for no reason. Priscilla had prayed hard for God to take away her anxiety about the wedding, but sleep eluded her anyway.

She kicked a pebble in the road, but quickly picked up her pace when she noticed the clouds darkening above her and felt the sting of the wind's chill on her cheeks. Leaves on either side of the road started to swirl in small brown and orange tornadoes around her, and within seconds she felt raindrops splashing her face. Rose's house was in view, so she sprinted toward the porch. By the time she reached the steps, she was soaked.

"Priscilla King, what in the world are you doing?" Rose pulled Priscilla into the living room. "Wait here. I'll get you a towel."

Priscilla stood dripping on the hardwood floor until Rose returned. "Sorry, I got water on the floor."

"That's okay. Let's move into the kitchen and sit at the table." Rose pulled out a chair for Priscilla, who then sat down on top of the towel. Droplets of water spilled onto the top of the table, and

Rose handed her a kitchen towel for her face. "Didn't you know we were in for rain this afternoon?"

Priscilla shrugged as she patted her face. "Where is everyone?"

Rose sat down across from her. "*Mamm* and *Daed* went to Strasburg Tractor Supply to get a part for the plow, James and Ben are in the barn, and *Aenti* Tabby is visiting a friend. So this is a *gut* time to talk." She put her elbows on the table and dropped her chin into her hands. "What's wrong, Priscilla? You look like something's bothering you."

Priscilla shrugged again. "I—I don't know." She scratched her nose, then fumbled with the damp towel on the table. "Just so much to do before the wedding."

Rose put her palms flat on the table and sat taller. She lifted her chin. "Priscilla, you've had everything for this wedding planned out for months. What's *really* bothering you?"

Priscilla smiled. Rose knew her better than anyone, so her prodding wasn't surprising. Still, she felt silly. She rubbed her eyes for a moment, then looked up at her friend. Leaving out no details, she told how she had been getting the hiccups as a forewarning of unwelcomed events. When she was done, she waited for Rose to comment. But Rose just stared at her.

"I know you think I'm *ab im kopp*, but isn't it strange?"

Rose folded her arms across her chest and grinned. "*Ya*, I do think you're off in the head. That's just plain silly, Priscilla. Those things can happen to anyone." She leaned forward to reach for Priscilla's hand and squeezed it. "Don't worry, *mei maedel*. Everything is going to be fine. Trust the Lord's will."

Priscilla forced a smile. "You're right." She eased her hand from underneath Rose's and stood up. She pointed a finger at her friend, whose nuptials were set for December. "I just hope you don't have all the problems we're having, come time for your wedding."

Rose raised her shoulders, then dropped them slowly. "If we do, we will put our faith in God and work through it. Which is what you should do."

Priscilla walked to the window and took a peek outside. The sun was slowly lifting above blue-gray clouds. "I guess I better head home before it makes wet again." She turned to Rose, gave her a hug, and darted down the porch steps.

She was determined to put her trust in God's will and not fret about silly superstitions.

Chester pulled the stool up close to the workbench in the barn and sat down. He took off his hat and reached for the clock he'd been working on, picturing it on the mantel in his and Priscilla's home. His future *frau* loved clocks, and he wanted her to cherish this wedding gift. He ran his hand over it gingerly, pleased that the last coat of stain was dry. Now he just had to apply the glossy finish and install the clockworks.

He took great care applying the lacquer, making sure it was smooth and didn't leave any bubbles. He'd spent most of the day working on the roof with Zeke, and he hoped to finish the clock in time to take it to Priscilla tomorrow when she cooked for him at her house. He tried to picture the deacon announcing to the congregation that he and Priscilla would be married. They'd been formally engaged since July, and traditionally the publication of their engagement would have been a surprise to most of the community. But both he and Priscilla had been guilty of spreading the word from the moment she had agreed to become his *frau*. Chester reckoned a few folks weren't sure of the date, but Priscilla's father would announce the day and time after the deacon spoke. He couldn't wait until November when they would take their vows before God, friends, and family.

As much as he would like to hear the deacon and Priscilla's father speak about their upcoming wedding, he wouldn't give up tomorrow afternoon with Priscilla for anything. It was rare that they were allowed to spend time alone, and Chester wanted it to be a day to remember.

He set the clock off to one side so that it could dry. By morning, it would be dry enough to install the parts.

"Done with the clock?"

Chester turned to see Abe walking into the barn, his wrist still in a cast. "*Ya*, almost."

"Sorry I haven't been able to help you more with the *haus*."

Chester started to answer, but then he noticed something holstered to his brother's hip. "You know Bishop Ebersol doesn't like us using cell phones unless it's for business. And neither do *Mamm* and *Daed*."

Abe put his good hand on his hip. "*Ach, ya*. But I'm in *mei rumschpringe*. Besides, everyone has one."

"I never had one before I was baptized, and I still don't." Chester frowned. "I'd put that in my pocket if I were you. No need to rub it in *Mamm*'s and *Daed*'s faces."

"They've already seen it, and they didn't say nothing." He reached down and touched the phone. "I wouldn't need one if *Mamm* and *Daed* would allow an answering machine in the shanty. We miss calls all the time, and I never know what's going on."

Chester elbowed Abe as he brushed past. "Don't play trickery with me. You just want to be able to call Linda. Bet she has a phone, too, no?"

Abe grinned. "How'd you know about Linda?"

Chester turned to face him. "Everyone knows about you and Linda. You've been carting her home from singings for weeks, and you get a goofy look every time you're around her."

"I do not." Abe stood taller and raised his chin.

"*Ya*, you do." Chester chuckled as he walked out of the barn.

Abe was on his heels. "What do you mean, goofy look?"

Chester kept walking but did his best to imitate the look Abe got when he was around Linda. He lifted his nose and squinted his eyes. "Like this."

"You look like a pig."

Chester laughed. "Exactly! So do you when you give Linda that *dumm* look."

They were walking up the porch steps to the house when Chester heard the vibration coming from Abe's hip. Abe unlatched the phone and brought it to his ear.

"At least you got the good sense to keep it on vibrate," Chester mumbled, shaking his head.

As he reached for the screen door, Abe nudged him with his elbow. "It's for you."

"What? Who is it?"

"Mr. Turner."

"Huh?" How on earth had his boss tracked down his brother's cell number? For that matter, how did he even know Abe had a phone? Chester dismissed the thoughts as he brought the phone to his ear.

Mr. Turner was up in years, but generally he was a likable

fellow, even though he'd been acting a bit out of character lately. But Chester had never heard him scream the way he was hollering into the phone at this moment. He held the phone out a few inches from his ear, shocked at what Mr. Turner was saying.

CHAPTER 5

Priscilla lit the bayberry-scented candle that she'd saved for this occasion. Then she arranged some chrysanthemums in a vase, ones she'd picked that morning. If she had any regret about the ways of the Old Order Amish, it would be that flowers were not allowed at weddings. She wished her special day could be filled with them.

She breathed in their scent as she eyed the two place settings she'd carefully laid out for her dinner. *Mamm* insisted she use the good china, white plates with ivy delicately etched around the edges, and she put them atop lace place mats that were more for looks than anything else. Cream-colored napkins, silverware, and company tea glasses finished off the setting.

She and Chester would have about two hours alone while everyone else was sharing a meal after church service. After spending the morning preparing, everything was ready. Chester had requested "underground ham" for the main meal, a recipe her mother often carted to social events. Chester loved the cheesy ham and potato dish that was baked and topped with crumbled bacon. Earlier that morning, Priscilla had baked two loaves of bread and a butter pecan cake. Chester liked the cream cheese filling and rich, flavorful icing. She planned to spend the rest of her life tending to him, their house, and eventually their *kinner*.

Now, as the fragrance of the candle mingled with the rewarding smell of her cooking, she stepped back and smiled. And no hiccups. She'd convinced herself that her superstitions were unfounded, and she refused to let worry block her heart from the voice of God. He was in control. She pushed loose strands of hair up underneath her prayer covering and smoothed the wrinkles from her black apron. Chester liked her burgundy-colored dress the best, so she was happy to wear it. She closed her eyes and thanked God for all He'd blessed her with.

As she heard the *clippity-clop* of hooves coming up the driveway, she took another look around the kitchen. Joy bubbled inside her as she moved through the living room. She pulled the wooden door open, but when she looked through the screen at Chester, her elated spirit floundered. She knew when his smile was forced. She pushed the screen door open, and he handed her a box wrapped in yellow and tied with a white bow.

"Danki," she said as she accepted the present. She bit her bottom lip. *No kiss?*

"You're welcome." Chester took a deep breath. "It smells *gut* in here." He took his hat off and hung it on the rack by the door. His blue shirt brought out his eyes, which met with hers as he finally leaned down and kissed her.

"Is everything okay?" Priscilla held her breath, praying nothing else was wrong with the house.

"Sure."

They stood there for an awkward moment, and Priscilla was certain that everything was not all right.

"I made your favorite, underground ham." She reached for

his hand and pulled him into the kitchen, cradling the package in her other arm. "It's keeping warm in the oven."

"You're the best, Priscilla. I love you."

As he kissed her again, Priscilla slowly eased away and placed the present on the table. "What's wrong, Chester? I can tell something's not right." Her stomach rolled as she watched his face fall. "Please tell me." She pulled out her father's chair at the head of the table. "Here, sit. I'll pour you some tea."

After she poured them each some tea, she sat down beside him on one of the long wooden benches and waited.

"I know how much you've been looking forward to this day." He smiled, looking at the flowers and the candle flickering in the jar on the table. "I don't want you to be concerned or sad about anything."

She cupped one hand over her mouth. She *did* want this to be a special day, but it wouldn't be if something was bothering him.

"I talked to Mr. Turner today." Chester ran a hand across his forehead as he sighed.

Priscilla lowered her hand and placed it on her chest, trying to speculate why this would upset Chester.

"Abe got a cell phone, and Mr. Turner went to a lot of trouble to find Abe's phone number. He evidently called all over town until someone said to try Linda's parents' phone in the barn. So, long story short . . . he found me."

"What did he want?"

Chester locked eyes with her, and she wanted to look away. She couldn't stand to see him so sad.

"He accused me of stealing money." Chester stared at the wall to their left. "Two hundred dollars."

Priscilla's eyes grew round. "What?"

Chester put his elbows on the table and dropped his forehead into his hands. "How could he think I would do that?" He kept his head down as he spoke. "Then he fired me."

"What? That's not fair!" Priscilla jumped up from her bench, hands on her hips. "Did you tell him that you would never do such a thing?"

Chester leaned back in his chair and reached up for her hand. Gently, he pulled her back down until she was seated again. "Of course I did. But he said I was the one who closed the store on Friday, which I was, and that the money didn't just walk away. He said he had two hundred dollars cash from a customer in an envelope inside his desk. And it was gone Saturday morning when he opened the store." He let out another heavy sigh. "I'm upset about losing my job, but I'm even more bothered that he thinks I stole from him."

Priscilla folded her arms across her chest and tipped her head to one side. "This just doesn't make sense. Mr. Turner has always liked you . . . and trusted you. He obviously misplaced the money."

"*Ya*, he did."

"Was anyone else around? Maybe someone else took it."

Chester shook his head, and Priscilla sat quietly for a moment. Mr. Turner had been good to Chester since he started working there almost two years ago. The elderly man had always been kind and fair. He said it was a big step for him to hire help after thirty years of running the business by himself. Turner's Furniture was a small store with a variety of furniture, but Mr. Turner often commented about how well Chester's pieces—especially his rocking chairs—sold. And Chester did a lot of other things for Mr. Turner . . . inventory, stocking, and even some ordering.

"Don't you think it's strange that he would track you down on Abe's phone instead of talking to you in person?" She shook her head. "I just can't believe he accused you of stealing."

"Mr. Turner hasn't been himself lately. I don't know what to make of it." Chester paused with a faraway look in his eyes before turning back to her. "I'm sorry to dump this on you today, but it really has me down." He eased his hand over to hers and squeezed. "But let's don't talk about this anymore. I want you to open your present."

She tried to clear her mind and focus on their special time. "Why am I getting a present? It's not my birthday."

"It's my wedding present to you. I couldn't wait."

She gasped. "But I don't have your present ready yet." She'd been sewing Chester a Sunday vest and matching pants, but they weren't finished.

He stood up, pulled her into a hug, and whispered in her ear, "I love you, Priscilla. Let's don't let worry plague our hearts today." He kissed her on the cheek. "Will you open your present?"

"*Ya!*" She eyed the box on the table.

Chester picked up the package, reached for her hand again, and they walked into the living room. Once they were settled on the couch, Priscilla delicately worked the white bow from around the package and carefully peeled back the yellow paper. She pried open the top of the box. Tears welled in her eyes as she lifted the beautiful clock from the box, and when the scent of freshly stained wood filled her nostrils, she knew right away that Chester had made it for her.

"It's the most beautiful thing I've ever seen." She ran her hand gingerly along the smooth casing of the clock.

"Not from where I'm sitting." Chester cupped her cheek and

kissed her on the mouth, lingering for long enough to give her a glimpse of what their time as husband and wife would bring, and she kissed him back.

She forced herself to ease away from him and looked down at the clock again. "This will look beautiful on our mantel."

Chester smiled—a real smile. And she was glad that he seemed to be forgetting about Mr. Turner.

"Are you ready to eat?" She stood up from her spot on the couch.

"*Ya*. It smells mighty *gut*."

They strolled hand in hand into the kitchen, and once Chester was seated, she refilled both their tea glasses, placed a jar of chowchow on the table, and put out a loaf of butter bread and two kinds of jam. Then she carefully pulled out the underground ham from the oven and placed it on the table.

They bowed their heads in silent prayer before Chester dived in, eating like a man who hadn't had a meal in a month.

"Chester Lapp, you act like you've never had underground ham before." Priscilla's insides warmed as she watched him devour her cooking. She pushed the bread and jam closer to him. "Don't forget some butter bread and jam. It's rhubarb."

Chester nodded, his mouth stuffed. He was doing his best to show Priscilla how much he appreciated the fine meal she'd laid before him, but he didn't have much of an appetite, and his mind was filled with worry despite his best attempts to clear his head. The roof and wiring on the house needed repairing, he was getting married in just over three weeks, and now he would start his married life without a job. Even though he planned to grow hay on his sixty acres, it wouldn't provide enough income to live. Mr. Turner had paid him more than a fair wage for the thirty hours per week he put in at the store.

Still chewing, he glanced up. Priscilla was pushing her food around on her plate. He knew that this news was weighing heavily on her. He swallowed, then said, "Priscilla, I can see the concern on your face. Please don't worry."

She offered him the hint of a smile. "I know everything's going to be fine."

She sat taller, scooped up a forkful of ham, and he watched her take the bite. Surely, her appetite must have left her when he shared his news, but Chester knew how important this time was to Priscilla. And to him.

After the main meal, Priscilla served them each a slice of cake, and Chester was pretty sure it was the best cake he'd ever had, but he continued to fight the anxiety that roiled in his stomach. It seemed like he and Priscilla just couldn't catch a break. Everything leading up to the wedding was going wrong—the house, Abe breaking his wrist, Priscilla's dress, her favorite aunt and uncle not being able to attend, and now . . . he didn't have a job. If he didn't love Priscilla as much as he did and know that she was the one for him, he might question the challenges the Lord had laid before them. His father said that too much opposition meant that you weren't on the path God intended for you. But Chester trusted God's will, and lots of good things in life came with opposition.

Then why did *Daed*'s words keep lingering in his mind?

He was jarred from his thoughts when Priscilla hiccuped.

CHAPTER 6

No. Not now.

Priscilla clamped her hand over her mouth. Slightly embarrassed, she reminded herself that superstitions were not to be heeded. Chester raised his brows a bit as he bit into a slice of cake. She hiccuped again. "Oops," she said, and raised her eyes to Chester's. "I don't know why this keeps happening."

"I think it's cute."

"It's not cute, Chester." She hiccuped again, and he grinned, which caused her to smile back at him. "It's bothersome."

Chester laid his fork on the small plate in front of him, not even a crumb of cake left. "I have to go to the bathroom. Be right back."

She watched him walk through the living room and down the hallway. She held her breath, but when that didn't help, she stood up and began clearing the dishes from the table, hiccuping off and on. As she filled the sink with soapy warm water, she tried to focus on something other than her hiccups. Her wedding. She envisioned the scene for the hundredth time this week, and pictured herself and Chester promising to love each other for the rest of their lives.

After she slipped their dishes into the water, she returned to the table and carefully picked up the casserole dish with the leftover ham. Her father would eat it the next day for lunch. With great care, she covered the dish with foil. It had belonged to her grandmother and was her mother's favorite, oblong and white with three-inch sides, and a farm scene around the sides that had faded over the decades. Priscilla pulled the door of the refrigerator wide, bent down, and scanned inside for a place to store the dish.

"Boo!"

Chester's fingers poked her in the ribs, and the dish crashed to the floor. Priscilla stared at the broken dish as the sauce from the underground ham flowed slowly onto the wooden floorboards. She slowly raised her eyes to Chester's.

"Priscilla, I'm sorry." He squatted down and picked up the broken dish, which continued to drip as he lifted it. "I was trying to scare away your hiccups."

She put the broken dish on the counter and covered her face with her hands to hide her tears.

"Priscilla, I'm so, so sorry." Chester put his arms around her and pulled her close, but she jerked away.

"Everything is going wrong, Chester! Everything!" She swiped at her eyes and kept her head down.

Chester let out a heavy sigh. "I thought you were just looking in the refrigerator. I didn't see that you were holding the food."

She sniffled as she looked back up at him. "It's not just this. It's everything. If I didn't know better, I'd think God was sending us a message that we're just not meant to get married." When Chester's jaw dropped, she knew she shouldn't have voiced her thoughts. "I shouldn't have said that," she said as she reached out to him.

He backed away, his expression strained. "Maybe you're right."

"No, Chester. I love you." A tear slipped down her cheek as she realized that her hiccups were gone. "I'm sorry I said that." Her stomach knotted as she watched him take another step back.

"I love you, too, Priscilla. But maybe you're right. Everything is going wrong. I don't even have a job now. It's been one thing after the other, and . . ." He took a deep breath as he thrust his hands on his hips and stared at the floor. After what seemed like an eternity, he looked up at her, and his eyes softened like the sound of his voice. "I love you," he repeated.

She ran to him and threw her arms around his waist. "I love you, too, Chester. And no matter the challenges, I want to be your *frau*." She lifted her eyes to his. "The most important thing is our love for each other."

His lips met with hers, and Priscilla closed her eyes, melding into his arms and refusing to let pre-wedding stress come between them.

All the way home, Chester thought about Priscilla's fears, a mirror of his own. It was hard not to question if he and Priscilla were on the right path. But how could their love for each other be a mistake?

By the time he got home, his thoughts were resolved. No more fretting about the wedding, the house, or a job. God would provide in His own time. Right now, he wanted to get home before his folks and Abe returned from church, climb into bed, and take a rare nap—even if only for an hour. He hadn't slept much the night before, and by the time he kicked off his shoes and hit the bed, he fell fast asleep.

Less than thirty minutes later he opened his eyes and saw Abe standing at the end of his bed. He rubbed his eyes, then leaned up on his elbows. "How long have you been standing there?"

"Long enough." Abe shifted his weight and grinned. "I hope Priscilla can put up with your snoring." He nodded his head toward the door. "*Daed* wants you to come downstairs. He said he needs both of us to help him carry something in the barn."

Chester groaned as he swung his legs to the side of the bed. "It's Sunday. No work on Sunday." He ran a hand through his hair, blinking until he felt alert. Then he noticed an envelope in Abe's hand. "What's that?"

Abe pushed the envelope toward him. "Something from Rachel Zook."

Chester took it, smiling at the pink drawings all over the envelope. Rachel was a special girl.

"*Ach*, and she told me at least a hundred times to tell you not to open it until your wedding day." Abe grimaced as he rubbed at the edge of his cast with his good hand.

"Hurting, *bruder*?" Chester stood up and laid Rachel's gift on his nightstand.

Abe shrugged as he dropped his hand to his side. "A little. But it mostly just itches under the cast."

Chester grabbed his hat from the bedpost. "Well, let's get downstairs and help *Daed* with whatever project we shouldn't be doing on the Sabbath." He patted Abe on the shoulder as they left the room.

∽

Priscilla's eyes glassed over as she showed her mother the broken casserole dish. "I'm sorry, *Mamm*."

"It was an accident, *dochder*." Her mother cupped her face in her hands and smiled. "Don't be sad, *mei maedel*." She kissed her on the forehead, then opened the refrigerator and pulled out a pitcher of tea. As she poured them each a glass, she told Priscilla about church service, how the deacon announced their engagement, and how her father informed everyone about the date and time. She handed Priscilla a glass. "It might be wrong to be prideful, but today . . ." A smile lit her mother's face. "Your *daed* was a proud man as he announced your wedding. It was very touching."

They both sat down at the kitchen table.

"Hannah and Leroy weren't at worship today. We stopped by there on the way to church, and Hannah is just miserably huge, so I talked them into keeping her off her feet today." *Mamm* took a long drink of tea. "But your sister said there is no way she is missing your wedding."

Priscilla forced a smile, figuring that Hannah would probably go into labor right in the middle of the ceremony. "Where is everyone else?"

"Your father and Sarah Mae are outside in the barn, and Naomi's in the *daadi haus*." Sarah Mae skipped into the kitchen from outside, swinging Lizzie Lou at her side—wearing, of course, her new blue dress. Priscilla tried to calm her heartbeat as she thought about how she still had to finish sewing her new wedding dress.

"*Mamm*, I'm going to give Lizzie Lou a bath." Sarah Mae held up her rag doll with smudges of black underneath her hand-painted blue eyes. The days of faceless dolls were long gone, except for the tourists, and Sarah Mae's doll was handmade by a woman in town. A Christmas present last year.

"I think we better just give Lizzie Lou a sponge bath." *Mamm* walked to the counter and came back to the table with a damp kitchen towel. She dabbed underneath Lizzie Lou's eyes until Sarah Mae was happy and skipped back outside. A few moments later her mother snapped her fingers together. "*Ach*, I almost forgot to tell you. Rachel Zook talked to me after worship, and she told me over and over again to make sure you open the envelope she gave you on your wedding day, and not one day before." *Mamm* paused. "What did she give you?"

"I'm sure it's a picture. You know how Rachel is always drawing everyone pictures."

Mamm nodded. "She's such a sweetheart . . . and she looked so pretty today dressed in a new pink dress."

They were quiet for a few moments, but Priscilla couldn't hold it in any longer. "Today wasn't as *gut* a day as I'd hoped, *Mamm*." She ran her finger along the rim of her tea glass. "Chester lost his job."

"Honey, I'm so sorry." *Mamm*'s voice was soft and comforting. "But marriage will be filled with *gut* and bad days, to be sure." She shook her head and blinked her eyes a few times. "But wait a minute. Why did Chester lose his job?"

Priscilla felt her face flush. She knew Mr. Turner's accusation wasn't true, but she didn't even like to say the words out loud. "He said Chester stole two hundred dollars."

"Well, that's hogwash. We know Chester wouldn't do that." She shook her head. "Poor boy. I know it comes at a bad time."

"We've had a lot of bad timing lately." Priscilla searched her mother's eyes. "You don't think we're going against God's plan for us, do you? I mean, so many things keep going wrong, and—"

"Priscilla . . ." *Mamm* placed her hand on top of her daughter's. "I don't think that at all. Sometimes we can't understand the life lessons that God sets before us. But everything that happens puts His overall plan in motion." She gave Priscilla's hand a squeeze. "And it is normal to be nervous this close to your wedding."

"I'm not nervous about marrying Chester. I'm nervous about the fact that things keep going wrong."

"Focus on the love in your heart for Chester and your future together." *Mamm* eased her hand away and stood up. "And think about Sisters Day Thursday." She smiled before she left the room.

Priscilla stayed at the table for a while. She was excited about Sisters Day. Normally, it was a time for the women to get together for baking, quilting, canning, or another planned activity. It was always a fun day, but Priscilla suspected that there was something entirely different planned for this Sisters Day.

Something for her.

CHAPTER 7

Priscilla sat up front with her mother in the buggy while Naomi and Sarah Mae huddled together in the back. A cold front had blown in this week, and temperatures were low enough to require a jacket over their dresses, as opposed to the capes they had been wearing so far this fall. Priscilla rubbed her hands together, wishing she'd brought her gloves. But the chill in the air couldn't thwart her excitement about Sisters Day.

She knew what was coming, and she couldn't wait.

Please, dear Lord, I pray that everything goes well today. Please keep any worry from my heart. And . . . I pray I don't get the hiccups.

Anna Ruth Smoker was today's hostess, and although everyone who attended brought a dish, Anna Ruth always made extra desserts when the event was held at her house. Priscilla smiled as she counted the number of buggies parked out front.

The Smoker residence was beautiful inside and out. It was a new home built to resemble an old farmhouse, but every time Priscilla visited, she could still smell a hint of fresh paint, even though there was always a lingering aroma of freshly baked cookies in the air.

Her stomach tickled with butterflies as *Mamm* knocked on the door. Her heart raced as they stepped inside the roomy living room.

"Surprise!"

Priscilla threw her hands to her mouth and pretended to be surprised, the way all brides-to-be did when Sisters Day was transformed into a party before someone's wedding. Bridal showers like the *Englisch* have weren't part of the Old Order Amish ways, but instead someone hosted a Tupperware or Home Interior Party, and the hostess credit went to the bride-to-be so that she could pick out whatever she wanted for free. Priscilla had been to dozens of these parties over the years, dreaming of one day being the guest of honor. Everyone always bought lots of items to ensure a plentiful shopping spree for the bride. She was anxious to see what type of party they'd planned for her.

"Danki, danki," she said as she made her way through the crowd, which included Chester's mother, Irma. Mary Zook and her girls were there, too, including Rachel.

"Pre-Ceelia! Pre-Ceelia!" Rachel pushed her way to Priscilla and threw her arms around her. Once Rachel's mother finally coaxed Rachel to step aside, Priscilla saw Rose, all her friends, and . . . "Hannah!"

She walked briskly to her sister, who looked incredibly uncomfortable in a recliner in the corner. But a smile stretched across Hannah's face. "I wouldn't have missed this, Priscilla."

Priscilla leaned down and hugged her very pregnant sister, then glanced around the room, still anxious to see what type of party had been planned for her. *Yes! Tupperware!* She eyed the food containers and fancy gadgets lining a table against the wall in the living room.

"Let's go have a look." Her mother tucked her arm in Priscilla's, and together they walked to the table while the other women chatted amongst themselves. *Mamm* picked up a Whip 'N Prep, and Priscilla filled with excitement at the thought of owning the nonelectric appliance that could whip egg whites, creams, and all kinds of sauces.

"*Ach, Mamm.*" Priscilla accepted the item from her mother and inspected it. "I've always wanted one of these, ever since I saw Linda Petersheim get one at her party." She slowly placed it back on the table, knowing it was expensive.

"That's why I'm buying it for you." *Mamm* stood taller and grinned. "The *Englisch* don't have anything on us, my dear. That is a fine kitchen tool, and no electricity needed."

Priscilla smiled. "*Danki, Mamm.*"

Her mother nodded as they walked back to the living room, making sure they greeted everyone. Priscilla didn't notice the smell of fresh paint today, only the wonderful aromas of freshly baked goods. She couldn't wait to see what was in store for her in the kitchen, that her friends and family had prepared for this special day. For her.

Thank You, God.

Chester and his father sat on the back of the plow eating sandwiches Chester's mother had made that morning. Abe was in town getting supplies since he wasn't much help on the plow with his broken wrist. Chester was glad that the last of the harvest was in, and as he ate his ham and cheese sandwich, he hoped Priscilla was having a good time at her party. He was pretty sure she'd known about the event, but it would have been improper for her to have mentioned it, and Priscilla played by the rules. He knew that the mishaps lately were causing her grief.

Please, Lord, I pray that things go gut at Priscilla's party today.

"Chester, I'm planning to help you as much as I can with your *haus*, but . . ." His father ran his hand the length of his beard. "I just don't see how we are going to be able to finish everything in time for you to move in by mid-November as you and Priscilla were hoping. You might need to stay with her folks for a couple of months, at least."

Chester's heart sank, but he knew his father was right. There was just too much work to do. "*Ya*, I know."

They were quiet for a few moments.

His father stored his trash in the same black tin lunch box he'd been carting around for as long as Chester could remember. Chester stuffed his garbage in something a bit more modern, a small vinyl ice chest no bigger than his father's lunch box, but with a cooling block. He'd offered to buy his father one—Abe had one too. But *Daed* insisted his old box was just fine.

"You going to talk to Mr. Turner about getting your job back?" *Daed* tipped back the rim of his straw hat. "Just don't make no sense, him firing you like that."

Chester jumped off the plow. "He thinks I stole that money, *Daed*. I think that bothers me more than anything else." He turned to face his father. "How can he think I would do that?"

His father eased his way off the plow as he pulled his jacket snug around him. "I don't know, *sohn*. That's why I think you should go talk to him."

Chester thought about the hurtful words Mr. Turner spewed at him on the phone. "*That money was there! Now it's gone, and I know you took it! I don't want you back in my store. Ever! Do you understand me? I will mail you your final check . . . minus the two hundred dollars!"*

"I don't know, *Daed*."

They were quiet again as they readied the plow and mules to resume work.

"Guess you'll be going to meet Priscilla at the shanty tonight?" *Daed* grinned. It was the first time his father had openly admitted that he knew where Chester went on Tuesdays and Thursdays. "Soon enough, you'll have your own home."

Chester forced a smile, but he sure did wish things were different. He wasn't looking forward to living with Priscilla's family for longer than the two weeks they'd originally planned, plus he didn't have a job. It wasn't the way he wanted to start their married life.

Daed put his hands on his hips and scowled. "Did you know your *bruder* got a cell phone?"

Chester twisted his mouth to one side. "*Ya*. I'm not sure exactly how long he's had it."

"He knows we don't like that." *Daed* shook his head as he stepped onto the plow. "I would say he came to his senses and decided to get rid of it because it's just not our way, but . . ." *Daed* grinned. "He found out what it was going to cost him every month. I overheard him tell Linda that he was getting rid of it." His father chuckled. "But turns out it ain't cheap to get rid of those things either. Something about a cancellation fee."

Chester smiled. Abe was always the first one to be interested in a new gadget, but he didn't like to spend his hard-earned cash unless he had to. Abe only worked about fifteen hours per week in Bird-in-Hand behind the counter at an Amish-owned deli.

"I know that the temptations of the outside world are many. And I know that more and more folks are putting phones in their barns and even carrying mobile ones." *Daed* shook his head. "But if we're not careful, we'll become just like the *Englisch*— never a peaceful moment."

Chester nodded. Almost everyone they knew had a phone in the barn, some with ringers in the house. And even though Bishop Ebersol frowned on cell phones, lots of folks in the district had them. He and Priscilla had talked about the convenience of having a phone in the barn, but in the end they decided they wanted their *kinner* to experience Old Order life as it should be: detachment from the rest of the world. Chester knew that times were changing and more and more of their people were converting to the ways of the *Englisch*, but even if just for a while, he and Priscilla wanted to share the same phone shanty with their folks, the Dienners, and Petersheims. The same phone shanty that they'd shared for so many Tuesday and Thursday evenings.

He smiled as he thought about holding Priscilla in his arms tonight.

Priscilla left Sisters Day elated. There was so much going on that she didn't have time to worry about everything that had been going wrong lately. Her friends and family had spent lavishly on Tupperware items for their own homes, increasing the hostess credits. Priscilla used her gift credits to purchase a vast assortment of kitchen utensils, tools, and containers, although her mother had insisted on buying the Whip 'N Prep.

She spent the afternoon working on her wedding dress,

which was coming along nicely, and she was pretty sure she could finish it this week. With the wedding only two and a half weeks away, she'd be busy with final preparations. For the first time in days, her heart was free of worry, and she silently thanked God for the many blessings in her life.

After supper and cleanup, she pulled her black coat on and topped her prayer covering with her black bonnet to protect her ears from the early evening winds.

She ran across the field, anxious to tell Chester about her day. Blue-gray skies with only a hint of orange signified that the day's end was near. She could see Chester waiting for her in the distance.

"I take it you had a *gut* day," he said as she flung herself into his arms.

"*Ya*, I did. It was *wunderbaar!*" She eased away from him, feeling light and peaceful. "Sisters Day was my bridal party, and I got so many wonderful things for our new home. I can't wait to be your *frau*, Chester, and I refuse to let worry fill my heart. Our wedding will be beautiful. We will get the *haus* done, and you will find a new job." She exhaled a long sigh. "Everything will work out according to God's plan."

She stepped back from him, met his eyes, and smiled. "So! No more fretting!" She'd let no shadows cross her heart today.

Her husband-to-be smiled down at her, and she could see joy and approval in his blue eyes.

"*Gut.* I'm glad to hear that you will let go of worry. And you're right. Everything is according to His plan. We'll be fine."

Chester leaned down, and as the cool wind breezed against her cheeks, his kiss warmed her all over. She kissed him back, ready to be Mrs. Chester Lapp.

Then the phone rang.

CHAPTER 8

Chester wasn't sure he'd ever seen a person transform so suddenly. As the phone in the shanty rang over and over again, Priscilla's face had changed to something—frightening.

"Chester Lapp, don't you *dare* answer that phone. Don't pick it up! Pretend it's not ringing." She squeezed her eyes closed and pinched her lips together.

Chester gently took her by both shoulders until she opened her eyes. She glared at the ringing phone as if it were evil. "Priscilla . . . what is wrong with you?"

She let out a heavy sigh. "Every time that phone rings, there's a problem." She cut her eyes at him, and he tried not to grin. "Don't answer it, Chester."

"Okay, okay," he finally said, holding his palms up. "I won't answer it. But I think you're being a little crazy. It could be for someone else."

"Or it could be someone calling to tell us something else is wrong with the house! Or some other catastrophe relating to our wedding." She hiccuped. "Oh no! Oh no!"

She slapped her hand over her mouth so hard that Chester was sure it must have stung.

"See! This is what happens! Bad news and hiccups always go together!" She took two steps back. "I have to go."

Chester glanced back and forth between his somewhat *ab im kopp* fiancée and the phone. "Listen." He held up one finger. "It isn't ringing anymore. You don't have to go."

"*Ach! Ya*, I do!"

She hiccuped again, and Chester couldn't keep from grinning.

"This is not funny, Chester. I have to go before something happens to mess up this day." She turned and ran, but looked over her shoulder. "I love you!"

Still grinning, he watched her run across the field. "I love you, too, Priscilla!"

She didn't turn around, but waved a hand in the air.

Life with his Priscilla would never be boring.

Priscilla bolted up the porch steps, ran through the living room, and hit the stairs two at a time. She bumped into her mother on the way up.

"Priscilla, what are you in such a hurry for? Come back downstairs. I have some things to talk to you about, things about the wedding, the food, and—"

"No! Not today. I can't, *Mamm*. We'll talk tomorrow."

"But, Priscilla—"

She slammed her bedroom door and didn't hear the rest of what her mother said. Flinging her bonnet and jacket on her bed, she placed both hands on her chest and took a deep breath. The hiccups were gone.

She sat down on the edge of the bed and thought about

how ridiculous—and childlike—Chester must have thought her behavior. The bedroom door flew open.

"Priscilla Marie King . . ." *Mamm* stood in the doorway with her hands on her hips. "What in the world is wrong with you?"

Priscilla cringed, knowing she shouldn't have been so snappy with her mother . . . or slammed the door. "Sorry, *Mamm*."

"I thought you'd be excited to hear what I have to say about plans for your wedding." She dropped her hands to her side. "Not rush to your room and slam the door."

"Sorry." She hung her head for a moment, but then superstition flooded over her. Even though she didn't have the hiccups anymore, she was still afraid to ruin this day. "Can we talk about it tomorrow?"

"What's wrong with right now?" *Mamm* edged closer to the bed and scowled. "This isn't like you, Priscilla."

"It's been such a nice day, and I don't want anything to spoil it, and . . ." She glanced at her mother for only a moment before she hung her head again. "Every time I get the hiccups something goes wrong. Something to do with the wedding." She looked up. "I know it sounds silly, but I just don't want to talk about anything to do with the wedding."

Her mother just stared at her for a moment. "You don't really believe that, do you? Silly superstitions, that's all."

"I guess not." She silently prayed that if she was lying, God would forgive her.

Mamm jumped up and clapped her hands together. "Well, my news was not bad news, but it can wait until tomorrow. And tomorrow, young lady, you and I are going to take a little trip to town."

"For what?"

"You'll see. The public library opens at ten o'clock. So plan to leave here around nine."

Priscilla stood up. "Why are we going to the library?"

"Because I suspect I know what is causing your hiccups, and I want to see if I'm right. And it might help you."

Friday morning *Mamm* parked the buggy in front of the Pequea Valley Library in Intercourse. After she tied the horse to the hitching post, they walked briskly to the building, their heads tucked to avoid the nip in the air. On the way to the library, Priscilla's mother had given her the wedding updates she'd tried to give her the night before—mostly about the food and the cake Naomi was planning to make, very close to the one her aunt would have baked.

"We're looking for a book about hiccups," *Mamm* said to a library clerk when they entered the large room filled with rows and rows of bookshelves.

"Okay . . ." The young woman, about Priscilla's age, motioned with her hand for them to follow, but then stopped. "What exactly are you looking for?"

Mamm stood taller and repeated herself. "A book about hiccups."

"Like how to get rid of them?" The woman's mouth tipped up at one corner, and Priscilla was embarrassed. But *Mamm* was undeterred.

"No. What causes them."

"Oh. Okay. Follow me to the computers. I'll see what I can find."

"Thank you." *Mamm* smiled, and she and Priscilla followed the woman to a row of computers on the far wall. After a few minutes, they were given the names of three books.

"That's a general health book." The librarian pointed to the second book on the list. "That's probably the best one. I'll show you where to find it."

Once *Mamm* had the book in her hand, she thanked the woman and walked to a long table and sat down. Priscilla sat next to her and folded her arms. This was a waste of time.

"*Mamm*, everyone gets the hiccups. I don't know why we're doing this."

Her mother didn't look up as she flipped a page. "But not everyone believes that their hiccups are a warning of something bad to happen." She glanced at Priscilla and narrowed her eyebrows. "I don't think God would like that."

Priscilla sighed. "I'm not trying to make God mad. It just seems like more than a coincidence that—"

"There are no coincidences in life, Priscilla." *Mamm* glared at her for a moment. "Everything is His will. You know that."

She knew her mother was right, and there was no point in arguing, so she sat quietly while her mother flipped through the pages. She glanced around the room at the few patrons whose heads were buried in a book. Occasionally, one of the *Englisch* would nod in her direction and whisper to someone, but overall folks in Lancaster County were used to seeing Plain People.

Mamm tapped her finger to one of the pages in the book. "Here you go. Read this." She slid the hardcover book in front of Priscilla. She scanned the page, but followed her mother's finger when she leaned over. "Right here. Read."

Priscilla leaned her face closer to the page. *The most common triggers for short-term hiccups are: eating too much, drinking carbonated beverages, excessive consumption of alcohol, sudden temperature change, worry or emotional stress.*

Mamm started talking before Priscilla could process the information. "You eat like a bird, so that's not it. You don't drink sodas or alcohol, so rule that out. And there's been no sudden change in temperature. So! There you have it." *Mamm* slammed a pointed finger down on the page. "Stop *worrying*, and your hiccups will go away." She stood up. "Ready to go home?"

Priscilla sat in the chair and stared up at her mother. "That's it? Just stop worrying, and no more hiccups?" It couldn't be that easy.

Mamm frowned as she slid back into her chair. "Priscilla, worry is a sin, and it blocks the voice of God."

"So He's punishing me by giving me the hiccups." She regretted her sarcastic tone and knew right away from the scowl on her mother's face that she didn't appreciate it.

"You know that's not true. But you have worried about this wedding of yours since you were a little girl. Do you remember the large weddings your dolls used to have? You would place them in their proper positions all over your bedroom. Then you would go through the ceremony. And you've always had the perfect plan for your own wedding."

Priscilla smiled as she remembered.

"But, Priscilla, only God's plan is perfect. So worrying about what might or might not go wrong before, during, or after this wedding is doing you no good. Everything is in His hands." She squeezed Priscilla's hand. "Do you love Chester and want to be with him the rest of your life?"

"Of course."

"Then stop worrying. Not only will your hiccups stop, but you will hear God's plan for you more clearly. Just follow Him, Priscilla." *Mamm* stood up smiling, as if she had conquered the evils of the world. "Now, let's go."

Priscilla, still skeptical, followed her mother out of the library. *God, is she right? Is worry troubling my heart and keeping me from trusting Your will?*

CHAPTER 9

Priscilla sat at the kitchen table as her mother paced in the kitchen. She was still seeing Chester at the phone shanty on Tuesdays and Thursdays, but they'd only spent a short amount of time together. Chester looked exhausted each time, but insisted he was fine. She knew he was still upset about losing his job and frustrated by the slow progress of their house.

"Naomi has everything ready to make your cake on Monday." *Mamm* read from a list and checked as she went along.

"Where is Naomi? She seems to go missing a lot."

Mamm tapped her finger to her chin. "Zeke Lapp was here the other day. I didn't think too much about it, but now it wonders me if maybe they haven't taken a fancy to each other. But now, of course, he's back in Middlefield looking after his *daed*. You know his father cut his leg while chopping wood."

"*Ya*, Chester was disappointed that Zeke had to leave, so he's planning to ask his friend John to fill in as an attendant."

Mamm was back to her list. "And everyone knows their duties as far as the food preparation. It will be a busy day on Monday with everyone coming here to get things ready. The extra propane ovens will be delivered on Monday also." *Check.*

"Your father and several other men are finishing up the temporary structure next to the house for the reception." *Check.*

Priscilla nodded. Her family had a large farmhouse with an especially big living room to host the service, but like most Amish homes, theirs wasn't nearly large enough to accommodate almost four hundred guests. So her father, cousins, and friends of the family had built a framed structure right next to the house, and today they would cover the top and the sides with heavy blue plastic to keep it warm for guests. Additional tables and benches would be set up underneath. It was a common practice in their district, and Priscilla was glad to see that the temporary shelter hadn't blown away. She shook her head to clear the negative thought as her mother went on.

"You said you finished your wedding dress, *ya*?"

Priscilla nodded.

"And Naomi and Rose have both tried on their dresses?"

"Naomi has. Rose is coming over this afternoon to pick hers up."

"Make sure she tries it on."

"I will." Priscilla fidgeted with the ties on her prayer covering. She was thankful that she hadn't had a case of the hiccups since their trip to the library, but things still weren't coming together as she'd hoped. Chester said there was no way the house would be finished in time for them to move in two weeks after the wedding. She'd cringed when he told her it could be a couple of months, or longer. She knew that many newly married couples spent the first few months with the bride's parents, but Chester had built them a lovely new home, and she was anxious to begin their life together in their own house.

Chester, his father, and even Abe with his broken wrist had been working late into the night on the new home. But Chester said to be prepared for an extended stay with her parents. Another thing that wasn't in her plan.

She took a deep breath. *God, I know that everything is in Your hands, and I will not question You.* It was a prayer she had repeated daily, but she sometimes still felt disappointed. But she figured disappointment was better than worry. Worry had gotten her nowhere, it was a sin, and she knew her mother was right—it blocked the voice of God. She was resolved in knowing that her wedding and her life were in God's hands.

"Your father, Chester, and Abe will oversee the group arranging the benches, tables, and chairs." *Mamm* walked into their large living room, then returned to the kitchen. "Naomi, Rose, and I will make sure the *eck* is positioned correctly for you, Chester, and your attendants."

Members of the church district would spend most of the day on Monday cooking, getting things ready, and also show up at six o'clock the morning of the wedding to help.

"Oh. I also wanted to ask you if you want *Aenti* Mary Katherine to bake her special red velvet whoopee pies? I know Naomi will be making a special cake, and there will be lots of other cakes and desserts, but . . ."

"Everyone loves *Aenti* Mary Katherine's whoopee pies. I think that would be *gut*."

"Great. Let's see . . ." *Mamm* tapped her pen to the pad, but they both looked up when they heard a buggy coming up the driveway. Priscilla walked to the kitchen window and peered outside.

"It's Rose." Priscilla pulled the wooden door open and watched through the screen as Rose walked across the grass— clawing at her arms with both hands. She pushed the screen open and stepped aside so that Rose could come in.

"Why are you scratching yourself like that?" Priscilla cringed as she watched her friend rubbing both arms atop her green dress.

Rose shook her head as she continued to scratch. "I've got this horrible rash all over my arms." She lifted one sleeve of her dress to show Priscilla the red bumps covering her arm from the elbow down. "It's on both arms."

Mamm walked over. "How did you get this, Rose?" She eased Rose's sleeve up farther and inspected.

"It's a long story, but let's just say that a bouquet of flowers unexpectedly had some poison ivy in it."

"Are you putting anything on it?" *Mamm* asked as she lowered Rose's sleeve.

"*Ya. Mamm* got me something at the drugstore." She pinched her eyes together as she began to claw at her arms again.

"Wait right here, Rose." *Mamm* turned to leave the room, but glanced over her shoulder. "I have something that will help."

"I have been itching all morning." Rose's face twisted into a deep frown.

Priscilla watched as Rose scratched, and a minute later both turned as Priscilla's mother came back into the room.

"This is from the natural doctor, a blend of herbs and ointment." She handed Rose a small plastic container. "Take this with you. Sarah Mae wandered into some poison ivy last year. This helped her a lot."

Priscilla remembered how miserable her sister had been. "How long will the itching last?"

"I don't know." Rose lifted her sleeve again. "See how bad it looks." She shook her head.

Mamm patted Rose on the shoulder. "I'm so sorry, Rose. I

hope it's better by the wedding so you can enjoy yourself." She smiled. "Use the salve. It should help."

After her mother excused herself, Priscilla went to get Rose's dress. She returned a minute later and handed it to her friend. "*Mamm* said you should try it on."

Rose scratched at her arms. "I'm sure it's fine, Priscilla. Do you mind if I don't try it on right now? I am itching so much, and I want to go home and try this ointment."

Priscilla shrugged. "Sure. I understand." *It probably won't fit because that just seems to be how things are going.* She struggled to push the negative thought out of her mind.

After Rose left, Priscilla pulled a loaf of bread from the oven, then tinkered about the kitchen. She put two glasses in the sink, wiped down the counter, and thought about what the next few weeks would be like.

As was traditional, she and Chester would help with cleanup the next morning, and it was always the new bride and groom's duty to wash all the clothes and linens. Her mother had laughed and said it was usually the only time an Amish man would do the laundry during his lifetime.

She turned around when the screen door in the kitchen slammed and Naomi entered. Her sister walked straight to the refrigerator and pulled out a pitcher of tea. She poured herself a glass and sat down at the table with a sigh.

"Too bad Zeke had to go back to Middlefield," Priscilla said. "Have you heard from him?"

Naomi took a drink. "Why would I have heard from him?"

"Oh, I just thought you might have." She grinned at her sister.

"I'm not going to talk to you about this, Priscilla." Naomi hurried toward the living room, but there was a new bounce in her sister's step. Priscilla smiled. Naomi had been playing match-maker for everyone else for as long as Priscilla could remember. She hoped that Naomi had found someone special.

Friday evening Chester was tired after working on the house all day. He'd spent the early morning hours looking for a new job in town, but he wasn't having much luck. He didn't know how to explain to potential employers that he was fired for stealing money, so he just didn't mention working for Mr. Turner, which left him with little work experience to take under consideration, other than farming.

He'd just pulled his suspenders off his shoulders when Abe walked into his bedroom. He quickly asked his brother if he was done in the bathroom. A hot shower was going to feel mighty good.

"*Ya*, I'm done." Abe ran a comb through his wet hair. "*Mamm* wanted me to remind you to put your marriage license in a place where you won't forget it on Tuesday." He shrugged. "I guess you could give it to me."

Chester stood perfectly still as he scanned his bedroom. *Where did I put it?* He and Priscilla had gotten their marriage license almost two months ago. He pulled open the drawer of his nightstand and rummaged through some papers, then quickly moved to the top drawer of his chest.

"You lose your license, *bruder*?" Abe chuckled, but stopped right away when Chester glared at him.

"It's here somewhere." He yanked open the second drawer, pretty sure he didn't store it where he kept his underwear. Closing it, he turned to face Abe. He could feel the color draining from his face. "Priscilla will have my hide if I've lost our marriage license." He shook his head. "I know it's here somewhere."

"It wonders me if *Mamm* won't have your hide too." Abe grinned as he backed out of the room and shut the door.

Chester sat down on the bed and scratched his forehead. *Think, think. Where did I put it?* He looked around his small room again and spotted Rachel's envelope atop his nightstand. He'd managed to keep track of a picture from Rachel, yet he'd lost the one document necessary for him to marry Priscilla in four days.

God, why is everything going wrong? He knew how important it was for Priscilla to have everything in order. It was just part of who she was, and this wedding was definitely an event that she wanted to run smoothly. He might not have questioned whether or not they were on the right path if she hadn't, but with so much opposition . . .

He let out a heavy sigh, knowing that he loved Priscilla with all his heart. She was everything he'd ever wanted in a wife and mother, and they balanced each other, with her necessity to have things organized while Chester so often focused on the moment to moment. And sometimes Chester was able to push back a little and let Priscilla know that the world would not come crashing down if everything didn't run smoothly all the time. He knew that Priscilla trusted God's plan for their lives, as he did.

There'd been the problems with the house, her wedding dress disaster, change of plans for the cake, Chester losing his job, and now this. What else could possibly go wrong?

CHAPTER 10

Priscilla tried to stay focused on church service this brisk Sunday morning, but her mind kept drifting. They were gathered in the Petersheims' barn because Elizabeth and Elam's house was small and couldn't accommodate over a hundred people. Priscilla wasn't sure how it housed Elizabeth, Elam, and their five children.

This would be her last time to attend church as a single woman, and tonight would be her last time to attend a Sunday singing with Chester. Soon they'd start their own family, and someday their teenagers would gather on Sunday evenings.

She glanced around the barn. As usual, the women were sitting on long wooden benches facing the men on the other side, and the bishop and deacons were in the middle. Priscilla smiled at Chester, and he returned the smile—sort of. Priscilla sensed by his expression that something was wrong. She hadn't had time to talk to him before the service, but after lunch she'd see if something was bothering him.

Naomi sat next to *Mamm*. Priscilla was disappointed that Zeke had been called back to Middlefield to tend to his *daed*, but she certainly understood. She had hoped Naomi the matchmaker might have found a match of her own. Rose sat two rows in front of Priscilla. She felt sorry for her friend, who scratched her arms through most of the service, but despite her poison ivy, Priscilla caught her and Luke exchanging smiles.

She stifled a yawn and refocused on the service . . . though visions of her wedding in four days challenged her attention span, and within a few minutes her mind trailed. Chances were good that things were not going to go as she'd planned. She tried to recall when she'd become such a perfectionist, needing things to run smoothly all the time. Yes, she'd always dreamed that her wedding day would be special, but it was more than that, and Priscilla knew it. She thought back to what Naomi had said to her.

When there was order in her life, she felt like she was on the right path, God's path. When things fell apart, she questioned her actions, inactions, and everything that did or didn't happen to cause the upheaval. As she pondered her past up to now, Bishop Ebersol's voice suddenly boomed, and her eyes rounded as she held on to his words.

"To question the Lord's will is to not believe in His perfect plan."

Priscilla locked eyes with the bishop, then hung her head, knowing that his words were the essence of everything she'd been taught her entire life. *Why haven't I been living by that?* Her perfection was not God's perfection. She closed her eyes.

I'm sorry.

Chester helped the men rearrange the benches and set up tables after the church service ended. It was chilly in the barn despite the propane heaters placed throughout, but Chester's forehead dripped with sweat. How was he going to tell Priscilla that he couldn't find their marriage license? There was a three-day waiting period in Pennsylvania, so even if they went tomorrow to get a new one, there was no way they could get married the following day.

He helped Abe set out some additional folding chairs in preparation for the meal, although he didn't have much appetite.

"You find your license?" Abe grinned, and Chester felt his blood start to boil. He reminded himself that smacking Abe went against their ways.

"No. I didn't." He shoved the last of the chairs up against the table. But when he turned back toward his brother, Abe wasn't smiling.

"Seriously? You didn't find it?" Abe stroked his clean-shaven chin as his eyebrows drew inward.

"No."

"What are you going to do? The wedding is in two days, and that ain't long enough to go get another one."

"I don't know, Abe!"

"No need to holler, *bruder*." Abe put a hand on Chester's shoulder as he glanced around the barn at the other men. "I'll help you look some more tonight."

Chester lowered his head, rubbing his forehead. "I don't know where else *to* look."

"Will you tell Priscilla?" Abe lowered his hand and sighed. "Maybe you should wait."

"I've looked everywhere, Abe. It just isn't there. I'm going to have to tell her." He dropped his chin. "So much has already gone wrong, and now this." He looked up at Abe. "We can't even get married without that license, and everyone is already coming on Tuesday, tomorrow everyone will prepare the food, and . . ." He stopped when he caught movement out of the corner of his eye. *Priscilla.* She eased her way through all the men setting up tables and benches.

"How's my favorite husband-to-be?"

Abe made a dash for the barn door. "See you later."

"They're getting ready to bring out the food, so I was sent to make sure the tables were ready."

Chester looked around. "I think so." He forced a smile and wondered how he was going to tell Priscilla that the wedding would have to be postponed.

Fifteen minutes later he was seated next to Abe and his father, picking at his food while Priscilla and the other women scurried about, making sure everyone was taken care of.

After the meal, he had the perfect opportunity to tell her. They were standing off to the side of the house, but when Priscilla started detailing the plans for Tuesday, he just didn't have the heart to interrupt. She seemed to have made some sort of peace with the fact that so much had gone wrong.

"It's God's will for us to be challenged," she said. "But I love you so much, Chester. I can't wait to be your *frau.*"

Now as he rode alongside Abe in the buggy on the way home, he knew that he would have to tell her the truth tonight at the singing. It would only make things worse if he kept putting it off.

Priscilla bathed herself in lavender bubble bath that she and her mother had made recently, and the sweet smell reminded her of spring. By then, she would be Mrs. Chester Lapp.

As she towel-dried her hair, she thought again about how this would be her last official Sunday singing. Lots of older folks still attended from time to time, but mainly it was the younger people, those who were of dating age.

She'd prayed hard about the challenges that she and Chester had faced as the wedding drew closer, but she hadn't had any more hiccups, and she was doing her best not to worry. She'd felt much more open and able to hear God's guidance. Nothing was going to stop her from becoming Chester's *frau*.

After she dressed, she gathered up the Sunday vest and pants she'd made for him. If anything had gone right along the way toward the wedding, it was the clothes she made for Chester. Each seam was lovingly sewn and straight, and she couldn't wait to give them to him.

"I'm going, *Mamm*," she said when she walked into the living room downstairs. She reached for her heavy black coat on the rack, then pulled her arms through the sleeves. "I saw Chester pulling in from my window."

"Enjoy yourself." Her father looked above his gold-rimmed glasses and smiled. Her mother got up from the couch and gave Priscilla a hug.

"*Ya*, have fun, dear." She kissed Priscilla on the cheek. "Sarah Mae is with Naomi at the *daadi haus*, so your father and I are going to enjoy this nice fire and some quiet time."

Priscilla smiled. Her parents were still so much in love. "I won't be too late." She pulled on her black bonnet and headed outside, glad that the Petersheims' house was close by. Close enough to walk if it hadn't been so cold.

"You look beautiful," Chester said when she climbed into the buggy.

"*Danki.*" She handed him the vest and pants. "They're not wrapped, but I couldn't wait to give them to you." She grinned. "I hope they fit." She'd asked Abe about sizes, so hopefully he'd given her the right measurements.

Chester ran his hand gingerly over the vest, then the pants. "I'm sure they'll fit perfectly," he said, but just like this morning, she sensed something was wrong. He clicked his tongue, and they started toward the Petersheims'.

When they arrived at the singing a few minutes later, Chester leaned down and kissed her as soon as they were out of the buggy. "I love you."

"I love you too." She gazed into his eyes. "Chester, is everything okay?"

"*Ya.* Why?"

"I don't know." She shrugged. "You just seem . . . like . . ." She reminded herself not to fret. "Never mind. Let's go into the *haus.* Looks like lots of folks are here." She squeezed his hand as they made their way up to the front porch. "Our last Sunday singing before we're married."

Chester smiled, but Priscilla's stomach was beginning to churn. *I trust God's will. I will not worry . . .*

Chester stayed by Priscilla's side, smiling when it was required amidst the talk of their upcoming wedding, but for the most part he kept quiet. How was he going to tell Priscilla that her special day was not going to happen? At least not this Tuesday. He took a deep breath as he listened to his fiancée describe the cake her sister was planning to make the following day.

"*Ach*, Rose. Wait until you see it. Naomi makes such beautiful cakes." Priscilla's smile was radiant, and Chester didn't think he'd ever seen her look so happy. Rose didn't look quite as happy as she scratched her arms continuously. He'd heard about her run-in with some poison ivy.

There was a plentiful spread of food on the table in the Petersheims' kitchen. Under different circumstances, Chester wouldn't have been able to stay away from the many snack trays and desserts, but his stomach churned with anticipation. And dread.

About an hour into the singing, he couldn't take all the wedding talk anymore.

"Priscilla, I need to talk to you." He gently coaxed her away from Rose and whispered, "Privately."

Her face registered the appropriate amount of concern. *If she only knew.*

"What's wrong?"

"Can we please go? I really need to talk to you." He edged through the crowd in the kitchen.

"Chester, you're scaring me." Priscilla blinked her eyes several times.

Please don't start crying.

He brushed past Lena Petersheim and gave her a quick thank-you for hosting the singing.

"See you on Tuesday," she responded with a wink.

Chester hurried out the door and down the porch steps toward his buggy. He could hear Priscilla calling behind him. Once he got to his buggy, he opened the passenger door for her to get in. Even in the moonlight, he could see her beautiful blue eyes filling with tears. *I'm so sorry, Priscilla.*

"Chester?" Her eyes were wide and glassy as she stared up at him. "Please tell me what's wrong."

He gently grasped her shoulders. "Everything is going to be fine, Priscilla. Here, just get in, warm yourself with the heater, and we'll go talk."

She sniffled a bit, but climbed inside the buggy. He waited until they were on the road before he said anything.

"I'm going to pull over up here off the main road."

Priscilla was quiet as he edged off of Blacksmith Road and onto an unmarked dirt road that he knew was a dead end. An almost full moon lit the area around them, and he twisted in his seat to face her. He reached for her trembling hand.

"Are you cold?"

She shook her head. "Just concerned. What's going on, Chester?" She blinked her eyes a few times, and her lip trembled.

"I'm so sorry for what I'm about to tell you." He pulled his eyes from hers and hung his head. "We can't get married on Tuesday."

She jerked her hand out of his grasp. "What? Why?" Her voice shook as she spoke. "It's because everything is going wrong, isn't it? God must not want us to get married!" Her voice rose an octave as a tear slipped down her cheek. "I've tried not to worry." *Hiccup.* "Oh no! I should have known . . ."

"Priscilla—"

"Stop!" She held up one palm toward him. "I know what you're going to say. You love me, but there is just too much going against us. We're not on the right path." She lowered her face into her hands and sobbed.

"Priscilla, that's not what—" He reached for her, but she pulled back.

"All my life, I've needed everything perfect, even though

we're taught to trust His will when things don't go as we've planned. Just when I realized that everything happens on God's time frame and in His way, you"—her voice grew angry as she swung her hand in his direction—"decide the challenges are too much for you." She shook her head, crying hard. "It just wasn't meant to be."

"Maybe not." He regretted the words the moment they hastily slipped from his tongue, but it hurt him that Priscilla would feel this way. Yes, they'd had obstacles, but he never thought that it was enough for her to not want to marry him.

"Take me home." Her body shook as she cried.

"Priscilla, wait. You're not understanding me. I'm trying to tell you that we can't get married on *Tuesday*. That doesn't mean that I don't want to marry you."

She sniffled. "What?"

Chester reached for her hand again, and this time she didn't pull away. "I love you, Priscilla. I want to marry you more than anything." He took a deep breath. "But I've lost our marriage license. I can't find it anywhere." He shook his head as he talked. "I'm so sorry. We don't have time to get another one by Tuesday."

Priscilla stared at him with her mouth hung open. "That's it?"

"That's enough, isn't it? We'll have to postpone the wedding, and I'm not sure how we're going to let everyone know, and I can't believe I've blundered so badly."

"Chester." Priscilla's voice was firm as she said his name. Her brows rose, and a slight grin formed at the corner of her mouth. "*You* never had the marriage license. I have it safely put away at my house."

He didn't move as Priscilla's comment soaked in. *How could*

I have forgotten that? He thought back to their trip to the courthouse to get the license. "You put it in your purse that day, didn't you?" He slapped his forehead with his hand as she nodded. "I can't believe I didn't remember that until now."

Relief washed over him. About the marriage license, anyway.

They'd said some hurtful things to each other. Was Priscilla really just about to give up on them?

CHAPTER 11

Priscilla sat quietly as they rode to her house. Her heart was heavy. She'd reacted much too quickly and said things she didn't mean—once again forgoing what she knew to be true and falling back to her old ways. Chester was the man she wanted to marry, and that was much more important than the challenges they'd faced up to this point. But he was quiet. Too quiet.

When he stopped the buggy, she turned to face him. "I'm sorry."

"Me too."

"Do you still want to marry me, Chester?" She fought back tears.

"Do you still want to marry me?"

That was not the answer she'd hoped for. She quickly swiped at a tear that rolled down her cheek. "Of course."

"I want to marry you, too, Priscilla. There's just been . . ."

She braced herself and didn't breathe as she waited for him to go on. When he didn't, she finished his sentence. "There have just been a lot of things going wrong."

"*Ya.*"

Chester pulled to a stop, got out of the buggy, and walked

around to where Priscilla was standing. He leaned down and kissed her, but despite his words earlier, his lips betrayed him. She could feel it in his touch. Something had changed. He was having doubts.

"I love you." She wrapped her arms around his waist.

"I love you too."

She pulled back and stared into his eyes for a long while. "See you Tuesday?"

He smiled a little. *"Ya."*

Priscilla walked across the yard to the house, turning back twice to look at Chester and wondering if he would actually show up.

Monday morning Priscilla watched as Naomi put the yellow candied roses on the cake she was making. Within the hour, their house would be bustling with church members who would set up for the wedding tomorrow.

"It's beautiful." She sat down at the kitchen table across from her sister.

Naomi adjusted the tiny roses along the edge of the cake and looked up. "What's bothering you? For someone who is getting married tomorrow, you seem down in the dumps."

Priscilla shrugged. "I don't know. I guess it's because Chester and I had harsh words last night." She took in a deep breath and looked up at the ceiling for a moment, then blew it out. "I mean, I think everything is fine, but . . ." She touched the corner of the cake and pulled back a tiny dab of cream cheese and pineapple icing.

Naomi slapped her hand. "Priscilla, that is something I would expect of Sarah Mae. Stop that." She grinned and went back to work. "Now tell me . . . but what?"

She tried to organize her thoughts. "We've had so much go wrong. You don't think it's God's way of telling us not to get married, do you?"

Naomi didn't look up. "What do you think?"

"Don't do that, Naomi." Priscilla gently tapped the table with her hand. "I want to know what *you* think."

Naomi stopped what she was doing and walked around to sit down beside her. "Here's what I think." She put her hand on top of Priscilla's. "Life is not perfect. And sometimes in your world, Priscilla, you need things to go exactly as you've planned, even though you know it is our belief that life should not be easy. But you forget . . . we are here living God's plan. Sometimes things might seem like they are falling apart or going wrong because God has something better planned for us around the corner." She tipped her head and smiled. "Life is a learning journey, Priscilla. But sometimes I think you forget the lessons being taught."

Priscilla knew that Naomi was right. *Please, God. Let me trust Your plan for my life.* She knew that it was just a wedding and that the meaning behind the event was far more important than the affair itself. She hoped Chester could forgive her outburst, and she hoped that God would calm her heart as she fought the fear that Chester was now having doubts about their future.

Chester had a surprise for Priscilla, even though he wouldn't be able to tell her until two weeks after they were married. But even though he was excited about it, worry threatened to weigh him down. He loved Priscilla more than anything in the world, and her desire to have things organized and orderly was one of the things that drew him to her. But if the past month was any indication of how their wedding might go tomorrow, he worried that she would be disappointed. He'd prayed long and hard last night after he dropped her off at home, and through communion with God, he asked the Lord to fill his heart with faith. Surely love was the right path, even if it was paved with challenges. And today, Priscilla seemed to be working things out in her heart and mind. The day before they'd both reacted out of fear and worry, both emotions that they knew kept God's wisdom just out of reach. He hadn't been able to talk to her much with so many people around getting things ready, but she had smiled most of the day. And things were looking up in other areas too. Zeke had made it back from Middlefield tonight, saying his father was doing better. Even though John had been ready to step in as an attendant, Chester was glad that his cousin was back.

Chester finished towel-drying his hair, tossed the towel into the hamper, and sat on the bed. He noticed Rachel's envelope on the nightstand. As he picked it up and ran his finger along the seam, he remembered how he promised Rachel that he wouldn't open it until the day of his wedding. Smiling, he put it back down, then fluffed his pillows and got comfortable in bed. A subtle breeze blew through the opened window, enough for him to crawl underneath the covers. He slept so well when the nights were brisk. He wondered if Priscilla liked to sleep with the window cracked this time of year.

He snuffed out the lantern, pulled the covers up to his neck, and stared at the ceiling. A glimmer of moonlight spilled through the window and into his room, producing tiny specks of light on the ceiling. He connected the dots in his mind as he thought about how this was the last night he would sleep in this house as a single man. That was the plan anyway. He sure hoped Priscilla wasn't having doubts. Despite his determined attitude that he wouldn't let worry plague his thoughts, the nasty emotion kept creeping up on him just the same. He squeezed his eyes tight as if to will it away.

I trust You, Lord. I'm not going to worry.

But an hour later he was still awake, and still playing connect-the-dots above his head. They were supposed to be at Priscilla's house at six o'clock to help with last-minute setup, and the wedding would begin at eight o'clock. He finally dozed off around eleven, but awoke with a startle at three. His eyes bolted open as he tried to recall the dream he'd just had. As he sat up in bed, he remembered. They were at the wedding, and Priscilla was crying. It was raining on her special day, and the food was cold because they ran out of propane. Naomi dropped the special cake she'd made for Priscilla. His heart raced.

Please, dear Lord, don't let all that happen.

He lit the lantern and ran a hand through his shorter curls, glad his mother had cut his hair the day before, then edged his legs over the side of the bed. Rubbing his arms to warm himself, he shook his head. He didn't believe in premonitions or predictions of doom and gloom, but the dream felt so real that it shook him up. Was this what he had to look forward to in a few hours?

Deciding that sleep was out of the question, he got dressed in his wedding clothes. A new crisp white shirt his mother made, black slacks, and . . . he picked up the black vest he'd planned to wear, but hung it back on the rack and chose the clothes Priscilla had made. He slipped on his black suit jacket and walked to the mirror carrying the lantern. He placed it on his chest of drawers while he looked in the mirror and carefully fastened his bow tie. Today he and his attendants would don the bow ties, as was tradition. He finished off his outfit by putting on a brand-new black hat with a three-and-a-half-inch brim.

Dressed and ready to go, he still had two hours before he needed to leave. Abe had already said that he would take care. of the morning chores today. Chester sat down on his bed, his stomach churning with anticipation, excitement—and a tinge of worry. Then he remembered Rachel's envelope. He picked it up and slid out a single sheet of paper, expecting one of the pink-colored pictures Rachel was known for. He pulled the lantern closer. It was pink all right. But it wasn't a picture. And Chester's eyes filled with water as he read the words scribbled on the page.

Priscilla awoke to the sound of Rusty the Rooster crowing. Sarah Mae had named the rooster, who was clueless about when he was supposed to crow. Every other rooster they'd had announced a new day when the sun came up. Not Rusty. He sang when he saw light. Any light. And that meant that someone was already up downstairs with lanterns lit. She glanced at her clock, which showed four a.m. She was much too anxious to try to sleep for another hour or so.

After she cleaned up and brushed her teeth in the bathroom, she dressed for her wedding. As she slipped her dress on, she was pleased. Every stitch might not be as perfect as her first dress, but the navy blue dress fit well. She pulled her hair into a tight bun, then pinned it beneath a new black *kapp*, a gift from Hannah. She eased to the mirror in her room with the lantern in her hand. She looked at herself in the mirror in her black prayer covering, which was to differentiate between the white *kapp* she normally wore.

I am a bride. Today is my wedding day.

She smiled, walked back to her bed, and sat down. As she pulled on a new pair of black socks and new high-topped black shoes, she sighed, knowing she was dressed way too early. Folks wouldn't start arriving to help for another couple of hours. She carried the lantern out into the upstairs hall, glad that Rusty must have gone back to sleep, but she wondered if anyone was up downstairs. She eased down the stairs, careful to skip the creaky third step on the way down. There was a lantern lit in the kitchen, but no one was downstairs at the moment, so she walked back upstairs and sat down on her bed, unsure what to do with herself.

Her muscles tensed. Despite her prayers and communion with God, she couldn't seem to shake the apprehension that festered within her heart. She bowed her head. *I know in my heart that You have a plan for me and that I shouldn't worry so much about what this day might bring, so please, God, wrap Your arms around me and Chester today, and let us not lose sight of what is most important.*

Priscilla lifted her head as she recalled the times in her life she'd heard the voice of God. In those instances, she had known that she was right with God in her heart and mind, fearful of her Lord, but without fear in her heart of human actions and reactions. She knew the difference, and she knew that human fear and worry had overcome her as of late, as hard as she'd fought it. She lowered her head again and prayed for renewed faith and total trust in God and His plan for her. When she was done, she stood up and decided to go back downstairs. There still wasn't anyone in the kitchen, but maybe she'd try to eat a bowl of cereal. She didn't think she could stomach a big breakfast this morning.

When she got to the doorway, she turned around and looked back at her bedroom, knowing that tonight Chester would share her room. She walked toward the bed, placed the lantern on the nightstand, then pulled up her covers on the bed and smoothed the wrinkles. She loved her Lone Star quilt with its brilliant red, but her mother had made her a new quilt to take to her new home—a lovely white wedding quilt with the traditional intertwined rings. She only wished she didn't have to wait months to start keeping house in her new home.

Her head swirled with thoughts. She was excited and nervous about spending her wedding night with Chester, but she loved him with all her heart. No sooner did she have the thought when she wondered if Chester would for sure show up today.

Of course he will.

She took a deep breath. Then she noticed Rachel's envelope on her nightstand. *Sweet Rachel.* And Priscilla had kept her promise. She picked up Rachel's envelope, slid her finger along the seam, and gazed at the white piece of paper with large pink lettering. Then she began to cry. How could Rachel have possibly known that this what exactly what she needed to hear at this very moment?

Chester read Rachel's special gift three more times.

> God say you shoud not be scard Chestr. True *lieb* stop scared-
> ness. You *lieb* wont be perfect if you scared Chestr.

Following the written words were two pink hearts, and underneath Rachel signed it, *I lieb you, Chester.*

Chester smiled as he blinked back tears. He knew the
Scripture well. *There is no fear in love; but perfect love casteth
out fear: because fear hath torment. He that feareth is not made
perfect in love.*

At that moment, worry and fear fled his heart and mind,
and all he wanted to do was get to Priscilla. Even if it was four
o'clock in the morning.

CHAPTER 12

Priscilla brought Rachel's letter to her heart as a tear rolled down her cheek. God used someone so simple and pure as Rachel to speak to Priscilla through Scripture. She read it again.

> To Pre-Ceelia, I *lieb* you. Today is you happy marreage day. I happy two. God go befor you and withs you and He not gonna let u down. So dont be scard Pre-Ceelia. I think it Gods perfect plan. ☺☺☺

Priscilla swiped at another tear as she translated Rachel's message.

And the Lord, he it is that doth go before thee; he will be with thee, he will not fail thee; neither forsake thee: fear not, neither be dismayed.

She closed her eyes and wept, knowing she was going to marry Chester Lapp come rain or shine, and no case of the hiccups or any other unplanned occurrence would make her wedding any more perfect than the love that she and Chester shared. She wanted to tell him she was sorry, that this day would be perfect no matter what, because it was a union to be blessed by God. Her heart filled with gratitude as she pressed Rachel's letter back to her chest.

Then she heard a noise outside, and next thing she knew, her windowpane broke. Tiny pieces of glass spilled onto the hardwood floor. She stepped back and wondered if a bird hit her window, but then she saw . . . *a rock*?

Easing slowly toward the window, she heard someone calling her name. She edged around the broken glass, then heard her name again. *Chester?*

"Priscilla, are you up there? I have to talk to you. It's important."

She peered out the window. "Chester, what are you doing?" It was a loud whisper, but she wasn't sure he heard her, so she spoke a little louder. "You broke the window. What are you doing?"

"I have to talk to you, Priscilla."

A few hours ago she might have wondered if Chester was here to call off the wedding, or she would have worried about what he had to say. "I have to talk to you too."

Her bedroom door flung open, and she spun around to see her father standing in the doorway, barefoot and in his long pants and pajama shirt. His hair was sticking up on the top of his head, and he had a scowl on his face.

"Tell that boy to come into the house like a normal person." He turned to leave, scratching his head, but turned back. "And tell him I expect him to replace that window." He narrowed his brows, but a grin shone on his face. "You two only have a few more hours before you're married and together all the time. He had to break *mei* window?" He shook his head and left.

"Chester! I'll meet you downstairs."

Priscilla sprinted down the stairs, out the front door, and across the yard to where Chester was waiting in the darkness. In the moonlight, she could see his blue eyes calling to her, and she jumped into his arms. He cupped her face in his hands, kissed her on the mouth, the cheek, the forehead, then back on the mouth again.

"Priscilla, I love you with all my heart. It doesn't matter what happens today or—"

She gently put her finger against his lips. "I love you, too, Chester, and I'm not concerned about anything." Her breath clouded in front of her from the cool night air, but inside she was warm and peaceful. "Today will be a wonderful day even if it rains, nothing goes as planned, and I get the hiccups . . . It doesn't matter. It's perfect because I love you!"

"Priscilla," he whispered as he drew her close again. "In a few hours you will be *mei frau*."

"*Ya*. I will." She gazed into his eyes and touched his cheek. "And I can't wait."

They both turned around when they heard footsteps on the front porch. *Mamm*.

"Chester Lapp, I don't know what you're doing here at this hour on your wedding day, but both of you get in here out of the cold. I'm heating up a breakfast casserole, then there is much work to be done." *Mamm* shook her head as she turned and went back into the house.

Priscilla and Chester both chuckled as they made their way slowly across the yard hand in hand.

Three hours later Priscilla watched as almost four hundred friends and family gathered inside the living room area, spilling into the temporary addition her father, friends, and family had built. *Mamm* had opened all the window blinds early that morning. An orange glow filled the horizon and lit the fields with golden hues as rays of light filtered through the house. Priscilla could feel God's presence all around her.

The ceremony began right at eight o'clock, and the congregation sang several songs in German. From her place on a backless bench in the front row, Priscilla sat almost directly across from Chester, and he'd never looked more handsome. She searched his face for any sense of hesitancy, but he sat tall and confident, and he looked as at peace as Priscilla felt. Forty benches filled their large living room, and more benches and chairs were in the extra space connected to the house, with the double doors from the living room open so everyone could hear the ceremony. A fire roared in the fireplace, and the smell of *roascht* filled the house. Her attendants, Rose and Naomi, sat to her left. Chester's attendants, Zeke and Abe, sat to his right.

The bishop presented stories about the Old Testament, followed by several Scripture readings, and then a lengthy sermon that focused on the bond and commitment of marriage. It was over two hours later when the deacon asked Priscilla and Chester to step forth and join him.

Priscilla choked back tears as she listened to Chester. "I, Chester, take you, Priscilla . . ."

Then with a shaky voice, she vowed to love Chester for the rest of her life, and Bishop Ebersol blessed their union. He took Chester's right hand and Priscilla's right hand and joined them together, placing his hand on theirs. After he pronounced them husband and wife, he asked if either of the fathers would like to speak or offer words of wisdom for the new bride and groom.

Chester's father stood up and reminded them that the man is the head of the household and that Priscilla is his helpmate, but as he looked at Chester, he also emphasized to his son that he is responsible for providing for his family. For a brief moment, Priscilla thought about how Mr. Turner had fired Chester, but she quickly tossed the thought aside.

Priscilla's father spoke to Priscilla and Chester next. A knot formed in Priscilla's throat as she listened to words from her *daed*.

"*Mei dochder*, I pray you will find much happiness in your life with Chester, and that you will keep God in your heart as challenges arise, as they most certainly will." Her father swallowed hard as he turned to Chester. "A man will leave his father and mother and be united to his wife; and the two will become one flesh. So they are no longer two, but one. Therefore, what God has joined together, let man not separate." *Daed* looked back and forth between Priscilla and Chester, and she could see her mother and both attendants dabbing at their eyes. "Be *gut* to each other. Follow the ways of the Lord in all you do."

With tears in her eyes, Priscilla nodded at her father before her eyes met with Chester's, and she knew that God's love was shining on them.

A final prayer by the bishop drew the ceremony to a close. Priscilla smiled as she glanced at Rose—whose dress fit perfectly, and who wasn't scratching her arms. She looked at Hannah, still pregnant and with no signs of labor today. What a party they would have now.

A rush of women headed toward the kitchen, and the men wasted no time as they began transforming benches into tables and setting up a table in a U-shape under the temporary shelter.

The corner of one table, the *eck*, was for Priscilla and Chester, along with their wedding party. As was customary, they would be served first. Priscilla's attendants sat to her left, along with other young unmarried women. Chester's attendants sat to his right, next to more unmarried women. Young married men sat on the remaining side of the formation.

Soon they were served the traditional *roascht*, mashed potatoes, gravy, creamed celery, pepper cabbage, applesauce, rolls, and homemade bread and jam. Women bustled about, and after everyone at the *eck* was served, the women tended to the first group seated. As a courtesy, folks ate as quickly as they could so that setup could begin for the next group, then the next. Usually, it took three shifts to feed the wedding guests.

After everyone had eaten, Priscilla and Chester, along with their attendants, returned to the *eck*. Priscilla was excited to see all the desserts and sweets that her friends and relatives brought. And, of course, there were "wedding nothings"—the cookies always served at weddings. After she and Chester inspected the items, they passed them around the table for the others to see. Many of the cakes had something written on top specifically for Priscilla and Chester, often an inside joke of some sort. She laughed when she saw that Naomi had added something to her cake—in between the candied yellow roses she'd written *Skydivers Forever*.

Chester reached over and squeezed her hand under the table as he smiled. "I love you, Priscilla Lapp."

Her heart warmed as she squeezed back, but suddenly Chester's smile faded and was replaced with a scowl.

Chester stared across the room at the man who had caused him so much heartache and wondered what he was doing here. Then he remembered. Chester had invited him a long time ago.

"What's wrong?" Priscilla's voice was tight.

He forced a smile. "Mr. Turner is here." He rubbed his chin for a moment. "It just wonders me why he would come after the way he talked to me."

"I'm surprised too." Priscilla paused as she squinted in Mr. Turner's direction. "And isn't that Mrs. Turner with him?"

Chester sat taller. "*Ya*. It is." He watched the older man and his wife take a seat across the room as he pushed aside the conversation they'd had awhile back. "But that's okay. Don't give it another thought." He focused on his food, his new bride, and the blessings God had bestowed on him, but he could feel Mr. Turner's eyes on him. He avoided holding eye contact with the man, but as soon as they were through looking at all the cakes and candies, he was going to go talk to him.

About thirty minutes later he excused himself after he saw Mr. Turner walk outside with his wife. He wasn't sure if they were leaving or just getting some fresh air. Outside, a cluster of people gathered on the porch, and it took him a minute to locate Mr. and Mrs. Turner sitting in the double porch swing, eating dessert. He moved through the crowd, past a portable heater on the porch, and approached them slowly, unsure what he would say.

"Chester!" Mr. Turner set his plate down on a table beside him. "I'm glad you found me. I have much to say to you."

Mrs. Turner also put her plate down. "Chester, it was a beautiful ceremony. Just lovely."

Chester's mind spun with confusion as Mr. Turner stood

up and extended his hand. Hesitantly, Chester shook his hand. Then Mrs. Turner stood up.

"I owe you a huge apology, son." Mr. Turner lowered his head for a moment, then looked back up at Chester. "I—I . . ." He shook his head as Mrs. Turner put her arm around her husband. She rubbed Mr. Turner's back as she spoke.

"Chester, what my husband is trying to say is that he made a terrible mistake by accusing you of taking that money." She turned toward her husband, frowning, although she continued to rub his back. Then she turned back to Chester. "I told him that there had to be some kind of mistake."

"I've been trying to call you." Mr. Turner met eyes with Chester as his brows drew downward into a frown. "No one ever answers at the phone shanty, and your brother's phone says it's been disconnected." He lowered his gaze. "I should have gone out to your house, but . . ." Mr. Turner looked up again, his eyes soft and glassy. "I was ashamed."

Chester thought about the couple of times that he and Priscilla just let the phone ring at the shanty, fearing bad news. He waited while Mrs. Turner went on.

"Mr. Turner is having some—some medical issues." Her expression fell, and Chester hoped she wasn't going to cry. "He didn't remember putting the money in a jar at home. I found it when I was cleaning."

"Chester, I'm so sorry." Mr. Turner stepped forward a bit. "I'm an old man, and I reckon I'm forgetting things left and right." He paused as he let out a heavy sigh. "And I'm only going to get worse."

Mrs. Turner blinked back tears. "We're hoping the medication will help, but we both know that we can't run the store anymore."

"I'm so sorry, Mr. Turner, that you're sick." Chester took a deep breath as he thought of an uncle he had who suffered from Alzheimer's. "Is there anything that I can do to help?"

"As a matter of fact there is," Mr. Turner said, standing taller. "We'd like for you to run the store."

Chester's voice echoed the hope he felt in his heart. "Really?"

"We understand if you can't forgive me, Chester." Mr. Turner shook his head. "I reacted so hastily. Just not like me to do that." He sighed again. "Anyway, we were wondering if you might want to buy Turner's Furniture Store. You're such a fine carpenter, and we'll be glad to finance it for you."

"Buy it?" Chester's eyes grew round as saucers, and he wondered if this day could get any better. "I'd be honored, sir." He held out his hand.

"Wonderful!" Mrs. Turner hugged Chester. "And as a wedding present and apology, we'd like for you to take over the store right away and not worry about any payments for the next six months until you and Priscilla get settled."

"Thank you both." Chester smiled as he silently thanked God as well for his good fortune and offered a prayer for the Turners.

By late afternoon plans were already underway for another meal. Following a day of socializing and fellowship, some guests had slipped out to attend other wedding receptions. Since everyone in their community married in November or December, it was almost impossible to have a date exclusive to one bride and groom. As was customary, Priscilla was the one to choose what they would have for the evening meal. She'd chosen chicken and wafers and steamed peas.

Finally the day came to a close around nine o'clock, and Priscilla and Chester said good-bye to the rest of the guests. Priscilla hugged Hannah.

"I made it through your wedding, Priscilla." Hannah smiled as she patted her large belly. "Now, I'm going to go home and coax this baby into having his birthday on your anniversary."

"I can't wait!" Priscilla said as Hannah slipped past her with her husband. Rose and Luke were behind Hannah. Priscilla was glad to see that the dress fit and that Rose didn't seem to be scratching anymore. She hugged her friend good-bye. Out of the corner of her eye she could see Naomi and Zeke standing outside talking, and she smiled to herself.

"It's been a perfect day," she whispered to Chester as they watched the last of their guests leave.

"*Ya.* It has."

Now it was time to go upstairs with her new husband.

For the next two weeks Priscilla and Chester visited family and friends, sometimes hitting four or five houses in one day. They ate dinner and supper with someone different each day, and they received some wonderful wedding gifts. One of her favorites was a small red suitcase that was filled with towels, washrags, and homemade lavender soap—a gift from one of Chester's cousins.

In the evenings, Chester worked on their new house while Priscilla continued to help her mother with the regular chores. He was scheduled to start back to work at the furniture store the following day, but this evening he was home from working on the house earlier than usual.

"I want you to come see the *haus*." Chester kissed her after he looked around and saw that they were alone.

Priscilla hadn't seen the house since the wedding, at Chester's insistence. He had been very tight-lipped about it, which made her wonder if they'd be staying even longer than the anticipated two months with her family.

"I thought you didn't want me to see it until everything was ready for us to move in."

He shrugged. "I changed my mind."

"Okay." She was anxious to see how much progress had been made.

A short while later Chester pulled into the dirt driveway. He jumped out, then went around and opened the buggy door for Priscilla. She glanced up at the roof and wondered if they'd made all the repairs. And what about the electrical issues and touch-up work that still needed to be done?

Chester scooped her into his arms and laughed.

"What are you doing?" She laughed along with him as she clung to his neck.

"The *Englisch* aren't the only ones who can carry a new bride over the threshold."

Chester eased his hand to the doorknob and turned. Then he pushed the door open with his foot and set Priscilla down in the entryway.

She blinked her eyes a few times to make sure what she was seeing was real. "Chester . . ." She cupped her hands to her mouth as her eyes scanned the living room. On the floor, on the built-in shelves, and on the fireplace mantel were vases full of flowers.

She swiped at a tear as she fell into Chester's arms. "*Danki! Danki!* They're beautiful!"

"All for you, my sweet Priscilla." He hugged her tight and kissed her lips.

Priscilla took a closer look. There was a rocking chair from Chester's house in the living room. She eased away from him and moved toward the kitchen. There was a pitcher on the counter, two canisters, and some kitchen towels laid out. Around the corner, she could see their bedroom. She hurried that way. Chester's bed and all his furniture was in the room.

"Why did you move some of your things in when the house isn't finished?" She met his eyes, but he just smiled. Priscilla took a closer look. The fireplace mantel was sanded and finished, and it hadn't been before. The floor wasn't covered in sawdust anymore, but instead shone with a fresh layer of wax. All the little things that hadn't been completed were done.

"The roof and the electrical issues are fixed too."

Priscilla ran from room to room. Not one thing was left unfinished. "How did you do this?"

"Several nights last week, about two dozen members of the community met me here, and we finished everything." He winked. "Kind of like a mini barn-raising." Then he walked to Priscilla and pushed back a strand of hair that had fallen across her cheek. "Tomorrow we will get your things. It's completely ready to live in."

Priscilla swiped at a tear. "I love you, Chester."

It was all a part of God's perfect plan.

A CHRISTMAS MIRACLE

PROLOGUE

Bruce fumbled behind his ears, adjusting the elastic band necessary to hold his Santa Claus beard in place. His salt-and-pepper hair was mostly white around his temples, the only places not covered by a traditional Santa hat, so he fit the part well. Running a hand across his overly inflated stomach, he sighed. Joan had insisted he stuff a throw pillow under his red jacket at the last minute, but now the extra padding stretched the black buttons to a point where he feared they might pop.

He took a deep breath and eyed the eager children waiting to sit in his lap. A long line ran the length of the toy aisle before it disappeared around a corner and returned to Bruce's view near the sporting goods section.

"I know this is a far cry from the boardroom, but I feel sure this is the best option out of the choices you were offered for community service." Joan leaned close to his ear and spoke in a whisper, the familiar smell of an orange Tic Tac on her breath. "You're lucky the judge is a friend of yours."

"He's not really a friend." Bruce brushed white lint from the left sleeve of his red suit. "More of an acquaintance." He rested his hands on the armrests of the throne he'd been assigned for the day.

Joan scowled as she pointed a bright red fingernail at him. "But I didn't get awarded community service, and dressing as an elf isn't part of my job description."

Bruce locked eyes with his longtime assistant. He had been her employer for twenty-five years, but there was no question who the boss was in their relationship. *Her.* "Your Christmas bonus will reflect your generous spirit." He smiled at her. "And isn't this better than being at the office?"

Joan rolled her big blue eyes as she blew a strand of short, silver hair from her face. "I suppose."

Bruce remembered when those locks were a mass of brown waves that fell well below Joan's shoulders, tresses that were sun kissed a deep shade of blonde during the summer months. But a year ago, she'd stopped coloring her hair, and it had grown into a lovely shade of silver that complemented her youthful glow yet exemplified the wise woman she'd become.

"You'd just better be sure I'm out of here by six o'clock or you'll be answering to Phillip." Joan tugged at her hat until it was snug on her forehead, the length of the green cone falling to one side, anchored by a bouncy red ball. "I haven't worn this outfit since I served Christmas dinner at the women's shelter years ago, and I must have been a bit thinner then." She pulled on the green skirt she was wearing, then adjusted the black belt around her waist. "Anyway, you know how Phillip doesn't like to miss a meal."

Bruce grinned. "That one's never going to leave the nest, is he?"

Joan had raised four kids, mostly by herself. Her husband died when her oldest child was only seven. Her children were all thriving and on their own, except for Phillip.

"I'd bounce off the walls in that big house if Phillip wasn't there. Besides, he's only twenty."

Bruce had ventured out on his own at seventeen, with barely a hundred dollars in his pocket. But times were different forty-five years ago. He couldn't begrudge Joan wanting to keep one of her children nearby. A house was lonely with only one occupant.

Bruce started counting the kids in line. *Five . . . ten . . . fifteen . . .* But those were only the ones he could see before the line disappeared around the corner. "If we're late, I'll spring for your and Phillip's dinner out somewhere."

She smiled, her cheeks dimpling beneath an extra layer of rouge for the occasion. "Well, then I'll hope we're late."

Bruce smiled. He'd paid Joan well for years of hard work and loyalty, and she'd put three of her four children through college. That hadn't been easy for her.

"It's a good thing you're doing here." Joan's eyes twinkled in the bright lights before she narrowed her eyebrows at him and frowned. "Even though I'll tan your hide if I ever hear of you driving under the influence of alcohol again."

Bruce breathed in the smells of Christmas—a display of evergreen branches hanging on a rack nearby, comingling with the aroma of cinnamon coming from the bakery—all filling the store with holiday fanfare. But months after his run-in with the law, Bruce still carried a heavy dose of guilt about what he had done.

He'd been out to dinner with three happily married couples, and he'd missed Lucy more than usual that night. Bruce wasn't a drinker, and given his state of mind that evening, he should have passed on the cocktails. His emotions didn't give him the right to put lives in danger.

Thankfully, he'd been pulled over not long after he'd gotten behind the wheel of his car. He had deserved his brief stay in jail, and Joan was right—he'd gotten off easy by paying a fine and playing Santa Claus for a week, as opposed to being assigned a week of picking up trash alongside the highway.

"Look at that cute little Amish girl." Joan nodded toward the fifth child in line, dressed in a blue dress, black apron, and the traditional white prayer covering.

Bruce had been in Lancaster County his entire life, so he knew the Amish folks didn't participate in the whole Santa Claus thing. They were Christians and celebrated the holiday in a modest way, but he'd never seen an Amish child in a line to see Santa Claus.

"Rather odd," Bruce said softly as the photographer approached them to signal that he was ready.

"Maybe she wants something really big." Joan smiled, clasping her hands together in front of her. "You know, like the girl in *Miracle on 34th Street*. Remember? She wanted a house and a family."

Bruce himself was a wealthy man, but the Amish were simple people and would never ask for anything like that. Bruce was on the lookout for children whose families might need a financial hand. That's why he'd brought Joan along, to take notes if opportunities were presented. He supposed he'd been playing Santa Claus for a long time, just never in this capacity. He enjoyed helping others this time of year.

He lifted his hand to scratch his chin, forgetting a long white beard covered it.

"I know you didn't really want to do this," Joan said. "But do a good job. Some of these kids will remember this visit to Santa for the rest of their lives."

Kids. Decades ago Bruce had come to terms with the fact

that he and Lucy wouldn't have children, but he was never going to accept the Lord calling her home two days before her fifty-fifth birthday. He and Lucy had plotted out five years of travel plans, and Bruce was getting ready to retire when Lucy had a heart attack at home by herself. Since then he'd extended his retirement a couple of years, not ready to be completely alone. At least his business provided him normality and contact with other people, something he had needed after Lucy's death. But he was ready now. Ready to pass the baton to a snappy young partner who had more of a technical grip on the ways the world was changing, which included the architectural components necessary to run a successful real-estate development firm.

Yes, God, I'll do a good job for these children. And I'll do my best to be a good person. But I will do these things in my own name, not Yours. You no longer strengthen me. And I no longer accept my fate and destiny as Your will.

Bruce had considered himself a blessed man prior to Lucy's death. He had a loving and devoted wife of thirty years, more than enough money to sustain them for the rest of their days, and plenty of available cash to share with others. But as it turned out, Lucy didn't have enough days left to see their retirement dreams to fruition.

He'd gone through his own stages of grief following her death—denial, anger, and resentment. His final phase was blame, and the blame phase was where he remained now, years later. God was to blame. Sometimes he could picture Lucy looking down on him, shaking her head. They'd both been good Christians up until her death, before Bruce turned from his once beloved Father. He couldn't seem to find his way back, nor had he tried very hard.

Bruce turned his attention back to the present, to the excited children. He would let each of them sit in his lap to tell Santa about the items on their Christmas wish list, hopefully creating memories that they'd cherish. Bruce could do that.

After the first four children had seemed satisfied with Bruce's imitation of Santa and his promise that he'd do his best to get them their requests, the little Amish girl approached tentatively, her eyes cast down at her black leather shoes.

When she finally got within a couple of feet of Bruce, he held out his arms like he'd done for the others. "Would you like to sit on Santa's lap?"

Her brown eyes met his as her eyebrows knitted into a frown. "*Nee.*"

Bruce slowly dropped his hands to the armrests of his chair. "Okay. Is there something you'd like for Christmas?"

The girl edged closer. "*Ya*, I would like to ask for something for *mei mamm*. My *Englisch* friend said you grant wishes."

Amish children were taught Pennsylvania *Deutsch* until they started school when they were five. Bruce figured this girl to be five or six, and her vocabulary was a mixture of English and their traditional dialect. "And what does your *mamm* want for Christmas?"

The small girl blinked her eyes a few times but lowered her gaze back to her shoes. "She needs help," the child said, barely above a whisper as she closed the remaining distance between them. She looked up at him and laid a gentle, tiny hand on Bruce's knee. "Can you get her some help?"

Bruce didn't want to dash this child's dream any more than the other children's, but his first thought was that her mother was sick. And that thought led him to visions of Lucy on their living room floor, and for a few moments, he was lost in his own memories. Until the girl tapped his knee.

"Are you really Santa Claus?" She blinked her eyes again as her lip trembled.

Bruce swallowed hard. He suspected this girl knew he wasn't. Surely her parents had told her that Santa Claus was a legend that only English children were led to believe in—"English" being the title reserved for anyone who wasn't Amish. "Yes, I am," he finally said, recalling Joan's encouragement to make this a memorable event for each child.

She opened her other hand, the one she'd had fisted at her side, and she slid Bruce a piece of paper. "This is our address. If you can help *mei mamm*, please send the help to this address."

The child sucked in an unusually long breath of air, as if she was straining to fill her lungs. *Maybe she's the one who is sick, instead of her mother. Maybe the family needs money for medical bills, regardless of which one is ill.* Bruce glanced up at Joan, then returned his gaze to the child.

"Is your mommy sick?" Bruce spoke as softly as he could, glancing over the girl's shoulder at a restless little boy who was tapping his foot, his arms crossed over his chest.

"*Nee.* She's not sick. But she needs help."

Bruce stared at the child for a few moments. "What's your name?"

"My name is Rachel Marie King." The child took another long, deep breath, and Bruce felt certain she was the one who needed help.

He nodded, smiling. "Help is on the way, Rachel Marie King."

CHAPTER 1

M ary glanced around the room, evaluating which one of her five children needed her attention the most. She started with her youngest, one-year-old Leah, who wailed from where she was nestled on the couch. *Probably a soiled diaper.*

Next, her eyes drifted to Katie. Only a year older than Leah, Katie was the quiet one, known to sneak off when no one was looking. Mary was glad to see her sitting quietly on the floor thumbing through a picture book.

Her oldest daughter, Rachel Marie, was the chatterbox of the family, and at five years old, she'd already decided that she was going to be an *Englisch* doctor when she grew up. Mary attributed that to the fact that Rachel had been going back and forth to Lancaster, to the same doctor, since she'd been born with a congenital heart defect. But Mary thanked the Lord that Rachel's cheeks were rosy, not pale or bluish, and that she was content building a tower out of blocks in the corner.

Mary scooped Leah into her arms and headed to where the diapers were folded on the coffee table when she remembered that John and Samuel were home from school sick. Not really sick, but with pinkeye, which was contagious to the other children.

Mary prayed that her three daughters didn't come down with it. She'd done everything she could think of to prevent it. Each child had his or her own towel and washrag, and she'd taken care to keep the girls away from the boys as best she could.

Mary walked to the landing at the base of the stairs and hollered to her seven-year-old twin boys. "John! Samuel! Can you please come downstairs?"

Mary could smell the trash in the kitchen from where she was standing in the living room. Her boys were supposed to take turns taking the trash to the burn pile, but it was a constant battle to get them to do so. She called their names again.

"They aren't here," Rachel said as she carefully placed another block on her tower.

"What do you mean they aren't here?" Mary hoisted Leah up on her hip, the feel of the heavy diaper against her arm. She walked the length of her living room until she could see into the laundry room. Mary cringed at the laundry basket overflowing with dirty clothes that needed to be run through the wringer washer. She wound around to the mudroom in the back of the house before she returned to her two daughters.

"Rachel, do you know where John and Samuel went?"

Mary's daughter nodded, still focused on her building. Mary waited a reasonable amount of time before she said, "Can you please tell me where they are?"

The *Englisch* doctor had said that Rachel needed to avoid as much emotional upset as possible, so Mary tried to keep her voice calm and steady, even though John and Samuel were known for mischief. Then her heart hammered against her chest.

"And where did Katie go?" Mary had barely taken her eyes off the two-year-old to look for her boys.

Leah began to wail in Mary's ear.

"Rachel, where is Katie?" Mary's heart thudded even harder against her chest. John and Samuel were older, but Katie was only two. "Rachel!"

"Stop yelling!" Rachel slammed her hands against her ears, shaking her head back and forth. "Don't yell at me! Don't yell at me!"

Sometimes Mary wasn't sure if Rachel took advantage of her health situation, but Mary wasn't going to take the chance. "I'm not yelling," she said, much calmer. "But Katie is just a baby, and I need to know where she is." Hurrying from room to room, Mary wasn't convinced Katie wasn't hiding somewhere in the house, but a gut instinct pulled her out onto the porch. She didn't see Katie and was almost back inside when she heard noise coming from overhead. Her heart thudded against her chest as Leah sobbed in her arms.

Mary hurried down the porch steps and turned to see the twins on the roof.

"*Ya!* I promise. You will fly. Just jump!" Samuel stood behind his brother, grinning.

"No one is jumping. Sit down right now where you are, and don't move." Mary waited until both boys were sitting on the slanted roof before she ran back inside. Leah cried harder and threw her head back so far that Mary almost dropped the baby.

"Rachel Marie, can you please help me find Katie?" Mary didn't even look at her five-year-old as she began walking from room to room again. Strands of dark hair were coming loose from under Mary's *kapp*, so many that she finally yanked it off and put it on the coffee table. "Katie!" she yelled.

Mary spotted movement out of the corner of her eye, so she charged toward the kitchen as the foul trash can odor assaulted her nostrils. She set Leah, still sobbing, on the wood floor, her diaper hanging almost to her knees, and she reached for Katie underneath the kitchen table, grabbing her hand and easing her around two kitchen chairs. The soup warming on the back burner of the stove was boiling now, splashing onto the cooktop surface.

She turned off the burner, scooped up Leah, and took hold of Katie's hand again. As she hurried across the living room, the front door swung wide.

She gasped, her feet rooted to the floor. "Gabriel," she said above Leah's cries as her eyes rounded with surprise. Her husband gave Samuel and John each a gentle push forward. "They were on the roof." His eyes blazed with fear and worry as his forehead crinkled beneath his cropped brown bangs.

His accusatory voice made Mary want to lash out at him, but instead she stayed quiet. She wasn't a good mother, and Gabriel had reasons to be angry. Only a week earlier, Mary had lost Rachel Marie at the store. The boys were in school then. She'd had Leah and Katie in a double stroller, but after she'd paid for prescriptions for Rachel at the pharmacy, she'd turned to see her daughter gone. Store security had to make an announcement, and eventually a lady dressed like an elf had returned Rachel Marie to Mary. She recalled how their hired driver shook his head most of the trip home that day also. Mary couldn't blame him. They'd been late meeting him in the parking lot as planned, and Leah's diaper had been dirty, leaving an unpleasant smell in the ten-passenger van.

"Mary, it's starting to rain outside. Why were the boys on the roof? They could have slid off and broken a leg." His eyebrows furrowed. "Or worse."

"They got out of my sight." She raised her chin slightly, determined not to cry. Leah, still in her arms, was sobbing enough for both of them. "You're home for lunch." Mary fought the lump building in her throat.

Gabriel took Leah from his wife and carried her into the living room. He'd never seen his father change a single diaper, but Gabriel had changed hundreds. Gabriel's mother had handled four children just fine, kept a clean house, and prepared three tasty meals each day. How much harder could it be with five children, as opposed to four?

He stilled his hand on Leah's leg and sniffed the air, cringing. He wasn't sure which odor was strongest—his daughter's diaper, the smell of old garbage in the kitchen, or something burnt on the stove.

He pulled back Leah's diaper and felt the weight of the situation pressing down on him as he eyed the baby's diaper rash. After he cleaned her and rubbed ointment on the red whelps, he put on a new diaper and went back to the kitchen. Mary was making ham sandwiches. Again.

Gabriel slipped Leah into her high chair before he pulled the trash from the can and took it outside, hard pellets of rain stinging his face. He tossed the trash into a pile, hoping stray animals wouldn't get into it before he had a chance to burn it. Pulling the rim of his straw hat down to protect his face, he ran back to the house, then slowed his pace across the living room, taking deep breaths to calm himself.

"Are you sure you don't want me to have *mei mamm* come

by to maybe help you a little?" Gabriel already knew the answer. Mary resented his mother—her clean house, the aroma of bread and cookies baking when you went inside, and the line of clothes hung promptly each Monday morning before being folded and put away that evening. *She doesn't have five children to tend to,* Mary always said, *that's why her house is always perfect.* But Gabriel remembered things always running smoothly, even when he was a child.

"*Nee,* I don't need any help. I just got a little behind today, and with the twins home from school, I just lost sight of them for a few minutes." She placed a sandwich in front of Gabriel as she blinked back tears.

He hung his head in prayer, thanking the Lord for his many blessings and the food that nourished their bodies. Even if it was his fourth ham sandwich this week, he was thankful to have food for his family. Then he asked the Lord to help him see a way to help his wife. *Please, Lord, she needs help.*

Mary had just gotten all the children settled and was about to sit down across the table from Gabriel when someone banged on the door. Gabriel glanced toward the living room, then back at Mary. "Are we expecting someone?" He started to stand up, but Mary walked toward the living room.

When she returned, she stood behind her chair and stared at the envelope in her hand, pressing her lips together, studying it. He hadn't even noticed her *kapp* wasn't on her head until now. Dark strands of hair flowed almost to her waist. Even now, she was still the most beautiful woman on earth. Gabriel loved her with all of his heart, as much today as when they got married eight years ago. But he worried about her and the children when he was at work.

Gabriel finished chewing a bite of his sandwich. "What is it?"

Mary lifted her eyes to his. "It's a letter that I had to sign for."

"From who?" Gabriel couldn't recall ever having to sign anything to get mail.

Mary grinned a little. "The return address says it's from . . ." She paused, glancing at the envelope again. "It's from . . . Santa Claus."

Rachel squealed, then slammed her hands over her mouth, bouncing in her chair as her eyes grew round as saucers. "He *is* Santa Claus."

Mary and Gabriel exchanged glances before both of their gazes landed on their oldest daughter. "Rachel Marie, what are you talking about?"

The child slouched into her chair as her bottom lip rolled into a pout. She shrugged. "Maybe just open it."

Gabriel walked to his wife and looked over her shoulder as she peeled open the envelope with her finger, then pulled out a letter, along with something else.

Mary brought a hand to her chest as she gasped.

Gabriel stopped breathing.

CHAPTER 2

Mary and Gabriel awoke more exhausted than usual. They had spent much of the night discussing what to do about the contents of the letter. Mary, blinking her eyes, bounced Leah and Katie in her lap, praying both girls could hold off on a diaper change until they'd left the fancy waiting area they were in. There were white chairs with chrome legs against one wall with a glass table in between them. On the other side of the room, a tall white shelving unit was filled with sculptures and models of big buildings. She glanced at the twins who were sitting quietly for the moment. Mary felt the boys were over the pinkeye, but Gabriel had thought it best to keep them home one more day, to be safe. *Easy for him to say.*

Mary dreamed of the day all her children were in school. There would be a short window of time. Leah would start her studies in four years. The twins would be eleven then, with three more years to go. Since Amish children only went to school through the eighth grade, Mary would have three glorious years when all her children were away at the same time. *I'm a horrible mother for even thinking that.*

But this morning, Gabriel had placed enough fear into the

boys that Mary's sons seemed to have taken heed. Rachel Marie was breathing more shallowly than usual, which was heavy on Mary's heart, but the doctor had said her new medication might cause such a reaction. Rachel Marie was focused on breathing, and not much else.

Mary had asked her mother-in-law if she might be able to watch the children while she ran this errand. All of Mary's errands had to be done by hiring a driver, even when the boys were in school. Two babies and a five-year-old were too much to handle while she was driving a buggy. Although she'd already heard—repeatedly from Gabriel—how plenty of mothers manage to drive a buggy with several small children in tow.

Elizabeth had declined to babysit, saying she couldn't keep her grandchildren because she'd come down with a cold. Gabriel didn't understand how hard it was for Mary to ask for help. Most of the women in their district did just fine without assistance. But what Gabriel also didn't realize was that Mary asked Elizabeth for help much more than he was aware of. Mary didn't have the heart to tell her husband that his mother wasn't interested in babysitting or spending time with her grandchildren. But the woman had successfully raised four *kinner*. Maybe she'd earned her quiet time.

"Remember what the doctor said." Mary spoke to Rachel as she continued to bounce Leah and Katie on her lap. "Slow and easy breaths."

Rachel nodded.

Mary was thankful no one else was in the waiting room besides her and the children. She planned to handle her business here quickly, to be gone less than a minute.

"Why are we here?" Rachel spoke softly as she continued to take slow breaths.

"Remember, I told you. I have a business meeting." Mary had never been to a business meeting in her life. The closest comparison might be the annual meeting of women to discuss the mud sale held in Penryn.

Rachel Marie had eventually confessed to having waited in line to see Santa Claus. But Gabriel and Mary had decided not to tell Rachel that they were returning Santa's gift. Rachel's actions had been wrong, but her heart had been in the right place, Gabriel said. After a gentle scolding, Rachel promised not to do such a thing again, even though their daughter had insisted that she never asked Santa Claus for money, only help for her mother.

Mary could still see the way Gabriel had looked at her when Rachel told them what she said to the Santa man. Mary's humiliation had suffocated her. Even her five-year-old daughter thought Mary needed help raising her family. But it was Gabriel's sad eyes that stayed in Mary's mind.

She would have to endure one more dose of embarrassment today by returning the check in her purse, but she'd never have to see this man again.

Bruce scratched his forehead as he leaned back in his chair. "Why do you think they're here?"

Joan stood on the other side of his desk with her hands clasped together in front of her. "I don't know, but I recognize the little Amish girl." She chuckled. "She called me the elf lady, and I had to confess that I had another job, in addition to being Santa's helper. And now the mother and all five children are waiting to see you. Maybe she just wants to say thank you."

"How did she know the money came from me?"

Joan sighed. "Remember, I told you that Michelle, the young woman who helps me a few hours a week, used company letterhead by mistake. I have special Santa Claus letterhead for that type of check, and I even have a post office box and separate account for these things." She clicked her tongue. "I should have handled it myself."

"Oh well. I think I give you too much to do anyway." He smiled, then motioned with his hand. "Go ahead and send them in."

"I'll keep an eye on her children." Joan smiled. "So you two can talk."

Bruce closed the file that was in front of him and retrieved a yellow notepad from inside his desk. It was only a few weeks until Christmas, so he already had a short list going. His employees received monetary gifts, but he always got something for the young couple who had lived next door to him for the past few years, along with toys for their two children. And he always sent something to Lucy's parents, although communication between Bruce and his aging in-laws had slowed down over the past year. Bruce wasn't sure whether that was due to their declining health or the pain associated with the memories they all shared.

Joan pushed the door open and stepped aside so the Amish woman could enter. She wore a traditional dark-blue dress, black apron, and black shoes and socks. Her black purse had a short handle and was draped over her arm. She looked mighty young to already have five children.

Bruce stood up and walked around his desk. "Mrs. King, I presume." He extended his hand, and after a long hesitation, the woman latched on but withdrew quickly. She pushed an envelope at him.

"Mr. Hanson, while I appreciate your generosity, it would be unthinkable for us to accept money from you."

Bruce took the envelope, knowing he could convince her to take it back. "Mrs. King, when your daughter visited me, I sensed that—"

"She should have never been in that line." The woman raised her chin. Not a wrinkle on her face. Dark hair peeked from beneath her prayer covering. "I apologize for any inconvenience Rachel might have caused you."

Bruce smiled. "I assure you, it's no inconvenience. But I must ask you, Mrs. King, is Rachel sick? She seemed to have a little trouble breathing that day."

The woman hung her head for a few moments, and when she looked back at Bruce, her face was bright red. "It's very embarrassing for *mei* husband and me that Rachel would ask a stranger for any type of help. We aren't quite sure why she did this."

Bruce scratched his chin and asked the question again. "Is your little girl sick?"

Just when Bruce thought this young woman couldn't raise her chin any higher, she did. "Rachel has a heart condition, but all of her medical expenses are taken care of by our community fund. Thank you again for your offer, Mr. Hanson." She turned to leave.

"Just so you know . . ."

She turned around, her hand on the doorknob.

"Rachel didn't ask me for money. She, uh . . . asked me for help for her mother. So I assumed that either you or the child might have a health issue." Bruce took a few steps toward her and held out the envelope. "I'd like for you to take the money. You never have to pay it back. It's a gift."

She dropped her hands to her side, clutching her small black purse in one. "*Ya*, I know that Rachel didn't specifically ask for money. Again, I thank you for your generous offer, but I cannot accept." She tipped her head. "Many blessings to you, Mr. Hanson. I'm sure another family can benefit from your generosity."

Bruce rubbed his chin as she closed the door.

Mary started her trek to the waiting room, her heart pounding, hoping the woman she'd left in charge of her children hadn't pulled her hair out. Mary recognized the *Englisch* woman as the elf who had returned Rachel Marie in the store. Mary held her breath, reached for the doorknob to the waiting room, and braced for chaos.

The elf woman was sitting in a chair with her legs crossed, Leah in her lap, Katie in a chair beside her, the two boys on the floor in front of her, and Rachel Marie was right behind the twins. The woman was reading to her children, and you could have heard a pin drop. Mary had tried countless times to gather her children so she could read to them, and she had deemed it impossible to entertain five children at the same time in a quiet manner. But here was proof that it could be done. Apparently it was only Mary who couldn't master the task.

The woman smiled. She was older, probably Mary's mother's age if her mother were still alive. And she was pretty with wavy, silver hair that framed her face and went almost to her shoulders. But it was trusting gray eyes that Mary homed in on. She desperately wanted to ask this woman how she'd gotten five little ones quiet and entertained.

"You have lovely children." The woman closed the book she was reading and lifted Leah up to Mary. "And they are so well behaved." She glanced around at each of Mary's offspring. "Just lovely, each and every one of them." She gently put a finger to Katie's nose, which got a smile out of Mary's two-year-old. She stood up and faced Mary. "I hope you and Mr. Hanson were able to get your business handled."

"*Ya*, we did." Mary forced a smile, but her own failures as a parent reared up and smacked her in the face again. "*Danki* for keeping an eye on the children while Mr. Hanson and I talked."

"Oh, you are very welcome. My three daughters and grand-children live in Texas, so I don't get to see them much. I miss them tremendously." She smiled again. "It was nice to be around these angels for a while." Waving a hand around the office, she said, "Mr. Hanson doesn't have many appointments today, so it's quiet."

"I saw on the door that this is a real-estate company. Does Mr. Hanson build houses?" Not that it mattered much to her what the man's occupation was. She just wasn't ready to leave the quiet comfort of this room or this woman who seemed to be an angel herself.

"No, not exactly." The woman reached down and touched Katie's nose again, invoking another smile. "This is a commercial real-estate development company. He builds office buildings, like the one you're in."

Mary looked around. "It's very fancy."

"Well, it hasn't always been. Bruce is a smart man, and he

built a strong company with barely any startup." She stuck out her hand. "By the way, I'm Joan."

Rachel had stood up from where she'd been sitting on the floor and walked to Mary's side. "She's the elf lady," Rachel said, smiling.

"*Ya*, I know." Mary propped Leah up on her hip and shook the woman's hand. "I'm Mary King." She glanced at her children, then back at Joan. "Thank you again."

"Do you and your family need a ride home? I'm assuming this would be quite a haul in a buggy?"

Mary shook her head. "*Nee*, we have a driver waiting." *If we didn't scare him off on the way here.*

Bruce was pacing, the check still in his hand, when Joan returned.

"Who turns down three thousand dollars?" He held up the check, shaking his head.

Joan sat down in one of the chairs facing his desk, so Bruce went and sat down across from her.

"The Amish are simple people. You know that." Joan locked eyes with him. Something was different about her, even though Bruce couldn't put his finger on it. Maybe different makeup? He didn't think she'd done anything new with her hair. But there was something. "You can't always throw money at a problem, Bruce."

He grinned. "Well, it can't hurt the problem." When she scowled, he tried again to figure out what was different about her, but when she didn't stop frowning at him, he said, "I hear you, Joan. I know money can't fix everything." If that had been the case, he'd have spent his entire fortune to save Lucy.

"Do you know what that little girl told me?" Joan sat taller, and for a split second, he thought he saw Joan's lip tremble, but his assistant wasn't one to cry. He could count on one hand the times he'd seen her cry over the past twenty years. "She said she wasn't supposed to know that her mother was here seeing Santa Claus, but she overheard her parents talking. Then she said that Santa Claus had misunderstood her, that they don't need money. She said they needed help, that her mother needed help."

Bruce raised both shoulders, then lowered them slowly. "What kind of help?"

Joan folded her hands in her lap and squinted one eye at him. "I suppose I can guess. The kind of help a young mother needs when she's got a crew of little ones close in age."

"Isn't that just something you get through?" Bruce wasn't sure since he'd never had any kids of his own.

"Yes, of course. And we all have meltdowns in the process." She paused, a faraway look in her eyes. "But this is something else, I think." Refocusing on Bruce, she said, "I'd like to take a day off later in the week and go visit that young woman and her children, if that's okay with you."

Bruce didn't think he'd ever denied Joan time off. "Sure."

"It's something else the little girl said to me. It greatly disturbed me, and I'd like to just pay them a visit."

Bruce nodded. "Okay." He waited for her to elaborate about what the child said, but Joan just sat there. Bruce was still trying to peg whatever it was that was different about her, squinting as he tilted his head to one side.

"Why are you looking at me like that?"

He grinned, pointing a finger at her. "Because there is something different about you today, and I can't figure out what it is."

She chuckled. "Well, you are very observant." She tapped a hand to her knee. "Okay, I'm heading back to my office. It's my day to play collection agency, so I have lots of calls to make."

After she stood up, he said, "Aren't you going to tell me what's different?"

"Nope." She raised her chin, followed by a thin-lipped smile.

For the second time in the past thirty minutes, Bruce rubbed his chin, lost in thought. Joan was an open book. She'd always been that way, transparent. Now she wasn't telling him what the little girl said, and she wasn't telling him why she looked different.

He shook his head and buried himself in a file. But he couldn't concentrate on the drawings he was supposed to be reviewing. Something niggled at him in a strong way.

Something about Joan.

CHAPTER 3

Gabriel's stomach began to churn on his way up the porch steps, triggering guilt. He should be excited to come home to his family after a hard day's work. But he was always afraid of the chaos that awaited him. Would all of the *kinner* be accounted for? Would supper be burnt and a sandwich in its place? How many children would be wailing or in need of attention? He could cope with all of that, even if it made him fearful at times. But the one thing he dreaded the most was the misery in his wife's eyes, as if she'd been sentenced to prison for a crime she hadn't committed. And with each day that passed, he felt them slipping further and further away from each other.

He took a deep breath, filling his lungs with cold air before he opened the door. The fire in the fireplace was barely flickering, mostly orange coals glowing amid a heap of ashes. Sidestepping a pile of toys, he slowed his pace and stopped. It was quiet. Eerily quiet. By the time he reached the kitchen, his heart hammered against his chest. *Where is everyone?* He eyed the pot on the stove, and when he lifted the lid, a pleasant aroma wafted up his nostrils, but when he put a finger to the side of the pot, it was cold. *They've been gone awhile.*

"Mary?" he called out when he was back in the living room. "*Wie bischt!* I'm home." Gabriel hurried to the stairs, taking them two at a time as he called his wife's name again, but after a quick look in all the bedrooms, he was sure they weren't home. He looked out the window in the boys' room. It was close to dark, but he could see Mary's buggy in the barn. And in the distance, he could see a buggy coming down the narrow road to their house. The churning in his stomach relocated to a burning pain in his chest as he ran down the stairs, out of the house, and across the yard to meet the visitor.

Breathless, he stared into his father's eyes. "It's Rachel Marie, isn't it?"

His father nodded. "*Ya.* Mary called a driver from the shanty, and once he arrived, she piled all five *kinner* into the van and went straight to the hospital." *Daed* reached through the open window of the buggy and touched Gabriel's shoulder. "The girl is going to be all right. I think she just gave Mary a scare when her face turned a frightening shade of blue, like it does sometimes, but they've already put Rachel Marie through the normal drill, and Mary will be heading home with her soon. We have the other four *kinner* at our *haus.* Big Jake's boy works at the hospital. You know, he went *Englisch* and all, and he delivered the other children to us when he could see Rachel and Mary would be awhile. He will also drive them home."

Gabriel tried to slow his breathing as his teeth chattered. *Thank You, God.* "*Danki* for coming out here to let me know, *Daed.*"

"Your *mamm* and I knew you'd be frantic when you didn't find them at home."

Gabriel nodded, swallowing back a lump of worry that had

been forming in his throat. "We'll make arrangements to get the rest of the *kinner* tomorrow morning."

Daed lowered his eyes for a few moments before he looked back at Gabriel.

"Um . . ." His father ran his hand the length of his beard. "Jake's boy is picking up the rest of your bunch from our *haus* on the way home."

Gabriel's heart sank to the pit of his stomach as more guilt scurried to the surface. He loved his children, but it sounded heavenly to have only their oldest daughter at home tonight. No bath-time squabbles, no mound of dishes in the sink overnight, and only Rachel to tend to. Maybe Gabriel and his wife could even spend some time in the bedroom doing something besides sleeping. Mary's head barely hit the pillow each night before she fell into a deep slumber.

"*Danki* again, *Daed*." Gabriel gave a quick wave before his father backed up the buggy, and he cast his eyes to the darkening sky. *And thank You, God.* How many times had they prayed for Rachel Marie's good health? The Lord continued to bless them, and Gabriel was going to keep that in mind when his exhausted wife and five children got home.

As he cleaned the dishes in the sink from Mary's supper preparation, he thought about his parents. Gabriel had three sisters, all considerably older than him and living with their families in Philadelphia. Gabriel was an uncle to their combined fourteen children. He could recall his parents babysitting his sisters' children often before the girls and their families chose to leave the district for something less conservative. The move had been hard on his parents, but his folks were grounded in Old Order traditions, with no desire to relocate somewhere more liberal.

He dried his hands on the kitchen towel, then turned the burner on to warm up the stew. *Women's work.* But Gabriel had learned long ago that Mary had trouble keeping up with the household and the children, so he tried to help when he could. His thoughts drifted back to his parents. It was clear they didn't want to babysit Gabriel's children. Gabriel thought he knew why—his home and family life were just too disorderly for his aging parents. But his acknowledgment of that fact stung and brought forth a lump in his throat.

"I'll only be a few minutes," Mary whispered to Jake as Rachel slept on one of the long seats in the van. Her heart had sunk when she'd heard she had to pick up the other four children tonight. What would one night with just Rachel Marie have been like? Maybe a quiet supper, devotions with Gabriel, and an early night to bed? What would an extra few hours of sleep mean? *Everything.* But Rachel Marie was okay this time, and she silently thanked God for that.

Elizabeth answered the door holding Leah as Katie tugged on Elizabeth's blue dress. Leah was trying to catch her breath from crying. Her youngest always cried. The corners of her mother-in-law's mouth edged up for a few seconds, but barely enough to even call it a smile. Mary saw the twins rolling on the floor in the background.

"*Danki* for keeping the *kinner,* Elizabeth." Mary reached out her arms to take Leah.

"*Ach,* you're welcome, Sarah. I'm sorry we can't keep the *kinner* overnight." Elizabeth picked up Katie before she closed the door behind Mary and Leah. Sarah was Gabriel's sister's name, but Mary didn't say anything about the name slipup.

Mary waited for her mother-in-law to give a reason why the *kinner* couldn't stay the night, but Elizabeth practically ran to the couch and began stuffing diapers, baby wipes, snacks, and two bottles into the diaper bag. "Time to go, boys." She walked to where the twins were rolling around.

Once Elizabeth had herded them all toward the door, Mary thanked her again as she swallowed back tears in her throat. As she walked to the van, she cried out to God in her mind. *Please, Lord, help me. I need help.*

Bruce fluffed his pillows behind him and began flipping TV channels with the remote. He landed on *It's a Wonderful Life. Jimmy Stewart at his finest.* He reached for his cup of raspberry tea. Lucy had loved this classic Christmas movie—and raspberry tea. Bruce could still see her in bed next to him, but the vision wasn't as strong. The first few months, the scent of his wife had comingled with memories in a way that was awful and wonderful at the same time. But now he seemed lost in a time warp where he was unable to move forward, but the past was fading. He'd never forget Lucy, and he'd love her until the day he died, but he couldn't see her as clearly in his mind's eye.

Joan. His longtime assistant and friend was at the forefront of his mind this evening also. He pictured her dressed as an elf and smiled. After a few moments he picked up his cell phone and found her phone number. When Phillip answered, Bruce held the phone out to make sure he'd dialed the right number, and he had.

"Hey, buddy. Your mom around?" Bruce remembered when Phillip was born. He'd always been a good kid. *Is twenty a kid?* It seemed so to Bruce.

"Hey, Bruce. No, she's not here right now, and she forgot her phone."

"Oh, okay."

"But actually, I'm glad you called." Phillip exhaled a heavy breath of air. "I'm moving out in a couple of weeks. A guy at work has a room for rent. His roommate got married, and he's making me a good deal. It'll be closer to work too. But I'm worried about leaving Mom alone. Maybe you can help me soften the blow." He chuckled a little.

"Well, it sounds great to me, but you'll be the last kid to leave the nest, so I suspect it will be a little rough on her. But I think she'll be okay." Bruce paused as he pictured Joan shuffling around that big house by herself. "I'll keep an eye on her."

"Thanks, man. I appreciate it."

Bruce glanced at the clock on his nightstand. "Where's your mom at this time of night anyway?" Joan avoided nighttime driving if possible.

"Well, can you believe this . . . She's on a *date*."

Bruce stiffened as he sat up. He couldn't recall Joan ever going on a date. She probably had when she was younger, but Bruce hadn't known about it. "Uh, oh. Anyone I know?"

"Yep. That guy at your office. Matt."

Bruce searched his mind. There were sixty employees at his company, and the name Matt wasn't ringing a bell. "I can't place anyone named Matt. What department is he in?"

"I'm not sure, but he's an architect."

Bruce let out a half-hearted grunt. "Well that narrows it down."

"Hey, man . . . it's your company. You'd know better than me." Phillip chuckled. "Yeah, she was pretty excited. She got her hair done and bought some new makeup that she said would cover her wrinkles." He laughed. "I figure since the guy works at your company, he's probably pretty safe."

So it was her hair and makeup that looked different.

"You want me to give her a message?"

Bruce scratched his forehead. "Um, nah. That's okay. It can wait."

After he'd wished Phillip a good night and hung up, he swung his legs over the side of the bed. He'd bought a huge bag of chocolate chips since late-night sweets had become a habit. But he wasn't hungry. He tried to force a yawn, but he wasn't tired anymore either. His chest was so tight he could barely breathe. *Maybe I'm having a heart attack.* He took a deep breath and quickly ruled out a heart attack, even though he'd never had one. But his stomach cramped and churned like he'd been punched in the gut.

Joan . . . and Matt. The churning worsened.

CHAPTER 4

Mary sat on her bathroom floor with the door shut and the water running in the sink. She could still hear Leah screaming from her playpen, and she'd left Katie in the playpen also. Rachel Marie was keeping an eye on the twins, who were rolling toy cars across the wood floor in the kitchen. It didn't take long for the boys to find mischief, and Rachel Marie liked to feel in charge even though she was younger.

She covered her face with her hands and cried. The soothing sound of the running water calmed her and kept her children from hearing her. She only needed a few minutes. Sobbing never helped. It almost always left her with a headache. Then she'd return to her children and do her best to meet all of their needs.

After a couple of minutes, she stood up and turned off the water as a wave of nausea wrapped around her. Mary tried to recall if she'd eaten this morning. *Yes, I had eggs and a biscuit.* Then she brought both hands to her chest, stared at herself in the mirror, at the dark circles, then cried again. *Am I pregnant?* The thought caused her knees to go weak, and Leah's cries were becoming louder. Mary blew her nose and dried her tears as best she could before she went to the baby.

"There, there," she said as she picked up Leah, who was wet again. Katie was on her back in the playpen sucking her thumb, her eyes heavy. Samuel and John were still in the kitchen, and Rachel Marie was now lying on the couch resting. Mary thanked God again that her oldest daughter was okay, just tired. As she set to changing Leah's diaper, she heard a car coming. *Oh no.* She glanced around the living room. Two plates on the coffee table, a spilled glass of milk, and toys everywhere. Leah was only in a diaper, Katie had a spill on the front of her light blue dress, and the boys had dressed themselves. Mary hadn't paid attention to what they were wearing. Rachel Marie was covered with a blanket on the couch.

Mary walked to the window with Leah on her hip. A woman stepped out of a maroon car, and Mary tried to place where she'd seen her. The older lady was within a few feet of the porch when Mary recognized her. The *Englisch* woman who read to her children earlier in the week, the one who had dressed like an elf in the store. Mary could feel her face turning several shades of red when she opened the door.

"*Wie bischt.* Hello." Mary pushed back strands of hair that had fallen from beneath a *kapp* that was surely on crooked. She couldn't recall the woman's name. "Can I help you?" She hoped the woman wasn't here to convince her to take her boss's check.

"I hope you don't mind me stopping by. I was in the neighborhood, and I couldn't resist dropping off these apple turnovers." The *Englischer* held up a box. "I know that all of you Amish folks are wonderful bakers, but these are different." She laughed, which lent a more calming effect than the running water in the bathroom had done. "You'll just have to trust me."

Mary remembered the woman's name. *Joan.* With Leah still

on her hip, quiet now, Mary accepted the box. "That's very kind of you. *Danki*."

"Hello, sweet Leah. How are you today?" Joan smiled, then Leah did too. Mary almost smiled, which would have been the first in a while.

Mary could already feel the burn of embarrassment rising in her cheeks, but she couldn't leave Joan on the front porch shivering. "Would you like to come in?" *Please say no.*

"Well, I wouldn't mind spending a little time with these angels, but I don't want to impose."

Leah couldn't have picked a worse time to bolt from Mary's arms and into Joan's, who chuckled as she took hold of the baby.

"Please come in." Mary stepped aside, watching Joan closely, waiting for a look of disdain to cross her features, but if she'd noticed the state of Mary's living room, she didn't let on.

Rachel Marie sat up. "You're the elf lady."

"Why, yes I am." Joan's blue eyes glowed as she bounced Leah on her hip. "And you are Rachel Marie King."

"Did you come to help *Mamm*?"

Mary gasped as she scowled at her daughter. "Rachel Marie. Please hush." Then she turned to Joan. "I'm so sorry, and I apologize for the mess. We were at the hospital last night with Rachel Marie, and I'm just . . . a bit behind."

Joan stopped bouncing Leah, and almost instantly Leah began to cry.

"I think she has a wet diaper. I was just about to change it when you arrived." Mary walked toward Joan to retrieve Leah, but there was a loud crash in the kitchen. "Excuse me." Her heart thumped in her chest as she walked faster, stopping just over the threshold. Samuel and John stood over a broken fruit bowl, their rounded eyes lifting to hers as they both mumbled apologies.

"Both of you, carefully step to your right and sit in a chair until I get this glass swept up." Mary worked as quickly as she could. She'd left her three daughters with a stranger in the next room. When she returned, breathless, she smiled. Rachel Marie was sitting up, Leah was in Joan's lap, and Katie was sound asleep in the playpen.

"I hope you don't mind, but I could hear that you had a situation in the kitchen, so I went ahead and changed Leah's diaper." She tapped a finger to the end of Leah's nose, which produced another smile. "And Rachel has been telling me about her ordeal at the hospital last night." She winked at Rachel. "You're a very brave girl."

Mary opened her mouth to say something, but speaking was going to bring forth crying. She was so tired, and feeling like a failure as a mother was a heavy load as well. Mary and Joan locked eyes. For a split second, she was sure she saw her mother, and a tear slipped down her cheek. She tried to talk again but just lowered her gaze. The anniversary of her parents' death had been the week before. The buggy accident was nine years ago, and as much as Mary wanted her mother to speak to her from heaven, she was sure *Mamm* would be disappointed in Mary's mothering abilities.

"Don't cry, *Mamm*." Rachel's tender, sweet voice echoed in Mary's head, but instead of looking at her daughter, she found Joan's kind eyes again. Still holding Leah, the older woman sat down beside Rachel Marie on the couch.

"Sometimes even mommies cry," Joan said softly. "And your mommy probably does need a little help right now." She winked at Rachel. "Maybe an angel whispered that in my ear."

"Or Santa," Rachel said in a whisper. Mary would have to make sure Rachel understood that only God made things happen, not Santa Claus. But as she glanced around at her messy house and dabbed at her wet eyes, it seemed like something she could get to later.

Joan smiled as she stood up with Leah. "You know, I find myself with nothing to do the rest of the day." She moved a little closer to Mary. "Do you remember me telling you that my grandchildren lived far away?" Mary nodded. "It would mean the world to me if I could just spend a little time with these precious children today."

Mary thought about her mother-in-law and the way she seemed to avoid her grandchildren. But this woman was a stranger. And she could already hear Gabriel saying, "She's not Amish." Her husband's parents were more traditional than most, not having evolved with the times, and Gabriel had followed their lead, despite the bishop's leniency about some things. None of them had cell phones, which had become more popular over the years. Neither Gabriel nor his father relied on gas- or diesel-powered farm equipment. Elizabeth used outdated kitchen tools even though battery-operated mixers and such had been available for a long time.

Rachel excused herself to the bathroom, and Joan waited until Rachel was out of earshot before she spoke.

"Perhaps you could take care of some other things while I'm here. Or even take a nap." Joan smiled.

Mary couldn't nap. She didn't trust this woman enough for that. But having someone watch the children while she caught up on household chores would be a welcomed gift. It should have felt wrong, but it didn't. "Are you sure?"

"I raised four children. We all need a little help from time to time. It's the hardest job on the planet. And I really would love to spend some time here. But first"—Joan chuckled—"we're going to need an apple turnover and some coffee."

Mary felt lighter for the moment. And again, for a split second, she thought she saw her mother in this woman's eyes.

Bruce leaned back in his chair and tapped a pencil against his desk. He'd planned to talk to Joan first thing this morning, but he'd forgotten she'd taken a day off. Dating employees wasn't something he encouraged or forbade, but he was curious about the man who took Joan on a date on a Thursday night. He'd already scanned the employee roster. There was only one Matt employed at Hanson and Associates, and Bruce had only been around the guy a few times. He was an architect who had been on the payroll about a year, a single guy who had to be ten or fifteen years younger than Joan.

He set down the pencil, wondering how this Matt fellow could be a good fit for Joan. She was his employee, but also a good friend with a heart as big as Texas, where she was from. Maybe she'd suspected her son would be moving out soon. Perhaps she was afraid of being alone. Bruce could understand that. *But why a man so much younger than she?*

Bruce began tapping the pencil against the desk again. Joan's youthful glow and contagious smile made her look younger than fifty-two, even with her silver hair. He could see why any man, even one a decade younger or more, would be interested in her. But what could she see in him? Bruce supposed Matt wasn't a bad-looking man, but what could they have in common? Joan had buried a husband at a young age and raised a family, with the last child about to be on his own.

All the analyzing had kept him unfocused on work for most of the day. Looking at the clock, he was surprised it was almost five. He wondered how Joan's day had gone with the Amish woman and her children. It didn't surprise him that Joan would reach out to someone in need, but there seemed to be an urgency in Joan's mission that Bruce couldn't grasp. He knew it was something the little girl had told Joan.

But right now he was more concerned about why Joan had gone on a date with Matt.

He was going to call her this evening. Just to chat, the way he'd planned last night. But first, he was going to find out more about this Matt fellow.

CHAPTER 5

Gabriel got his horse settled in the barn, then crossed the front yard toting his lunch pail. He'd made himself a ham and cheese sandwich that morning for lunch and tossed an apple in with it. Occasionally he longed for the taste of his mother's chicken salad, which she used to send with him for work when he lived at home. But those days were years behind him, and he'd gotten used to making his own lunch after the twins were born.

As he pulled his black coat snug around him, breaths of cold air reminded him that it wouldn't be long until Christmas. But as soon as the thought came and went, he silently prayed that this would be a good night, one filled with less disorder and maybe a little calmer than the usual way of life they'd settled into.

He opened the door, and a beefy garlic aroma filled his nostrils as he walked into a tidy living room. At first his chest tightened, recalling the empty house he'd come home to when Rachel Marie was in the hospital, but he turned an ear toward the kitchen and heard voices.

Gabriel felt as if the clouds had parted and revealed a slice of heaven to him, showering him with blessings. Leah and Katie were each in a high chair nibbling on crackers. *When did we get a second high chair?* Rachel Marie was helping Mary set the table by placing a steaming loaf of freshly baked bread in the middle. Gabriel couldn't recall the last time he'd had anything besides store-bought bread, unless his mother sent some their way.

The twins were sitting at the table, quiet and patient. Gabriel could practically see the halos around their heads, and for a brief moment he wondered if he was dreaming.

"Good afternoon." Mary smiled as she carried a pot filled with something that smelled wonderful. "Beef stew," she said. "A new recipe."

Gabriel's wife resembled the seventeen-year-old girl he'd married, her cheeks rosy red, a smile on her face, and not a hair out of place from beneath her *kapp*. She looked happy, and a warm feeling settled over him. He'd felt like a failure for so long. Mary's shortcomings when it came to family were his burdens to bear as head of the household. But at this moment he'd never been prouder of his wife, even if pride was frowned upon. He eyed the scene, hoping to capture it like a picture to take out and remember later if things went back to chaos.

"*Mamm's* new friend spent the day with us, and she showed *Mamm* how to cook and clean and take care of babies." Rachel Marie sat down in a chair beside Leah and wiped the baby's mouth with a napkin before helping her drink from a small plastic cup.

Gabriel wished the friend who helped was his mother, but Rachel Marie would have referred to Gabriel's mother as *grandmammi*. "What new friend?" Who in their district would have time to spend the day with Mary and the children? Gabriel should have told Mary how good everything looked and smelled, but in his mind he was already thanking God for this new friend, whoever she was.

"She's *Englisch*." Rachel Marie took in a long, deep breath, a reminder that she wasn't well, but her cheeks were filled with color like Mary's today. The hairs on the back of Gabriel's neck prickled. He wanted to be grateful to this person who'd helped his wife, but he'd also worked hard to teach his children that they were unequally yoked with outsiders, thus they should always be polite to the *Englisch* but not seek close relationships.

Mary sat down at the table and didn't say anything, so Gabriel took off his coat and hat, joining the rest of his family. After they'd bowed their heads in prayer, Gabriel reminded himself to be appreciative and grateful. Perhaps God had answered his prayers, but as often happens, not in a way Gabriel would have expected.

"So, who is your new *Englisch* friend?" He held out his bowl when Mary nodded to it. She spooned several ladles of stew for him. Next she filled Samuel's bowl.

"She's the elf lady from the mall." Rachel Marie offered her bowl up next.

Gabriel raised an eyebrow as he looked across the table at Mary.

"Santa's elf." Mary winked at Gabriel, which would have been a welcomed gesture under different circumstances. He knew Rachel Marie had visited a Santa Claus at the store, and he knew about the check that had arrived—a check that he instructed Mary to return immediately. "She works for, um . . . Santa. The children and I saw her when we went on our errand. Remember me telling you we were going?"

Mary was talking in code to keep Rachel Marie from knowing about the returned gift, but Gabriel's hunger pains transformed into churning balls of worry. "Why was she here?"

"She was in the neighborhood." Mary shrugged. "And she wanted to drop off some apple turnovers for us. She ended up staying."

"She has two jobs." Rachel sat taller, smiling. "Working for Santa Claus and in a tall building too."

Gabriel didn't respond to his daughter as he stirred his stew. "She was here all day?" A stranger had spent all day at his home with his family. He glanced around the table at his clean and well-mannered children and at his lovely, calm wife. Was this woman an angel of mercy or . . . trouble? Gabriel suspected the latter. He recalled the last *Englischer* they'd gotten too close to, and things hadn't ended well.

Mary pulled her white nightgown over her head, brushed her teeth, and headed to bed. Gabriel was already lying down. Normally he would have a book in his hands and then read for a while until he fell asleep—or so he said. Mary fell directly to sleep each night, so she was never sure how long he stayed up. But Gabriel didn't have a book tonight. Instead, his hands were folded in his lap. It had been such an extraordinary day for Mary, and she was bubbling with leftover energy she planned to share with her husband. She snuggled up to him and kissed him on the neck.

She was confused when his neck tensed and he didn't reciprocate any affection. Early nights with all the children tucked in and sleeping were rare. She eased away.

"What's wrong?"

Gabriel twisted to face her, running a hand through her

hair. "You look beautiful," he said in a whisper, his eyes flickering from the light of the lantern, which met with the moonlight streaming in through the window. "And everything was great tonight, the meal, the *kinner*, the clean *haus* . . . all *wunderbaar*. But . . ."

Mary swallowed back the knot forming in her throat. Joan had lent her a much needed helping hand today, but she'd also given Mary ideas about how to organize her time and tend to her children. Mary wasn't going to have a perfect house tomorrow, and things would still be in disarray, but she was hopeful she could take control of her life by applying some of Joan's suggestions.

"What's wrong?" she finally asked as her lip quivered.

Gabriel reached for her hand and squeezed. "I'm just worried that you let a stranger into our house, that she was with you and the children all day, and . . . she's *Englisch*."

Mary had grown up in a home that encouraged friendships between good people in general, whether Amish or not. It wasn't how most of the families in her district thought, but Mary's parents didn't grow up Old Order. They'd been Beachy Amish—or New Order as some called it—prior to making a choice to join the Old Order. Some of her family's less stringent rules and beliefs had carried over from that district to here.

Gabriel's family was the opposite. For generations the Kings had adhered to the teachings of the *Ordnung*, with little leniency, even if the bishop approved a new and more modern way of life. Most Amish families were allowed use of a cell phone for business and emergencies, but Gabriel's parents didn't have one and neither did Gabriel and Mary.

"She didn't feel like a stranger," she finally said as she tucked her dark hair behind her ears. "She felt more like a . . ." She paused, reconsidering whether to verbalize her thought.

"Like a mother?" Gabriel frowned when she nodded. "You have a mother, *my* mother."

She clenched her teeth. "Your mother has never tried to teach me how to run my household. I didn't have siblings. I didn't have an example to follow. Joan raised four children, and she gave me some great ideas about how to balance all of the things in my life, as well as suggestions about how to discipline the twins."

Gabriel grunted as a twisted grin took over his features. "You are taking advice about disciplining our *kinner* from an *Englisch* woman you barely know?" He threw his hands in the air. "I'd rather put up with a messy house, burnt suppers, and dirty children before we let an *Englischer* tell us how to run our household."

"Put up with . . ." Mary blinked back tears. She knew how he must feel about her role as a wife and mother, but hearing him say the words still stung. "And I don't want your mother coming over to teach me how to run our household." She bit her tongue, chiding herself for what she was about to say. "Your mother doesn't want to be around our *kinner.*" Mary wanted to hurt him as badly as he'd wounded her, and as he lowered his head, she breathed in success—but it didn't taste very good. "I'm sorry, but you know it's true."

He lifted his eyes to hers. "It's not true. You're just too stubborn to accept help."

Mary's lip trembled as she tried to think before she spoke. "I'm not stubborn. Running a household and taking care of five children is a lot of work."

"Everyone else does it."

A tear slipped down Mary's cheek as she pressed her lips together, vowing not to say anything else. She was a failure, even if for a day a kind stranger had made her feel otherwise.

Gabriel hung his head for a few seconds before he looked up at her. "Mary, I'm sorry. I know you do your best. I love you, and . . ."

She pushed him away when he reached for her.

"Fine." He rolled over onto his side.

Leah started to cry from upstairs. Katie chimed in a few seconds later. Samuel yelled that the babies were crying, and then faint grumblings from John and Rachel Marie could be heard.

Mary waited to see if Gabriel would offer to help her now that all five children were awake. As their children called out, she waited another minute.

Then she climbed out of bed to take care of their children. By the time she got on her robe and slippers, Gabriel was snoring.

CHAPTER 6

On Monday morning Joan tapped twice on Bruce's door, then walked into his office before being invited, the same way she'd done for years. But today he shifted uncomfortably, loosened his tie a little, and picked up the familiar yellow pencil he'd taken to tapping on his desk lately.

"How was your weekend?" Joan smiled, glowing in a way that caused his breakfast from earlier to churn in his stomach, and his pressure on the pencil became so taut, he feared it might snap in two.

Bruce leaned back against his chair, reclining slightly, and he put himself in check with the reminder that Joan was free to do whatever she wanted on her own time. Nevertheless, a muscle in his jaw flicked. "Well, I didn't have a *date* over the weekend." He forced a smile to see if she'd offer up information about her and Matt.

"Nor did I," she said as she sat down in the chair on the other side of his desk, folding her hands in her lap.

Scowling, Bruce stared at her. He couldn't recall a time Joan had ever lied to him. "What about Matt? That wasn't a date?"

She pressed her mouth into a thin-lipped smile, which felt

like she was mocking him, and Bruce could see an invisible line of defense building. "My date with Matt was last Thursday, *not* over the weekend."

Bruce felt the kick in his shin all the way to his heart. *Yep, she's right.* He straightened, moved forward in his chair, and folded his hands on his desk. "We're friends, right?"

"The best of friends." Her smile was more genuine now.

"Then why didn't you tell me you were dating someone here at the office? Did you think I'd give you a hard time about it?"

She raised an eyebrow, barely grinning. "It sounds like you're giving me a hard time about it now." She paused, squinting a little. "And we aren't *dating*. It was just one dinner."

Bruce let out the breath he'd been holding as relief swept over him, which was confusing, and it left him with a brain fog he wasn't used to. "Oh." He was going to need more time to process this, so he decided to change the subject. "How'd it go with the Amish family Friday?"

Joan's posture fell as she lowered her gaze. "I thought it went well." She looked back up at him. "The little girl had told me that she often heard her mother crying in the bathroom with the water running. I didn't say anything to you because I didn't want you to think Mary was crazy or something. But Billy, my oldest, did that when he was a teenager. He had severe anxiety, so much so that it became debilitating for him. So I was worried about Mary, and I wanted to see if I could help her. Some people have more trouble than others coping with stress. I wasn't a perfect mother"—she chuckled—"but I was forced to learn as I went along, and I made plenty of mistakes." She cringed. "Bad mistakes, like I guess all parents do. But something about Mary, what Rachel said . . ." She shrugged. "I don't know. I felt called to lend a hand. I thought that if my mistakes might help Mary, then there was a purpose for them. I just felt very strongly that God wanted me to go to her."

God. It was the one subject Bruce and Joan didn't agree on. "It sounds like you did a good thing by helping her family."

"Apparently not. I was planning to visit her again this Friday." She lifted an eyebrow again, as if waiting for Bruce to comment about her taking off another day. Of course he didn't. "I got a call from Mary on Saturday. She was at a nearby shanty. She thanked me for spending time with her on Friday, but she said she didn't need me to visit anymore. When I asked her why, since I thought we'd had such a good day, she said her husband didn't approve of her spending time with an outsider."

Bruce shrugged. "Does that surprise you? You know the Amish like to keep to themselves."

Joan slumped into her chair a little more. "I know. But I'm telling you, I felt a definite calling to help that young woman."

Bruce scratched his chin. "Some people don't know how to accept help, Amish or otherwise." He thought about the check that was returned. And right away he recalled what Joan had said about not always being able to throw money at a problem. Joan was one of the most giving people he knew—of herself and her time. "But you tried," he added.

She shook her head hard as she captured his eyes and leveled a penetrating dose of confidence his way. "I'm not giving up. That's the enemy at play. I feel sure I'm being called to—"

Bruce let out a heavy sigh accompanied by a grunt he wished he would have suppressed.

Joan squinted at him as she folded her arms across her chest. Then up went her chin. "What was that about?"

"I'm just not sure God *calls* us to do anything." Bruce shrugged. Joan was as good a Christian as he'd ever known. She didn't just talk the talk. Joan walked the walk in everything she did. The last thing Bruce wanted to do was to hurt her feelings, but he'd come to believe that God doesn't call on us any more than He listens when we call on Him.

Joan stared at him long and hard. "You know, Bruce, you are a good man. But more than once, I've heard you say something negative about the Lord. You and Lucy were always Christ-centered, faithful people. Now that she's gone, I can understand that you would still be grieving, but I can tell you blame God for Lucy's death."

"He is God. He could have saved her."

Joan smiled slightly. "Maybe He did save her."

Bruce frowned but waited.

"I think about these things, and I wonder—you and Lucy were planning to travel. What if Lucy had survived the heart attack but the two of you were in an awful accident or some other catastrophic event happened that caused even more pain for Lucy . . . and you?"

Bruce shook his head.

"Just hear me out. Maybe God saved Lucy from something far worse. It's impossible to know. I'm not simplifying or minimizing her death at all." As Bruce shook his head again, she went on. "We can't know God's plan, but I will pray that you lose the bitterness you feel."

"In your analogy, the situation remains the same. God is God. He could allow us to avoid an accident or other event altogether."

Now it was Joan who shook her head. "I believe that when

something bad happens, there has to be a reason for it, and we aren't always meant to know."

Bruce wondered how they'd gotten so off topic, away from the conversation about the Amish family. But Joan's supposed calling in that regard had brought them here.

She stood up and turned to leave.

"Are you mad?" Bruce leaned forward, scowling at her speedy departure.

Her expression dropped as she spun around and locked eyes with him. "No. Not mad. Just disappointed. Everyone questions God's will, but we can't foresee His plan during our time on this earth. Only someone who has lost a spouse could possibly understand your grief."

Bruce took a deep breath.

"So, imagine my horror at losing my husband, with four young children to raise. I understand your pain. But you can blame the Lord, or you can give your all to Him and trust that He has your best interests at heart." She paused. "You will be happy again, Bruce. I know it."

Bruce wasn't so sure about that. Right now he felt worse than ever.

By Thursday evening Gabriel struggled to retrieve the picture he'd stored in his mind. The one where supper was on the table, the children were clean and orderly, and his wife was glowing and happy.

Mary was scrambling to get bread and jam on the table. Katie was busily pouring juice onto the floor from a cup with no lid on it. The glasses rattled as one of the twins kicked the other under the table. Rachel and Leah were quiet, but probably because Rachel was giving her baby sister pinches of a cookie that was surely going to spoil both their suppers.

Gabriel closed his eyes, but he still couldn't find the fond recollection in his mind, and he wondered if he'd made a mistake by forbidding the *Englisch* woman in their home. But the safety of his family came first. The lady might have been a kind person, but was she committed to the Lord? That was something that Gabriel didn't have to worry about with members of their community. But worse, would the woman try to con Mary the way an *Englisch* woman had done to his mother? He shivered just thinking about it. An *Englisch* woman had wormed her way into his mother's life years ago, pretending to be someone she wasn't, and she'd stolen money from *Mamm*. He could still remember how hurt his mother had been, more about the dishonesty of the friendship, and not so much about the money.

Gabriel took a bite of roast. A memory of last Friday's stew surfaced, and it was hard to ignore when compared to this roast, with little seasoning and maybe not quite done.

"Forgive me." Mary bolted from her chair, holding her hands across her stomach as she left the kitchen.

Gabriel glanced at Rachel Marie. "Is your *mamm* sick?"

His oldest daughter shook her head. "*Nee.* She's not sick." Rachel took a long, deep breath, and when she let it out, Gabriel heard her chest rattle a little. "She's going to have another *boppli.*"

Gabriel dropped his fork on his plate as his jaw fell open. *Nee, Lord, nee.* A baby was a gift, but as he looked around the table at his five children, he didn't see how he and Mary could possibly handle one more.

"How do you know your mother is in a family way?" He found Rachel Marie's eyes. "Did she tell you that?"

"*Nee*. Samuel told me." Rachel pointed to the twin on her right. "Right, Samuel?"

Gabriel looked at his son and waited.

"She didn't *tell* me that," Samuel said. "But she was sick like this before Katie and Leah were born."

Gabriel felt relief wash over him as his heartbeat slowed. Mary might just have a bug, a bout of stomach upset.

He forked a piece of roast, stuffed it in his mouth, and chewed hard, nodding his head once. Ya, *just a stomach flu.*

Mary wiped her mouth, stared at herself in the mirror, and turned on the water in the sink. She sat down on the floor and pulled her knees to her chest, wrapping her arms around her trembling legs. *I can't be having another baby.* She just needed a few minutes to gather herself, but she jumped when there was a knock at the bathroom door.

"Mary, are you sick?"

She glanced at the doorknob and wondered if Gabriel would walk in. There wasn't a lock on the door. Her eyes darted to the water running in the sink, and as she contemplated getting up, the door opened. Gabriel's sullen expression said it all.

"Sweetie . . ." He squatted down beside her. Mary couldn't remember the last time he'd spoken to her using any type of pet name, and it caused a tear to slide down her cheek.

"I'm pregnant," she said as her lip trembled. "It's a gift, I know."

Gabriel hung his head, then looked back at her. "Are you sure?"

"*Ya.* You left the babies unattended."

"Samuel and John are in charge; they will keep an eye on them."

Mary smiled a little. "The same boys who were contemplating jumping off the roof to fly recently?"

"They're fine." Gabriel placed a hand on Mary's leg, and she fought the urge to slap it away. "Why is the water running?"

Mary shrugged. "I don't know."

Gabriel reached up and stretched his arm until he had hold of the faucet, then turned off the water. "We'll get by. I know six *boppli* is a lot, but many of the families in our district have a lot of *kinner*, and they do just fine."

Mary began to sob. "Gabriel, I am *not* doing just fine."

He swallowed hard as his wife cried.

CHAPTER 7

Gabriel stood facing the elevator, waiting and double-checking the address on the piece of paper in his hand.

Two women passed behind him. "Look at the Amish man. I wonder what he's doing here."

Gabriel took a deep breath when the elevator doors opened, then slipped in beside three men dressed in black suits. Two of the fellows were talking in another language. The third man looked Gabriel up and down. *This is Lancaster County. Haven't you ever seen an Amish person?*

He took a deep breath and forced himself to stow his frustration. As he stuffed his hands in the pockets of his black trousers, two of his fingers slid through a hole in his left pocket. He jumped when a bell rang to signal he'd reached his floor. He took his hands out of his pockets, tucked his head, and slid past the three men into a large corridor.

A few moments later, he walked into suite 308 and made his way to a lady at a desk, assuming she was the person who received visitors.

Smiling, the young woman asked, "May I help you?"

"Uh . . . I am here to see someone." He paused and removed his hat. "Um . . . a lady."

The woman at the desk raised an eyebrow, waiting.

"I, uh . . . I'm here to see the elf lady."

Grinning, her eyebrow rose even higher. "I'm sorry. Who?"

Gabriel felt a flush crawling up his neck, pretty sure his face was turning bright red. "She is Santa's helper. The lady. Can I talk to her?"

"Sir . . ." The woman smiled broadly. "We don't have a Santa Claus or an elf who works here." She glanced around, as if looking for someone.

"Oh." Gabriel shifted his weight, then dropped his hat. He scooped it up. "Um . . ."

The woman stood from her seat. "Wait right here, please." She disappeared behind one of two doors in the room. A few moments later, she returned with an older man. He was tall with salt-and-pepper hair.

"Hello, sir." The man extended his hand, and Gabriel slowly shook it. "I think I know who you're looking for. I'm Bruce Hanson. Follow me."

Gabriel followed the man down a long hallway. On either side hung big framed pictures of tall buildings. Gabriel wondered how long it took to build something like that. The man slowed his stride at a closed door on their left, then opened the door and motioned for Gabriel to go inside, closing the door behind them.

"You must be looking for Joan. She's the woman who was dressed as an elf in the store." He nodded toward a couch against one wall. "If you'd like to have a seat, I'll go find her for you."

"*Danki*. I mean, thank you." Gabriel sat down, and after Mr. Hanson was gone, he scanned the fancy office space. There was a big desk with a high-back chair behind it, and behind the chair was another type of desk with files, a phone, and several pictures of Mr. Hanson with a woman—his wife, Gabriel presumed.

He set his hat on his knee as his foot tapped wildly against the wood floor. The shiny flooring was nothing like the wood floors at home. Gabriel wondered how they got it to glisten like that. He took in a deep breath and waited.

Bruce opened the door to Joan's office, but she wasn't there. He checked the lounge and the copy room, then tapped lightly on Amanda's office door, knowing the two women were chummy. "Have you seen Joan?"

Amanda looked up and shook her head. "No, I haven't seen her this morning."

He smiled, left, and headed down the hallway as his heart pounded in his chest. He picked up his pace, then stopped outside Matt's door. He turned the doorknob and stepped over the threshold without knocking. He recognized the back of Joan's head as she sat facing Matt.

"Joan, there's someone here to see you," he said in a voice he didn't recognize, almost crackly like a teenager's.

Joan twisted to face him as Matt smiled from behind his desk. Bruce wanted to fire him on the spot.

"Oh." She put her pen atop a yellow legal pad in her lap, and right away Bruce wondered if it was just a prop, if there was really any work going on in this room. Joan walked toward Bruce, wearing a dark-brown knee-length skirt that flowed as she moved, and a white shirt that was belted at her waist. She moved quickly in her flat brown shoes, and Bruce wondered if he'd ever inventoried Joan's apparel before now. "Who is it?" she asked when she got within a foot of him.

"I, uh . . . forgot to ask his name." Bruce owned this building, everything in it, and the business. He shouldn't feel like a visitor, like a person interrupting something that shouldn't be going on anyway, but as he stammered, his pulse picked up even more. "I forgot to ask," he repeated.

Joan scowled as she tucked a strand of hair behind her ear. "Okay. Where is he?"

"In my office. He's Amish."

Joan left the room ahead of Bruce, but he was quickly on her heels until he was walking beside her. "I don't care what you do on your own time, Joan, but try to keep your little office romance from interfering with your job." A knot the size of a golf ball formed in Bruce's throat. He didn't think he'd ever reprimanded Joan for anything.

She kept walking, her eyes straight ahead, her expression unreadable and flat. "Shame on you for even saying that." Her chin lifted slightly.

What does that even mean? Bruce wasn't sure if Joan was saying again that nothing was going on, or if she was just angry that he'd pulled rank on her. But before he could analyze it further, she walked into his office and slammed the door behind her.

Bruce stood perfectly still as he faced his office door and the sign that hung on it. "Bruce Hanson, CEO." *The man in charge. That's me.*

Bruce had never felt less in charge in his life.

What is happening to me?

Mary wiped milk from Leah's mouth and lifted her from her high chair, the one Joan had given her. The *Englisch* woman had recalled seeing a high chair at a garage sale, and during their visit, Joan had left to go buy it. Mary was thankful to have two now.

Katie was in her playpen, and Mary sat down with Rachel Marie, Leah in her lap. Mary was glad the twins were well enough to go back to school, and a tinge of guilt nipped at her for having the thought.

"Have you tried to read the first few pages of your new book?" she asked Rachel Marie.

Rachel would have been in school with her brothers, but Mary and Gabriel had decided to hold her back until next year, hoping her health would be more stable.

"*Nee*, but I will." Rachel drew in a deep breath, her face paler than normal.

Mary stared at her beautiful daughter for a few long moments. "How are you feeling?"

Rachel lifted one shoulder, then lowered it slowly. "Not so *gut*."

Mary put her hand against Rachel's forehead, thankful it was cool to her touch. "Maybe just rest today. Or do you need one of the pills the doctor gave you?"

Rachel shook her head before she spoke to Mary in Pennsylvania *Deutsch*.

"Use your *Englisch*." Mary had been working with Rachel on her *Englisch* because most children learned it during their first year of school and Rachel would be a year behind the others. But with two older brothers, Rachel had picked up on most of the second language early anyway.

"*Nee*, I'm okay."

Mary kissed Rachel on her forehead. When Rachel's heart defect was first diagnosed, the doctors had assured Mary and Gabriel that Rachel would live a full life, but that she might require medication to treat her symptoms until she was old enough to have surgery.

When Leah began to yawn, Mary placed her in the playpen with Katie, who was already asleep. She was thankful that Leah drifted off to sleep quickly. She'd have about an hour to clean things up while they slept. As she recalled her conversation with Gabriel the night before, she wished she hadn't said anything to him. Today was a new day, and she was going to do her best to be a good wife and mother.

After she'd put another log on the fire, Mary picked up two plates the twins had left on the coffee table, along with a cup Rachel had used earlier. She was on her way to the kitchen when she heard a car coming up the driveway. After she set the dishes back on the coffee table, she went to the window. She recognized the black van with a dent on one side. It was her mother-in-law's driver. Mary was forced to use a driver most of the time because she had so many children in tow, but she'd never understood why her mother-in-law didn't travel short distances by buggy. Gabriel didn't have an answer either, saying only that his mother used to drive a buggy all the time. Mary remembered when Elizabeth started hiring a driver, around the time the twins were born.

"*Mammi* is here," she said softly to Rachel, then sighed.

Rachel twisted around to see out the window. She waited until Elizabeth was coming up the steps, then waved.

"What brings you out in this cold?" Mary opened the door for her mother-in-law and stepped aside, quickly closing the door behind her as a burst of cold air entered the room.

Elizabeth's eyes quickly found Leah and Katie, who were sleeping in the playpen. She stared at them for a long while before she looked at Rachel. "*Wie bischt*, dear. How are you feeling today?"

"I'm fine, *Mammi*." Rachel smiled a little.

Mary fought the awkwardness swirling around them. She'd prayed for years that things would be different between her and her mother-in-law, but she'd decided long ago that Elizabeth wasn't interested in having more than a polite relationship with her son's wife and children.

"I can't stay," Elizabeth quickly said in a whisper as her eyes drifted to Leah and Katie again, as if she were watching them grow in their sleep.

Of course you can't. Mary folded her hands in front of her and waited to hear the purpose of Elizabeth's visit.

"I wanted to let you know that Isaac and I will be traveling by bus to see the girls and their families for Christmas. We'll be gone two weeks."

Mary nodded. Gabriel's sisters lived in Philadelphia, and Elizabeth and Isaac visited them often. Even more so lately. It seemed they went every few weeks to spend time with them. "*Danki* for letting us know." Mary swallowed hard. Gabriel didn't usually say much about his parents' trips to Philly, but Mary knew it hurt him.

Elizabeth opened her mouth as if she were going to say something but snapped it closed. Instead, she hurried to Rachel, squatted down, and wrapped her arms around Rachel in a tight hug, kissing her tenderly on the cheek.

Mary thought she heard Elizabeth whisper that she loved Rachel, but it was so out of character for Elizabeth that Mary shook the thought away.

"Do you want some coffee?" Mary wasn't sure she had any coffee since she hadn't been to the market recently. But she knew her mother-in-law would decline.

"*Nee*. I must go." Her eyes drifted to Leah and Katie again, and she kept her gaze on the girls for a few seconds before she turned back to Mary. "Be well, dear."

Elizabeth wrapped her arms around Mary and squeezed tightly. Mary was too stunned to move at first, but she eventually embraced her mother-in-law.

"Safe travels," Mary said when Elizabeth finally eased out of the hug and turned to go. There was a part of Mary that wanted to lash out at her mother-in-law, to scream and holler that they all needed her as much as Gabriel's sisters did, probably more. But another part of Mary longed to rush after Elizabeth and beg her to stay—to show Mary how to be a better mother, maybe even provide some mothering to Mary.

Gabriel's sisters' children were all teenagers now. Maybe that was the problem, those children were older and well behaved. Mary had a troop of wild monkeys.

But I love my monkeys.

Mary stared as the van pulled away, then she picked up the dirty dishes from the coffee table and carried them to the kitchen. Gabriel had said repeatedly that the children shouldn't eat in the living room. But some days it was just easier to give in to them. *Choose your battles*, Joan had told her.

As she got a whiff of Samuel's leftover boiled egg on the plate, she hurriedly placed the dishes in the sink, then threw an arm across her stomach, hoping she made it to the bath-room.

I can't believe I'm having another child. She recalled her conversation the night before with Gabriel, when she'd cried and been pitiful. *Why can't I handle my family the way other mothers do?*

CHAPTER 8

Gabriel stood up when Joan walked into the room, closing the door rather loudly behind her. "I'm Mary's husband."

After they'd exchanged greetings, Joan folded her hands in front of her, lifted her chin, then asked how she could help him.

"I think you are friends with my wife."

She smiled slightly. "Well, I thought we were becoming friends, but then I was told you weren't comfortable with that."

"I, uh . . ." Gabriel scratched his forehead, wishing he had better prepared what he would say. "Do you want to come back to our house to see my wife?"

Joan stared at him for a few seconds, and Gabriel wondered if she was going to throw him out. "Let's sit down." She nodded toward the couch.

Gabriel sat down, his foot tapping again. He stilled it when Joan cut her eyes in his direction and lifted an eyebrow.

"Mary is a lovely girl," she said. "I felt called to reach out to her. But I've lived in Lancaster County my entire life, and I do realize that some Amish folks prefer to keep to themselves." She sent him a thin-lipped smile. "Having said that, I was told that you would prefer I not visit. What has changed?"

"I made a mistake." Gabriel lowered his gaze for a few seconds before he met the woman's eyes again. "Can I beg you to come back and visit with my wife sometime? I'm worried about her."

Joan's blue eyes softened as her smile took on a more genuine look. "Hon, you don't have to beg me. I'd be happy to pay her a visit soon."

"I don't know why she can't seem to tend to our household, but she said you helped her organize her time."

Joan scowled. "What exactly do you do? I mean, you work, right?"

"*Ya, ya.* After we pull the harvest in, I work at the lumberyard through the holidays and until it's time to plant our crop."

Joan nodded. "I see. And then at home, you help with the children at night, right?"

Gabriel straightened. "Sometimes I have to. Mary just can't keep up with our home and family." He shook his head. "I'm hoping maybe you can help her more with that organizing of her time."

Joan grinned, but it was that funny-looking smile that didn't show any teeth. "Oh, I think I can help her line out a schedule."

Gabriel felt a wave of relief. "*Gut.* That would be kind of you. She hasn't really had anyone to learn from. Her folks have passed, and she didn't have any siblings, so having a big family isn't familiar to her. And my parents are, um . . ." He looked past her, not sure how to explain his parents. "They're busy." Gabriel's heart got heavy when he faced the truth, that his parents didn't want to be around his unruly children. "I feel like if Mary is less stressed, then things will be better all around, especially since she's in a family way again."

Joan's jaw dropped. "You people *do* know how that happens, right?"

Gabriel's eyes rounded as heat radiated up his neck and surely filled his cheeks with color. "Sure. *Ya.* But a baby is a gift."

"Of course it is. But a woman must be able to maintain her sanity too." Joan stood up, and Gabriel figured that was his clue to do the same. "I'll be by next Friday to visit with Mary."

"I'll let her know. *Danki.*" Gabriel was on a tight budget, but he wondered what he was supposed to do in a situation like this. "Should I pay you for this?"

She tapped him once on the arm. "No, hon. Kindness is free." She smiled and walked toward the door, opening it for him. "Take care now."

He left the room and nodded to the older man who had been waiting in the hallway.

Bruce walked into his office, but he wished he hadn't. Joan was all bristled up, her chin high, her eyes blazing as she peered at him. He reminded himself that he was the boss, but like always, it didn't feel like it.

"Everything okay?" He held his breath, mostly referring to the Amish man who had visited, but also wondering if he had a verbal lashing coming.

"That was Mary King's husband. He has decided that maybe it's not such a bad idea for me to stay friendly with his wife."

"It's very nice of you to take an interest in her well-being."

"I told you—and Mary's husband—that I feel called to help

that young woman." She shook her head, frowning. "She's pregnant again, with her sixth child."

"The Amish always have a lot of kids."

"Yeah, I know. But some mothers, even Amish ones, need help." She pointed a finger at Bruce, and his heart rate picked up. "I am very disappointed in you for the way you spoke to me earlier. If I was in a relationship with Matt or anyone else, I certainly wouldn't carry on in the office." She leaned forward a little. "And I'm not in a relationship with anyone. It was dinner with a colleague, that's all."

Bruce took a cleansing breath. "Okay, that's good."

Joan took a step closer to him and tipped her head to one side, squinting slightly. "But Bruce, I would like to spend the rest of my life with someone. I've been alone for a long time."

Bruce hadn't been alone for as long as Joan, and sometimes he could barely stand to be in the same room with himself. He'd started talking to Whiskers at home recently, but his finicky feline didn't pay much attention, mostly yawning when he heard Bruce's voice. "I hope you find someone," he said softly. *Glad it's not Matt.*

"Me too."

After she'd left his office, Bruce poured himself into his chair, then spun around to look at the pictures of Lucy on his credenza. "Should I be trying to find someone too, Lucy?" He counted six framed pictures as he studied each one, the events scanning decades. A trip to Oklahoma for a friend's wedding. Another at the Mexican Riviera. His favorite was a close-up of just Lucy sitting on their deck at home, her dark hair swept up into a loose bun. He looked at the other photos, allowing himself to feel the sting from her absence, and then his eyes drifted back to the close-up. Leaning closer to the picture, he whispered, "What should I do?"

Pray.

He heard the word loud and clear in his mind. Did he imagine it?

"I haven't prayed in a long time," he said softly as he reached out to touch the photo. "Maybe I'm not worthy anymore."

Pray.

He closed his eyes, leaned his head back against his chair, then opened them and looked back at the picture. "I don't know what to pray for."

Mary finished bathing Leah and Katie, and as she dried Leah off, she could faintly hear Samuel and John in their room. They'd missed devotion time this afternoon, but when Gabriel wasn't home to pray with them, things tended to fall apart. And Gabriel was working late this evening, taking inventory at the lumberyard.

She kissed the babies before she lay each one in her respective crib, knowing Leah would cry for a while before she slept. Joan had assured Mary that was okay, as long as it didn't go on for too long. Mary closed the door to the girls' room, and Leah started to whimper right away, but Mary forced herself down the hall. She picked up a pair of black socks in the hallway, checked on Rachel Marie, who had fallen asleep early, and then peeked into John and Samuel's room, telling them each good night.

As she trudged down the stairs, she was pretty sure she could have sat down where she was and just fallen asleep. But when she hit the landing at the bottom of the stairs, she made her way to the couch and curled up at one end. A few minutes of sleep before Gabriel got home would do wonders, and she could devote quality time to her husband.

She wrapped a hand across her stomach as she wondered if this new life would be a boy or a girl. Gabriel would want another boy, someone to help in the fields when he was older. Before she even closed her eyes, she heard Gabriel's buggy coming, so she forced herself up and into the kitchen. She'd kept a pot of chicken and dumplings warm on the stove for him.

Despite her exhaustion, she was grateful that the children were fed, clean, and in bed. She met Gabriel with a hug and a kiss, then served him his supper.

"Aren't you eating?" He took a big spoonful of the soup, blowing on it before he slid it into his mouth.

"I already ate." Yawning, she kept her eyes on him, hoping for the tiniest compliment, that the soup was good. Or maybe he would notice that all of the children were tucked into bed. The house wasn't particularly clean by Gabriel's standards, but it was tidy, void of toys or other miscellaneous items strewn here and there. But he was quiet.

"I spoke to your friend Joan today," he finally said, glancing up at her. "She'll be here next Friday to visit with you."

Mary took in a sharp breath and held it before she blew it out slowly. "To *visit* with me?"

"*Ya*. I told her I made a mistake by forbidding you to see her." He shoveled another spoonful of soup into his mouth. "She'll help you organize your time again."

Mary tapped a finger to her chin as her bottom lip trembled. "It was one thing when my friendship with Joan progressed naturally, but it embarrasses me that you would go to her that way. I basically cut her out of my life before we'd even had a chance to get to know each other. Because of you."

Gabriel paused his full spoon and set it in the bowl. "Well, I made things right today. I thought you'd be glad about that."

Mary and Gabriel rarely had words. Mostly because Mary just went along with everything Gabriel said. But tonight she wasn't feeling so compliant. She was tempted to tell him to go see Joan again and to cancel the visit, but somehow that seemed like she'd lose in the end. Joan really had shown kindness and compassion to Mary, and Mary had looked forward to getting to know Joan better.

She decided to change the subject. "Your *mudder* was here today. She wanted to let me know that she and your father are going to Philadelphia for Christmas."

Gabriel cast his eyes down and stirred his soup. "*Ya*, okay."

"Don't you think it's odd that they spend so much time with your sisters and their families, even though they must travel by bus to do so?" The issue of Gabriel's family never coming around was usually an off-limits topic, but Mary wasn't up for any charades this evening. "I know they love us, but they also seem to avoid us for the most part."

"They don't avoid us." Gabriel's voice was louder than before. "Maybe they just don't feel comfortable here."

Mary sat taller, the quiver in her lip returning. "What is that supposed to mean?"

Gabriel shrugged before he resumed eating.

He was placing blame on her, and she couldn't help but wonder if he was right. Had Mary done everything she could to have a good relationship with his parents? *I thought I had.* Then she recalled the way Elizabeth had behaved earlier, how she was overly affectionate.

They were quiet for a while, then Mary said, "Do you think anything is wrong? I mean, maybe someone is sick, one of your sisters, or even one of your parents." She paused, thinking of Rachel Marie. "I hope it's nothing with one of the *kinner.*"

"I'm sure everyone is fine."

Mary put two fingers against her lips, thinking and knowing she should just leave the subject alone, but there was plenty of history to rebuke Gabriel's comment. "We didn't know for almost a month when your father fell and hit his head. And we didn't know for three months that your mother miscarried a baby. We also weren't told about the fire in the kitchen until after all the repairs were made."

Gabriel put his spoon in his empty bowl, hard enough that Mary feared it might have cracked the china. "They are private people, but that doesn't mean anyone is sick." He pushed his chair back from the table and left the room.

Mary called after him, but he didn't turn around. She should have known better than to mention the possibility of an illness to Gabriel. Her husband was a strong man of faith, but ever since Rachel Marie's heart diagnosis, he was sensitive—and terrified—about anyone getting sick. Mary understood that, but if any of their children got so much as a cold, Gabriel panicked.

As a tear slid down her cheek, she folded her arm across her stomach again. All she'd ever wanted was a big and loving family. But no one ever told her how much work it would be. And no one ever told her how hard marriage could be.

By the time she'd readied herself for bed, Gabriel was sleeping. She eased into bed beside him, lay on her side, and faced him.

What has happened to us, Gabriel?

CHAPTER 9

Bruce was finishing up a phone call when Joan walked into his office, her hands on her hips, a scowl on her face. He hastily ended the call with a potential client.

"What's wrong?"

"My car won't start." She rolled her eyes. "Again. I just got it out of the shop, and they assured me the problem was fixed. I'm supposed to go visit with Mary King today, the Amish woman."

"Just take mine." Bruce reached into his pocket, but Joan was already shaking her head.

"You know I can't drive a stick shift."

Bruce had never understood how someone their age had never learned to drive a standard. "I'll take you over there."

Joan let go of her hips and dropped her hands to her sides. "That would be great. I told her I'd be there around ten. I had a few things to catch up on here this morning."

Or maybe you just wanted to see Matt? Bruce stowed the thought, deciding not to borrow trouble this early on a Friday morning.

"I'll be ready in about an hour, if that works for you."

Bruce nodded, then realized he was looking forward to

getting out in the sunshine, even if it was just for a drive down the road to Amish country.

Joan rubbed her hands together in Bruce's car, so he adjusted the heater to a warmer setting. Through his dark sunglasses, he navigated his way down Lincoln Highway, noticing the glittery wreaths and swags of Christmas lights strung overhead blowing gently in the breeze. He recalled his Christmas last year, another holiday without Lucy. He'd spent it sitting in his recliner looking through old pictures, having told the world that he had plans on that day. Including Joan. He'd regretted lying to her ever since. He hoped she didn't ask what he was doing this year. Although, with Phillip gone, she'd be facing her first Christmas alone in years. *Or maybe she'll spend it with Matt.*

He pulled into the driveway where the young woman and her family lived. A section of the fence was down on one side. A modest pile of firewood was stacked in a rack by the house.

"So, what will you do today—babysit or help her clean house or cook?" Bruce eyed a scooter leaning up against the white clapboard house, the wheel resting beside the bike with enough dead grass around it that Bruce assumed it had been that way for a while.

"Mary is overwhelmed. I just want to help her learn the skills to run her household in a more efficient way. She's very young to have so many children and another one on the way."

Bruce smiled. "You're the woman for the job. I've never known anyone more organized and with such a keen ability to multitask."

She smiled. "Can you pick me up around three?"

Bruce nodded but then took another look at the fence, the bike, the lack of firewood. It had been a long time since he'd done any outside chores. He had a yard man who came when his lawn required attention, and lucky for him, he hadn't had to make any serious repairs lately. But there was a time when he enjoyed working outdoors with his hands, and with retirement looming, maybe a little physical work would be refreshing. "I don't have much going on today. Maybe I could help out around here outside while you're inside with Mary."

Joan lowered a pair of pink-rimmed sunglasses, then peered over them, grinning. "In a suit when it's forty degrees?"

Bruce shrugged. "It feels warmer with the sun out."

"Suit yourself." She laughed. "Pardon the pun."

Bruce followed Joan across the yard and up the porch steps. He recognized Mary when she opened the door, carrying a small child, with another little one standing by her side, clutching her mother's maroon dress. Peeking from behind Mary was the child who had come to see him, asking for help for her mother.

When Joan had told him about the little girl's mother hiding in her bathroom with the water running, Joan's eyes had been moist from recollections about her son who had suffered from anxiety. She was surely trying to keep Mary from slipping into that same bad place. Bruce was glad he'd tagged along.

Mary tried not to let shame and embarrassment wrap around her as she smiled at Joan and Santa Claus. Mary couldn't remember his real name.

"Joan, it was very kind of you to come out to see me today,

especially after our last phone call." Mary ducked her chin for a few seconds before she met Joan's eyes again. "But my husband shouldn't have come to see you. I'm embarrassed about it."

Joan chuckled, then winked at Mary. "Men. They have no idea how to act sometimes, do they?" She reached out her arms for Leah, who had stopped crying. The baby went right to her. "The truth is, I've been looking forward to our visit and spending time with these little ones." Glancing over her shoulder, she said, "Do you remember Bruce Hanson? He gave me a ride because my car isn't running at the moment."

"*Ya*, of course." Mary forced another smile.

Joan nuzzled noses with Leah, then leaned down and cupped Katie's cheek.

Mr. Hanson cleared his throat. "Uh, if it's okay, I thought I'd stay awhile." He pointed to the section of the fence that was down. "I'm pretty handy with a box of tools." *At least, I used to be.* "I'm sure your husband works long hours. Maybe I can get a few things done around here since I find myself caught up at work."

"*Nee, nee.*" Mary shook her head. "Your kindness and generosity are too much. I can't accept."

"Nonsense." Joan glanced at Mr. Hanson. "A little outdoor work will do him good, keep his middle from going soft."

Mr. Hanson scowled, but only for a moment before he smiled. "Ha, ha."

Mary grinned at their playful banter. There was a time when she and Gabriel teased each other.

"I've got a heavy coat in my trunk in case my car ever breaks down. I'll just slip out of this jacket and put it on. Does your husband have tools in the barn?"

Mary's jaw fell open. Her own in-laws had never offered to help them, and now two strangers were gleefully getting to work. What would Gabriel say when he got home and saw that two strangers had transformed their home into a place of order and peace?

Gabriel worked through lunch, then left a bit early and headed to his parents' house. Things needed to be said. His wife was falling to pieces, and Gabriel had never in his life felt more like a failure. He wondered how things were going at his house, if Mary's new *Englisch* friend was there like she'd promised, helping Mary to better manage the household. But something was niggling at Gabriel, tearing at him from the inside out. His father was on the front porch reading the newspaper when he pulled up in his buggy.

"*Wie bischt.* What brings you here in the middle of the afternoon?" His father closed the newspaper and crossed one leg over the other, setting a pair of gold-rimmed reading glasses atop the newspaper.

Gabriel pulled his coat snug and closed the distance between them, surprised his father was sitting outside. He was a man who barely tolerated cold weather. "I took off early today, and I wanted to talk to *Mamm*."

"Your mother is resting. Can I help you with something?"

Gabriel took off his hat and scratched his forehead. He wasn't sure he'd ever had a real heart-to-heart talk with his father. The few instances he'd felt compelled to unload emotionally, he'd sought out his mother. Gabriel didn't have the kind of relationship with his *daed* that made him comfortable seeking guidance. Isaac King was a strong man that made raising a family look easy, and he seemed to have done a good job.

Gabriel sat down in one of the two rocking chairs on the porch. The sun was just starting to set, and sunshine slipped right below the porch rafters, providing rays of warmth. He took a deep breath as he considered what he wanted to say. "I'm worried about Mary."

His father ran his hand the length of his dark beard. "Is she ill?"

Gabriel shook his head. "*Nee*, I don't think so. She's with child again, though."

"I see." The man's forehead creased as he continued to stroke his beard. Gabriel waited for his father to tell him that a baby was a blessing, a gift from God, but his eyes stayed in the distance as a cow made itself known in a far-off pasture.

"Mary has trouble running our household and taking care of the *kinner.*" He glanced at his father, who was still lost in a faraway gaze. Gabriel lifted an invisible leg and prepared to step over a line he'd never crossed before. "I don't understand why *Mamm* hardly ever visits or wants to babysit. She's never showed Mary how to properly run a household."

His father's expression remained flat, his eyes far away. Gabriel worried he'd overstepped. When his father didn't respond, he went on, figuring he'd gone this far.

"*Mamm* always babysat for *mei* sisters, especially Sarah's *kinner.* She kept them a lot. I know our children can be unruly and a handful, but . . . ." Gabriel shrugged. "I don't know what to do anymore. Right now there is an *Englisch* woman with Mary.

A woman she's taken a liking to who seems to help her organize her time. I don't like the idea, but I want *mei fraa* to have some help if she needs it."

"We all need a little help sometimes."

Gabriel stared at his father, surprised at his calm admission. "I don't even know if the elf lady is Christian."

His father turned to Gabriel, frowning. "Elf lady?"

Gabriel shook his head. "Well, she was an elf when Rachel first met her." Once again, Gabriel couldn't remember the woman's name.

"How did Rachel meet this elf?" *Daed* raised an eyebrow.

Gabriel took off his hat, scratched his head, and slipped the hat back on. "You know how the *Englisch* take their *kinner* to see Santa Claus at the store?"

His father nodded. "*Ya, ya.*"

"Well, Rachel Marie got away from Mary, and she stood in line to see Santa Claus. She'd heard that he grants wishes." Gabriel slunk into the rocking chair, and he saw that there were no Christmas decorations on the porch. Modest decorations were tradition, and his mother usually had greenery on the porch railing and a festive wreath on the door.

"Only the Lord grants wishes through prayer and faith." *Daed* shook his head. "But it's hard to shelter this generation of children from the outside world."

"Rachel Marie asked Santa Claus—the man who was pretending to be him—for help for her mother." He lowered his eyes, not wanting to see the disappointment that was surely to be found in his father's gaze. "The man sent us a check for three thousand dollars." He glanced up, but his father's eyes had returned to the pasture. "We sent it back, but that wasn't the kind of help Rachel meant. She wanted to know if someone could come help her mother tend to her family, I guess."

His father scowled. "How bad are things at your house, that a child would do such a thing?"

"Bad enough that a five-year-old can tell her mother can't cope with her responsibilities." Gabriel shamefully hung his head.

"And what do you do to help Mary?"

Gabriel's eyes shot to his father's. "Sometimes I have to help her bathe the *kinner* or clean up the kitchen." He shrugged. "Or other things that are her job. I just want her to be happy."

His father chuckled. "There's such an age gap between you and your sisters that I doubt you remember the routine when your sisters reached an age that could have done your mother in. *Sohn*, there is no his job or her job, no matter what you hear. Marriage and child-rearing are a partnership. *Ya*, traditionally, the women have certain things expected of them and the same for the men. But at the end of the day, it's all about what works for each family."

Gabriel's jaw dropped as he wished he'd reached out to his father sooner. "But everyone else makes it look so easy."

Daed laughed again. "No one knows what goes on behind another family's closed door. I assure you that raising a family isn't easy, but the rewards are many." His father grinned. "I used to sweep floors in the evenings after you kids went to bed."

Gabriel stared at his father. "I don't remember you ever doing that."

"*Ya*, well . . . I did. I went through a spell when I couldn't sleep, so I'd sweep all the floors to try to wear myself out. And ninety percent of the time, I got up with any child who woke up in the middle of the night."

Gabriel lowered his gaze, then looked back up at his father.

"Why can't *Mamm* help Mary, though, the way she did Sarah, Marie, and Lizzy? Mary didn't have siblings, so she doesn't understand, and she refuses to spank the children for anything."

Gabriel had grown up fearing the pine tree by the fence, the one his father always chose a switch from.

"Times are different, I reckon." His father tipped back his straw hat, scratching his forehead, then he locked eyes with Gabriel. "Your mother is sick, Gabe. She has a form of dementia that causes her to lose time, sometimes hours, and she's afraid to be around you or your family much because of this. She isn't herself when it happens. It's been going on for years, but she didn't want you to know about it." His father looked away. "I should have told you sooner."

"Do the girls know?"

His father nodded. "*Ya*. We travel there often for special treatments your mother receives in Philadelphia. She sees a specialist, a type of therapist that works with her, and sometimes it helps. Your *mamm* is a *gut* woman but a stubborn one. She doesn't want folks around here to know, so she refuses to take money from our community health care fund, and she wants to go far enough away from our district so that she isn't found out."

Despite the knot forming in Gabriel's throat, recollections washed over him like rainwater pooling in a forgotten place in his mind. How many times did his mother miss church? What about all the times she'd missed Sister's Day, the monthly gathering of women in their district? And there were plenty of times people had stopped Gabriel to say they hadn't seen his mother in a while. *It isn't just us she avoids.*

"Your *mamm* knows that Mary struggles. It's just part of

raising a big family. Your mother didn't want to add burdens for either of you. I told her she was making a mistake and that you and Mary would think she was avoiding you and the *kinner* for other reasons." *Daed's* eyes clouded in a way that Gabriel hadn't seen before. "Sometimes, she doesn't even know me." After a few moments, Gabriel thought he saw his father's lip quiver. "I'm sorry I haven't been to visit more often, but it fears me to leave your *mamm* alone for long."

Gabriel's chest tightened as fear gripped him the same way it had when Rachel had been diagnosed. "Will she get better?"

His father blinked his eyes a couple of times and shook his head. "*Nee.* The treatments help a little. But Gabe, she won't be cured of this. And when the disease takes hold of her for good, she will go down fast."

Gabriel tried to swallow back the lump that had been building in his throat, but his eyes filled with tears just the same.

CHAPTER 10

With his legs spread wide and his hands on his hips, Bruce's stance made him feel like a lumberjack or other strong and capable man. It had been a long time since he'd performed any real physical labor, and getting the fence repaired and grounded had left him sweating and winded. The temperature had risen to a cool forty-five, but without a cloud in the sky, the sun shone brightly, deceiving him about how cold it actually was.

He looked toward the house just as Joan stepped onto the porch. For a split second, this was Bruce's house, and Joan was his wife, calling him in for lunch. His chest tightened as guilt squashed the thought like it was a bug trying to burrow inside of him. He'd loved Joan for decades, but not the way that provoked this kind of thought pattern, and it confused him.

"We've laid out some cookies if you need a break." Joan smiled. Her silver locks bobbed atop her shoulders as she waved.

Bruce had the vision again, and by the time he reached Joan on the porch, his face burned with embarrassment. What would she think if she knew he was having such daydreams of them playing house together?

"All that hard work has left you red-faced and tuckered out, I see." Joan shivered, then rubbed her hands over her arms, which were covered by a black sweater.

"I've got to keep my tummy from getting soft." He smiled as he marched up the steps.

Joan laughed. "I reckon you do." She winked at him, which sent Bruce off balance, causing him to trip, then grab the hand-rail before he fell.

"Careful, fellow. You're not used to doing manual labor."

He followed her inside as the aroma of freshly baked cookies welcomed him. The two babies were in high chairs, and Rachel Marie sat in a chair at the table. Bruce slipped into a seat beside her. Mary and Joan were chatting quietly in the corner of the kitchen. It looked like Joan was writing down a recipe on a pad of paper and explaining it to Mary. Joan had already told him that the couple had twin boys, but that they'd be in school most of the day.

"We don't believe in Santa Claus." Rachel Marie spoke to Bruce in a whisper as he reached for a chocolate chip cookie. "But *danki* for helping us."

Bruce smiled. "Happy to help out."

The little girl stared at him. "We believe in God. He makes miracles happen."

I used to think so. Bruce nodded, letting his eyes drift to Mary and Joan. Their newly found friendship made him smile. It was nice to hear laughter. He glanced at the two babies—one with an upturned bottle, the other eating a cookie—then he looked back at the little girl. Rachel was staring at him. He raised an eyebrow, anticipating a question from her.

"Do you pray when you wear your Santa suit?" The child scratched her cheek with one hand as she dangled a cookie in the other.

Bruce's faith might have slipped, but he hadn't taken to lying to children, so he wasn't sure how to answer—that he wasn't praying much these days.

"I, uh, believe that the tradition of Santa Claus carries a bit of magic, I guess. When I wear it, sometimes I can make nice things happen." He recalled the checks he'd had issued to lots of children whose families had seemed to need help. Then he recalled Joan saying how you can't just throw money at a problem. He glanced at the two women chatting and laughing, at the babies, at Rachel, then thought about the good day's work he'd put in. He was tired physically but didn't remember feeling so emotionally gratified at the end of a day. He hadn't answered the child's question, but maybe she'd let it go.

Rachel shrugged. "Just think of the magic you could have if you prayed while wearing the Santa suit." Then she pushed away from the table and left the room without another word, and Bruce heard the front door close.

Two young boys came into the house, followed by the man who had visited him looking for Joan.

Mary held her breath as Gabriel walked into the kitchen behind Samuel and John. The twins said hello to Bruce and Joan, put their lunch pails on the counter, then left the kitchen, each taking a cookie with them.

"I told them to clean the henhouse," Gabriel said before he extended his hand to Bruce. "Nice to see you again." He nodded to Joan.

Mary was still waiting for some type of wrath from her husband, even though he'd set up this visit.

"Wonderful about the boys," Joan said. "Mary and I were just talking about a firm list of chores she could assign to them. If they like the outdoors, let's factor that in."

"Mary, can I talk to you for a minute?" Gabriel's tired eyes locked with hers before he looked at Joan. "*Danki* for your time today, for this visit. Would you mind keeping an eye on the babies while I speak with Mary privately? We won't be long."

And here comes the wrath. Mary tucked her chin and followed Gabriel to their bedroom. He closed the door behind them, then threw his arms around her. "I love you," he whispered. "And things are going to be different. I'm going to help out more, and . . ." His voice trembled as his sentence trailed.

Mary eased away from him. His eyes were filled with tears. "Gabriel, what is it?"

"*Mei mamm* is sick."

Mary was quiet as her husband explained about Elizabeth. A typhoon of emotions engulfed her. Fear for Elizabeth, regret she hadn't known sooner. But her mind bustled with ways she might be able to help her mother-in-law.

It took a few moments for Gabriel to gather himself, but when they walked back into the kitchen, both Mr. Hanson and Joan were fussing over Leah and Katie, playing peek-a-boo and laughing. Mary smiled at the way the babies responded to their new friends. Even Rachel Marie was in on the game, covering her eyes and laughing.

"I'm sorry about that," Gabriel said. "I learned today that my mother is ill, and I needed to tell Mary about it."

"Oh dear." Joan's eyes widened as she focused on Gabriel. "I'm sorry to hear that. Is there anything we can do?"

"*Nee*. Thank you, though." Gabriel hung his hat on the rack by the door, then sat down in an empty chair by Leah, taking time to kiss the baby on the cheek. "They have been traveling to Philadelphia for my mother to get therapy for dementia, but they'd been trying to spare us this news."

"That's a long trip," Bruce said as he leaned back in his chair. "And it's not a trip that can be made by buggy, I'm sure."

Gabriel shook his head. "*Nee*. They have to hire drivers, but *mei* sisters and their families live there, so at least they have a place to stay. But it is still a hardship on them." Her husband had already told Mary privately that his mother didn't want folks around here to know about her condition, so she was a little surprised that Gabriel shared with these people he didn't know well. But maybe that was why he felt comfortable telling them—they were outsiders. Although, as Mary glanced at Joan, the woman didn't feel like an outsider at all.

"I will pray for them, Gabriel." Joan smiled a little before she looked at Bruce. "We should probably be on our way."

Mary cleared her throat. "You should stay for supper. There's more than enough, and it's the least we can do for the kindnesses you've shown us." She glanced at Gabriel and wondered if she had overstepped. Her husband wasn't going to change his opinion about outsiders overnight, no matter how kind and helpful Bruce and Joan had been, but he nodded.

"*Ya*. Please stay."

"Well, I do enjoy these babies." Joan touched Katie on the

cheek and smiled, and then she winked at Bruce. "Seems like someone else does too."

Rachel Marie coughed, and everyone turned her way, but she took a sip of water and didn't seem to notice that all eyes were on her. Mary wondered if there would ever be a time she didn't worry about her oldest daughter.

But for today, she was going to be grateful for her family, her husband's honesty and change of heart, and she was going to pray for Elizabeth. A sense of strength was wrapping around her, a need to be stronger.

Bruce thanked Mary for the meal, and when their hostess asked if they would like to stay for devotions, Joan said yes. Bruce wasn't sure how to get out of it. Gabriel asked if Bruce wanted to join him in the living room while the women cleaned the kitchen, but then he said, "Actually, I think I'll bathe Leah and Katie while the women take care of the kitchen. But please, relax on the couch. I'm very appreciative of the work you did around here today." He paused, looking away. "Always so much to do, and I just hadn't gotten to that fence."

"It did me a world of good to work outside." Bruce smiled, and after Gabriel was gone, he looked down at the tear in his trousers. He chuckled a little. Working in a pair of eighty-dollar slacks and fixing the fence for an Amish family he barely knew when it was forty degrees outside hadn't been on his radar. But he'd enjoyed the work, and the family was kind. Joan was right to follow her calling. Bruce thought again about the forthcoming devotions, unsure if he was ready to commune with God, but he was considering it.

Gabriel laid Leah in her crib upstairs. Mary joined him and got Katie settled in her crib. He'd told Mary that things were going to be different, that he was going to help out more. Mary said that she felt stronger when Joan was around, and that the older woman encouraged her to keep to a schedule that allowed for flexibility. Gabriel still wasn't sure about close friendships with outsiders, but his heart had been warmed to see Bruce—as he insisted they call him—and Joan interacting with their children, and Gabriel shouldn't let one past event define who they were friends with. His mother's incident might have been Gabriel's first recollection of the outside world when he was young, but he had to believe that not everyone outside of their community was dishonest.

"Do you think Bruce and Joan are Christians?" he whispered to Mary as he carried the lantern, both of them tiptoeing out of the girls' room. "Bruce looked uncomfortable during devotions."

"*Ya*, they are Christians. Joan even prayed with me earlier in the day. But she told me that Bruce struggles with his faith. Apparently he took the loss of his wife quite hard, and Joan said he turned away from the Lord."

An alarm sounded in Gabriel's mind, but he wasn't going to allow it to control his choices right now. "Maybe we can help him find his way back."

Mary threw her arms around him in the hallway. "I love hearing you say this, and I think the changes we are both making will benefit all of us. But"—she eased away—"I feel badly for all the ill thoughts I've harbored about your mother. I just assumed she didn't want to be around us because the children weren't well behaved and because I'm not the best housekeeper. But I'm going to do better, and I'm thinking of ways I can help your mother."

They started down the hallway but slowed their pace when they got to the twins' room. Both boys were tucked in bed. Samuel had a flashlight under the covers, but Gabriel chose to let it go. The boy liked to read and seemed to drift to sleep with a book, much like his father.

When they got to Rachel Marie's room, they paused again. Joan was softly reading a passage from Rachel's Bible to her as Bruce looked on.

"Look at the way Bruce is watching her." Mary spoke so quietly that Gabriel could barely hear her.

"Who? Rachel?"

"*Nee.* Look at the way he is watching Joan. I've seen the way she looks at him too."

CHAPTER 11

Bruce was nearing Joan's street when his longtime friend said, "What a wonderful day this was." She chuckled. "Some hard work, but helping that girl feels right to me. She won't get it all figured out overnight, and I suspect those twins have plenty of mischief up their sleeves, but she needed to know she wasn't alone. Parenting is the hardest job on the planet."

"You're a good woman, Joan." Bruce glanced in her direction before he turned onto her street. Even in the darkness, her eyes sparkled. Plenty of people had told Joan that she had "the light" over the years. Bruce wasn't sure he ever understood what that meant until today. She lit up a room with her smile, she had goodness to a fault sometimes, but she also seemed to walk in God's light. Bruce wanted to stay in her shadow on that trek.

She touched his arm. "And you're a good man," she said. He'd hugged Joan hundreds of times over the years, he and Lucy both, but the feel of her hand on his shoulder was different today. His heart beat faster than normal. His jealousy over the time she'd spent with Matt was more than just a protective instinct. He loved Joan. Lucy had loved her too. *So, what's different?* Something was different.

"I guess you and Phillip will go to Texas for Christmas?" Bruce didn't relish the thought of spending Christmas alone again, but it seemed better than the alternative—making small talk and pretending to be festive. He was sure a colleague or friend would ask him to dinner, like the past few years, and he'd decline again this year. But if Joan invited him for Christmas, he had decided he would go.

"Actually, this will be the first Christmas without my family. Ever." She moved her mouth from one side to the other, ping-ponging her dimples from one cheek to the other. "Phillip informed me that he is planning to move out, but it won't be until after the holidays. But he is going skiing in Colorado with two other young men over Christmas break. And the rest of the kids are taking their children to Disneyland over the holidays. They asked me repeatedly to join them, but that's just not my thing. So, we will celebrate after the first of the year."

"Hmm . . ."

"What about you? Will you choose to be alone on Christmas again this year?" Joan pointed a finger at him. "Yes, I know you were by yourself last year, even though you said otherwise at the time. Lucy wouldn't like you being by yourself. You know how much she loved the holidays."

Bruce flinched. "Sorry. I just wasn't ready to be around anyone on Christmas Day." He tried to construct a sentence in his mind, a way to ask Joan to spend Christmas with him, but his nonverbal attempts didn't sound right in his head.

"Didn't you love spending time with those children? They are just precious." Joan paused. "You know, they invited me to have Christmas with them. Gabriel's parents will be with his sisters in Philly, so it will just be Mary, Gabriel, and the kids."

Bruce smiled. "They invited me too. I was surprised since I barely know them."

She touched his arm again. "Good people recognize good people. And I think we should go."

Bruce put the car in park. He considered shaking his head and telling her he couldn't, but a small inner voice whispered, *Go.*

Mary threw up her breakfast before she'd even had time to clean the kitchen. She suspected her morning sickness would take hold of her for the first three months, as it had with her other pregnancies. The boys were out of school since Christmas was only two days away. After she'd gathered herself, she told the twins to sit at the kitchen table, that she needed to talk to them.

"We are going to do things a little differently around here." Mary put her hands on the back of a kitchen chair, glancing back and forth between Samuel and John. She pointed to a piece of paper on the table. "That is a list of chores that each of you will take care of. On the right side of the page is an empty box. When you complete the task, you get a star in that box. Once you have ten stars, you get a special treat."

It was the first of many changes Mary planned to implement in her effort to run her household more efficiently. She'd been concerned that a reward system for the boys wasn't in line with a proper upbringing, but Joan had just chuckled. "We do what we can to keep our sanity," she'd said.

For the first time in her life, Mary didn't feel alone. She could be a good mother and a good wife, and most days would never run perfectly, but she would do her best through prayer and patience.

After the boys joined Rachel Marie in the living room, Mary set to baking two loaves of bread that she'd kneaded earlier. Gabriel came into the kitchen and wrapped his arms around her waist, tickling her neck with his beard.

"Katie and Leah both have clean diapers, and they are in the playpen." He kissed her softly behind her ear. "I have an idea for Christmas."

Mary turned to face him, and he kissed her tenderly, like a whisper at first, then with enough passion for her to consider abandoning the dishes. But she knew the babies wouldn't be napping for a while. "What's that?" she finally asked.

She listened as her husband told her his thoughts about the holidays. "I think it's a wonderful idea," she said, kissing him again.

Bruce woke up Christmas morning to the first snowfall of the season, and by the time he'd showered and eaten a light breakfast, a blanket of white covered his yard and car. He picked up his keys from the hutch by the front door, lingering at Lucy's picture smiling back at him. Hesitating, he wondered if he should stay home.

Go.

Smiling, he eyed himself in the mirror, all repacked into the Santa Claus suit, by special request of Miss Rachel Marie King. The child had gone to a nearby shanty and called Bruce the day before, asking if he could please wear the Santa suit when he came for Christmas dinner. It seemed strange that she'd make such a request since Santa wasn't part of Amish tradition. But it was Christmas, so Bruce figured he would indulge her. He'd asked her on the phone if it would upset her parents, and Rachel had assured him that it wouldn't.

He drove slowly to Mary and Gabriel's house since a light layer of ice was forming on the roads. Large snowflakes cascaded from above, sticking to his windshield. He couldn't remember the last time he'd seen a white Christmas.

When he arrived at his destination, Joan was carefully stepping on the stone slabs that led to the porch, holding her hands out to each side for balance, a plastic grocery bag over her arm.

Bruce caught up to her. It wasn't until then that he realized he'd forgotten to stuff a pillow under his Santa jacket.

"I wasn't sure you'd make it." Joan turned to face him, smiling. Her hair was in a tight ponytail, her rosy cheeks dimpling as she spoke. She wore a black coat that fell almost to her knees, and it was buttoned to her neck. But the green hose and pointed green shoes gave her away along with the elf hat she was carrying. "Why in the world do you think Rachel would call and ask us to dress up?" She laughed. "Very atypical for an Amish girl."

Bruce instinctively latched onto her elbow as they walked up the icy steps.

"Oh my." Joan looked above the door at a sprig of mistletoe. Bruce felt his face turning red. Then she knocked on the door.

"There's a note." Bruce pointed to a piece of paper behind the screen, attached to the wood door.

Joan opened the screen door, then leaned closer to the note. Bruce glanced at the mistletoe and cleared his throat. She turned around and met his gaze, and then she also looked up but quickly handed him the note. "It says to let ourselves in."

"I hope there's not a problem. With five kids, you'd think we would hear some activity, even from out here."

Joan turned the doorknob and walked into a dark, quiet living room, Bruce following her.

"I feel like someone is going to jump out and say, 'Surprise.' Or 'boo.'" Bruce chuckled.

"Mary? Gabriel?" Joan crossed through the living room toward the kitchen. "Anyone?"

Bruce caught up with her. "I smell food."

Both their eyes landed on a larger piece of paper on the kitchen table. "Another note," Joan said as she picked it up and read aloud.

Dear Joan and Bruce,

A driver picked us up early this morning to take us to Philadelphia to be with Gabriel's sisters, their families, and his parents. Especially now, having learned his mother is ill, we want us all to be together. We are sorry if we deceived you, but we were afraid that the two of you would each stay home on Christmas Day. And that would never do for Santa and the elf lady.

Joan laughed.

There is a turkey with all the fixings inside the refrigerator, ready to be warmed up. Samuel and John stacked plenty of firewood outside the back door. There is even a bottle of eggnog in the refrigerator.

We are thankful to know you. And we hope that you will enjoy this occasion to celebrate the birth of our Lord.

Peace be with you, and Merry Christmas,

Mary, Gabriel, and the children

P.S. It was Rachel's idea to ask you to dress up. She said you would understand.

Joan looked up at Bruce and locked eyes with him, and then she lifted her gaze overhead as she walked around the kitchen. Someone had hung mistletoe in various places throughout the room.

"You do realize this is a setup, right?" Joan lowered her eyes and found his. She pointed to the middle of the table. "Those candles aren't normally there."

Bruce nodded as he picked up the box of matches that had been left on the table, and he lit the candles. But he couldn't take his eyes off of Joan for more than a few seconds. He felt like he was seeing her for the first time, in a new and confusing way, but a cocoon of hope calmed his racing heart.

"Why do you think Rachel wanted us dressed up like this?" Joan waved her arms the length of her body.

Bruce smiled. "I told her I believed in the magic of Christmas." He paused. "Rachel told me that she believed in the power of prayer and that I should think about how much magic I would have if I prayed while wearing the Santa suit."

Joan folded her arms across her chest, grinning. "Smart girl. How's that working out for you?"

"Well . . . I guess I'm about to find out." He dropped the matches on the table and stared at her. "I don't want you going out with Matt."

Joan's lips puckered as her eyebrows slanted inward. "Is that so?"

"He's . . . he's not the man for you." Bruce could almost feel Lucy nudging him on, saying, *She's your best friend. It's okay to love her.* But he looked away, lost in a singular world that longed for companionship, and not from just anyone. He wanted Joan by his side on the remainder of his journey, but he had no idea if that was even something that might interest her. But when her hand cupped his cheek, he felt the warmth in her touch all the way to his soul, and as he locked eyes with her, she smiled, then pointed above their heads.

Bruce wasn't sure he remembered how to kiss, but as he leaned down and found Joan's lips, he lingered there, drawing her close to him, knowing their friendship was evolving into something more intimate.

"I've been waiting a long time for you to do that." Joan smiled up at him. Somehow her hands were in Bruce's as they stood facing each other.

They spent several more moments in each other's arms, and Bruce was sure they had lots to talk about, maybe curled up on the couch in front of the fireplace later, but they both laughed when Bruce's stomach growled at them.

"Let's get Santa some food." Joan gazed at him one last time before she took off her coat and made her way to the refrigerator. Thirty minutes later, they had the food warmed and on the table. Bruce bowed his head when Joan did. And this time he had plenty to say. He thanked the Lord for allowing him to see Joan in a way that lifted his sorrow. He would always miss Lucy, but somehow a void was filling, and God was responsible for the joy he felt.

"What a wonderful meal." Joan closed her eyes, took a deep breath, and blew it out slowly. "They were insistent on no gift giving, and I respected that, even though it was hard. But now I wish I'd broken the rules and gotten them at least a little something in appreciation of not only this great meal, but for . . ." She clamped her mouth closed, her cheeks dimpling.

"For setting us up like this?"

Joan smiled. "I only went out with Matt to light a fire under you. But I also let him know that it was just a friendly dinner so he didn't think otherwise."

Bruce almost spewed tea when he chuckled, then said, "It certainly worked."

"I hope Mary, Gabriel, and the children are having a wonderful time. Family is so important."

Bruce smiled on the inside, keeping his eyes on his plate. "I think they will all have a wonderful Christmas."

Joan squinted her eyes at him and grinned. "What have you done?"

He couldn't look her in the eyes. Bruce never wanted to lie to her about anything. But Rachel was right. Combining the magic of Christmas with prayer could certainly work miracles.

Smiling, he finally locked eyes with Joan and winked at her. "Santa never tells his secrets."

CHAPTER 12

G abriel stacked wood in his arms alongside his father, and
then they began the trek from the barn back to his sister's
house, fighting random gusts of snow, careful to keep their footing as they walked across the frozen yard.

"I'm glad you, Mary, and the *kinner* came. And I'm glad your
mamm is having a *gut* day."

Gabriel was still adjusting to his mother's illness. "Will she
remember this day?"

His father offered up a weak smile. "I hope so."

They walked quietly for a while before his father spoke
again. "Your *mamm* wants to talk to you and Mary privately.
She feels bad that she didn't share about her condition with you."

Gabriel enjoyed getting to know this more intimate side of
his father, but he dreaded having a conversation with his mother
about her illness.

He and his father set down the wood they were carting, placing it right outside the front door for easy access.

"How's Mary's new elf friend working out?" His father
grinned.

"They've become *gut* friends. She works for an *Englisch* man that has come to visit us also. He even did some work around our *haus*. They like our *kinner* real well."

His father smiled. "A child can never have too much love."

They were quiet again, shivering, and Gabriel's bottom lip trembled, but more from fear than cold. "Is Mom going to . . . to, um?"

"Die?" His father's eyes left Gabriel's as his gaze drifted to a place somewhere over Gabriel's shoulder. It was several long seconds before his father said anything. He stared into Gabriel's eyes, and Gabriel braced for the worst. "That was the initial diagnosis, that your *mudder's* dementia would continue to take her downhill, to a point where she didn't remember or know much at all. But something has happened. Something that has given us far more hope than we've had."

Gabriel raised his eyebrows and waited, even though his heart still hammered in his chest.

"I'll let your *mudder* explain. She's waiting for you and Mary in the downstairs guest bedroom."

Mary sat down beside Elizabeth on the bed. Gabriel eased into the rocking chair nearby. The sounds and smells of Christmas wafted underneath the closed door. Hot cider simmering on the stove. Turkey baking in the oven. And children's laughter could be heard from the living room. The love of family everywhere.

A tear rolled down Elizabeth's cheek, and Mary reached for her mother-in-law's hand and squeezed. "Please don't cry. I wish I had known all along that you were ill. I could have tried to help more, or—"

"*Nee, nee.* You have your hands full with young *kinner,* so please don't say that. I'm just very sorry that you thought we didn't want to be around your children because of their behavior. They are just children, lively and full of energy. I was just always fearful of not being up for the task. What if something happened, if I had a bad spell or something, and I was watching the children at the time?" She covered her face with her hands. Mary didn't think she'd ever seen her mother-in-law cry before, and such an outpouring of emotion soon had Mary in tears as well.

"But it isn't all doom and gloom." Elizabeth swiped at her tears and smiled. Then she told Mary about a new medication she would be starting to take soon. "Isaac and I had ruled out the medication because it is very expensive and not widely available. Even my doctor said it's hard to get. But . . ." She paused, shaking her head. "My doctor received word that an anonymous donor is paying for this medication for as long as I need it." Her eyebrows drew inward as a confused expression took over. "I just don't know anyone who would be able to afford such a thing,"

"Then there is hope that you will get well?" Mary brought a hand to her chest.

"*Ya,* there is hope. It is a blessing we couldn't have foreseen. And there is more. We love visiting your sisters and their children, but traveling to Philadelphia every two or three weeks is expensive and hard on us. But now we have a doctor, a therapist type person to work with me, who will come to our *haus* as often as need be." Elizabeth drew her eyebrows together until her eyes were thin slits. "And it's all paid for. We don't have to pay anything, which means we can travel to Philadelphia when we want to, but not nearly as often. And it's confidential, so I can choose to tell members of the district what I'm going through, or not. I'm leaning toward telling some of my close friends. Even my doctor said the support will be helpful.

"Who would do such a kindness for us?" Elizabeth asked again.

Mary glanced at Gabriel, his eyes wet with emotion. But they both smiled, and Mary was pretty sure her husband was thinking what she was thinking. *Bruce.*

She reached for a tissue in her apron pocket, dabbing at her eyes, just as Rachel Marie came bursting into the room, closing the door behind her. "I'm hiding," she said, snickering, but her smile faded when she realized Mary and Elizabeth were crying. Gabriel sat taller and quickly swiped at his eyes. "What's wrong? Why are you crying?" She slowly edged closer to the bed.

"We're fine," Elizabeth quickly said, sniffling.

"*Ya, ya.* These are happy tears." Mary smiled broadly. "We just got some very *gut* news. You know how our friend Joan helped Mommy and became my friend?"

Rachel nodded.

"Well . . ." Mary considered how to explain this blessing to a five-year-old. "Someone is helping out *mammi*, making things easier and better for her while she is trying to get well from this sickness."

"Who?" Rachel Marie's eyes grew round as saucers.

"We don't know," Elizabeth said. "The person wishes to remain anonymous, which means they don't want anyone to know about this blessing, about the kindness they are showing us."

Rachel Marie took a few slow steps toward Mary and Elizabeth, then tapped her finger to her chin. Then her face lit into a big smile. "Santa isn't magic, but when Santa and God get together, I think magical things can happen."

Mary smiled, even though her mother-in-law looked confused, looking back and forth between Rachel Marie and Mary.

Rachel Marie took another step closer to Mary, whose Christmas blessing was also seeing her daughter's rosy red cheeks today. "Do you think that our *Englisch* friends will get to become husband and wife?"

Mary suspected they were all hoping that their efforts at home would lead to Joan and Bruce seeing their relationship in a new light. "Maybe so. I hope so."

Rachel Marie grinned even larger than before. "I told him to pray while wearing the Santa suit. Maybe he did."

"I will fill you in later," Mary whispered to her mother-in-law before she looked back at her daughter. "All things are possible through—"

"—Christ who strengthens us."

A warmth filled Mary's heart from head to toe as she reached for Rachel Marie's hand, then her mother-in-law's. "Indeed," she said in a whisper as she squeezed their hands.

As Gabriel closed the distance between them, he wrapped his arms around them all, and somehow Mary knew everything was going to be okay.

CHAPTER 13

B ruce knocked on Mary and Gabriel's door, then glanced
down at his slightly enlarged waist. He'd packed on a little
winter weight, but with his retirement and spring around the
corner, he planned to take on some home improvement projects.
He'd even canceled his yard service, opting to reunite himself
with his lawn mower soon.

"I look forward to this day so much." Joan's face dimpled
and lit up as she spoke. She and Bruce had been having dinner—
supper as the Amish called it—with Mary, Gabriel, and their
children every Saturday evening for the past few months. "And
Mary is doing so much better."

"Thanks to you." Bruce squeezed her hand.

Still smiling, she said, "Oh, I think you had a hand in this
couple's happiness also."

"*Ach!*" Mary opened the door and ushered them inside.

March had arrived, yet the winter temperatures lingered.
Bruce was ready for spring, and he was happy to see a warm fire
going, orange sparks wafting upward. As always, Rachel was the
first of the children to greet Bruce and Joan, and today she had a
new faceless doll to show Joan.

"Isn't this lovely," Joan said as she leaned down to hug Rachel.

Bruce heard voices coming from the kitchen, and it sounded like either Leah or Katie banging a spoon on the table or high chair. Laughter was coming from that direction also.

Mary reached for both of Joan's hands, then smiled. "Elizabeth and Isaac are here. I hope that's okay. They've been spending more time with us, but they'd really like to get to know you and Bruce better."

Joan cupped Mary's cheeks. "Darlin', we are thrilled they are here."

Bruce smiled. Joan's Texas accent slipped out from time to time, even though she'd been in Pennsylvania for decades. Bruce was looking forward to seeing all of Joan's children in a couple of months. With the exception of Phillip, he hadn't seen the others in years. And he was eager to meet her grandchildren. Both he and Joan felt like grandparents to Mary and Gabriel's kids, but Bruce knew how much Joan missed her own grandchildren.

After introductions were made, everyone took their places at the kitchen table.

"That's my recipe," Joan whispered to Bruce as she slid into a chair beside him. "It's called chalupa casserole." She pointed and still spoke softly. "A bit spicy, but with a nice cheesy, Texas flair."

After the blessing, everyone dove in, and Mary was quick to give credit for the meal by announcing that the recipe was Joan's, who waved a dismissive hand at Mary.

"Each cook makes it her own recipe, with her own special touches," Joan said modestly.

Bruce tried to keep his manners intact as he gobbled up the chalupa casserole. If he had a weakness, it was cheese, and this dish was loaded with it. He glanced down at his stomach again.

Hurry up, spring. But he had another motive for his hastiness in finishing the meal. He waited patiently for everyone to finish eating. Only Leah had anything left on her plate. He'd noticed the children were all having ham and green beans, which made sense. As Joan had mentioned, the casserole was a little spicy.

Bruce cleared his throat, then formally tapped his fork to his iced tea glass. He hadn't realized until now how nervous he was. "I, uh . . . I have an announcement to make."

As the fire crackled and popped in the next room, Bruce waited for Mary to finish wiping Katie's face, and once all eyes were on him, he said. "I've asked Joan to marry me, and she has made me the happiest man in the world by saying yes."

Joan turned his way as a blush filled her cheeks. "I'm going to love this man for the rest of my days."

Mary was already standing up and rounding the table to get to Joan. Mary threw her arms around Bruce's fiancée. "We've been hoping for this." Then Mary hugged Bruce.

A round of congratulations was followed by embraces from everyone, and Elizabeth picked up Leah when all the excitement seemed to unnerve the child and she started to cry a little. But as Elizabeth nuzzled her, Leah quieted. Mary had already told them that the medication Elizabeth had received was working miracles. She still had an occasional bad day, but overall she was thriving and spending much more time with Mary, Gabriel, and the children.

"I'd like to offer a prayer for this union," Gabriel said with a taut nod of his head before he bowed. Everyone followed suit.

"Dearest heavenly Father," Gabriel began. "*Danki* for sending Joan and Bruce into our lives, and we pray their marriage will be filled with joy and love for all of their days." The young man paused. "And Lord, we thank you for the miracle of healing that you have bestowed upon *Mamm*."

As everyone lifted their heads and said amen, Gabriel locked eyes with his wife and smiled. The difference in the couple had been amazing. Bruce wondered how things might have turned out if little Rachel Marie hadn't braved the crowd and stood in line to talk to Santa.

"Who is ready for dessert? It's banana pudding." Mary pressed her palms together as she smiled and looked at her mother-in-law. "And this recipe came from Elizabeth."

Elizabeth's face grew a little red, and she also waved off Mary. "As Joan said, each recipe becomes your own, dear."

Bruce recalled what Joan had said to him awhile back about the many ways that God saves us all, the ways He works in all of our lives. He glanced around the room at everyone and smiled. *Thank You, Lord.*

DISCUSSION QUESTIONS

The Gift of Sisters

1. What were your feelings about Rachel at the beginning of the story? Did you sympathize with her? If not, what are some of the ways that Rachel changed throughout the story that might have softened your opinion of her?
2. Most women don't get through young adulthood without a run-in with a "bad boy." Did you know someone like Abraham when you were a teenager or older? How did you handle the situation?
3. Hannah and Rachel could feel it when the other twin was hurting or in trouble. Have you ever known twins who seemed to share this ability? Or, maybe not just twins. Have you known siblings with this type of instinct?

A New Beginning

1. What are some instances that the characters either took things out of context or misinterpreted an action? Has this ever happened to you, and if so, what was the outcome?

2. What do you think would have happened if McKenna wasn't involved with Paul and had been as infatuated with Noah as he initially was with her? Would Noah's love for Rebecca have won out in the end?

3. At various times in the story, there were reasons to root for each of the characters, and there were reasons not to in some scenes. But, in the end, did you end up rooting for all of them? Or, did one particular character steal your heart?

A PERFECT PLAN

1. Priscilla wants to have a perfect wedding day, but she loses sight of what's really important. How might things have been different if she hadn't let worry creep into her heart?

2. Chester likes that Priscilla is organized and structured, but is there ever a point when he wonders if her need for perfection will do harm to their relationship?

3. Rachel writes letters to both Priscilla and Chester, letters that hit on exactly what they are both feeling prior to the wedding. Do you think God is speaking to Priscilla and Chester through Rachel? Has this ever happened to you or to someone you know?

4. In what ways does an Amish wedding differ from a traditional *Englisch* wedding? Is there anything about an Amish wedding that you think should be incorporated into an *Englisch* wedding? Or vice versa?

A Christmas Miracle

1. Anyone who has parented a child knows that it is rewarding, but it can also be very challenging, especially having as many children as Mary and Gabriel. What do you think would have happened to Mary if she hadn't met Joan? Have you ever known anyone who struggled like Mary to raise a family?

2. The spirit of Christmas is prevalent throughout this story. How are some of the ways this is expressed?

3. What was your opinion of Elizabeth? And did your feelings about her change by the end of the story?

ACKNOWLEDGMENTS

As an author, I aspire to write stories that deliver what my readers expect from me—an entertaining plot combined with messages of faith, hope, and love. After writing these novellas, it seemed like the perfect opportunity to thank those of you who read my books. Thank you for staying with me, believing in me, and for all of the emails and letters I have received over the years.

To my publishing team at HarperCollins Christian Fiction, we've been on this journey for ten years now, and what a ride it has been. You are all awesome, and it's an honor to work with each of you.

Natasha Kern, my fabulous agent, what would I do without you? It's no secret that you are a fabulous agent, but you are also a wonderful friend. I'm blessed to have you in my life, professionally and personally. Thanks for all you do!

To Janet Murphy, "thank you" hardly seems enough anymore. But thank you, thank you, thank you for being my assistant, voice of reason, and my dear friend . . . and I know you always have my back, lol.

My husband, Patrick, and friends and family, a huge thank you. Yes, for your support, but also for loving me. I'm blessed.

My most heartfelt thanks goes to God. This was a journey I could have never predicted. When I tried to get published thirty years ago, I wasn't ready. I had a lot to go through before I would be able to write books that hopefully make a difference. Thank you for my life, my family, and an abundance of blessings. And also for nudging me to keep writing until I was ready and able to do Your work.

COMING OCTOBER 2018!

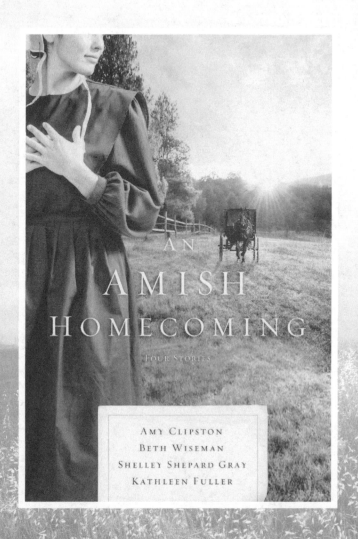

An

AMISH

HOMECOMING

FOUR STORIES

AMY CLIPSTON
BETH WISEMAN
SHELLEY SHEPARD GRAY
KATHLEEN FULLER

AVAILABLE IN PRINT AND E-BOOK

THE AMISH SECRETS COLLECTION

HER BROTHER'S KEEPER

LOVE BEARS ALL THINGS

HOME ALL ALONG

BETH WISEMAN

Daughters of the Promise
COLLECTION

PLAIN PERFECT   PLAIN PURSUIT   PLAIN PROMISE

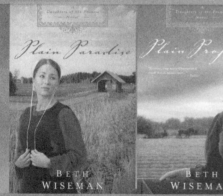

PLAIN PARADISE   PLAIN PROPOSAL   PLAIN PEACE

BETH
WISEMAN

Read more in these collections from our beloved authors!

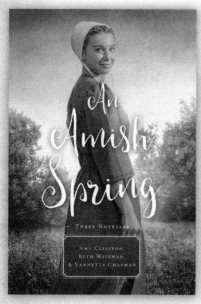
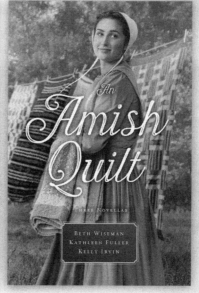

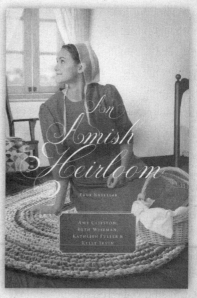

ABOUT THE AUTHOR

Beth Wiseman is the award-winning and bestselling author of the Daughters of the Promise, Land of Canaan, and Amish Secrets series. While she is best known for her Amish novels, Beth has also written contemporary novels including *Need You Now*, *The House that Love Built*, and *The Promise*.